THE FEAST OF THE NINE VIRGINS

THE FEAST OF THE NINE VIRGINS

by

Jameela Siddiqi

Bogle-L'Ouverture
London

Published by Bogle-L'Ouverture Publications Limited
t/a Bogle-L'Ouverture Press
P. O. Box 2186
London W13 9ZQ
England

Printed and bound in Malaysia

Text in Times Roman
Headings in Arial

Cover design by Mohssin Faraji
Photograph by Asia Maghouze

ISBN 0 904521 29 4

To all
my Teachers –
past, present and future

CONTENTS

ACKNOWLEDGEMENTS

A first novel is a difficult path strewn with slippery wet leaves. For making this journey easier, I am indebted to my many close friends and family who provided unending moral support and encouragement. Naomi Mobed was instrumental in sparking off some of the subjects covered in the story, and Zahid Dar's suggestions were invaluable in editing the final draft. I am particularly grateful to Susheila Nasta who had the unenviable task of being the very first person to read and assess the original, rather weighty manuscript. I am also grateful to Aniz Damani for his helpful comments and to Mohssin Farraji who patiently scattered sweets all over the cover. Last, but not least, I would like to thank Eric and Jessica Huntley of Bogle L'Ouverture Press for supporting my work.

1
QISMAT

Born in Bombay, raised in Mombasa, married in Kampala, educated in London, worked in Tehran, lived in New York, then Stuttgart, then Hong Kong, and died in Vancouver. Where was this person actually from? Where does anyone live these days?

Everyone lives in a space inside their head. To this space they add rules and regulations, do's and don't's. They reinvent the past, refurbish the present and then sit in fear of the future. They manufacture a unique culture born out of their own myth-ridden reality. They project this reality into a self-destructing future. They make sure their reality does not outlive them. Their culture dies with them. Their children can never carry it forward because the children live in their own space – inside their own heads. But sometimes, two different spaces, inside two different heads collide to create an even bigger myth ridden reality. It's called a perfect match. Sometimes it's called destiny – Qismat.

When destinies become intertwined, the world becomes a very small place. When those same destinies then diverge, the world seems as remote and as infinite as space itself. Destiny does not respect geographical boundaries. Small town African-Indian shopkeepers rub shoulders with glitzy Hollywood – and Bollywood producers when destiny so dictates. Impoverished descendants of yesterday's glamorous Lucknavi courtesans ride roughshod over the heads of British television producers when Qismat waves its magic wand. Yesterday's shit-sweepers are today's destiny-makers. Oppressed widows turn into dream merchants, and miserly "Dukavallas" want to spend every last cent of their money on a blockbuster movie. And babies, whether Black or Brown, or a bit of both, have a habit of growing up and demanding that you pick up that handkerchief you dropped all those years ago….

Destiny sees to all that. And it sees to a whole lot more. And the Moon God smiles His beaming, radiant smile, and He knows you will now have to feed another nine virgins….

2
THE FEAST OF THE NINE VIRGINS

There have to be nine of them, and they have to be virgins. To play it safe, you should really only invite the young ones, aged between five and nine. After that there was no knowing who was and who wasn't. After they had passed that age, there was no telling who had the "knowledge" and who didn't.

Nine virgins have to be fed as part of fulfilling a pact with God. You ask God for something, and if He grants it, you repay Him by feeding nine virgins. A special meal prepared by your own hands – give or take a few over-eager neighbourhood women, determined to interfere in the proceedings.

The preparation of the meal takes all morning amidst ferocious arguments as to how much water suffices to cook the rice to perfection, without having to face the arduous task of draining off excess liquid. Various women have their own method for getting the amount of water just right. It's all in the middle finger say some, while others maintain it depends on the size of the cooking pot. As it turns out, the senior-most woman present insists that her method is foolproof and the others buckle down. As a result, the rice remains gritty and uncooked. The hostess, she of the newly granted wish, blames the elderly woman, while the old hag blames it on the cooking pot.

The newly wish-fulfilled hostess mutters under her breath: "Yes, that's right. *Naachna na jaane....* When you don't know how to dance, just blame the tilted courtyard!"

The rice was uncooked, the potatoes were hard as stone, and someone had forgotten to add any sugar to the pudding. Each woman thought some other woman had done it. A thousand wishes were being granted but the pudding remained sugarless.

I didn't mind scoffing down the sugarless kheer. I just loved the novelty of eating in other people's houses. I was determined to enjoy myself. As far as I was concerned, it was a little girls' luncheon party. I was there because so were eight other girls nearly my age. It hadn't occurred to me that the fact of my being penetrated or not by someone of the opposite sex could have had anything to do with it. Not that I would even have known about anything like that.

I had become a regular fixture on these occasions. My virtue was an established fact. The more of these virgin luncheons I attended, the more I was invited to attend. These were not ordinary social engagements. One had a religious duty to attend. Even my snobbish mother always insisted I go, although more often than not, these events were held in the poorer neighbourhoods. Not the kind of areas my mother would normally have approved of. But class differences temporarily collapsed on such occasions, for this was an essential religious ritual. Here was some woman repaying God for His endless Benevolence. Her wish had come true, and she had to feed you, and eight others. It was one's religious duty to go and allow oneself to be fed – sugarless pudding and all.

The lunches were always on a Sunday. At one time I hadn't had a Sunday lunch at home for over six months. God was certainly granting a lot of wishes! Still, I completely failed to understand exactly what these women were getting from God. There was no evidence of new toys or games. It was very difficult to figure out just what grown-ups could ever wish for. Surely, they were grown up so they could have whatever they wanted? They didn't have homework or spelling tests. They could stay up as late as they liked. They could eat all the sweets they wanted. So, what was their problem?

But that's what I had thought with all the unadulterated wisdom of a six-year old. By the time I was eight, I realised grown ups could have a lot of problems – mostly of their own making. Take my own mother for example. Always whining about the sad state of the world. Where is the world? I know it's some place out there somewhere beyond the sun, but we live right here, in a different place. It's called the Pearl of Africa's Crown. Just Pearl, for short. So, what's her problem? Why is she always going on about the world? I try and tell her that WE don't live in the world. We live here, in this wonderful little Pearl in the middle of nowhere. What Suez crisis? Where is Korea? Does it rain in Vietnam? If the Arabs and Israelis want to kill each other, let them mummy. At least they aren't killing us. She would use mysterious words like Yew-en-O and Eye-arr-ay. Kashmir. Such a beauty spot, what a pity!

Where's the pity? All these places were in a place called World – "Duniya."

But we also live in this duniya, she informs me authoritatively. Pearl is also in this duniya. My mother is the original bubble-burster. I was devastated. All my illusions shattered into zillions of fragments with that one heartless line of hers.

Had she ever realised the extent of the damage this thoughtless piece of information had caused? All this time I had imagined there was somewhere called "world" high up in the sky somewhere, beyond the stars, or maybe even deep under the ocean, where all sorts of senseless atrocities happened so that melancholic people like my mother might read all about it. But we were not part of that. We were not from the world. We were from some other place where nothing bad ever happened.

In Pearl everything was just perfect. The sky was a semi-transparent dark blue, sometimes it was a light mauve, and the rainbows so crystal clear you could almost touch them. And warm rain fragrant with the sensuous smell of sun-baked earth. A deep red soil – where else could you see such red earth? How can this be world? This is Pearl. Here the breeze is deliciously fragrant with an indescribable scent, the kind that French perfume houses would've killed for and are still, unsuccessfully, trying to replicate.

And then the music. The mosquitoes made music. The crickets sang songs. Even the sewing machines played melodies to harmonise with the chorus of nature. And those glorious blood red sunsets were by themselves quite enough to make you thank your lucky stars you didn't have to live in a place called World.

But my mother had to go and spoil all that. Gradually and reluctantly, I had to accept the facts. Mother knows best. Gradually, the truth began to dawn on me. Yes, we too lived in the same world. It's funny how once I came to terms with the fact that our little paradise was not situated anywhere else but was also part of the world, I began to become aware of everyone's problems. It's then that I realised there was pain, and suffering and injustice. There was bound to be. How could there not be? This was World, after all. That same dreaded world about which my mother read and talked about so much.

I felt trapped. It was like waking up in the morning and thinking you were safely at home tucked up in your usual cosy bed, until someone unkindly informed you that you were, in fact, being held hostage in a five-star hotel.

I sank into a deep depression for about three days – an eternity in the life of an eight-year old – and then, having wallowed in my sad predicament for a full three days, I quickly bounced back. I'm a survivor. I emerged from my grief-ridden cocoon completely ready to tackle the world – this new place, where I'd just been told I lived. So, back to my usual routine of playing with the dogs and chatting to the flowers, and once again looking forward to my next Virgin Lunch invitation.

And it came. Only this time, it threw me into one of the most unfathomable mysteries of my early life, because believe it or not, this time the lunch was to be hosted by the Widow.

3
I'M NOT WHO I AM

The cleverest trick God ever pulled was to convince a vast majority of the human race that He doesn't really exist.

So they forgot all about Him and carried on with their empty lives. But I, the Widow, I refused to forget Him. I knew different. I knew He was real, and I dreamed. But they knew nothing of my dreams. They all felt sorry for me, but I knew something they didn't know. I knew about God. And I knew his many guises. They had given up on him, but luckily for them, God had a million ways of making a comeback.

The expulsion of Adam was just the beginning. Worse expulsions were planned. Adam may have been expelled from paradise, but some of Adam's descendants inherited another, altogether more heavenly paradise. It was called Pearl.

Paradise it might have been, but only for those who were a law unto themselves. Even heavenly Pearl had once fallen under the benevolent dictatorship of the Dukavallas. Heaven for them, but hell for the rest of us. Hell for the oppressed, overworked, underpaid indigenous population that had inhabited this paradise long before the Dukavallas arrived. Hell for those who believed in equality. Hell for the mosquitoes who were annihilated at the alarming rate of one per every second after sunset – thanks to DDT and the mosquito-servant. But most of all it was hell for me, the Widow.

But help is close at hand. The native Black population, the mosquitoes, and the Widow are about to be set free from the tyranny of the Dukavallas.

God can do anything – anything at all. He wears many disguises, and so do His agents. There was that one time when one of God's agents landed in Pearl in the guise of a mad military dictator....

4
THE TEACHER OF DREAMS

Zarine is no ordinary woman. She is a teacher. But she is no ordinary teacher. She is a teacher of dreams. She teaches people to dream. You might well ask, what use dreams? And Zarine will tell you that every reality is at first a dream. Only then can it become a reality. And if you learn to dream properly you learn to create your own reality. Forget I think therefore I am – I DREAM therefore I am!

Zarine will teach you this. And she will teach you a whole lot more. With her you will learn to see only what you want to see. You will hear only what you want to hear. You will feel only what you want to feel. And you will dream what you want to dream. And then you will learn to recall your dreams in your waking hours. Dreams and reality become one and the same as you are taught to weave them together.

And that's not all. You will learn to dream at will.

You have a choice. It's clear and simple. Either you learn to dream for yourself or you become a player in someone else's dream, and play out their reality for them. Which would you rather have? To dream for yourself, or to appear as an unpaid extra in someone else's dream?

Ash was dumbfounded. Sonia, his closest and oldest friend in London, was always full of the most wonderful, nonsensical theories of all time. So this was her new thing. In the ten years he'd known her she had always provided ready solutions to the most horrendous puzzles. As a result, she usually wore a contented, satisfied, I-know-better expression on her face. The expression never changed, but her pet subjects changed with alarming rapidity.

One month it was palmistry. Then God consciousness. Then astrology, followed by quantum physics. Then she'd got into the socio-political life of insects. And then abandoning her various glass jars of ants and spiders, she miraculously produced an authoritative textbook on the evolution of the office stapler. The book immediately gathered a cult following, causing Ash to observe that we did, indeed, live through very strange times. She followed it up with a mammoth 3-volume work on the life of an obscure saint, and was currently involved in writing the biography of an Indian musician.

"I don't give a damn about what Joe Public wants to read", she had declared at the time of the office stapler book. "I only want to write the sort of books that I would want to read." From superstition, divinity, insects and the design principles of the office stapling machine, she'd got into Indian musicians. Whatever next? The Top Ten sexual fantasies of the White Anglo-Saxon Male... or so it had seemed, given their last few phone conversations. But he knew there had been something else as well. So, this was it....

Dreams. He decided to play the game. She was full of this dream stuff, and as her best friend, he had a duty to ask all the right questions, to give her a chance to enthuse about her new favourite subject. That's what friends are for:

"OK, so I go to this Zarine woman and I learn to dream. Then what?"

"Then what? Just listen to you. What do you mean then what?"

"Well, once I start dreaming, where do I go from there?"

"Anywhere you like! You're free. You start to create what you want to be. All those years at film school, and you've done nothing. The trouble is you still even don't know who you want to be."

Her grammar suffered when she enthused about anything. But that didn't take his pain away. Whenever she hit at his non-career in films, he despised her. She had a way of twisting the knife. Yes, he had spent long years at the most prestigious institutions, thanks to his father's drug dealing activities, or whatever it was that he did to make so much money, it was that money that had paid for his obsession with film-making. But the obsession went as far as theoretical knowledge. Lots of books, lectures, presentations, endless discussions about other people's films. No actual film of his own. He never seemed to get started. His computer contained scores of unfinished film scripts – enthusiastically begun every time one of his acquaintances completed a project, and then dejectedly abandoned as soon as self-confidence deserted him. This had become a regular pattern over the years.

And so his best female friend had concluded that he didn't really know who he was or what he wanted. That was the problem with many would-be creative artistes, especially aspiring filmmakers. They didn't really know themselves, and when they did, they tried to cram all of their life's experience into one lousy project.

"Why does everything you know have to go into the same bloody script?" she would challenge aggressively. "Spread it out man, dish it out a bit at a time. One theme for each script. You're always thinly disguising everyone you know and then making them characters in your scripts. The same people crop up again and again. Why don't you invent characters? Why must they always come from real life?"

Nice one, he thought, coming from someone who doesn't read or write fiction, and someone who was proud to have never seen a film, or gone to the theatre. Sonia had always argued that her own life was so wonderfully weird and fascinating that no amount of fiction, however outlandish, could compete with the things that had happened to her for real. Novels were humdrum stuff compared to what she'd been through, especially the adventures she'd had in her studies about the intimate life of insects, to say nothing of the evolution of the typewriter. "When you learn to dream, you will learn just who you really are, and who you'd like to be. A thousand dreams bridge the gap between one's real self and one's distorted image of the self," Sonia was in full flow now.

He could tell she'd been reading pseudo-psychological dream analysis stuff: "But I'm already who I am," he argued.

"Yes, that's just my point. You can call yourself what you like. You can make films or you can bake bread. But inside you there's a real person who needs to be known. And Zarine's method helps you to identify the real you. That's why I'm telling you about her."

Zarine's client list, if one could have seen this top-secret confidential document, reads like a "Who's Who" of royalty, showbiz and politics. People have been known to fly Concorde just to keep an appointment with Zarine. Pop stars, politicians, Hollywood, Bollywood, international royalty – even religious leaders.

One by one, the dreamers arrive. They all have a dream – several dreams. And Zarine teaches them the art of actually dreaming what they only think they dream. Once they learn to dream properly, they learn there is no dividing line between dreams and reality.

Ash was always resentful of his best friend when she was newly enamoured with something. But it was so difficult to make friends in London. And where in this cold city of closed doors and drawn curtains could he find another friend who took such an interest in his work and considered it her duty to keep him well informed on all the latest fads?

Yet she was such an accomplished and down-to-earth sort of woman. How could she, of all people, be taken in with this dream thing? And who was this weird Zarine woman, who seemed to have done nothing with her life except dream and show others how to dream? Was she the reason behind the runaway success of his friend's latest boring book on the office stapler?

"But how does it actually work? Like I go in there and lie down and then will she put me to sleep or something? Does it involve hypnosis?"

"No. Nothing like that. You simply tell her what you want, and she shows you how to get it."

"What, anything?"

"Yes, anything."

"Like a Porsche or a Mercedes, or a mansion, or a rich wife...."

"If that's really all you want, I suppose that's all you'll get."

She was starting to get haughty again. She always assumed a detached, morally superior attitude when material possessions were mentioned. She resumed her attack mode:

"Look, let's get this straight! She can't *get* you things. She's not Santa Claus. If you want a Porsche go see a car dealer. If you want a rich wife go on an ocean cruise and net yourself a widow. Zarine can only teach you to first create and then tap in to your own reality. The rest is down to you. But you have to first learn about what you really want. What you think you'd like and what you actually need, are two entirely different things."

"Oh that's ridiculous! I already know how to dream about what I want."

"No you don't! You only know how to *day dream* about it. Fantasies only take you a million miles away from your goal."

"This is all getting too much for me. Let's talk about something else. I don't like this kind of talk... it scares me." Ash was clearly losing interest.

"Yes, I figured that. Still, it worked for me."

Suddenly he was interested again: "Really? You got what you wanted? What did you ask for?" Ash was always interested in anything that could shed light on Sonia's aura of success.

"I didn't ASK for anything. I simply learnt how to dream effectively and discover my true desires. The funny thing was, what I'd desired for myself was not in the end what I wanted – if you get my drift. And I'm very glad to say I want rather more out of life than BMW's or rich husbands."

Secretive. Smug. Superior. And sarcastic with it. Suddenly he hated his best friend. He'd show her! He would track down this Zarine woman and expose her as a fraud. Making people part with their money so that they can dream properly! Buggering bollocks!

"So, what does she charge? You dream your own dreams, but what's her cut?"

"Oh, lots and lots. But it's really worth it!"

"I don't know… I'm not sure… should anyone be allowed to make money out of other people's dreams?"

"How do you think Hollywood and Bollywood survive?"

Sonia always had a way of getting the last word.

5
DUKAVALLA

The Mohanji family had a shop in the main market square of a small African town. It was really a sort of shack with a corrugated tin roof, the midday African sun beating down mercilessly, resulting in a blinding dazzle on the outside, and an intense heat inside. I say shop, but it was more of a general store with a delicious smell of peppermints mingled with the aroma of freshly roasted groundnuts. This cocktail was made all the more appetizing with a strong scent of ground spices – haldi, chillies, dhaniya, all freshly hand-pounded in the backyard behind the shop. Except on those thudding, pulsating, chilly-pounding days, the hot afternoons seemed to stand still. Nothing stirred, except the battalions of flies buzzing around in the hope of making a landing on something sweet and sticky. The bulk of Mohanji's business took off with the decline of the afternoon equatorial sun, in the three hours or so before sunset. At sunset, the buzzing flies vanished and the high-pitched tones of the mosquitoes came into their own.

The Market Square was really the town centre and a major terminus and thoroughfare. An intricate network of arteries mostly consisting of mud roads linked all outlying villages to the small town. And a proper road linked the small town to the big town – the capital of this newly independent African country. At least that's what all the school textbooks said. What they omitted to mention was that, basically, all roads led to the Market Square, and consequently to "Mohanji & Sons, General Store For All Your Needs. Come One, Come All."

Any kind of business or shop at this strategic point where all roads met, was sure to be a huge success. Everyone was on to a winner here. And none more so than Mohanji. He knew all the tricks. Every saleable commodity was on sale in his shop – from bottles of ice-cold fizzy drinks to the odd piece of furniture. And he knew how to extract the largest possible amount of money from any customer. If he expected to get ten shillings, he would start by asking for sixty. Half an hour later the sale would be agreed at fifteen. This applied to everything except certain basic commodities on which the new Black African government had had the audacity to impose price restrictions – basic foodstuffs – sugar, maize flour, bread, cooking oil. The new government had insisted that basic commodities had to be price-controlled to prevent the largely Indian shopkeepers – or Dukavallas – from making obscene profits.

The "Dukavallas" were always at odds with the government. Who was the government to decide prices? The government didn't get up at five in the morning to fetch the goods from wholesalers. The government didn't stay up long after darkness had fallen to count the day's takings and stock up for the following day. What does the government know about running a business? What did the natives know about running a shop? No work ethic, these Blacks. Only Indians could do this sort of thing. It was in their blood. They were the descendants of the legendary Indian money-lenders – the Banyas, the Marwaris – and only they could know about running successful businesses because business was all about how to turn money into even more money.

Although each sale could sometimes take up to an hour, the turnover in the Mohanji shop was amazingly fast. In fact, if rumour was to be believed, Mohanji had a huge bank account in Switzerland, but continued to live like a pauper – always pleading poverty and looking crestfallen on the rare occasion, God forbid, when he had to concede any sale by even five cents. "What are you trying to do? You want my family to starve?"

It could be argued that Mohanji was really a very rich man but refused to believe it. And if you accept that wealth and poverty are attitudes of mind, then I suppose Mohanji was indeed really very poor. He had never got over being genuinely poor many, many years ago. But bit by bit, he had worked hard, and also had lots of children to provide free labour in his shop. Gradually he had a thriving business, but even when the money started rolling in, he couldn't stop believing he was still impoverished. Gradually, the shop did so well that he acquired the neighbouring property and opened a second shop adjacent to the old one.

The second shop was run by his daughter, the Widow. This was a different kind of shop. It carried the sign "Mohanji Fancy Goods for Ladies", meaning plastic jewellery, nylon lace, plastic flowers, plastic handbags and shoes to match. But the Widow's main earner was dress fabric, which she sold by the yard and then charged another ten shillings for making up the outfit. She was an expert dressmaker. She'd just picked it up by watching her mother, and by having to make her own clothes from a very young age. The orders came flooding in and she could hardly manage on her own. Eventually, after much pleading, she was allowed an assistant to help with the finishing stages of her garments – sewing on buttons, hemming and other finishing details that could only be done by hand.

Mr & Mrs Mohanji had ten children – nine sons, and one daughter. Being of the old school, Mohanji believed children, especially sons, to be wealth. Other Indian shopkeepers envied Mohanji for having nine sons. Most of them had daughters. And daughters had to be married off. And that could cost a lot of money. So what if you were in Equatorial Africa? Indian traditions still had to be upheld and weddings and dowries are an expensive business. Nobody would've dreamed of challenging the dowry system – that would have been tantamount to taking on the White culture of shamelessness. Why should any man accept your daughter into his family unless she could add to his wealth? And if nobody wanted your daughter then the whole marriage system would break down and shamelessness would set in. Our good Indian girls might find themselves reduced to running off with Black men. That was every Indian father's worst nightmare. Daughters had to be married off as early as possible.

Once a daughter was menstruating every drop of her menstrual blood descended on her father's neck like the blade of a guillotine, and to avoid death by such a gruesome method, elaborate dowries were arranged from day one. Things were gathered and stored virtually from the day a baby-girl was born. And then, if the father was lucky, the grown up baby left his house in her doli – a bridal palanquin – followed by cart-loads of goodies. Pots and pans. Furniture. Gold. Linen. Glassware. Every imaginable household item. For a while all this extra furniture, goods and chattels would be piled up over the existing furniture in her in-laws' home. In time, some of it would vanish as her husband's younger sisters' marriages were hastily arranged – now that their dowry could be completed. But one had to be careful. It couldn't all just be passed on. Everybody would've seen the dowry proudly displayed on Round One, so Round Two had to be varied somewhat. And if you played your cards really well, then what you'd given a daughter could easily be returned if you chose one of her sisters-in-law for your son. That's how the Dukavalla classes kept their property circulating amongst themselves, and the giving and taking of daughters was essential to the protection of property. Tradition dictated that daughters couldn't be kept back from marriage to help in the shop. Rival Indian shopkeepers thought Mohanji exceptionally fortunate to have a widowed daughter who was returned to him. OK, so the dowry had gone down the drain, so what? It was the Widow who had made the second shop such a success because she could do most of the sewing herself. But apart from all the advantages of a built-in seamstress, they were convinced that Mohanji's business was a success because he had all those sons to help him, whereas most of them had to pay real wages to hired assistants. Useless African fellows, stealing from the shop, and who knows, entertaining lustful thoughts about their daughters as well. These Black guys had to be watched – they couldn't be trusted. Lazy as hell. They just sat around in the sun laughing and talking and eating bananas. What did they know about work? Isn't that why the British had had to bring out the grandfathers of the Indian shopkeepers from India – to build the blessed railway that went all the way to the coast to help the easy movement of cheap raw materials out of land-locked Pearl and into Mother Britain and her many colonies?

The Market Square always managed to look and feel like the centre of the universe. A microcosm of creation itself, in all its contrasting colours. Always alive, expanding and persistently vibrant. Wonderful cacophonies of sound – car horns blaring to the syncopated rhythms of shoe-makers tapping away with all the pride of a repair-culture. Sewing machines screeching in tune with dozens of shop-radios blaring Indian film songs, and occasionally, very occasionally, the sounds of African pop music – Congolese bands – hastily lowered in volume, in preference to the orchestral sounds of Bollywood. It was proudly asserted by the likes of Mohanji that if his shop radio pumped out melodies from Shankar-Jaikishen and O.P. Nayyar, then his Black customer volume doubled. This was cited as proof that the Blacks, the indigenous native population to whom this beautiful country belonged, were, after all, capable of understanding and appreciating the finer things in life. "Look, look how they move to our music – such rhythm these native totos!"

Professional middle-class Asian grown-ups found the whole scene most stressful, and only necessity would drag them away from their breezy, leafy suburbs and verandahs in the surrounding hills to the sweltering heat of the market area and the stench of its drains. But then grown-ups are so stuffy about cleanliness. They don't understand that you have to get down there in the dirt – you have to put up with some sort of muck to get a good story. I thrived on the millions of stories the Market Square and its surrounding shops had to offer. For me, it was a gateway to the real world and an exhilarating contrast to the sanitized environs of my own dwelling, rather ridiculously called the "European Residential Area". Ridiculous because only Asians lived there now. Most of the Europeans had long left. They weren't going to hang around and be bossed around by the new Black government. They left the Asians behind to cope with that sort of thing.

The Africans called all Asians "Muhindi", but the upper middle-class professional Asians who lived in these so-called European areas, thought of themselves as European. European, in this part of Africa, invariably meant British. The British themselves never managed to think of themselves as European – and still have difficulty accepting the concept of belonging in Europe – but as far as the Asian professional middle-classes were concerned, anyone with a white skin was a European. And it was the done thing to take on as many European mannerisms as possible. So they lived like Europeans, or what they imagined was the European way of living. They replicated the attitudes of the Europeans they had seen in the motherland, and recycled whatever memories they had of how a lighter-skinned race behaves when it lives alongside a darker-skinned one: keep yourself to yourself. Forks and knives and toilet paper. Don't mix with the natives. The only Blacks with whom they ever have dealings are sometimes their students or patients, but mostly they're servants. It's easy to feel naturally superior to servants.

The tameness of the Muhindi European areas offered peace and quiet, cool breezes and huge gardens fenced in by high neatly trimmed hedges, but for me it held little charm. Nothing much to see. No stories. Nothing new to learn. The Market Square by comparison, was a sort of theatre of life. Traders, buskers, stuntmen, witchdoctors, prostitutes, courting couples and once, I even saw a woman and her dog wrapped up in a blanket being rushed to hospital. It was the strangest thing I'd ever seen, but when I asked about it, I was merely told that they were both very sick and had to go to hospital together. "But why in the same blanket – why wrapped up like that?" Everybody ignored the question and carried on whispering amongst themselves. People whisper a lot when they don't want children to know things. The Square also served as a taxi rank – not taxis in the European sense of the word, but long distance taxis connecting the town to rural areas. These taxis were usually Peugeot 404 or 504 Estates, officially meant to seat a driver and four others, but it was more usual to see them bursting with at least fifteen, plus livestock. Often there would be one or two people with cloth bundles on top of the luggage rack, and on one occasion, even a big fat snake coiled up in a half-closed wickerwork basket. And all that against a backdrop of loud arguments between would-be passengers and drivers haggling over fares. There were fights between different drivers vying for passengers, who in turn went from taxi to taxi to negotiate fares. A taxi seldom departed until it was overflowing with people.

Most of the passengers were Black, and so were the drivers but there was one exception and that was Mohanji's second-born, green-eyed son. He was his father's favourite and as such had been absolved from putting in time at the shop. Mohanji, realising that his favourite green-eyed one had not been overly blessed with academic ability, had generously bought him a Peugeot 404 Estate so that he could contribute to the Mohanji treasury by driving his long-distance taxi from dawn to sunset. He was the nicest looking of all the Mohanji boys, and many Dukavallas hoped they would acquire just such a son-in-law via their virgin daughters. But the green-eyed one disappointed everyone by falling in love with a Black African girl. Mohanji maintained she had used "Jadoo" – witchcraft – to ensnare a good-looking Indian boy. Mohanji secretly went to the town's top Jadoo-maker and purchased a spell to counteract the original spell. The girl ended up committing suicide and everyone was satisfied. Whatever was she thinking of? Surely she didn't think she'd be marrying the fair skinned, green-eyed one? Not with her jet-black skin and frizzy hair and flat nose, (nice teeth though,) no, never! For him, we'll find a really nice, tall, fair-skinned, long-straight-haired virgin Indian girl.

6

UNOFFICIAL APARTHEID

Like all the other Dukavallas, Mohanji too had received a free drinks cooler from the manufacturers of the world's leading fizzy drink, Soda Baridi. From time to time, the manufacturer's especially appointed Askaris were sent to all the shops disguised as customers, to ensure that the drinks cooler was not being used for any purpose other than cooling bottles of Soda Baridi. This was a vital monitoring process in a strategy aimed at ensuring that the newly independent Blacks would become addicted to the sugary soda, in preference to plain water. But in these hot steamy equatorial climes where the tap-water was invariably tepid while the sugary Soda Baridi ice-cold, no prizes for guessing which one was set to be the winner.

Mohanji was astute enough to know that most of his customers could not afford Soda Baridi at one shilling per bottle. So he cheated, and sneaked in a few bottles of tap-water to become illegally ice-cold in the special chest. He then charged Black Africans ten cents for the privilege of being able to drink an ice-cold version of the sweet water of their own land, a land abundant with rivers and fresh water lakes. But if an Indian stopped by for a drink of cold water, there was no charge. And on the rare occasion that a European traveller happened to get thirsty in the area, forget water! Shopkeepers vied with one another to be the first to offer him a free bottle of Soda Baridi or beer. It was, after all, a Godly act to quench the thirst of a wayfarer.

Unofficial apartheid manifests itself in the strangest of ways. The Africans were sold their drinking water in empty jam or fruit tins, complete with jagged edges where the tin had been clumsily and primitively cut open. It required real skill to drink from such a container without shredding your lips. The Indians got their free drink of water in a stainless steel cup, but good manners dictated that the mouth should not be allowed to touch the cup – a simple precautionary exercise to prevent the contamination of both. Head thrown back, the Indians poured the water into their mouths from a safe distance above the face. But European hippies received a real glass into which to pour their free beers and sodas, which were then sipped from multi-coloured, candy-striped straws.

Although subscribing to this de facto apartheid in terms of respecting White supremacy, Mohanji was, nevertheless, a God-fearing man and as such felt justified in his subversive action of selling tap water to the natives on the grounds of helping to preserve their dental health. After all, the whole world knew the Whites had rotten teeth and were now bent on trying to corrupt the high dental standards of the low-sugar, low-salt, fat-free, noble African savage. And he considered it his God-given duty to make ice-cold tap water available for sale in his shop, in complete defiance of the wicked soda manufacturers and their world-conquering schemes aimed at spreading shamelessness and tooth decay.

7
THE LETTER "R"

"Hi, it's me." Ash always identified himself as 'me'.

"Yes I know," Sonia replied sleepily.

"How do you know? You know the way I ring, right?"

"Who else could it be at this ungodly hour?" She stated the rhetorical question good-humouredly. Curiosity always had the effect of making her wide-awake: "So what's up? Writer's block? Which Speilberg eat-your-heart-out block-buster are you working on now?"

"D'ya know, I'd have married you if it weren't for your unending cattiness?"

"Yes, I know. Miaoww.... That's why I have to be so horrid in case you fall in love with me... anyway what's the problem?"

"No problem. Just wanted a chat... what word would you use if you couldn't use 'horrendous'?"

Here we go, she thought. "Oh, I don't know... check your Roget."

"Can't. Never figured out how to use it. Is "momentous" a good substitute?"

"No, it means something else entirely. What's the context?"

"Something terrifying, horrifying, bizarre...."

"So use one of those instead...."

"Can't. They've all got 'r's' in them. Can't use anything with an 'r' in it. The 'r'-key on my keyboard isn't working. Don't laugh! How long do you think you could survive without typing a word with the letter 'r' in it?"

"Hmm, interesting. There ought to be a special mathematical formula for working out that sort of thing. Must work on it one day. Anyway, have you woken me up at four-fifteen in the night just to ask me that?"

"No, not really. I just had a strange dream. It was all about you."

Suddenly she was interested: "Oh, what what what? Erotic?"

"Come off it! You're about as erotic as that non-existent mathematical theory which stipulates how many words can be typed into coherent prose without resorting to the letter 'r'!"

"Fine. That's what friends are for. Anything else? Any other little problem

I could help you with since my sleep isn't so important and I can lie in bed as late as six-thirty because my first meeting isn't until eight?"

"Who are you meeting?" Ash suddenly felt threatened.

"I'll tell you about it after it's happened. Don't know what he wants."

"Stop being so secretive. We promised never to hide our projects from each other. I'm also meeting a potential funding contact tomorrow afternoon. That's why I called you. I was trying to get this synopsis into some sort of shape – just to have something to show him. And now the 'r' won't work. Anyway, what's your mysterious meeting about?"

"No mystery. I just don't have anything to tell you yet. Just a meeting with some rich guy. He probably wants a coffee-table book on all his rich ancestors, featuring all of their gaudy jewellery in macro-close-up. Anyway, if you're seeing someone tomorrow, then why haven't you got something ready? Why do you always leave things to the eleventh hour?"

"Don't change the subject... tell me, who are you meeting?"

"Just some Indian businessman. Says he has a project that might interest me. Who knows? He probably just wants a ghost-writer for his boring autobiography. Anyway, I don't mind... there's no harm in this kind of work. It usually brings lots and lots of material for other things, like real books."

"Don't do it. Don't go and see him. I have a bad feeling about this. And remember you have a difficult Mercury movement at the moment...."

For the thousandth time she wished she'd never got him interested in astrology. She had got into it two years ago and then abandoned it, but Ash lived by it now, and worse still, tried to make her live by it. She had moved on since her astrology days. She was now into Quantum physics and applied mathematics, and men's sexual fantasies. But he was still stuck on astrology.

"Dear Boy," she said, "You just concentrate on your hundredth unfinished block-buster script, and let me worry about my own career. Bit by bit, big or small, I know what I'm doing. I don't have a job – I just have an approach. I bring that approach to everything I do. I try and have the same enthusiasm – whether it's for a thirteen-volume dictionary of world mythology or a half-page blurb on AIDS. What's it to you?"

"I am worried about you. I feel he might ask you for something... well you know... something difficult..." he broke off uneasily.

She knew her friend well enough to know that he was never really optimistic about anything. The word enthusiasm – although conveniently without an 'r'

– had never formed part of his vocabulary. That, she reckoned, was the reason for his complete lack of success at anything he tried.

Ash had nothing to show except dozens of unfinished film-scripts. Everything had to be abandoned at some stage on the grounds that the heavens had not produced the ideal celestial moment during which to launch something new. Saturn was in the wrong place. Or Mercury was retrograde. Or all new projects had to wait until the Spring Equinox, but the Equinox by itself wouldn't do. Jupiter would also have to form an appropriate angle to the Sun. Why had she taught him all this? Was she mad? No, it wasn't really her fault. She had only enthused about it – as she enthused about everything else. She wasn't to know he'd disappear into a northern Californian institution for four years and then emerge completely zombified with ideas about good days and bad days, and the universe being for you and against you – and planetary energies flowing this way and that.

She was fully awake now. She knew she wouldn't be able to go back to sleep. So she had to keep him chatting. The last thing she wanted was for him to ring off and leave her sleepless and uneasy about her morning meeting. Why didn't he want her to go and meet this man? What did he know about it?

"Now, tell me the truth. Why should I not go to this meeting? How do you know anything about it? Is this just a feeling, or have you actually seen something in my birth-chart?"

"Just a feeling, you know...."

"A proper feeling feeling, or a knowing feeling?"

"Neither, just a of sense of impending doom. Something I can visualise but can't yet verbalise, you know? I'm a film person, so I see things in my head. You're a book person so you see things in words... oh, I don't know. I'm sorry. Sorry to have woken you up. I'm getting sleepy now. I'll let you rest...."

He'd always wanted to do this, but she usually got the better of him. Perhaps it was the late hour and her lack of sharpness, but suddenly he realised he'd managed it. He'd have liked to do this more often. Make some cryptic remark. Get her interested and alert, and then himself feign sleepiness, knowing fully well that she was hooked. And Sonia was indeed hooked.

"OK, cut out the crap! And don't you dare go to sleep! If you put the phone down, I'm driving over to your place right now and I'm going to sit there until you explain yourself. Come on, come clean. What do you know about my meeting?"

"I know nothing. Forget it. I was just a little jealous that you were about to land some big job, yet again. I was making it all up. Honestly. Hope it goes well, whatever it is. Tell me about it tomorrow if you want to. Ciao!"

"No... wait, please listen to me.... I'll try and coax him into a documentary or something like that, and then pass it on to you if you like. I've always tried to fit you in somewhere. But you refuse to direct other people's scripts. And you never finish your own. So what am I to do?"

"Hey, don't worry about it. I don't want a slice of the action. I'd have to be desperate to direct an Indian jewellery commercial. Grotesque looking yellow stuff! Not in the least photogenic. Anyway, I might be onto bigger and better things soon. Good night! Sweet dreams!"

8
I WANT FILLUM

"Make me a film," he said, with the casual air of one who was ordering a back street Bangkok tailor to make him a silk shirt.

There was no reply. A stupefied face just stared at him – big round eyes, wide open under scraggly fringe of bleached hair.

"Don't look so stupid – just tell me how much money you need and make me a film." He hated it when people refused to be impressed with money.

And she hated these self-styled millionaires. She was prejudiced about most things and most people, but this particular breed always left her massively angry with herself. Why did she have to deal with them at all? These Indians who cared nothing for their own history or literature, while she, a White woman, had worked her guts out at being an expert on all things Indian. These rich Indian men usually came from somewhere in Africa where they had lived in small cramped rooms backing onto their miserly fathers' thriving shops and businesses. They would get to Britain somehow, have three jobs as well as a mini-cab business on the side, and eventually they would own a chain of shops and restaurants and open-all-hours grocery stores. Then they would start to play big boss man. Ready to buy anything, even if it wasn't for sale. Unlike the host British community, she had no respect for their hard work and their so-called Protestant Work Ethic. Hard work invariably meant no time to read books. What use people who didn't read?

The nouveaux riches African-Indians were insufferable enough here, but when they visited the old motherland – not Africa, but the original Mother India – then their phoney act came into its own. They yelled at the servants, they were rude to hotel receptionists and they only spoke in their own atrocious English to anyone they considered beneath them – in money terms of course – and in India, that was almost everyone.

Everyone that is, except anyone with the slightest whiff of glitz and glamour attached to their name. Actors, actresses, dubious models, wannabees and has-beens were respected and adored. These greasy self-made millionaires used hard currency to wangle their way into any set-up at which anyone, however remotely connected with the Bollywood Dream Machine, was likely to be present.

When she had been approached for a meeting, she had imagined all sorts of things, but not this. You didn't just send for a woman you didn't even know, a woman without name or fame, and then order her to make a film.

She went on staring at him. He looked around sixty years of age. Very normal and ordinarily dressed – M & S trousers and pullover. Faint smell of Old Spice, or was it Brut? You could have run into him in a supermarket and never guessed that he was a regular occupant of the best suites in the best hotels. Her anti-Asian billionaire businessmen rage gradually turned to curiosity. Curiosity always had the effect of activating her vocal chords. At last she found her voice:

"I don't get it – what is it that you want exactly? A film, you said, what sort of film... why?"

"Why does anyone ever make a film? What's it to you? Too superior to make an ordinary, entertaining film for a Gujarati businessman? Look, I'm a very straightforward man. I play straight. You take as much money as you want and make a lavish film. You know, the sort of film that everybody talks about, long before they've even seen it? Publicity – lots of interviews, photos splashed everywhere... nice music... that sort of thing."

"Oh, I see. You want to be a producer, but don't know how to do it, so you want me to make the film for you, and you take all the kudos. I know, like a ghost writer. Anyway, what's it about? Is it your life story, that sort of thing... right?"

"No, wrong. Completely wrong! I must never be associated with the project. My involvement is top secret. You hear me? Top Secret!"

This was turning out to be an uphill struggle for the poor little rich business-man. He had expected her to squeal with delight and fall at his feet at the mention of the word "film". What was the matter with her? Was it his English she didn't understand? Was it his accent? He returned from his momentary despair, and tried again:

"Just tell me, will you do it?"

"But what are you exactly? I mean who are you? Do you usually finance films for high returns, or whatever?"

She would have to get him checked out – yet again. Her sources had suggested various possible angles, but not this one – not billionaire aspiring to film maker.

He switched into his Gujarati accented Urdu:

"Look daughter, do you want to eat the mangoes or do you just want to count the trees? What is it with you educated people? Why does everything have to be so complicated? I'm a rich man. And all I'm saying is please get a good script or whatever else you need, and make a film with my money. But for God's sake leave my name out of it!"

"So what's in it for you?" She thought it was a perfectly valid question.

"That's none of your business. How I choose to spend my money is nothing to do with you! You should only complain to me if you run short of money."

"But what kind of film exactly? We're not talking hard porn... are we?" she trailed off uncomfortably. Now that wouldn't be such a bad idea. What a challenge! She'd always wanted to make a pornographic film, but she would have wanted it to be viewed as artistic, erotic, tasteful. She'd had lots of ideas about Indian equivalents of frilly black suspenders and red stilettos.

He seemed genuinely shocked at the idea: "No, no, please definitely not pornographic! What do you take me for? Look, listen, what kind of film you make is up to you. I really don't want to interfere with that, but I would prefer it if you made an ordinary kind of family entertainment film – perhaps something historical. Clean romance. Boy meets girl, that sort of thing... nice songs... whatever you like... something all the family can enjoy – a little kissing if you like... but nothing more!"

"Why if I like? Why whatever I like? It's your money. Why not something you like? Surely you must have some idea. Maybe there's a subject on which you'd like to see a film and no one's making it so you've decided to pay for it yourself. Why bother with a film at all? I could do it quite cheaply on Compact Digital. You only need it to sit and watch at home, right? On your VHS machine, right?"

He rose from the leather settee in his expensive London hotel suite, his face crumpled with exasperation, his hands waving despair: The conversation switched once again into his Gujarati accented Urdu:

"Look, I spent a lot of money tracking you down. You seemed to fit the bill. Your discretion is legendary, your obscurity unmatched. I was assured you could be trusted. Yet all I see before me is a fairly stupid woman. Here I am, offering you the best opportunity you'll ever get, and you're talking about doing it cheaply on Video? What's the matter with you? I'm talking film. You know, "filllum" – big screen, big budget, big stars, long-long songs, shiny costumes, dancing, fighting, good story. I know you only make slow, boring films which nobody ever sees. So here's your big chance. Make a real film."

"What do you want me to do exactly? Write you a story? Manage the production, or direct it myself? What?"

"I don't know. How do I know how it's supposed to work? That's your business surely? You mind your business and I'll mind mine. Hire who ever you have to hire. Nobody else must know of my involvement. They'll only deal with you. So, are we talking now? How much money do you want?"

"Oh come on, I haven't even got a script yet. We do things systematically you know. I have to work it all out. How much money can I have?"

"Whatever you need," he replied without the slightest hesitation.

She shook her head in hopeless despair: "I still don't get this. What's this about? Come on, please, what's the catch?"

"No catch. Have all the money you want. Just make me a film."

"Oh, I see," she said, none the wiser. "Look Sir, there are better ways of losing money. If you're having tax hassles, why not just make charitable donations, or better still set up some sort of educational foundation, lots of prestige in that. Perhaps a new research centre on...."

He jumped in before she could finish suggesting all the honourable ways in which to lose large amounts of money:

"I didn't ask for your advice on how to spend my money. All I want to know is will you do it or won't you? Why must you take your hand round the back of your head to hold your nose?"

She took a long sip from her glass of water, and lit another cigarette truly at a loss for words. No text book had ever prepared a film-maker for such an eventuality. A mad man determined to risk a large amount of money as long as there was some kind of song-and-dance film at the end of it. She calmed down and made another serious attempt at getting some sense out of Mr Moneybags, as she had now christened him in her head:

"Please try and understand. I'm not being difficult. This is just a very unusual brief. It's almost unreal." She had switched into flawless Urdu. He was impressed – an Englishwoman with such good Urdu! Gujarati-speaking people were always impressed by Urdu, thanks to the rebirth of the ghazal music industry.

She continued: "This is so bizarre – please tell me, why are you doing this?"

"Keep your nose out of my affairs! Find a good story – spend a lot of money – get all the best people. At no time must they think they might be working for me. Only the best – megabucks and lavish sets and costumes and lots of media hype! The works! But it's your film, remember, officially, OK? Only you and I know that, OK? And everything you shoot, just give to me… everything…."

"Edited, or unedited? Neg. or Print? I mean do you want only rushes or can I actually cut the film and mix the sound…?"

"Rushes? Neg? What's that? Never mind, whatever… you just do everything – whatever you need to do. Only I get to keep everything… I'll hold onto everything until we are ready to release it – or even not to release it… do you understand?"

"But what's this kind of fiasco going to do to me – to my reputation?"

"What reputation? You are an obscure writer and an even more obscure film-maker, who cares? OK, so you had a go at directing a major film and then it was never heard of again – so what? Hollywood is full of completed films not yet released. Why do you care what happens afterwards? I'm paying you well enough – not only to produce and direct it, but also to keep your mouth shut!"

She was silent for a while. This was impossible! She had expected all sorts of dubious ventures – but not this. Could it be that he was mad? That sometimes happened to people who suddenly came into money. But he hadn't suddenly come into money. She knew that he'd worked his way up from virtually nothing. Dedication and slog had been his motto. He'd built up his businesses slowly, systematically. And now he had a stake in virtually every kind of business, from oil to hotels and motels, from weapons to funeral parlours. Here, and over the Atlantic Ocean. From here to eternity he was supposedly coated with thick layers of money. His was a well-known success story.

After a few minutes' silent contemplation she tried again:

"Look, it would be much easier if you just told me what this was about. Anyway, what makes you think I can even work to such a brief? I'm used to limitations. I like restrictions. I operate best with budgetary constraints. I like cutting corners. I've never ever made a bad film…."

"You've never made anything, period!"

"I don't make films for people like you – my films are serious – well researched, well scripted, well shot and thoughtfully edited. I don't make song-and-dance films – I only deal with reality."

She was off on a favourite tangent, defending her career as an obscure documentary maker. One film, every three years or so, usually about some equally obscure place in the world where people did unimportant, but fascinating things. Well, fascinating for documentary festival goers.

He cut in impatiently: "I'm not asking for your CV – I know you only make the sort of thing that gets seen at film festivals and nowhere else – I don't care about that. Look, I'm paying you the compliment of singling you out as an intelligent film-maker – someone who's smart enough to go through all the motions, but also clever enough to ensure that it gets nowhere. I don't know how you manage that exactly, but you should know your work."

"That's a very difficult brief. To get the best people to work on it, I'd have to have a very good script to show them. Then while shooting, they're not stupid you know. Good actors always insist on re-takes, even if the director is satisfied."

"So let them have as many re-takes as they want… I'm giving you enough money…."

"You really don't understand about film-making…."

"No, that's why I sent for you. I'm a businessman. I only know about business. I only know that sometimes businesses have to look good, but they're really only a front for something else…."

She frowned. What was it all about? Just what was he up to? There was only one way to find out:

"OK, I'll do it…" she began, carefully, with a sense of walking into a long tunnel with a "NO EXIT" sign at the end.

"By the way, there's one condition," he said casually.

"Ah, here it comes…" she thought, relaxing a little. There's nothing quite like having a suspicion confirmed, to bring on a feeling of self-satisfied righteousness.

"The condition is this. Your story must centre on a female character. And she must be fat!" So that's it! She heaved a sigh of relief. He's besotted with some overweight starlet and wants to give her a lucky break. He wants to sit on the film until she does whatever he wants her do, and then, and only then he agrees to release the film. It made sense. Sex is a powerful motivator. Even ordinary not-so-rich men launched pathetic campaigns in the interests of hunting down female prey – but seriously rich men, with unlimited financial resources at their disposal, did positively idiotic things just to get some bimbo to part her legs. The tension lessened within her as she began to get the picture.

He continued: "This must be a very strong and challenging role for an actress – the whole film must hinge on her... it must be HER film – she must be all over it. It must be the story of a woman – any woman...."

She relaxed. Now this crazy scheme made a bit more sense – or so she thought, quite forgetting that it was still a pretty weird brief. And inevitably, relaxation brought its own inspiration.

She suddenly leapt up knocking over a flower vase and screamed: "But I've got it! I've got just the right script. It's wonderful! It's perfect! It's something I wrote years ago about a courtesan from Lucknow. Oh, I've been dying to shoot that script... oh, I can't believe it! What a perfect opportunity – just wait till I tell you about it. It's totally centred on the courtesan and she's an amazing, powerful character. And because she sings and dances, there's plenty of scope for some outstanding original music...."

She stopped suddenly, remembering that she had just been asked to make a film about a fat woman, that would probably never even be released....

It was too depressing. The best script she'd ever written – how could she throw it away on crazy Mr Moneybags and his secret plans? His film-making scheme was obviously part of some really complex seduction strategy.

She fell silent again, totally deflated. In the very next moment a kind of recklessness took hold. This was the nearest she had ever got to actually realising her courtesan project. This was a God-sent opportunity! What was this man to know? She could convince him he'd get his lousy film, and she could secretly try to make a really good film. Keep copies of everything. Duplicate every thing... yes... keep the best takes... how was he to know? He didn't even know what rushes meant. What could he do? He couldn't take legal action against her – not without admitting that he had asked her to make a non-existent film, and that would surely raise the question of why he wanted someone to deliberately make a film destined to sit in the cans forever? In any case, they were no laws against making good films. Yes, she would do it! And she would double cross him. She would make the best film ever. In any event, it would be impossible to make a bad film with a script as good as her Courtesan script. On the other hand, it might turn out bad, but then he didn't care anyway. It was a win-win situation.

"OK, agreed," she said at last, a plot already hatching in her mind.

"Let's drink to that." He got up and poured the drinks, completely forgetting she had already said she never touched the stuff. She carried on sipping water.

"So, what's this story of yours about? A courtesan you say...?" he began chattily.

"Yes a real one – the legendary Tameezan Bai of Lucknow. Have you heard of her?

"No, not really, but go on... what's her story?"

"The story is really about a television film crew from London, making a documentary-drama on the life of Tameezan Bai. Her story unfolds through the story of the filming of this documentary and involves various situations with the film crew. Various things happen to them while we inter-cut back and forth from the actual life of Tameezan. There are three time-frames, you understand? The present-day TV crew, the reconstructed life of Tameezan – late 19th century – being portrayed by present-day actors for the drama-doc sections – and then, wait for this, flash-backs to her *real* life, being played by another set of actors, of course. You get it? It's all inter-cut between differ-ent time frames – the personal dramas of the TV crew and the actors which parallel major episodes from Tameezan's life. It all gets very complicated, but it's told with stunning simplicity. Only I can write like that. I love having lots and lots of different realities going on at the same time. I'm a brilliant writer, you know?"

She stopped for breath and noticed him dozing off. She wrapped up her breathless verbal synopsis: "Anyway, it's that sort of thing. You can read it if you like. I'll bring it in tomorrow."

"Sounds terrible – very boring... but lots of potential for media-hype. I hope it looks interesting enough for your actors and actresses to fall for ...." He laughed uncontrollably, and the sinister expression returned to his face.

She felt put down. He was also getting quite drunk now. He'd gulped her untouched drink as well and was now slurring a bit.

"Really nice," he said. "It sounds really arty-farty and pointless. Just what I wanted... 'twill keep everyone busy busy busy, but then nothing, nothing, at the end... very nice. Sorry, sorry, please go on. Tameejjan, eh?"

"Well, basically, there was a big mystery in Tameezan the Courtesan's life and it centred on her involvement with a certain very well known musician of the time. The Grand Ustad – 'He Who Lights up the Universe' – that was the official title bestowed on him by the rulers of the State. The theme of my script is to give a possible explanation of that mystery – but it has to be disguised as fiction otherwise there could be problems with the Ustad's descendants. Oh, by the way, there's this grandson of that same universe-lighting Ustad, Shohrat Khan, you know? He's the best known Indian classical musician today. I think I'll approach him to play all the solo sitar pieces for the film. I'm sure he'll be thrilled to play the sitar for an actor portraying his very own legendary grandfather. That's rather neat, don't you think? Quite a coup."

The millionaire had heard of Ustad Shohrat Khan, the classical musician. And he knew what a sitar was, but basically he had a lot of difficulty differentiating a sitar sound from a sarod sound. They twanged in a similar way – that's all he knew. He frequently got them mixed up. And as for the surbahar and the veena... well let's stop nit picking.

The millionaire couldn't really be expected to know much about classical music. He had grown up on Bombay film music, and for him all music was boring unless it had words – easy words that could be memorised, and tunes that could be hummed. Even so, in the interests of appearing cultured to potential business contacts and junior diplomats he had, on numerous occasions, sat through hours and hours of excruciating boredom, pretending to be moved by some or the other Ustad or Pandit. Mostly he just fell asleep on these occasions.

She was chattering away about possible recruits for her new venture. All of a sudden, she was a person with a real project – with all the euphoric enthusiasm that marks the birth of artistic projects. There was no stopping her now. She was gushing forth with a torrent of ideas. There's a famous Arabic proverb – the longest distance in the entire universe is the distance between words and deeds!

"And then there's this World's Number One Composer. He can look after all the background music. And he can compose the central ghazal. Oh, I forgot to tell you the most important thing – the whole plot hinges on this one ghazal recital by Tameezan the courtesan, you know? Everything happens that night."

"What night?" He wished this woman would leave now. He really didn't want to go on hearing about her wretched script. He just wanted to wallow in his scheme.

"The big night. Oh, you'll see it in the script. The night the courtesan finally comes face to face with her beloved Lighter Up of the Universe. Years of waiting, years of longing and pining, and then finally, she gets to see him. That's the night she sings the ghazal. I'll get a special ghazal composed by the World's Number One Composer. Do you know, he has a huge following of groupies... in a surreal sort of way he's almost like a present-day courtesan. I mean he's real, but he could almost be imaginary – you see what I mean?"

"I love it. I love it. Yes, yes, very confusing – all the makings of a flop so far. Well done! It's getting rather late. My next meeting's in about half an hour and I must change."

His next "meeting" was his favourite call girl. He always called her when he was in London. She was like an old friend. Very often they'd just sit on the bed and chat until he got very drunk and very sleepy. He still paid her the full amount. The girl would be here soon, but this boring Producer Director Documentary turned Drama person with her script to end all scripts looked like nowhere near shifting her arse.

"Then there are various other characters – it's a huge cast. The TV camera-man falls in love with the producer, while she herself is obsessed with the courtesan – you know, emotional lesbianism by proxy – that sort of thing. The actress who is playing the courtesan in the reconstruction is in love with the guy who's playing the musician in the original life story. That's different from the dramatised reconstruction you know. No, perhaps it's not different. Anyway, stuck on a long shoot in an excruciatingly hot and dusty North Indian summer, they all keep lusting after one another – all except the producer. She only loves herself."

"Yes, just like you," he thought, and started to get up.

"If you like I'll bring the script to you now. It'll only take a few minutes. You can read it for yourself."

"Er, no, no, please don't trouble yourself. I don't need to read it. You've described it beautifully. It's good. Start casting for all the other parts you need and next time, I'll brief you on who's going to be your courtesan...."

"What on earth do you mean?" (Ah-ha, so at last he's coming clean, she thought.)

Best to play dumb: "You're not going to foist some Bombay starlet on me, are you? I want to hold auditions properly. And then if you want to try them all out on the casting couch – that's fine, I don't care. But I'll choose my own courtesan. I'm not having some starlet-model Miss World look-alike, who'd really like to work with children, diamond stud in the nose, bimbo lip-gloss and lacquered-hair."

"It's my money," he reminded her. "And anyway, she's not a starlet. She's a major star! Top of the league. Perfect for the part. You will pay her a decent advance and sign her in an exclusive five-year contract. During that time she works for no one else. You hear me? You must make sure she has loads of work, all the time. All her social engagements should bring maximum publicity for our film – nothing else. Loads of interviews. Magazine features. Big photos. Parties. No time for other producers, OK?"

She began to see the light – so he had some kind of score to settle with this actress woman. Talk of revenge – what a way to go about it!

"But who is she? You know my script requires a flawless Urdu diction. Unless she's got that, forget it!"

"Well, she can spend the first few months of her contract period getting herself tutored for a nice Urdu accent. What do you call it? Vocculation? Electrocution? Something like that...."

"It's called an erection. Look, what's this about? You've got a gripe against some Bombay actress, so you want her tied up in this film for a full five years. And then what happens?"

"Wait and see," he had started to open the door to let her out. "Call me next week. You need to sign a contract with me, and then I'm setting up this special company so you've got someone to pose as your boss. A full five-year contract, OK?"

"What if she refuses to sign?"

"She'll sign all right. As far as she's concerned it's her Moggaley-ajjam, her Pakeeja, or Gone Vith The Vind. But we know better, don't we?"

"Do we?"

9

MOHANJI PRODUCTIONS (PRIVATE) Ltd.

Each and every Mohanji son, from the oldest to the youngest, assisted in the shop during the school lunch-break, and again after school. Lunchtimes could get very busy, just before the afternoon lull, and Mohanji would not himself be able to get lunch unless the boys took over the lunchtime shift. The boys were happy enough to do this. It was a welcome change from school, and serving in a shop gave them a sense of being grown up and powerful. They had learnt all the haggling techniques from their father and they did him proud in terms of milking the maximum amount of money from customers. But the boys had all assumed that this would only be a temporary arrangement, only until such time as they had real careers of their own. They had all imagined they would ultimately be going to university – if not in England, then at least in the Big Town.

But Mohanji had other plans. They were all to be educated to secondary school level, and then as each boy became available, another unit would be added to the shop. Gradually, with nine sons, he would take over two entire sides of the Square. Every son would have a shop unit of his own to run, and behind that, a couple of rooms for himself and his future family. Mohanji had worked it all out. But what he liked best about the plan was that it would save him thousands of shillings in further education, and more important it would also save him the expense and hassle of hiring staff. How could he ever forget all that business with Kasoga, the radio-gramophone repairman? In any case, how could his boys ever imagine they would pursue independent careers of their own? How would all the shops function then? Surely, doing well meant having lots of shops – not spending lots of money to send your children to English universities so that they married shameless White women and remained in England forever.

There were many tales of Mohanji's stingy ways. For instance, there was a well-established town tradition of Sunday cinema. Bombay Talkies was Indian-owned and usually featured the latest 1960's gaudy masala from Bollywood. Evening shows were reserved for the professional middle-classes, those that didn't have to get up as early as the shopkeepers on Monday mornings. Cinema tickets were also more expensive in the evenings, a built-in safeguard to prevent Asian teachers and doctors and lawyers from sharing their air-space with the Dukavalla plebs.

The huge cinema, surprisingly plush for a small town, had originally been built by the British so that homesick Brit. expats could feed their nostalgia with Ealing comedies and Hollywood musicals. It stood on one of the streets that ran off the Square. Everything that was said and sung in the melodramatic Bollywood offerings could be heard outside the cinema if you positioned yourself correctly. Youths, both Black and Asian often loitered around outside just to listen to the songs. Lots of screechy noisy high-pitched female vocals, dhishum-dhishum sound effects from fight sequences (choreographed as painstakingly as the elaborate dance sequences), heroes in ketchup blood, star heroines in glycerin tears and vamps sprawled in garish costumes, legs apart in fish-net tights and heaving bosoms entrapped in sequined Gossard Wonderbras.

This money-spinning art form from Bombay was generally considered good, clean family entertainment. Nothing rude, no kissing, and generally, no loss of virginity. And most definitely no nudity except through the wet-sari technique. Boy meets girl. Boy and girl sing together. Forced to separate by parents and or villain. Both sing again – separately, in a slower tempo. In the end, good triumphs over evil and all assemble for a happy family photograph. Gigantic posters depicting this weird and wonderful world of singing together and singing apart, were splashed on corrugated tin fences around the Square, leaving passers-by with no option but to step in and check out the offerings.

And that was exactly what all the Dukavalla families did on Sunday afternoons, all except the Mohanjis that is. No way was he paying for twelve cinema tickets. Even if the parents didn't go, it still meant paying for ten tickets – more than thirty shillings in all, sufficient for a whole month of electricity for the shop.

So Mohanji came up with a brilliant scheme whereby ONE son, on a strict rota basis, would be bought a ticket each Sunday, and in return for this privilege, would have to come home and act out the entire film. This involved narrating the story and acting out the songs to the rest of the family over supper. The fact that the average Bombay film of this period didn't carry anything even vaguely amounting to an original story-line didn't enter into the Mohanji brand of logic. (So what if all the stories are the same? Just play them out differently, you stupid boy!) And so, all the Mohanji boys, one by one, Sunday by Sunday, became brilliant story-tellers in their own right – narrating, acting and translating the visual experience of a song-dance-fight film into their own amateur theatricals. Needless to say, these performances had to include a complete and accurate rendition of all the ten or so songs, including the screechy orchestral bits, at the appropriate moment in the proceedings.

When I heard about the Mohanji home-spun Sunday theatre and supper tradition, I decided to excuse myself from the Sunday evening cinema outings with my snooty family and their friends, and decided instead, to attend the Mohanji re-enactments. I had the good fortune of being friends with a Mohanji son who was nearly my age, so I pleaded that I wanted to play with my friend instead of going to the cinema. My mother, surprisingly enough, allowed this. The cinema was only down the road from the Mohanji premises, so I would be dropped off at the shop while the others proceeded to the cinema. Here, they would sit enthralled with the latest gaudy Bombay blockbuster, while I (lucky me!) was able to sample a more tasteful home-made adaptation of the same. It brought a whole new dimension to what would otherwise have been a passive visual experience.

Soon the Mohanji boys were in great demand as story-tellers of Indian film. Even those who had seen the real film invited the boys to come over and do their own version of it, complete with song, dance and fight sequences. I thrived on these sessions. Sometimes one of the boys would forget a particular song, and I would quickly make up another one in its place, and we'd sing that instead. My songs were sometimes even better than the originals.

This was real art and I had the good fortune of sometimes being part of the team. We called ourselves Mohanji Productions (Private) Ltd. I played all the "extras", assisting the storyteller with some of the more feminine gestures. Inevitably, but much to my mother's delight, my flat-chested, awkward, eight-year-old tom-boyish ways gradually took on the exaggerated grace and pseudo-elegance of the Bombay film heroine, albeit minus the heaving bosoms.

10
FRENEMIES

Great friendships are sometimes the result of mutual dislike – not only a dislike for one another, but a general malaise with the rest of the world. The world then becomes the common enemy and the protagonists in this kind of friendship relate to one another only in terms of the things they detest.

Sonia despised films. And so did Ash. Only in his case, the resentment was based on not having made it into films, while hers was from a sense of superiority. She worshipped the powers of imagination, and books provided the most fertile ground on which to nurture the imagination, with music coming a close second. And then there was Radio. That was fine, as long as one was engaged in some other productive activity while listening to the wireless, as she insisted on calling it. And Television?

"Oh please, give me a break! Unless you're sixteen-something, what on earth can you watch on television these days?" she would ask.

As for films well, they did the exact opposite of books. They stagnated the powers of the human imagination, because they SHOWED it all. They showed one person's view of a given set of events. For Sonia, films were anaemic and one-dimensional but for Ash they were the high altar of all art and creation. If there was something to say, then it could only be said through a film and what's more, it could really only be said through one of HIS films.

Contrary to its outward appearance of an easy-going, companionable, platonic friendship, theirs was in fact a tense alliance based on the resentment of a common enemy – Film. And then there were various sub-plots, layered on top of one another to furnish an even richer texture to this enigmatic love-hate saga. Sonia's ability to actually finish the things she started left Ash feeling hopelessly inadequate. She seemed to produce ideas at the rate of almost one every ninety seconds. Most of these ideas she then proceeded to utilise in some mildly lucrative way. He, on the other hand, was always stuck for ideas. And on the rare occasion when an idea did strike him, he chewed it over for months, and then finally and reluctantly began writing yet another film script. Meanwhile someone else would have already successfully completed and released a film on the same subject.

"It's already been done," was his favourite excuse for doing nothing. He really believed that if someone had made a film called "Umrao Jaan", then no one else, anywhere on this planet had a right to make yet another film about any other courtesan in the world.

"Whenever I have a nice idea," he would moan, "just thinking about it seems to trigger off something and someone else gets there first. It's spooky I tell you! Almost like some kind of osmosis... my ideas seem to penetrate everyone's brain membranes before I've had a chance to...."

"That's ludicrous", Sonia would say. "You let them do it their way, and you do it your way, Ash. Just because Romeo & Juliet has been done once, doesn't mean it can't be done again. There are only three stories in the whole world anyway. All stories are born out of dispute – and at the root of all disputes are three things: land, wealth and woman."

She was always telling him what to do, but she sincerely believed it was for his own good. She felt sorry for him. He was after all, her best friend. He always listened to her sermons. He seldom lashed out at her. Sometimes she thought she should be kinder to him, ease him out of his blinkered view of art. Whenever she felt like this, she stopped barking and offered up feasible platitudes: "Art is born of sameness – it's nothing to do with uniqueness. It's because we're all the same we relate to the joys and fears of others. What you call pain, and what I call pain are one and the same thing – yet our pains are different. If we didn't use the same words to define the same emotions, how could one ever empathise with the work of a complete stranger, eh Ashy-Pashy?" she would cajole, lapsing into baby language.

But Ash refused to be consoled. No, it had to be film. Books? Who read books these days? But even as he reminded himself for the umpteenth time that books were a poor substitute for real art, he realised with a pang that most of hers usually managed to have a devoted cult following. Her last book, which he had thought a really stupid idea, had done extremely well. She had divided and sub-divided men into seven main categories of "Cassanova" and had written over two hundred and fifty thousand words providing a sort of early warning system for potential women victims on the art of identifying and classifying a womaniser.

Under aptly named headings such as "Tom Cat On the Prowl" and "Boy Child wanting a Breast Feed," she had actually produced an almost word-perfect script for the sort of things these men said when they set out to weave their magic spells. And her fieldwork had been meticulous. She had personally worked her way through a hundred and twenty-six different men in the short period of twenty months to gather material for the book.

Sonia and Ash had been friends for years, but they hardly ever met. Where was the time? Her hectic schedule of an idea a minute and six different men a month, and his endless moping about at home with the curtains drawn and Bob Dylan CD's blaring through yet another film script, when *could* they have met? But, luckily for them, the telephone had already been invented.

They talked on the phone at least once a day. They shared confidences. They talked about sex non-stop. They knew each other's sexual preferences and discussed their respective lovers in minute close-up detail. Or to use Ash's parlance, "unedited rushes" – no corny cutaways to flowers kissing in the wind. In a strange sort of way, they loved each other, but they were certainly not in love with one another. He didn't feel he was worthy of anyone's love, and she? Well she just loved herself. God had made her brainy and she knew it.

Ash adored her mind and admired her quick-witted bitchiness, but some-where deep down, he felt threatened by her. He lived with the perpetual dread that one morning, she would just leap out of bed and decide to make a film. That would finish him off for good. No film school, no training, no interest in films – she hadn't even been to the cinema for twenty-five years, yet if anyone had the energy and pig-headedness to pull it off, she most certainly did. She had just the right kind of personality for this game. Rejection excited her. She welcomed rejection as a cue to try again. She'd thump her fists on many desks until the money had been raised and she would not rest until it had all been done exactly to her liking. And that was the sort of personality a filmmaker needed. It wasn't fair. It was such a waste. She had the personality, yet she cared nothing about the film business.

Sonia considered herself vastly above all that sort of thing. So much so that once when she had agreed to do a small but vital role for a struggling young director, and the film had gone on to be a major success, she had not even bothered to go and see the film, never mind actually turning up at the glittering bash afterwards:

"Well, I helped him out, didn't I? I did what he wanted me to do. I'm glad it worked for him. What more does he want? I don't have to go and sit through all of it as well, do I?"

Just like that, the whole thing was dismissed. Everyone took it to be false modesty. How could you be in a film and then not even want to go and see yourself? But Ash knew better. He knew her nonchalance was genuine. He knew exactly what she'd say: "Who wants to sit in silence in a darkened auditorium? What's so social about that? You can't even have a conversation with anyone, so where the hell are you going to get material for your next book?"

So although Ash lived, breathed and ate film, without actually ever having made a film of his own, and Sonia had a complete disdain for any kind of visual medium, they managed to be friends – most of the time. There were times when he came dangerously close to wanting to end their friendship forever. There were times when she became ultra secretive about her activities. Actually, he was never quite sure what she did for a living. Sometimes, in the tense old days of the democratic-goodies and the communist-baddies, he was convinced she worked for MI-5. At other times he was sure she was a detective. Whether it was Caracas or Nicosia, she knew how to track people down.

She seemed to do everything and nothing. She seemed to know about everything and nothing. She wouldn't see films or read fiction, yet she knew exactly what was going on and who was who. And sometimes, in a spirit of early enthusiasm, when he showed her parts of a new script he had just started, she would go straight to some small detail and start pontificating like a Film School Lecturer:

"No point in seeing the hand first. First we should see the close-up of the face, crying. And then when we think she's crying, we should tilt the camera down to show that she's chopping onions. That will bring a sense of relief for everyone. They'll laugh. People love to laugh. Then you could cut to the close-up of the knife going through the onion to get you back to her wide shot in the kitchen... that's how it's done. And then when all the women are gossiping away and bitching, just inter-cut the knife close-ups... use a blunt knife on the onion – it will come out looking much more severe...."

This kind of talk he found extremely threatening. Why hadn't he thought of that? Then, when he'd incorporate her idea into yet another unfinished script, she would exclaim, with genuine surprise:

"Oh that's brilliant! I like that bit! That's really clever!"

What could one do with that sort of friend? She put you down, she patronised you, she gave you mind-improving books to read, but when you borrowed one of her script inventions, she just patted you on the back for being so clever and so original. And her compliments were anything but economical: "But this is prolific. What a metaphor! This is not a sentence, this is a symphony. It's orgasmic. A full 55.9 on the Richter scale – Oh Ash! The earth certainly moved!"

Then she would launch into her own latest passion. It could be almost anything – from plastic bangles to space travel, but whatever it was, of one thing he was always uneasily sure: it would earn her money somehow. While he, with his million unfinished scripts, had yet to shoot a frame. Thank God for his rich patron. Nearly thirty, and still financially dependent on his drug-dealer father. Or at least that's what he thought his father did for a living. What else could it be? How else did one have abundant funds in unlimited quantities for an indefinite period? He'd never actually seen his father, but received an ample, regular monthly income through a firm of lawyers while Sonia was completely financially independent.

But what did she actually do? Her books on all those obscure subjects could not by themselves have supported her lavish life-style. There had to be something else... but what?

11

FIRST, MUSIC...

For someone who had just been given a carte blanche to make a lavish film, she returned home strangely deflated. She wasn't even going to bother to figure it all out. God worked in mysterious ways. This semi-literate millionaire Moneybags upstart could be her big chance. Yet it felt completely unreal. But she resolved not to wallow in surrealism and just treat the whole thing like any other project. How did one behave when one had just landed a big-budget film? Celebrate! Go out and celebrate! But how? And with whom? And what could she say? Who would believe her? Had she been dreaming? Call up Moneybags to make sure he exists.

"Hello, it's me. We just had this meeting, and I'm still confused. I know I said I'll do it, but how do I... well you know... where do I begin? I need to set up procedures. Who do I deal with? And what about my own contract?"

"I thought we'd been thorough all that. I'm setting up a special company for this production. Someone will contact you when everything's ready." That was undoubtedly his own voice – so Moneybags did exist.

"So... er... is this other person officially involved? Does he know? I mean is he aware of your scheme?"

"Mind your own business. As far as you're concerned he is the Executive Producer, or Manager – or whatever you want to call him. He'll look after the business side. You just worry about your own thing. Make a film...."

"No, what I meant was, is his involvement official? Can my team know they're working for him?"

"Yes, yes of course, that's what he's for – the front man, the fall guy. He'll do all the official interfering. He'll turn up everywhere and get on your nerves. I've even asked him to give you a bad time on over-spending, just to make it look real. And sometimes he'll turn up on your sets with all his relatives who want to get a look at the stars. That sort of thing."

"For someone who claims to know nothing about the film business, you certainly surprise me," she said, genuinely taken aback with his attention to detail.

"I always do my homework. Anything else? Try not to bother me again. I'm leaving for India tomorrow," he said impatiently.

"Yes, OK, but what do I do next? I mean what...."

"We'll contact you when everything's ready. For now, you just get your end of it up and running. Start recruiting your team. Talk to your musicians. You know? Do I have to teach you everything?"

She still didn't understand any of it. The best plan was to proceed without worrying about what he was up to and why. Who cares? Some mad billionaire with a pash on a Bombay starlet. As long as she got to make her film what did it matter?

She started making plans. Such fun when the script is already in place. Down to the last detail. The film already existed on paper. And now at last, she could transfer it to celluloid. But sound first. Sound before picture.

The first thing to do was to secure contracts with all the musicians. Then record the music. That was the most important thing. This film hinged entirely on its music. If she could get that in the can, then even if Moneybags changed his mind or had some sense knocked into him by some do-gooder friend, then at least she could release all that original music. Yes, that alone would do. That by itself would make quite a satisfying project, film or no film. And then again, if things went well, and the money kept coming, she would shoot the final scene first. That ghazal scene would have to be done first. Do all the expensive stuff while he's in a spending mood. Sooner or later he's bound to tighten up. The rest could be done cheaply. Shoot the lavish climax first.

But first, MUSIC. She wrote out the word in large capitals on her notepad, reaching for the phone at the same time.

"Hi, it's me!"

"You? Hey, what a nice surprise! How did you find me?"

"I knew you had some concert bookings in Cyprus. So I knew it had to be Nicosia. How many hotels in Nicosia of the kind you would stay in? Just three. So I tried the first one, and here you are, elementary! How are you? What's all that noise?"

"Busy. I'm in the shower.... I've got fifteen minutes before a sound check. What's up?"

"Tameezan, that's what's up."

"Who? Is there a new potential groupie on the scene, and I haven't heard? Tell me, tell me."

"No dear, she can't be your groupie, sorry, she's dead. Nineteenth century courtesan, Lucknow."

"Oh that Tameezan! Tameezan Bai Lucknavi? The one who was obsessed with the Grand Ustad, the Ronson Lighter....?"

"The same. I'm making a film about her and I want you to do all the music. How does that grab you?"

"Wow! Great! I've always been fascinated by Tameezan... tell you what, I finish in Cyprus tomorrow and then I'm headed for Amsterdam. Send me a fax there."

"You could stop in London on your way and we could talk."

"Just talk? No action?"

"Oh, come on! OK, action as well if you want. But won't you be exhausted?"

"I perform best when I'm exhausted. My brain won't be working too well, but who cares about that? Who needs the brain, as long as other parts are in full working order... it'll be just like old times, right?"

"Yes, yes, OK. Just get yourself here first. I have lots to tell you. By the way have you been in India recently? I just wondered if you had come across a Bollywood starlet called Champakali?"

"Oh God yes! More like chhipkali! Have I come across her! She waited outside my hotel room for a full five days, and nights. Finally I took pity on her and let her in. Turned out she wanted to diversify into singing and was looking to various musicians for support, something like that."

"And? Was she any good?"

"Nothing to write home about. Not that I heard her sing. I like to check their sense of rhythm first, not bad. A bit clingy. Brought her own condoms, very considerate. Lovely eyes. She just wouldn't leave afterwards, and I had to call hotel security to escort her out."

"Oh no! You'd better get here quick, and I'll tell you the rest. It's quite a story."

"What what what?"

"Go and do your sound check first. We don't want some poor concert organizer to drop dead before his time.... I'll see you later."

12
MORALITY & CHILLIES

While it's true to say that Mohanji was mean with money and ever-alert to more money-making opportunities, it would be grossly unfair to suggest that he was heartless or unkind. He would be the first to help anyone in genuine trouble. His heart was as big as his fist was tight. For instance, he gave his services ungrudgingly and on a voluntary basis to a special town committee of elders, the "Panchayat", liberally translated as the Indian Morality Committee of Five Elders, sub-titled, "Custodians of Shame, Honour, Dignity and Female Chastity."

The Committee was in charge of Asian affairs within the mainly Black African town. Africans were not considered civilised enough to deal with the in's and out's of exclusively Muhindi problems. Indians had dignity. They had izzat. Izzat and Family Honour were definitions for a decent existence. Izzat meant everything. Scandal was worse than death. Asian problems had to be solved by morally upright Asians. For this, Mohanji and four other Asian notables were entrusted with the all-important task of making pronouncements on various moral dilemmas: family conflicts, mother-in-law problems, elopements and so-called "love marriages." None of these issues could be trusted to the Blacks, for they were as shameless as the Whites.

Mohanji was of the view that Blacks and Whites had no sense of izzat – no notion of family honour. No respect for elders. Only Indians knew about that sort of thing and they were in danger of fast losing it. Mohanji and his four colleagues, the custodians of family honour and dignity, ended every meeting with a general pronouncement on the shamelessness of Whites and Blacks – mini-skirts, the contraceptive pill, the Beatles' music, psychedelic drugs, and of course toilet paper. Only a shameless race could wipe its bottoms with paper rather than have a proper wash.

Their meetings were always held on Sunday afternoons and provided Mohanji with a focal point for his social life. This was the only day on which the shop was shut – it had to be, by law. The dreaded African government had now decided to start interfering in that sort of thing as well. In the old days, Mohanji had always opened on Sunday mornings. But to make matters worse, the Mohanji family Guru had sided with the government on this one, saying it was essential to have a day of rest to recharge one's spiritual batteries. Mohanji suspected the Guru's sentiments were more out of a need to keep the government sweet, in case they decided to slam the temple shut, rather than out of any grand spiritual considerations. But he felt guilty for thinking this. It was tantamount to blasphemy to question the holiness of the Guru. So, if it hadn't been for the Guru, Mohanji would probably have kept the door half-open, even on Sunday mornings, just in case any passer-by wanted to buy tap-water. In spite of all his stinginess, there was a feeling of abundance in the Mohanji household. I knew the weekly menu by heart, being a persistent hanger-on. There was something magical about the Mohanji meals. There was never a shortage of delicious food. The memory of even their simplest meals of vegetables, chappaties and rice still has a Proustian impact on me. The rituals governing the Mohanji meals were equally scintillating. Grace was said before every meal. Water was sprinkled on the ground. The parched earth had to quench its thirst before you could fill your stomach with the abundance it had provided for you. The family always ate on the floor, seated in a huge circle in the backyard – a short distance from the mud stoves on which their delicious meals were cooked by the Widow. To this day, as a tribute to Mohanji's memory, I detest the very concept of a dining table.

There was always plenty of food. Their meals were supposed to provide for twelve family members, but any number of guests or hangers on, like myself, could turn up unexpectedly and eat to their heart's content, making no difference to the family quota. For such a miserly family, this abundance of food was truly an anomaly. It wasn't until I came to the West, many years later, and realised how Europeans measure out everything and literally count every single potato and pea, that I fully appreciated the Mohanji food magic.

There were of course cynics who claimed that Mohanji's Widow daughter remained by the cooking pots ever ready with large jugs of hot water in case of unexpected visitors. But even if this were true, these dilutions certainly made no difference to the taste of the food. The curries were always a bright, bright red – not through excessive use of tomatoes, but through dried red chillies that were freshly pounded at home while still very red. (If left too long, they turn brown, which is why pre-packed chilly powder always has a muddy look.) But the home-pounded Mohanji chilly-powder always had a voluptuous red colour and a velvety glossy texture.

Chilly-pounding days were very special. Children were strictly forbidden from entering the yard when all the neighbourhood women gathered to pound the chillies. The yard would be dotted with dozens of huge stone containers in which loads and loads of shrivelled up red chillies would be mercilessly beaten to death with heavy wooden rods. Gigantic pestles and mortars emitting clouds of orange-pink dust, contaminating the moist equatorial air with pungent fumes. And the women, who would otherwise have been gossiping thirteen-to-the-dozen, remained eerily silent behind the ends of their saris, carefully held over their noses and mouths with one hand, while the other took alternate strokes with a partner in annihilating the wholeness of the poor chillies. The forced silence meant each woman was alone with her thoughts, and in the absence of what would have been therapeutic chatter to lighten the burdens of the heart, the women seemed to derive a sort of compensatory pleasure from beating the chillies extra hard. Their eyes watering and noses dripping, they re-lived some particularly outrageous act of injustice they had recently encountered at the hands of drunk husbands or imperious mothers-in-law.

Those pounding rhythms just entranced me. I was utterly hypnotised. I would hang around the closed outer door of the yard to compose my tunes. Even the women's incessant sneezing seemed to fit into my songs. I composed entire rhythm cycles around "Atishoooo, atishoo... dham-dham-dham-dham... khatt dham, khatt dham."

It was always a race against time – could I get to the end of a particular phrase before the next sneeze? Would I get another eleven dham-dhams before the next water-break? Needless to say, irregular rhythms became my speciality.

The women would pound enough for their own use, and then the excess would be sold off to Indian middle-class homes where no sane person would have dreamed of embarking on such a hazardous task. And then when it was announced that the chilly-pounding was complete, the powdered chillies were safely confined to large gunny sacks and the pungent air had settled down, the professional middle-classes arrived by the hordes to buy their supplies. My mother was sometimes convinced that Mohanji added sawdust to the red chilly powder to increase its weight. At other times she raved about the quality and freshness of Mohanji's own home-ground chillies. I always found her attitude confusing. Did she like the Mohanji's or didn't she? Like them, she too was Indian, but she considered herself a better sort of Indian. She was educated. She had a profession. She didn't run a shop. She only went to the shop to buy spices. Yes, spices, for however European these Muhindis might think they are, they never ever succumb to Europeanisation in matters of food. Indian food – the great uniter of all classes.

13
THE WISH LIST

Zarine wasn't a bit like he'd imagined. There was nothing even remotely spooky about her. No hint of new-age candle and incense rituals. No crystal ball. No salt circles. No birth-dates or times. She exuded the air of a highly competent, down-to-earth sort of woman who faced life head-on and somehow always got what she wanted. She carried around her an inexplicable quality of peace and calm and her face was radiant as one who might know the whole mystery of creation but wasn't telling. She could've been anything from 26 to 46 and immaculately groomed in a low-key sort of way. A smart leather brief-case crammed with case-notes lay half-open on a side table in her office, a small room in a New Age clinic in central London. Ash stared at the briefcase wistfully. Heaps of papers full of the hopes and aspirations of thousands, each dream revealing a hundred other dreams.

Ash was still in shock. So this was Zarine. Is this how dream-teachers looked? The bespectacled brown-haired young woman across the desk wasn't a bit like the fairground Gypsy he'd imagined. His annoyingly haughty, high and mighty best friend had a way of marketing people so that they sounded larger than life. Sonia had exaggerated as usual. Yet here was Zarine the dream machine, five foot nothing, small waist, petite, softly spoken, light make-up, unassuming manner. Ash was intrigued. He had paid a one hundred and eighty pound advance as an initial consultation fee and was determined to get his money's worth.

"So, tell me, what do I have to do?" he asked chattily, momentarily forgetting the clinical surroundings, and still half expecting to be given mantras and complicated salt, candle and mirror rituals to perform at bedtime.

Zarine looked at him blankly, fixing her soft gaze just somewhere above his hairline. Ash was beginning to feel intimidated when her soft, everyday-kind of voice put him at ease again: "You don't have to do anything. Just think in terms of what you'd like from life, and who you want to be – where you see yourself two years or five years from now… that sort of thing. And all I have to do is help you get there. So, first I'd like a wish list. Just write

down what you'd like – as many items as you like. In any order that you like."
She leaned over and handed him a form to fill out.

Ash was devastated. This was no magic. This was simply some sort of goal
definition exercise. He'd heard about young Americans who had become
billionaires by running courses in creative visualisation techniques. So, that's
her game, he thought, but aloud he said: "All right, item one, I'd like to make
a film."

He waited for her reaction hoping he had shocked and impressed her with
his single-mindedness.

Zarine's expression was unchanged. "Yes, please go on, as many items as
you like."

"No, that's all I'd like really. Can we just work with that for now, and if it
works out then I'll think of some more? Let's keep it simple."

He wanted to keep it as simple as possible, so that he could go back to
Sonia and triumphantly expose her Dream Teacher Contact as a trickster, a
fraud and a charlatan.

14
KALYUG

With the exception of the second-born green-eyed taxi-driver, all the other Mohanji boys were of above average intelligence. They sported brilliant school reports and entertained secret ambitions to be doctors, lawyers, engineers, accountants and computer programmers. But for now, they contended themselves with weighing out flour and spices, and home-pounded red chilly powder, while on Sunday evenings they faced the exciting but daunting task of re-enacting senseless Bombay films.

The Mohanji living quarters were spotlessly clean if you looked closely, but on first sight they always gave the impression of being nauseatingly squalid. The entire Mohanji family lived in four small rooms behind their two shops with a "sakati" – a concrete backyard which also served as an open-air kitchen. At the end of the sakati stood a roofless area partitioned by corrugated tin, which served as a communal lavatory. In another corner of the backyard a small partitioned room with a single cold water tap over a plastic bucket sufficed as bathroom. This too was roofless for Mohanji was a great believer in the health enhancing effects of a rain-bath. The boys would often pray for rain and then, as soon as it started, they would run helter-skelter towards the small bathroom. Not that they believed in the healing properties of rain water – it's just that the rain in this part of the world was often warmer than the tepid water which gushed out at a tricky angle from the rusty tap.

In the kitchen area, Mohanji's Widow daughter slaved night and day to cook for twelve people in between running the second shop and sewing almost non-stop. It was quite a common sight to see her finishing off the hemming on some garment while keeping an eye on the Sunday curry. When did she find the time to do her physics lessons? My Uncle was teaching her physics by post, and I was the postman.

She had been widowed quite early in marriage. She didn't want herself or her baby to be a burden on her father. She thought of him as a very poor man and so felt obliged to earn her keep. Apart from cooking, sewing and running the second shop, she also rolled out thousands of papards (poppadoms) for sale to Indian families. The papard money was said to provide good quality, imported milk-formula for her baby. Powdered milk was essential as the Widow's schedule didn't allow breast-feeding. In any case, it would've been considered immodest in the extreme to breast-feed a baby in public, leave alone in the presence of shop customers.

The Mohanjis were all deeply religious. They visited their temple every morning before opening up shop. They had a sort of family Guru who resided in the temple. He was petrifying to look at, but was said to be a very holy man who knew all sorts of things about the meaning of life.

From time to time the Guru would dish out wisdom on the proper way of doing things, and Mohanji waited on tenterhooks for his every word. It could be the smallest thing – like children must be in bed by eight o'clock. Or that you must make sure they clean their teeth properly. On one occasion, the Guru pronounced that western-style toothpaste was rubbish, and salt and household baking soda were the best substances known to man for the prevention of tooth decay and gum disease. Mohanji immediately took the cue and stopped the purchase of toothpaste, delighted at being able to make another saving in the household budget. Mohanji was the original conservationist. He believed if you could make something, you didn't go out and buy it. He detested waste long before it was fashionable to do so. In the language of the 1990's Mohanji was already a Green in the 1960's. Repair, don't replace, re-cycle and re-use everything. Luckily for him, none of his customers subscribed to this view. Mohanji often argued against the wasteful nature of paper tissues. But he had no objection to selling boxes of Kleenex in his shop. That was purely business. But in his personal life, he failed to understand how someone could pay five shillings for a box of flimsy paper, only to use once and then throw away. He argued that the same five shillings could buy the best quality muslin handkerchief that could be washed and used over and over again.

I've often wondered if Mohanji ever recognised his own personal waste-not philosophy being finally embraced, at least as an official stance, by the elite of wealthy nations. These lands of plenty – Canada, the USA, Britain, Germany, Austria, Sweden. He must be in one of these countries – or somewhere near them – after his tragic expulsion from his beloved homeland. True, it was never home, but it was the homeland. Real home was always India, Bharat. He had always asserted that as soon as he had enough money, he would return to Bharat. He'd said this for forty years. But in the Mohanji way of thinking, one could never have enough money. And he would never have left small town Pearl had it not been for his forced expulsion.

His crime? He was charged with exploiting the Blacks. Somewhere along the line, almost overnight, it had become a crime to exploit the Blacks. And Mohanji's name was first on the list of those charged with this brand new, heinous crime. All of a sudden it was a crime to make money out of Africans, or to refuse to marry your daughters to them. Mohanji was not alone in being wrenched from his beloved shop and transported to some cold inhospitable land dominated by shameless White culture. A few thousand others, all Dukavallas, soon faced the same end. But it was Mohanji who started the ball rolling, and in many ways, the general expulsion of the Dukavallas was aimed specifically at Mr Mohanji, who was charged with exploiting Blacks to the extent of openly and unashamedly selling them tap water in empty jam tins.

There was a drinks cooler in the Mohanji shop, but he refused to have a fridge at home. Cakes and pastries of all kinds, made by the Widow, were sold in the shop, but not consumed at home. These were baked on charcoal as Mohanji refused to have any electrical appliances in the house on the grounds that it would increase the electricity bill. There was no phone in the house, but he kept a padlocked phone in the shop – strictly for business. In the event of an emergency, he preferred to use one of his many sons as messenger.

Mr Mohanji did not subscribe to the "domestic and pleasure" category of car-ownership. He didn't believe in girls learning to drive because they couldn't earn money by it. If women knew how to drive, they only went out shopping and gossiping with friends. What was the point of wasting all that petrol, unless someone was going to pay you for it? Mohanji often cited by way of example all those middle-class Asian women who had their own cars and could drive. Never at home. Always out – tanga-tanga, loitering around and gossiping. Going from house to house like they have no house of their own. What a disgrace to womankind! And spending their husbands' money like water. It was nothing less than Kalyug!

Kalyug was one of Mohanji's favourite concepts for explaining the seemingly inexplicable. Any threat of a breakdown in moral values, any assertion of female rights, birth control pills, love marriages, any kind of shamelessness and any hint at racial equality. These were all invariably defined as signs of "Kalyug" – the age of darkness, and treachery – the penultimate chapter in the history of the world and a sure signal that the world was about to end.

15
PHYSICS, MATHS & THE MOSQUITO SERVANT

Mrs Seema Henara was at her wit's end. What on earth was one to do with such a daughter? Her only child was a source of continual disappointment. She had always given her the best – the best toys, even the best dolls' house, but the child still showed a preference for that so-called house behind the shop.

And now she was even turning down the Sunday cinema offering, flatly refusing to accompany her mother and her uncle and asking instead, to be dropped off at Mohanji & Sons General Stores to play with her friends. Try as she might, Mrs Henara completely failed to understand this latest whim. Only a couple of weeks ago, the Brat would've thrown the worst kind of sulk-and-hunger-strike tantrum to be taken to the cinema. And now, out of the blue, she was babbling something about it being a complete waste of time. "Much more fun," she would say. "Much better than the real cinema. In the cinema, it whizzes past, quickly, just once. At Mohanji's you can do it again and again."

Mrs Henara didn't understand any of this. What on earth could she mean? Maybe some sort of game they played again and again? Or was it that her daughter was just going through a clingy phase? Maybe she had made one of the Mohanji boys her hero, and wanted to spend every available spare moment gazing at him. Oh no! Such shame! Her only daughter in love with a shop-keeper's son, and that too at the tender age of eight!

How Mrs Henara wished her daughter would develop grace and charm – like other people's daughters, who could sew and paint and play the piano. Other people's daughters showed an aptitude for science and maths. Other people's daughters already behaved like young ladies. What would become of this girl? Why did she always show disdain for children of her own class? Why did she never even try to play with the few European children still left in the area? Mrs Henara had coaxed her a thousand times to go and play with the European children. European was a synonym for British. It would be good for her English. It would bring on a good English accent. She would learn good manners. She would learn to wipe her bottom with toilet paper instead of spilling water all over the bathroom floor.

Europeans meant "White" – a superior race that could do no wrong. The Blacks took them with a pinch of salt, but the Indians, otherwise known as Muhindis, and particularly the upper-middle-class educated types, just worshipped White skin. Mrs Henara, while pregnant with the Brat, had even religiously consumed warm milk and saffron every night. Such a drink is said to ensure that the baby will turn out to be milky white. But in typical unpredictable fashion, the Brat had emerged nearly copper-coloured. Still, it wasn't too late. If she played with the European children she might still catch their colour and whiten up a bit. Mrs Henara had never been able to explain how those supposedly superior English-speaking White children always flunked their English language exams while most of the Indians, including the Dukavalla children who spoke at least three other languages, always managed to pass with flying colours. Even so, Mrs Henara imagined that if her Brat-child befriended the European children she might cultivate a phony English accent. But the Brat sensed her mother's ambitions and instead worked on a ridiculously exaggerated Peter Sellers' Indian-English accent. It wouldn't be the first time the brat had done the exact opposite of whatever was expected of her.

In the privacy of her bedroom, safely concealed from the gawking eyes of her many servants, Mrs Henara shed tears of bitter fury at having produced such an awkward, obstinate, tomboyish daughter. Maybe she would change when she was older. What would her marriage prospects be? How could a girl who behaved like a boy ever have any marriage prospects? Boys certainly liked her, but they liked her for her boyishness. Mrs Henara was afraid this would go on being the case. They would carry on liking her because she was like them. Not because she was mysterious and elusive and attractive, but because she was one of the lads. Boys never married one of the lads. They just befriended them and confided in them, but for marriage they definitely preferred the girlies. Young men didn't get married to their friends. Generally they married unfriendly young women who kept them on their toes.

Mrs Henara despaired at the fact that her daughter had always shown a complete lack of interest in Muhindi children of her own class, while positively bordering on hostility towards European children. So where else would they find her a doctor-husband, or a lawyer-husband? If the girl only ever socialised with shopkeeper's sons, how could a young doctor find her even remotely attractive? And that ridiculous accent to top it all! True, the Brat was still only eight, but to Mrs Henara, she was already showing all the promise of an old maid. And although Mrs Henara's own marriage had been a monumental disaster, she still believed in marriage as a passport to adulthood.

The Henaras lived in a charming house in the town's best residential area, situated at the source of the River Nile. As a result, the area was infested with mosquitoes. But having more mosquitoes was also a status-enhancing symbol, for it proved you lived close to the river. And it meant you had a special mosquito servant, who came in just before sunset to close the shutters, spray the rooms and let down the mosquito nets. This was his sole job. He had no other work during the day. He was paid quite well for what sounds like a fairly simple task, but in a country where malaria can often have fatal consequences, his was a life-and-death duty. And later at night, if even one single mosquito were to be found buzzing within the nets, then his wages would be docked accordingly. Ten cents per every mosquito corpse caught and identified. Sometimes as many as five illegal-immigrant mosquitoes showed up and the servant had to forgo all of fifty cents, half his daily wages. A huge price to pay for not getting to work on time, or for not tucking down the nets properly, or having omitted to spray all the corners of the rooms with DDT.

Mrs Henara lived with her brother. Well, not a real brother, but a sort of a younger man friend. But he was always known as her brother. It would never do to say he was a "friend" – the Urdu language didn't even have a word for a friend of the opposite sex.

After her acrimonious divorce, and left all alone with a small baby-brat, she decided she needed a man about the house. So she sent for this man, a physics teacher from New Delhi. Mrs Henara always insisted on using the full English name of that homeland city. New Delhi, not to be confused with just plain Delhi, which to her was a dirty, decaying, over-crowded conglomeration of slummy villages, infested with narrow-minded and backward Muslim mohallas – enclosed neighbourhoods – featuring open drains and urinals. The "haveli" culture at its worst. She thought of the haveli as a sort of hovel, and was convinced the two words were related.

The so-called brother was a bright young thing, and within a few months of settling in Pearl, had the envious position of being Head Physics teacher at the one and only proper secondary grammar school in town. Mrs Henara herself taught A-level biology at the same school. Between them, they earned enough for a lavish life-style, as teachers usually did in this part of the world, their nice houses and most other necessities being provided by the government. It was all part of the British colonial system. Officially, they said education was a top priority, and if you were noble enough to devote yourself to the teaching profession, then you had to be amply rewarded for sharing your wisdom and knowledge. So why the hell didn't they follow this policy in their own country? Because it wasn't a real policy at all. It was an elaborate form of bribery.

The British depended on upper middle-class Muhindi teachers to spread the word. British was best – English was the only language in the world. These Indian academics, faithful servants of their colonial masters, and safely in possession of a British Raj education, were the true cultural ambassadors of British imperialism. Little wonder then that their job-related perks were on par with real diplomats.

Other Indians – lawyers and doctors and all those morality-ridden Dukavallas – had none of these special privileges. Some of them made a lot of money, but they were on their own. They had to pay their children's school-fees, build or rent their own houses, employ their own servants (including the mosquito servant), and pay the full amount for all utilities. The best of anything was always reserved for teachers. And Mrs Henara's house was certainly one of the best. The garden was abundant with rose bushes and fruit bearing trees – lemon, avocado, mango, guava – and various exotic tropical flowers, in every shade of colour that nature has ever made. The bright pinks, oranges, yellow, red and purples blazed away in the hot afternoon sunshine while the trees swayed in the evening breeze, willingly dropping their yield to the ground. An even bigger garden at the back provided all the fresh produce one could ever need, and Mrs Henara generously gave away the surplus to neighbours and friends. Peas, beans, yams, tomatoes, potatoes, lettuce, aubergines. A government-paid gardener and three assistants toiled day and night to ensure a generous yield of produce for the kitchen and flowers for the house.

The back garden joined on to the servants' quarters, lavish by any standards. Six medium-sized rooms with a communal sitting room, an open outdoor kitchen and a partitioned off bathroom, complete with plumbing. A flushing lavatory was one of the basic necessities of civilised living, even for servants. Mrs Henara often boasted that her servants – "mere servants," she would stress – lived in more luxury than the stingy Mohanjis and other mean-minded Dukavallas.

Mrs Henara liked her servants to live on the premises, but many others in her position had rented their servants' quarters to poorer Black families, forcing their own domestics to travel in to work from their distant villages early in the morning. Mrs Henara had nothing but scorn for this kind of meanness, and frequently stood in judgement against Muhindis mean enough to rent out their servants' quarters. Poor chaps. If they had to serve breakfast at seven, then that meant they would have to get up at five in the morning to walk or cycle into town. How could these bloody Asians be so heartless? Servants were human after all, and not all Blacks were bad. Some of them were very clean and obedient. Some even spoke perfect English. How could the Asians treat them like this?

Mrs Henara's moral crusading was typical of the schizophrenia of a lot of educated Asian women towards their over-worked Black servants. Completely and utterly dependent on them – sometimes God-fearingly kind, at other times mindlessly cruel. Hating their Black skins, but guiltily appreciative of their loyalty and hard work.

With wonder-boy Head physics teacher safely on base, and herself an Advanced level biology teacher, Mrs Henara thought of her household as a science household. "We are all scientists in my family," she often said with pride, as though it proved they all had some special secret brand of intelligence unknown to those who taught English or history. One of her more memorable pronouncements on this subject came while entertaining a couple who both taught history at the big university in the country's Big Town capital:

"Intelligence is about being able to do maths. All through history, the really intelligent were those who've had an aptitude for maths. Everything else is just secondary. It's not real intelligence," she said with undisguised relish.

The two history professors had felt suitably chastised as Mrs Henara, a mere school teacher, had gushed forth with names, past and present, of all the supposedly super-intelligent specimens of the human race. Just at that moment, the Brat daughter had woken up and come into the dining room for a glass of water. Her pink pyjamas, complete with bows and frills, always made her look deceptively angelic.

"Oh what a sweet little girl," the female history professor cooed, with all the typical wistfulness of the childless. "Come here, come to me little one. Do you also like maths, like your mother? What do you want to be when you grow up?"

"I want to sing and I want to dance and I want men to call me and give me lots of money so I can buy lots of sweets," the Brat had replied at jet speed and without a moment's hesitation.

"Oh, poor darling," said a breathless Mrs Henara. "She's still half asleep. Ayah! Where the hell are you? Can't you see the girl has got out of bed? Take her back and give her some water! Useless these African servants! These Blacks, they'll never learn you know. In India, New Delhi, you know, my ayah was like a real mother."

Why did the girl always take such pleasure in making her mother look bad? The same mother who had given her life. Two whole days she had been in labour while her monster-husband, a distinguished surgeon at the country's top hospital had gone to be with his new mistress, saying he couldn't face the trauma of childbirth. A surgeon! Unable to attend childbirth!

"It's different when it's your own," he had said lamely in his defence.

"But you won't be there as a surgeon. You'll be there as the father." she had reasoned, uselessly.

No. He couldn't. It was all too messy and unpleasant. The best place for him to be while she gave birth to their child, was to snuggle up to his latest mistress and be comforted. Then, when he finally came to see the baby, complete with new mistress in tow, bearing a gigantic bouquet of flowers (bought at the insistence of the mistress), he hardly looked at the infant. He spent most of his time gazing at his new floozy, clearly dying to get away from the maternity ward. Mrs Henara asked the mistress to leave them alone for a minute. When they were alone, she wept with humiliation and the added intensity of post-natal blues. "How can you be so cruel, bringing that woman here?"

"I like to be open about these things," he declared proudly. "You know about her so you may as well see her. She's quite pretty isn't she? Very fair. I like them fair. Anyway, what's it to you? You're going to be sexually indisposed for quite a while, so why do you grudge me a normal sex life? It's not natural for men to go without that sort of thing. When you're better, we will see."

No, we won't, she had decided there and then in a fit of post-natal reasoning. No way! She had put up with this for over a decade. She had never even wanted children. He made her have this one. He said he would stop womanising if their marriage had some focus – like a child. And stupidly she had believed him. Now there was a child, but still no husband. No, she would divorce him. That's what divorce was for.

Her gullibility and utter devotion to him in those early years of marriage had now made her a harder woman than she might otherwise have been. In those days, it wasn't done to kick your husband out just because he had a few mistresses. Wives were wives, and mistresses were mistresses – two entirely different roles. There was no competition and both were essential in their own place to make a man feel complete.

All married men had mistresses, if not officially, then certainly on a casual basis. That's what men were like, and you just accepted it if you wanted to go on being married to them. But if you actually found the courage to boot them out, then it meant you were someone very special, someone who was not afraid of being single and someone who was not afraid of the future. For this reason, Mrs Henara commanded a lot of respect in the local community. Other women, trapped in unhappy marriages, secretly envied her freedom. And the men admired her too, especially those who regularly cheated on their wives. For them, Mrs Henara was an exceptionally attractive woman who, by kicking out her husband, had surely made herself available on the good mistress-candidates list.

And that was the real reason she had invited her young man-friend to come over from India and live with her. A man in the house would make her less vulnerable to these "single-equals-available" prowlers. Although a snob of the first order and utterly class-conscious, she hated these amoral sexual norms of the educated middle class Indians residing in colonial Africa. In this respect at least, she respected the Mohanji classes. Those shopkeeper types usually only married one woman and stuck by her. Even if it was for all the wrong reasons, the Mohanjis of this world basically respected women. In return the women, whether wives or daughters or daughters-in-law, had to work hard and pull their weight in the family business. Sure, they worked like slaves, but at least they never had to face the indignity of being polite to their husbands' mistresses just a few hours after painful childbirth.

The Mohanji classes didn't believe in mistresses. They were an unnecessary expense. Much better to stick to the scriptures and be faithful to your one and only wife. Cheaper too. Make Money not Love!

It was with this particular fact in mind that Mrs Henara often thought that her daughter could do a lot worse than marry a Mohanji. But if only she didn't have to go and live behind a shop, and if only the brightest of the Mohanji sons could be allowed to have a real career instead of running a general store. But this was all wishful thinking. Her daughter wasn't even menstruating yet.

Menstruating... menstruating? The thought always made her uneasy. Oh well, plenty of time to sort out all that later. Leave things as they are for now.

16
A LANGUAGE FOR ALL OCCASIONS

Wrong class. Wrong occupation. Wrong language. But given the Mohanji boys' exceptional brightness and extreme subservience to parental authority, Mrs Henara reluctantly conceded to the Brat spending most of her spare time at the Mohanji shop-and-house. If nothing, she might at least pick up some tendency to parental obedience from the bright but submissive Mohanji sons. Still, it was too bad they spoke Gujarati all the time. And the brat had deliberately allowed a Gujarati tone to slip into her English speech, on top of the Peter Seller's accent. If they had to speak in the vernacular – as Mrs Henara in imitation of her White employers called it – why the hell couldn't they all learn Urdu? It was clearly a superior language, second only to English.

Language and occupation went hand in hand for the Indian immigrants to British colonial Pearl. The shopkeepers came from Gujarat, and spoke Gujarati. The building contractors and engineers invariably spoke Punjabi. They were mostly Sikh. The car mechanics and big garage owners also spoke Punjabi, being Punjabi of the Muslim variety. The jewellers were Sindhi. The bosses of the big insurance companies and banks always spoke Kutchi – whatever their religion. Primary school teachers were largely Goan and Parsee who officially only spoke English, while secondary school teachers were predominantly north Indian, whether Hindu or Muslim.

The doctors and dentists either spoke the Marathi language of Maharashtra or, in Mrs Henara's terms, one of those many horrendously ugly-sounding languages of south India. Mrs Henara, a typical Uttar Pradesh northerner, unashamedly and in a manner bordering on out-and-out fascist, despised all things south Indian: the people were dark skinned, their languages were gobbledygook, their saris gaudy, their food atrocious in the extreme: "Agram-Bagram-Bakamma-ay-yay-yo" she called it. The original junk food all deep-fried in smelly coconut oil. Makes you feel immediately bloated, and then twenty minutes later you're hungry again. But most inconveniently for Mrs Henara, the southies and their children were all brilliant at maths, and this caused her some consternation. Given her intelligence equals maths-ability theory, she couldn't write them off as superfluous to the Indian human race, even if their languages were a major turn-off.

Kutchi, Gujerati, Punjabi, Marathi, Tamil, Malyalam – these were grouped as the languages of the "riff-raff" by the other two main Indian language groups, both equal and always at odds with one another: Urdu and Bengali – formidable opponents for the throne of main Indian language of culture and learning. These two language groups had a virtual monopoly of all the cushy, perk-ridden academic posts this side of the African continent. They despised one another with an intensity that sometimes threatened to spill over into open hostility, but more often than not, given their exceptional pseudo-intellectual pretensions, they ended up socialising together.

Communication was strictly in English, of course, and consisted largely of consoling one another on the tragedy of having come from such mutually great literary traditions to the vulgar wilderness of Gujarati and Punjabi. On such occasions when they felt charitable towards each other, the Urdu group would rave about Rabindranath Tagore, and the Bengalis would claim that there hadn't been a poet greater than Mirza Ghalib in all the history of all the world's poetry.

This vast multiplicity of Indian languages was a big enough problem in the old motherland, India. But over there at least these languages were spread over a largish piece of land – an entire sub-continent, and by and large roughly divided region by region. But here, in small town Pearl, where dozens of Indian languages were often forced to co-exist within a town radius of less than five miles, it became necessary to work out some kind of compromise, lest linguistic rivalries erupt into open warfare. At least on the social scene, some sort of modus operandi was vital. And even though none of the languages held any official status in Pearl, it was imperative in the interests of social intercourse amongst the separatist Muhindis, to work out a communication ethic between the different language groups. So it was decided that one always relinquished to the superior language. If you addressed a native Urdu speaker, it was your duty to try and speak his language, to the best of your ability. The same concession was supposed to be made for Bengali, but the poor Punjabis and Gujaratis just couldn't manage Bengali, so everyone ended up speaking Urdu to the Bengalis as well. Whenever things got really difficult, everyone switched into English. But many Black African servants understood English. So if you had something really contentious to say, you had to have a mutually agreed common Indian language in which to bitch about the servants, or, in later years, the tedious Black government. And that language could only ever be Urdu – the lingua franca of North India, and now the Muhindi lingua franca of Pearl.

17
MR MOHANJI HE SAY...

Don't think that I don't know what they say about me behind my back. Miser – kanjoos-makkhi-choos-Marwari-Banya. And all because I don't believe in splashing money. I don't believe in showing off. God gives to those whom he wants to give. And He takes away just as easily as He gives. So, no point in getting big headed about money. Best to live in poverty. Hide all your money, then you can pretend you have none. Poverty is best. The greatest people were always poor.

It's true, I have a fair amount of money, and it's true I've transferred most of it abroad – in the good old days, when the Black government hadn't yet dreamed up currency restrictions. But I also keep a lot of my money at home. I don't trust those African banks. Who would? All these educated Asians who use government banks – you'll see, they'll suffer one day. Serves them right! Always acting superior to us uneducated shopkeepers! They never save much anyway. Shocking waste! The teachers, especially. The stupid government gives them all sorts of advantages, but instead of saving, they spend all their money on books and records and toys for their children. I don't believe in spending a lot of money on children. The sooner they learn nothing is free in life the better.

That arrogant Henara woman once came to my shop to buy her chilly-powder and started lecturing me on the advantages of sending my sons to British universities. University? Whoever needed university to run a shop? And my sons so well brought up, so obedient. Not like her Brat daughter who does nothing but hang around my shop. Always hungry and always greedy. She arrives just as we are sitting down to eat. Spoiling my sons. Wasting their time. Keeping them from their duties. She never has anything to do. Her mother never gives her any housework to do. Imagine, she's almost eight years old and still knows nothing about cooking or sewing. Poor kid. What is she to do? It's up to elders to teach their girls to grow up and be good wives. My Widow daughter was making perfectly round chapatties at the age of six! That's called training.

But these wretched educated Indians, just because servants and gardens are ten a penny in Africa, they think they're equal to Maharajahs! They look down on us, because we know the meaning of hard work. I get up at five in the morning. I go to the temple. I have a simple breakfast and open my shop at seven. If I didn't do that, what would the early travellers at the taxi rank do? Where would they buy provisions for their journey? Am I not a God fearing man? Would I let a poor traveller set out for safari without so much as a packet of Marie biscuits in his pouch?

It's all right for these teachers and doctors. They go to each other's houses for dinner and talk all night. Politics and poetry. Urdu and Bengali. Useless idle talk. When did poetry ever feed a family? What's the point of talking about all these clever things when you can't even keep your women in control?

I am a religious man. I like all religions, but I like mine the best. Other religions also teach good things, take Islam for instance. A good, simple religion, but nobody follows it properly. Double standards, all of them. Look at that Mrs Haq woman. All over town, always out, tanga-tanga, booray-booray, wasting money in beauty parlours and flirting with men half her age. Even making eyes at her boy students. Then she goes for Hajj! And her own husband – gutless, spineless fellow – always calling her Darling Darling and pretending to be afraid of her. And then he goes and spends all night with his boy scouts. Camping! Not normal that sort of thing. I don't like it. I don't agree with it. I have forbidden all my boys from joining the Scouts. All this Scout and Girl Guide rubbish is just another excuse of imperialists to snatch our children away from us and teach them to light fires and fill their brains with western shamelessness. Sleeping in tents! What for? Hasn't God given you houses?

Oh no! That girl has turned up again. I'm going to tell her the boys are busy. They have no time to play. She's like a stray dog – always poking her head everywhere, and yesterday I even caught her nosing around the toilets. Why does she hang around our toilets? Hasn't she ever seen a real toilet before? What's there to see?

18
BLOOD, SHIT & SONGS

I had just come to terms with the startling revelation that I live in a place called World. Yes, yes, I'm still in my beloved Pearl, but Pearl happens to be in the world. A huge pity that my equatorial African paradise was in World when all the time I had imagined it was somewhere completely different. Never mind. At least it was the same place I'd always known. But one thing really puzzled me. If we were indeed in World – you know, Duniya, then from what little I knew of the world, I knew it was supposed to be a round, rotating sort of globe. This was a source of constant worry to me. How could it be round when it looked flat? And how could it rotate when the ground beneath my feet stood still? Vital questions that I want answered, but all the grown ups keep asking me to shut up and not interrupt their important conversations about politics and poetry. So I guess I'll just have to figure it out for myself. I had only just resolved to single-handedly tackle all the mysteries pertaining to the spinning, whizzing world, when another distraction presented itself. Yet another invitation to attend a Feast of the Nine Virgins. Nothing unusual about that, because my virginity has long been a lunch-ticket, but this time the invitation has thrown me into one of the most unfathomable mysteries of my early life, even more mysterious than the alleged whizzing around of the round Duniya. This time, the lunch was to be hosted by the Widow. And she was holding it in the backyard of her house – not really a house but a sort of a backroom behind the second Mohanji shop.

With all the acute reasoning of an eight-year old, I wondered how the Widow could have any sort of pact with God? Surely God had forsaken her already by making her a widow in the first place? Even if He was able to grant her wishes, what could she realistically, wish for? Remarriage? Out of the question. There were more than enough young virgin girls looking for husbands. Who'd want to marry a widow? Surely her life was over in that respect? What on earth could she have wished for, and how in heaven's name could God have granted it? The Widow was the oldest of Mohanji's ten children. After the sudden and tragic loss of her husband she had moved back into her father's house. Her in-laws had refused to have anything to do with her. They held her directly responsible for her husband's death. They alleged she had brought bad luck on the family – "Kisrani" in Swahili.

The Widow and her small baby-boy shared a room with three of her younger brothers in the small, cramped living quarters behind the second shop. She paid for her keep by running the adjoining shop specialising in dressmaking and "Fancy Goods." She served in this shop from seven o'clock in the morning to six o'clock in the evening, taking only two hours off at midday to prepare the family lunch, the remains of which would be eaten for supper. She cooked for the entire family of twelve. Just as she'd done before being married off to the young drunk.

It had been generally assumed that the young drunk would improve once he was confronted with the responsibilities of husbandhood. His family ran a very successful business manufacturing bicycle tyres, and for Mohanji this line of work provided an opportunity for an ideal business alliance. It was clearly God's doing. His daughter would be marrying upwards. A Dukavalla's daughter married into a Factoryvalla's family. He would purchase bicycle tyres at a special price from his daughter's new in-laws and sell them at a huge mark up in his shop and his profits would double. And the profits did indeed double, and even redouble, during the ten months that his daughter was married.

Then it all came to an end. One night, after a particularly hard drinking session consisting of the local-brew distilled from pineapples, the young drunk fell onto a railway track on his way home, just in time to catch the midnight goods express to the Coast, travelling at top speed. Raw materials for the imperial masters had to be got out fast! And within seconds, the virtuous, duty-driven raw materials' fast train had minced his body beyond recognition.

The Widow was then six months pregnant. (Again it had been assumed the young drunk would improve once he was presented with the responsibilities of fatherhood.) The drunk's family decided the Widow was entitled to nothing, and escorted her back to Mohanji's house. At first Mohanji assumed that she had been returned for the birth of her first child. It was customary to return to your parental home for the first delivery. But after the birth of her son the months went by and no one came for her. Her in-laws expressed no interest in their grandson. Although quite wealthy, they had no intention of taking on an extra mouth to feed. They reserved their options for when the boy would grow up and be able to help in their business. Until such time as that happened, they didn't want to know.

So she remained in a small cramped room shared with three of her brothers, working by day and staying awake with the baby at night. Although still under twenty-one, she looked well over fifty. Her skin was wrinkled, dark hollows encircled her eyes and her hair had already turned dry and silvery. Her baby on the other hand, was the very picture of robust health. The kind of baby that sweeps up all the prizes at those European-organised baby-shows. Fat rosy cheeks, gleaming big black round eyes, long black eyelashes curling upwards and a wild mass of dark brown curls on his head. Every neighbourhood Dukavalla daughter yearned to have just such a baby. All sweetness and gurgles by day, but none of those broody girls really knew about his irritable, sleepless nights. They imagined he slept sweetly and angelically all through the night, long-eye-lashes sweeping chubby cheeks. Only his mother's tired face bore testimony to the fact that this was not the case – and then only for those who knew that babies tended to be anything but sweet at night.

Then one day, when the baby was two years old, the wife of her late husband's older brother, having failed to conceive after seven years of marriage, came to claim the boy. The widow's father-in-law accompanied the claimant and reinforced her claim on the grounds that children, especially male children, are always the property of their father's family. The Widow was utterly shattered, especially when her own family sided with the in-laws. Mohanji's reasoning was that with the hyperactive baby-toddler gone, the Widow could work harder. She could take on more orders for dressmaking and work right through the evening.

And so the Widow lost her one and only legacy from her dead, young drunk. They said she could visit him whenever she liked, knowing fully well that it would be quite impossible for her to travel to a village over fifty miles away given her seven-day working week.

No longer a wife, and now no longer a mother, she was always known as "The Widow." I sometimes got the impression that she had carried this title since before her marriage. Perhaps she was born a Widow. Sometimes they called her "Bechari" – not only helpless but also unfortunate and cursed. At certain ceremonials and weddings she was not allowed to step anywhere near the areas declared sacred for that day. She may not let her shadow fall on a new bride. She may not visit a woman who had newly given birth.

So, just a few months after her baby-son was forcibly wrenched away from her, and the Widow announced her intention to host a Feast of the Nine Virgins, I couldn't help but wonder which particular wish of hers had been granted by God. With the baby gone she worked harder than ever yet always managed to look peaceful and even-tempered. I never saw her hurry, or panic. I never saw her get angry with anyone. She never raised her voice. She never complained. Yet the blood in my eight-year old veins boiled when I thought of what she had been put through, the injustices that had been dealt to her – not by fate, not by some tyrannical government, but by her own nearest and dearest. For this reason, the Widow became my tragic heroine.

The front of the Mohanji shop opened onto a concrete verandah that gave way to two steep, roughly hewn stone steps, which stopped at the roadside. All through the hot sunny afternoons the Widow sat on the sewing machine placed in the shady verandah, treadling away at her Singer sewing machine. It was a shiny black machine with wavy patterns of gold. Voluminous folds of brightly printed cotton materials passed through her nimble fingers before being pierced with the savage in-and-out motion of the needle at the mouth of the machine. The machine-mouth reminded me of a snake with its tongue darting in and out, presided over by my beautiful, tragic heroine softly humming a tune.

Whenever possible, I just sat on the steps and watched, completely entranced by her singing and full of wonderment at such large quantities of material going in at one end and then coming out all joined-up at the other. There was always lots of fabric, for her main orders consisted of making up the local African outfit – the basuti – which required about nine yards of material for each ensemble. It was partly sewn, the rest draped, and all held together with a special contrasting sash wrapped over the hips and bum, to create the illusion of a big behind, a much cherished female asset in tropical Africa.

The colours of the fabrics were always garish, screaming purple and orange, boiling red and yellow, ice-cold sea-blue and fiery shocking pink – all well chosen by their wearers to complement and reflect the blinding tropical sunshine. The printed patterns were gigantic, usually flowers or leaves or huge blobs of mismatched colours like spilt paint pouring forth at random creating abstract shapes and textures.

The Widow sang to herself softly as she worked, in perfect time to the rhythm of her foot-operated treadle. I was drawn to her like a magnet. I was the moth of the Widow's melodic flame. She usually sang the same song for a few days and then changed to another song. Which song will she sing today? I'm hoping she'll sing my favourite one. But no, she has already moved on to another tune. I don't know what her songs are called but I have code-names for all of them. I've named them to match the pattern of whichever fabric was passing through her fingers at the time. I like the bluebells best. Bluebells on Black is my favourite tune. My second favourite is the Green Palm trees on White Sands. And that Orange-Pink-Yellow Spilt Paint isn't bad either. Oh, and I just love the Yellow Bananas Bunches on Red Mud. But on one occasion, I quite forgot myself, and urged her to sing the Green Palms on White. She looked at me strangely, as though she'd only just become aware of my presence. It was as though she didn't even know she'd been singing, leave alone holding captive a one-child audience. After that she stopped singing for a few days.

That day, I was suddenly and painfully reminded that my secret language was my own. How was she to know which song I meant? There is no pain in this world to match the pain that is born out of the loneliness of being the only speaker of a language.

A few days after that unfortunate incident, she resumed her singing. Thank God! Now, I must keep my mouth shut and just listen. No more thoughtless requests, or she might stop singing forever.

Around this time, it also became very easy to listen to her songs everyday as I had become a fairly frequent visitor to the shop. I had been enrolled in a special out-of-town school – my mother hoping my maths would improve – and the school bus terminated at the taxi rank in the market square across the road from the shop. From here I was picked up by car and driven home. Should the car ever be a little late, I was under strict instructions to not loiter around the market square, but, by special arrangement to go and sit on the shop verandah where my driver would find me.

Luckily for me, our driver had a pash on a fruit-seller woman in the market. I did my bit to help the lovers express their love and as a result, always gained about twenty-five minutes between leaving the bus and getting into the car. These were the most precious minutes of my long life of eight years – minutes in which to update my research on this fascinating family and the tragic Widow. I relished these opportunities to overhear Mohanji recommending various cost-saving techniques to his sons and neighbours, but most of all, I relished the unrestricted facility to just gaze at the Widow and listen to her sewing songs.

The rhythm of the Widow's sewing machine coupled with the crunching snake-like action of the in-and-out needle played the most wonderfully seductive and erotic tunes to me. I would try and compose my own words to go with the tunes. Then just as I thought I was getting somewhere, the rhythm would change. Sometimes she would just stop to undo a bit or to gather up more material. Sometimes she stopped for quite a while to change reels or even to stretch her tired arms. I am convinced these interruptions played their part in aborting some of my more beautiful compositions before they could take shape....

Electric sewing machines were becoming popular, but luckily for me, Mohanji would not hear of it. That would mean higher electricity bills. The shop had electric lighting, but he had never considered it necessary to light the house or its outer areas – the open-air kitchen, the one-tap and bucket bathroom or the partitioned roof-less tin-shed that served as a communal lavatory.

The lavatory consisted of a row of cement pedestals on which one squatted, placing one foot on either side. You then proceeded to do your business in the middle, from where it fell some distance onto the ground below. The special design of the pedestals allowed three or four people to go at the same time, squatting alongside each other – quite a sensible thing in a family of twelve. The excretions remained on the ground until they were swept away (every morning and every evening) by a special lavatory cleaner, in Dukavalla or Muhindi parlance, the "Bhangi".

In India, a Bhangi family would have been in that business for generations. It was a relatively well paid business, fairly well compensated in recognition of the fact that no sane person would ever want to clean up human shit twice a day. But in British African Pearl, the noble Bhangi profession was relinquished to the Black Africans, for Indians were too pure and too holy to touch their own shit. It was OK for an Indian Bhangi family to do that in India, but here, in this foreign "pardes" of shamelessness, there was a lesser race of humans to perform this unsavoury task, so it was only fair to give them a chance to serve their penance for past-life mistakes. After all, you must have done something really terrible in your previous incarnation to have been born Black in the first place. Karma, all karma.

When the Bhangi came to do his work, he was not allowed to pass through the house. He had to make his way to the backyard-sakati by way of a side-door. His bucket, cloths and brushes and cleaning materials were housed separately. There was a wonderful smell of Dettol every time he left. It carried for miles. Even from the other side of the Square, you could tell the Bhangi had just been. But I preferred to nose around the toilets just before the Bhangi's visit so that there would be something to see.

Visiting the toilet in that house was always an adventure – both revolting and fascinating at the same time. I never really did my business there. My mother had expressly forbidden me from ever using anyone else's lavatory. In dire emergency, Number one was OK, provided it could be flushed away, but under no circumstances was I permitted to allow my bowels to move in a house other than my own. So using the non-flushing Mohanji cement-pedestal toilet would have been quite out of the question. Controlling my bowels was no problem, but trying to control this urge to look at the contents inside the fascinating toilet was way beyond human capability.

In the normal scheme of things there wasn't much opportunity to study the intricacies of human excrement. In my own boring house it was just flushed away, and then the toilet pan miraculously turned blue – as though nothing had ever happened! But here, in the Mohanji way of doing things, there was an unrestricted opportunity to make a really detailed study. I did my best to time my visits in between the Bhangi's visits so that there would be some-thing to study.

One of my favourite games was to try and guess which shit belonged to which person. It's not easy. Shit, like blood, doesn't lend itself easily to that kind of analysis.

Another big mystery to solve. A round world, supposedly whizzing around, so many languages, so many skin-tones, so many people – Dukavalla-class, Mechanic-class, Upper class, Maths, Science, Mosquito Servants, but why does shit always look like shit? And why does everybody's shit always look the same? I guess it must be something to do with everybody's blood looking the same....

19
THE WORLD'S NUMBER ONE COMPOSER

Being the World's Number One Composer certainly had its upside. He had about as much sex appeal as a Brillo pad, but success and fame proved powerful magnets and women, particularly the wannabee-singer-actress bubble-headed bimbo variety were drawn by the lure of that Number One glamour. The result? An endless stream of followers wherever he went – all nobodies trying to be somebody by being seen with the World's Number One.

He was quite used to complete strangers coming up to him with the opening line of: "Shall I put my diaphragm in now, or should we talk first?" Unromantic perhaps, but romance had never suited him. Or at least it hadn't suited his public persona, which was a carefully cultivated image of a heartless womanising type of creature who never stopped in any one place longer than he needed to, and for whom there was a never-ending stream of willing bed partners. "Screw 'em and leave 'em" he gloated.

While on tour, the World's Number One would sleep with anyone who'd have him – and that was virtually everyone. Everyone except Sonia, that is. Not only would she be conspicuously absent from his concerts and other related festivities, she would quite often be in a completely different city at the other end of the world. The last time he'd actually seen her for more than half-an-hour had been at that accidental meeting inside a hotel elevator, in Rome. This delicious encounter had lasted exactly two hours and seventeen minutes owing only to the inefficiency of Italian elevator rescue services at weekends.

Until such time as fame had deposited a legion of beautiful women at his doorstep, the Number-One-to-be had been a struggling hand-to-mouth musician in an overcrowded Indian city, who went home to a temple backyard after each lowly paid job at a wedding or some other public function. Then came the lucky break that landed him in the affluent West of the early seventies. Younger generations in Europe and particularly in west-coast USA had got "India" rather badly. This was a sort of disease which sported secondary symptoms such as drugs, mantras, meditation, yoga, cheesecloth and veggie-burgers, but its chief symptom was an irrational desire to embrace Indian music – and an even more uncontrollable desire to embrace Indian musicians. There was this sudden craze for the twanging of sitar and sarod strings and the slapping of tablas. Positively erotic. But the craze didn't just stop at listening to hours and hours of these magical sounds. It also extended to an overwhelming desire to be penetrated by the teacher, in every sense of the word.

The World's Number One was a true product of this age. In its heyday he had been in his late teens. It would be true to say he had literally grown up in The-West-embraces-Indian Classical Music-Age. And his career had only really gelled into a successful multimillion-dollar business by being based in the West. Had he remained in India, he would've been another nameless musician – of whom there are thousands – surviving from session to session, or at best playing (un-credited) in those screeching backing orchestras without which no Indian film song would ever sound complete. He spoke with pride of his humble beginnings. You can only boast about the virtues of poverty when you're no longer in the midst of struggling with it on a day-to-day basis. He recalled the days of playing at weddings where nobody really listened to the music. He talked of providing background music for parties and weddings and then being fed in the kitchen with the servants.

His was the best Raag to riches story of its kind. A small town boy with a rudely interrupted education. But in those days he'd never cared about school so it didn't seem too much of a tragedy. He had learnt on the streets of Bombay and that, after all, was the biggest and best university. That was what prepared him for the life that awaited him. And that was where he had learnt the priceless technique of living for the moment. Even the most highly educated people had failed to grasp this point, but every street urchin in Bombay knows that the present moment is all we have – the past has gone and the future unknown, so why fret over either of those? Just live for the moment – that was the philosophy that prepared him for a high-speed, jet-setting career which required the best part of his working day to be spent reclining in the First Class cabin of a jumbo jet. Or sometimes, just for a change, accompanying a cabin-crew member (of either sex) into the confined space of an aircraft toilet, just to see what was possible.

The money and success had rather gone to his head, to say nothing of some of the world's most beautiful women scratching each other's eyes out just to get five more minutes alone with him. He sincerely believed that he had a right to use people – particularly women – in any way he liked, because he was Number One. Even the legendary Mughal court musician Tansen could not compete with him in the desirability stakes, however great his music may have been. Who needs the deer to come running out of the jungle when you can have groupies following you from airport to airport?

There was never a shortage of groupies – one Groupie in particular could always be relied on. But he wanted all those other women – the clever ones who read lots of books. The ones who vanished as soon as the music stopped. The ones who talked about Dante having read the original Italian and the ones who enthused about Chekov having read the original Russian. And Sonia was one such woman. She didn't want him, so he wanted her.

But what did Sonia actually do? If only she would stand still for just one minute so that he could try asking again....

When he was in London, then she was conveniently out of town. Then when he stopped over in Budapest for a night, she materialised out of nowhere, about to take her clothes off for him, and then (drat) called away by an urgent phone call. And then she'd be gone for another few months.

Believe it or not, he had even managed to marry her – briefly – but he still never really had her. Her unavailability proved the ultimate aphrodisiac. She had become his quest, his obsession, and no number of soothing blow-jobs from an ever willing succession of groupies could heal the wounds inflicted by his unrequited lust for a cold, heartless, well-read, multi-lingual woman.

Dante, Chekov, Goethe, Marx, Iqbal, Shakespeare, Faiz, Nietzsche. Those were the magic words. That's what educated people talked about. His own education was sadly lacking, because of poverty, and because of having spent his youth literally singing for his supper. Where was the time for books? Where was the time for a proper education? Where was the money? And when the money did come, years later in the West, he was completely caught up in a lifestyle of jetting from city to city and groupie to groupie. How does one improve one's mind with permanent jet lag, followed by pre-orgasmic tension followed by post-orgasmic bliss followed by more jet lag?

For that was the sum total of his existence when he wasn't actually making beautiful music.

20
TAMEEZAN

Tameez, Tahzeeb, Takaluff – strange words for a non-Urdu speaker. Basically very strange words for anyone who had not had the privilege of being from Awadh, the princely state that is now the badly decayed Lucknow. In its heyday, it was the seat of high culture – literature, poetry, music, and all things refined, actively encouraged and patronised by the ruling nobility. By a relatively rare historical accident, the ruling classes also happened to have exquisite taste and were genuine connoisseurs of the arts. Even today, the very mention of a now much-changed city, conjures up vivid images of a bygone age where everything was steeped in luxury and refinement. The last proper ruler of the Kingdom of Awadh had been an exceptionally gifted man – poetic, musical, and a first-rate dancer. And statesmanship? Well, you can't be good at everything!

A whole new style of dance emerged, evolving out of the Ruler's partiality to ribald love lyrics. Poetry, dance and music – in that order – formed a sizeable part of the whole way of life associated with Lucknow and the Lucknavis, and central to this way of life were the concepts of Tahzeeb and Tameez – etiquette, good manners, and a whole lot more. Refinement, nobility, dignity, cultured discernment and most important of all, a consciously self-effacing humility, in fact, just a short step away from self-parody. An integral part of the "Tahzeeb" mode of behaviour is a manner known as "Takalluf". A desire to (ostensibly), not cause another person even the slightest bit of inconvenience, or "zehmat" and to pretend to uphold his (non-existent) dignity and honour, or "izzat", at all times. This applied especially to adversaries. But only when they were present. Behind their backs one could be as vociferously venomous and abusive as one liked. But even abuse had to be delivered in a refined manner, in measured verse if possible, and in typical takaluff-ridden fashion, with a degree of restraint.

Tahzeeb may be untranslatable, but "Takaluff" readily lends itself to parable in the following conversation between two Lucknavi men, already late for a train, and both rushing to catch it. They both get to a carriage door just in time, but each man is too takaluff-bound to step on first.

"After you."

"No, no, you first."

"No, who am I to step out in front of you?"

"Please you first."

"No, after you."

"I'm worthless compared to you. Please, after you."

"No, all of Lucknow knows you. Who hasn't heard of your Greatness? I should feel lucky to be allowed to follow in your glorious footsteps, please, after you."

"Please accord me the dignity of crawling after you Huzoor (My Lord). Please accord me the privilege of following in your sacred footsteps. Don't deny me this one humble wish."

"No, no, please don't embarrass me. You first...."

"How can that be? It's unthinkable! How can I, a mere servant rush ahead of my Lord?"

"Oh no! I am the servant, you are the Lord. Please don't condemn my soul to hell for the sin of stepping out before you. How will I face my Creator? Please, after you...."

Needless to say, the train has long since pulled out of the station, but the conversation goes on. Names and addresses are exchanged, invitations to imaginary dinners issued.

It may sound ridiculous, but the story is an epitome of the Lucknavi invention of "takalluf" which was at its zenith in the old unhurried days – the days when ustads sang and played at the royal courts like there was no tomorrow.

It is important to grasp this context of takaluff, because then and only then, can one truly appreciate Tameezan the Courtesan's first "come hither" overture to the Grand Old Ustad, the "Lighter Upper of the Universe," and grandfather to the present-day Grand Ustad, he of the million recordings:

In the first instance, there was a verbal message conveyed by a long-suffering man-servant: "My esteemed employer Tameezan Bai the Great Courtesan – Great for the world but a worthless non-entity compared to you, requests that you subject your grand dignity to an enormous amount of discomfort and humiliating inconvenience in agreeing to call on her for a few minutes. She would like to bathe herself in the aura of your enlightened presence for just a few minutes. She fully realises that any longer than a few minutes would soil your noble and musical soul possibly, irreparably. In that case she takes full responsibility for your possible defamation – God forbid – and she would happily give her own life as a mark of her respect for your Greatness."

That's an almost exact translation from the original. That's how the message was delivered, in flawless Urdu, but did she really mean it? Or was it just takaluff? How would that message sound if it hadn't been devised in the language of takaluff? What was really going on in Tameezan's mind?

Just let him get his arse over here, then he'll see! He won't be able to keep away. Like the rest of them, he'll be bonded to these tresses like a noose around his neck. I'll show him! I'll have him eating out of my hand in no time at all. All I need is once, just once to come face to face with him, in private. Soon, he'll reach the stage when he can't ever bring himself to leave this house. He'll just lie around here all day while dozens of servants bring messages from his family imploring him to return home. Just let him see me once – my beauty will do the rest! Huh!

The Grand Ustad's unspoken, un-conveyed non-takaluff response was pretty clear-cut: Bloody whore! She's parted her legs for half of Lucknow and now she's hitting on me, using my God-given music as an excuse. Another besotted female fan! What is it about music that has women falling over one another to get to you? Flattering, but most tedious. Haven't got the energy to enter into a new affair. Quite enough problems in that direction already. Anyway who needs courtesans when you've got so-called respectable women ever ready for a dalliance? Royalty, nobility, even wives of magistrates and judges. No, I don't need a new affair – not with a courtesan. It's not as though I'm a struggling musician looking for a lucky break and living off a talented woman in the meantime. I'm the greatest! I light up the whole universe!

But after a few moments' deliberation, the following takaluff-ridden message was conveyed from the Lighter Up of the Universe, via the man-servant, to the Courtesan:

"Please tell your esteemed employer that her invitation is most kind, but circumstances beyond my control prevent me from being able to make such a call in the near future. Nevertheless, please thank her for her interest in my aura, and I would like you to reassure her that she is quite mistaken in the degree of honour and respect she accords to me. I'm really a very simple and humble musician and her desire for an audience with me is a great honour. I am extremely grateful that one as beautiful and talented as her should seek my company. My eyes have never been fortunate enough to rest on her beauty, but I have heard much about it. Who hasn't?"

That was the Grand Ustad's official response, and would have to be delivered verbally, word, for word. Those poor man-servants who always had to carry such messages, in time became quite eloquent themselves. Some were poets in their own right. Needless to say, their memory re-call was excellent. Their descendants would have probably carried on the grand tradition had it not been for that wretched invention known as the telephone.

If Tameezan the Courtesan was somewhat crestfallen at the Ustad's non-committal reply, or even slightly shocked that he hadn't immediately jumped at her offer, she refused to get disheartened by it. It was, after all, only a first attempt. She was an unrelenting, plucky sort and once she decided she wanted something, she thought of nothing else. No point in spending energy on anything else when the task in hand demands every single atom of energy that a human being can muster up.

And Tameezan was no ordinary human being. She was that rare breed – the ones who are even more energised by refusal. Obstacles are a turn on. Blockages provide challenges. Once she got it into her head that she wanted something, she meant to get it. But her operations would have to be conducted with extreme secrecy, taking the man-servant into her confidence. If her Madame-Keeper, a sort of maternal aunt, got a whiff that something was up, then she would hastily be sold into sexual service of the first mediocre nobleman who made a half-decent offer and then that would be that.

Tameezan's keeper guarded her imagined virginity like it was the State Treasury. After all it was her alleged virginity that would enable her to be sold for the maximum stakes. Once that hymen was officially ruptured, her price would be well below the top market rate. At least officially she was still considered a virgin, and indeed, technically speaking, she was one. That's why anal sex had been invented in the first place.

Tameezan continued with her pursuit of the Grand Ustad. At one point she sent a message nearly everyday. Then she started to write poetry – mostly ghazals – and sent them to him for critical appraisal. There was never an answer. She dug her claws into the man-servant. "But what did he say? How did his face look? Did he smile? Did you wait while he read the verses? You were supposed to watch his every expression while he read my couplets, did you? How did he look?"

The poor servant informed her for the umpteenth time that he had been asked by the Ustad's servant to simply leave the sheet of paper and a reply would follow later. He hadn't even seen the Ustad.

"You're useless! What other work do you have? This is all you have to do to earn your bread and you can't even manage that. Didn't I insist you should hand it over in person? Wretched man! Stray dog! Pimp! You're fed out of my singing and dancing money and you can't even deliver a message properly!"

The man-servant was used to such abuse. If he didn't get it from the beautiful, sulky young Tameezan, he got it from her hawk-faced middle-aged keeper-aunt. But he was devoted to the women he served. And he couldn't bear to see Tameezan so sad. So it was with much delight and a genuine desire to put things right that one day, he was finally able to provide Tameezan with what amounted to a ray of light on a pitch-dark night – some vital information.

The Grand Ustad visited a certain shrine every Thursday evening, to pay homage to the spirit of some Holy Man. He believed this Master was directly responsible for his own musical success and brilliance. He had vowed to personally lay flowers at the tomb of the Master every single Thursday, otherwise known as Friday's Eve, at sunset….

Tameezan managed to wrangle permission to do the same. The Holy Man's spirit was well known for its benevolence towards all practitioners of the arts. Her keeper imagined that such blessings could only add to Tameezan's singing and dancing prowess. So, Tameezan was allowed to go to the Holy Shrine every Thursday, closely guarded by two women, and all three of them escorted by the man-servant who walked a few yards ahead. All three women would be veiled and covered from head to foot, shapeless black forms rustling in the finest quality silk, faces shuttered behind diaphanous georgette veils, shielded from the lusty looks of all and sundry by that all-important aid to anonymity – the Black Burqa.

It was yet another Thursday evening. Many such evenings had come and gone without an iota of progress. Tameezan's life consisted mainly of counting the days from Thursday to Thursday – an eternity. And yet again, it was Thursday. What would this Thursday bring? Three women draped in black burqas winding their way through the crowd. Noise, dirt, chaos, confusion. Beggars and flower-sellers. The heady scent of blood-red roses. Petals strewn everywhere, mingling with the dust of the earth and the debris of its inhabitants. Somewhere in the near distance, the strains of a qawwali – a wide open red-stained mouth of a Sufi musician: "The path of true love is strewn with thorns, plucked from a garland of freshly-cut tears."

And then, at last it almost finally happened. Over the sea of heads, and threading through thousands of shoulders brushing past the folds of silk and georgette, Tameezan the Courtesan managed to catch a quick glimpse of his broad back.

Despite the throngs, the Lighter Upper of the Universe was easily identifiable because wherever he went, everybody stood back to make way for His Greatness complete with huge retinue of attendants, all carrying trays covered with shiny embroidered fabrics – various offerings for the shrine and flowers for the tomb.

That's all she saw – his broad back – nothing else. An actual encounter at such a Holy place, or even a few words of acknowledgement, would have been unthinkable, especially with her two watchful companions hanging on so close. These Thursday visits went on for about a year, and then Tameezan began to lose heart. How could you make a man fall in love with you if the one and only contact you'd ever had was a view of his back and that too from a few yards away?

One hundred and four Thursdays later – or two years later – she still only had that one and only, first and last glimpse of his back. Never mind. He who Lights Up the Universe with his music, could, at the very least, produce a small ray of light spelling hope with a mere sighting of his back. That was the only item on her score sheet – a poor show after so much effort and such single-minded campaigning. She began to feel she was fighting for a hopeless cause, and for the first time in her life, she experienced that indescribable void born of the despair that sometimes grates on the nerves of even the toughest fighters.

And that Holy Man? What about him? That Master's blessing was supposed to turn the most impossible wish into reality. It was said nobody ever left his shrine empty-handed, so what was all that crap? Wait, wait, O ye of little faith.

The Courtesan's last message to the Grand Ustad was conveyed by a letter in her own beautiful Urdu handwriting:

"This mere slave girl would consider it an honour if she could be permitted to enter into pupilage with you. If I could learn just one per cent of what you know about music, I would consider my life's mission accomplished. This knowledge would enable me to serve the rest of my days in the service of music, and your teaching would give me a little more confidence. At the moment I can do no better than just hum. That's the only gift that Allah has so far granted me. But recently, I have also been fortunate enough to receive the blessings of the Holy Man – the same Holy Man who has blessed you. I have presented myself at his shrine every Thursday for two years. He came to me in a dream, and commanded me to train with you. Now we are bonded you see, you and I. We share the same Spiritual Guide. So, unworthy though I am of your brilliantly talented attentions, I'm sure you will want to implement Allah's will and act in accordance with the wishes of the Holy Man's spirit, and take on the difficult task of teaching an uncouth chit of a girl like me to sing at least moderately well."

In her own non-takaluff-bound mind she knew that although he had never fallen for her come-&-see-me sometime line, or been drawn to comment on her efforts at composing ghazals, now, with the alleged intervention of the Holy Man, she stood a real chance. How could the Lighter Upper of the Universe turn down such a plea? Now he would have to take her into pupilage. The Holy Man had wished it. And he'd said as much in a dream. How could anyone argue with the wishes of a Holy Man – patron saint of music and musicians? Now let's see how he gets out of this one – tormentor of the soul, heartless torturer!

His response was conveyed verbally by his man-servant to her own long-suffering one. The Lighter Up of the Universe couldn't let her feel she was important enough to receive a hand-written letter from His Greatness.

"Please inform your graceful, eloquent mistress that there isn't a thing I can teach her about music. She's way ahead of me in that respect. All of Lucknow is under the spell of her sweet voice. My ears have never been fortunate enough to collide with her melodious reverberations, but I have heard much about her songs. I pray that she goes on singing more and more beautifully, and I sacrifice every string of my sitar to her one perfect note. Please ask her not to embarrass me by asking me to teach her. I should be learning from her. If only I had the time, I would ask to go into pupilage with her!"

His own thoughts, of course, were nothing like the ridiculous official message: So this is her new angle. Some women just don't give up. What a nerve! Astakhfirullah! Me, the greatest musician since Tansen, teaching a courtesan to sing – to entice and entertain men. What a notion! Sounds like she's got it really badly for me. Refuses to give up. Involving the Holy Man and all now. Poor thing, she'll get over it."

On receiving the official verbal reply, the Courtesan burst into tears. All day she had consoled herself with the fact that even if his reply was in the negative, it would at least be in writing, and then she would have something to treasure, written by his own hand. The verbal message itself, although couched in the usual elegant and flowery language of takaluff, was no consolation.

She had to think hard. Some new scheme was urgently required. It would come, somehow it would come. And then something called uncanny intuition stirred within her – suggesting that if she left everything to God and stopped making such huge efforts herself, it would surely come, all by itself, in the most unexpected way. It was called giving up the management of affairs. It would happen without her having to submit herself to the humiliation of approaching him yet again. And then, when it happened, she would invite nine virgins for a meal. And she would feed them with her own right hand. Yes, something had to happen. That intuition was absolutely right. But what that intuition didn't tell her was that her opportunity would come sixteen years later. Sixteen long years in which she would weep for him almost every day. Sixteen long years during which she would be sold to a distinguished member of the landed gentry, de-flowered properly, and then returned two years later. After that, she was given to another nobleman, and another and another, until finally, by her 35th birthday, she could do no more than return to her old home, laden with money and jewels, to sit back and watch younger girls being trained in the art of entertaining men.

In the meantime, her messenger, the man-servant who had faithfully carried the verbal messages between her and the Grand Old Ustad, had just published his first volume of poetry, inspired by his first-hand experience of Tameezan's unrequited passion. Every single poem in his book spoke of the sad, hopeless love of a lover for an unseen beloved. In her later years, when she was no longer the object of anybody's lust, he was her closest friend. And on that fateful night sixteen years later, when her opportunity to meet the Ustad finally came, it was one of these ghazals composed by the humble man-servant, that had saved the day. Or had it?

21
NO PLACE FOR MOSES

All through the tumultuous events leading up to 1947, leaders of India's nationalist independence movement had a cherished dream. A secular democratic India with complete freedom for people to worship whoever they wanted, whenever they wanted. Nehru's independent India was envisioned as a country where those who went to temples went to temples and didn't get in the way of those who preferred to go to mosques. It didn't quite work, and in the end those who preferred mosques had to have a land of their own. But it still didn't work, and the mosque-goers went on to divide their Holy land once again, in order to have Bengali mosques in the eastern half and non-Bengali mosques in the western half. What those Indian nationalists didn't know was that their dream had already come true, albeit not in their beloved land of hopes and dreams, but just across the Indian Ocean on the eastern coast of Africa. In the land affectionately known as Pearl, not only did people worship freely in their own religious institutions, but also came and went freely from each other's. No special religious occasion would have been complete in a mosque or temple without invited dignitaries from all other faiths, plus an open standing invitation to all members of the public. Hence a large part of Pearl's small town social life was a hectic round of religious rituals and ceremonies at mosques, temples, gurudwaras, churches and fire temples. In time, it was difficult to say which was which, and certain religious practices came to be part of all the different faiths.

The Feast of the Nine Virgins was among the first to acquire these hazy inter-faith boundaries. And from here it was just another short step for certain ways of life to seep into everyday behaviour. The Hindus were extra careful to not hold parties or weddings during the month of Muharram and the Muslims always avoided beef at all costs, although it would have been freely available to them. The Christians followed suit, out of respect for their Muslim friends, and soon the slaughter of cows was unheard of. And since Indian Christians in Pearl had already given up consuming pork out of respect for their Muslim friends, the only dead flesh ever consumed in Pearl was goat-meat, deer-meat, guinea fowl and chicken.

That's how things had always happened in Pearl. No legislation, no riots, no rules, no decrees – just considerate behaviour based on mutual respect. And since you could eat chicken or goat, why upset your Hindu neighbours by gloating over beef? And since you had the rest of the year in which to hold festivities, why upset the Muslims by holding a wedding during Muharram, or a luncheon during Ramadan?

Even money-minded Mohanji tore himself away from his shop to go and wish Eid Mubarak to all his Muslim friends, straight after their special prayers at the hill top mosque. He would not, of course, join the prayers, but would wait respectfully outside the main gate, handkerchief tied on head and then, as they emerged from their prayers, he would embrace them one by one, renewing brotherhood and friendship.

If only those blinkered Indian nationalist leaders and their descendants had taken the trouble to come and study the mechanics of multi-religious harmony in Pearl, then they would have found a perfect model of their cherished dreams. And they would have also learnt the vital lesson that this kind of give-and-take among the settlers from India, was only possible out of a sense of having a common enemy – the Black Man.

Indian religious harmony in Pearl was undoubtedly born out of a sense of superiority towards the Blacks, who since the departure of the British, were becoming more and more inclined towards tribal rivalries and hostilities. The Indians could stand aside from all this, and feel like a morally superior species. A more advanced race of human beings – an altogether more cultured one – a race given to feelings of shame and izzat. The mutual protection of daughterly hymens is a great uniting factor of class and religion.

How could such a superior race allow the inferior Blacks to stand back and watch them at loggerheads over their religious differences? No, that would never do. For Pearlite Indians 1947 never happened. And if it did, it had nothing to do with them. One had to feign tolerance for other faiths. And pretended tolerance and respect often turns into the real thing. Tolerance can become a habit. If you're forced to show respect and tolerance for all faiths, then, in time, you actually begin to believe in the one and only God and you accept there are many vocabularies with which to approach Him. "He is One, but His symbols are many," Mohanji was often heard to say. That was the single biggest lesson that the Black man taught the otherwise bigoted Asians. But it's one lesson for which he never received any gratitude. Daily early morning temple trips were a hallmark of the Mohanji classes – the Dukavallas.

Mrs Henara and her sort of educated Muhindi people only showed up at ceremonials and special occasions, particularly if there was a visiting dignitary or a special singer-cum-storyteller brought in especially from India. On such occasions, Mrs Henara would deliberately dress down for fear of being mistaken for a shopkeeper's wife. While the Dukavalla women turned up in red and purple and green and gold for these specials, Mrs Henara wore plain white and no jewellery, except for a simple watch. That was the only way to look highly educated and sophisticated, and to stand aside from the crowd.

She had her own corner. Whenever she made her majestic late entrance, cool as a cucumber and exuding Chanel No. 5 in the sweltering heat, her corner would be hastily vacated by anyone who had been presumptuous enough to occupy it.

Mrs Henara had a strict rule in temples – no talking. While other women used their temple outings as the perfect opportunity to exchange news and gossip, Mrs Henara sat in complete silence, refusing to even make eye contact with anyone. Her head remained bowed, and she seemed to be in deep meditation, or whatever. When she did look up now and then, she had a special face she wore for these occasions. Her eyes would appear faraway and dreamy, not noticing anything or anyone within her line of vision. And she made it a special point to never look up when anyone came in. Whenever there was a fresh arrival at the huge archway entrance leading to the main recital room, all heads would turn to take a look. Who was it? What were they wearing? Had they worn it before? Was it new? Had it been dyed pretending to be new? And an audible shuffle of whispers would form, moving like a wispy swirl of unseen mist amidst the gathered assembly of women seated cross-legged on the floor. Not for Mrs Henara such blatant curiosity. Only the lower classes were curious about other people. Us, the upper classes keep ourselves to ourselves and we don't care who comes or goes. We come here to be holy, and holy we must look, which means not looking anywhere at all. Gaze right ahead into empty space, or upwards at the ceiling, or fold your hands in your lap and look straight down. Show extra appreciation for that part of the song or story that nobody else seems to understand. Smile benevolently at the favourite bits where everybody else livens up, but don't show any signs of animation yourself. Little things please little people. Everybody likes that bit because they know the words. These people! Anyone would think Meera Bai had only ever written one song in her entire life!

Most of the time Mrs Henara carried her act with perfection. But now and then, if the Brat had decided to accompany her to the temple, and that was more and more often these days, then there was no telling what might happen....

"Oh mummy, look look! I want a red sari like that when I grow up! And see mummy, she's wearing those earrings AGAIN – the ones you said made her look like mutton dressed like lamb."

"Don't stare at people, it's not polite. We're in a temple. You shouldn't be looking at people's clothes. Your mind should be on higher things," she would whisper the reprimand, but inwardly hope that the women in her immediate vicinity had also had their characters improved.

"What higher things? Please tell me about higher things. I love anything like that. Tell me about God again."

"Not now, not in the Temple, later," Mrs Henara would say, hoping to silence the Brat for the rest of the session.

"But if we can't talk about God in a Temple, then where...?"

"Just shut up and listen! You can't always talk. It's only when we are silent that God can talk to us."

That did the trick. The Brat fell silent for the rest of the session and waited patiently for God to speak to her. But nothing happened.

She was devastated. She had remained silent for well over thirty-five minutes, a record-breaking feat for her, and yet God hadn't spoken. Why? She would have to solve this one later.

When the singing finished the children played on the temple steps while the grown-ups had tea and gossip and snacks in the adjoining community hall. The Brat slipped away to a room at the back where the Temple priest lived. He was also the Mohanji personal Guru. He would know how to make God speak. Gurus are supposed to know about that sort of thing. Yes, she would ask him. He was sure to know.

But how to ask him? He looked so spooky. Bald head with a thin pony-tail on top. Bare chest. Red and white marks on his forehead. She was petrified of him, especially since she had once seen someone bow down to him as though he were God himself. Perhaps he was? Well, in that case there was nothing to be frightened of. Her mother had said God was good to well-behaved little girls. All she had to do was behave and everything would be just fine.

"What is it child? Why are you standing there? This is my private room don't you know? If you want sweets just go to the hall – lots of things to eat there."

"No, I don't want... no, I mean, I just came to ask you about something. My mother said God talks. When we are silent he's supposed to talk to us. I was very, very quiet just now, but nothing happened. I didn't hear him at all. I just want to know why... I mean, what do you think...?"

"What are you babbling about... God talks? What do you want with God? You're just a child. Children don't need God. Just listen to your parents and do what they say. Don't bring shame on your family. Always be kind to everyone. There's no need to sit and talk with God at your age, huh! Out!" He barked with the kind of finality that should have told the Brat to make herself scarce, but the Brat was never one to buckle down easily if there was a mystery to solve.

"But I just want to know... I mean if I hear him just once I'll be quite happy. My mother took me to a film once and there was this man called Moses – The Ten Condiments, you know, and he wanted to see God, and then there was all this lightning on a mountain. I want something like that, but not too frightening, just some small sign, maybe?"

"Big talk! Such big talk for little girl! Mozis-Shozis nothing. We don't believe in all that. That is for Jewish people only. Now off with you!"

Owing to the shortage – in fact the complete absence of Indian Jewish settlers in Pearl – the Jewish faith did not enjoy the privilege of belonging in Pearl's exclusive Indian religious tolerance club.

22
TYPICAL, BLOODY TYPICAL

"If you could just trouble yourself to get off my body for a minute, I've got something I might want to tell you."

The Producer gasped from somewhere underneath the stranglehold of his lusty embrace. There was no doubt about it. Being made love to by the World's Number One Composer was indeed like being made love to for the very first time. Such a hectic schedule yet such a brilliant performance! How did he do it?

"Must you always talk?" he said at last. "Isn't this exciting? Doesn't this do anything for you? Women would kill to be held by me, and you, all you can do is talk."

The Composer was never in doubt about his desirability stakes. Women always wanted him, and he knew it. The best part of his working day was taken up with intricate campaigns aimed at the avoidance of groupies and similar besotted females. But, it was the Producer's couldn't-care-less attitude that did wonders for his erectile tissue.

The Producer had never really cared for sex. It was OK, but not quite on par with reading an exciting book about the mysteries of the pyramids, or the lost lands of Atlantis. Sex was sometimes necessary to get to know a person, to break down barriers, bare their souls and to reveal their insecurities. Essential material for scripts. She usually only had sex for reasons of research – or at least that's what she claimed. But with the Composer, even she had to admit to herself with a feeling of shameful inadequacy, that she could happily have done it all day and all night. But right now she was heavy with secrets, and the burden was becoming unbearable She needed to talk.

He was thrilled she had persuaded him to stop in London. True, he hadn't taken much persuading because this way he would get to Amsterdam just in time for the sound-check. Otherwise he would have got there a whole day too early. It was much more in keeping with his public image to arrive just five minutes before a performance. And how could he have turned down an offer to spend a whole night awake, with Sonia, in London? Well, that's the way it goes. You see, can't plan too much. Live for the moment. The present moment is all we have – that's what you learnt on the hot dusty streets of Bombay. You lucky devil you! For months you've been obsessed by this woman. She was never to be found anywhere. Yet here she is, right here, in a bed... with you. You haven't lost it clever dick, you haven't. Whoever you want, you can always get! And she wants to actually work with you. So that's what she does for a living. She makes films. But why haven't I heard of any of her films?

"I can't bear it any more. I have to tell someone, can I trust you?" Her post-orgasmic voice cut into his stream of self-congratulatory thoughts.

"What honey, what? You've fallen in love with me, I know, I know."

"No, not that you stupid big-headed – actually, I don't know if I should say.... Can I trust you? Promise me you won't change your mind about composing my music, first promise me that."

"Hey, come on, relax, of course you'll get your music. As long as the money is right, and you'll keep meeting me in bed like this, won't you? As long as we can be lovers, don't worry."

"I'm worried in case you... well... look, I can't really say anything, but can you tell me everything you know about that Actress – the chhipkali, you know that one who wouldn't leave your room and you had to call hotel security? Was she ever married or anything? To a very old man – much older than her... very rich?"

"How do I know? She may be, who cares? Actresses get through so many husbands what does it matter?" he said lazily, stifling a yawn.

"It matters because I feel someone is trying to get even with her. There's a very elaborate revenge plan – it's almost sinister."

"How do you know? And so what? Why do you care? Is she a friend of yours or something?"

"No no, not at all. I've never even set eyes on her. Didn't even know about her until... well... look, this is it: she's going to be Tameezan the Courtesan in our film.

"She's what? No, tell me you're joking. Are you mad?" He was sitting up in bed now, genuinely staggered by the revelation.

"I have no choice – the guy who's paying all the bills – let's just call him Moneybags for now – he's kind of foisted her on me."

"Oh God! What do you mean foisted? Who the hell is he, anyway?"

"I'm sorry I can't say – I really mustn't. Please understand. I know it sounds ridiculous, but I need whatever information I can get on both of them, but I can't say anything to anyone. Please help me."

"This is crazy! Forget it – not that I know anything about whoever since you won't even tell me... but what is this? Is it straight? Look, even if it is, I'm not, not, not working with her, you hear me? No way! She'll be all over me, don't you see?"

"Oh just belt up about your sex appeal for once. You don't have to work with her. I don't recall offering you an actor's part. You're just the composer, remember? Your work is in a different place – at a different time, you don't have to be anywhere near her, I promise you that. You'll deal only with me, and of course, the musicians of your choice – let me stress – YOUR choice. Whoever you want."

"Yes, yes, OK. But look, just speaking as a friend, or even as a friendly lover, how can you use a woman to play Tameezan when she can't even speak Urdu? Or is your film in English? But then she can't even speak English properly. She's only ever been in Hindi films and then too she speaks with the greatest of difficulty – so they usually just give her songs to move her lips to. How on earth is she going to cope with Tameezan's Urdu? Well, nice body and all that, but nothing else...."

The mention of her body brought a faraway look in his eyes. Yes, once or twice, it was OK, but who wants to sit and talk with the woman, leave alone work with her?

"I think you're mad," he announced, by way of summary.

"Look, I can't do anything about it, I'm committed. Anyway, we'll be training her to speak Urdu. We're paying for all that...."

"What a waste of money! Anyway, she can't act to save her life. She's only ever done those cabaret scenes – lots of gyrating belly and swaying hips... heaving bosoms... cleavage... Bust 42, I think, DD or E-cup."

He grew a little more wistful at some memory of her anatomy – wide pelvis, gyrating hips, heaving bosoms, 42-E cleavage, and who knows what else. Men! Typical, bloody typical! The Producer brushed off a vague sense of jealousy.

"Let's talk about our music," she said importantly, changing the subject. "This ghazal you see has to be...."

"Oh, I'll do it. I know what to do. One doesn't sit around – sorry lie around – talking about music. One just does it. And as for the Grand Ustad Ronson Lighter's solo pieces, I'll talk to his grandson. He's the best sitar player ever. But first tell me about this Moneybags person, who is he? What's going on?"

"Maybe I'll tell you some other day. First I need to find out some more...
oh, but let's talk about the music. I'm so excited about this ghazal, you know,
the one she sings on that fateful night? Imagine! Poor Tameezan has spent
sixteen long years waiting to see her wretched Ustad, and finally it's going
to happen. Right in the middle of that ghazal he's going to walk in and their
eyes are going to meet – oh! Doesn't it just kill you, even thinking about it? I
can hear that ghazal in my head. I wish I could sing it to you – just to give
you an idea! I hope this Chipkali actress has the right kind of face. I've got
an exact idea about how Tameezan should look that night – hopeful, defiant,
confident, apprehensive, nervous, beautiful, excited – but very cleverly con-
cealing all her emotions. So it's all got to come out through the ghazal alone
– musically as well as poetically. Oh, let's discuss it now. I need a melody
that conveys separation – a vague kind of Raag Des, do you think? You see
it's vital we build up that mood, because the audience doesn't know what's
going to happen, for instance...."

But the World's Number One Composer was already snoring in post-
orgasmic bliss – no doubt with a vague memory of the 42-E cup still playing
out somewhere in his loin area. "Typical! Bloody typical!" she thought, and
turned over to lie wide awake visualising her ghazal scene the umpteenth time.

23
GRANDSON OF THE UNIVERSAL LIGHTER

The Ustad who was to play the exquisite sitar solos for his own Grandfather's role was a man of immense stature, in every sense of the word. Now in his sixties, he had been undoubtedly one of the best sitar-players for over thirty years. Portly, balding, and laden from head to toe with gold chains, bracelets and diamond rings, not forgetting the numerous amulets containing special Quranic verses, especially designed and engraved in gold for his protection. Protection from what? From enemies – other jealous, less successful musicians. Evil eye, you know. Bad-Nazar. One poisoned glance might kill.

The Ustad sat comfortably in his private living room overlooking the sunny side of the huge garden attached to this large Hampstead mansion. The house belonged to one of his students, a man of about forty, who had been in pupilage with the Ustad for about twenty years. During that time, he had learnt neither to sing nor to play an instrument, but had become extremely good at going to all the Ustad's concerts, as well as showing up at various private recitals at mansions even bigger than his own. A standing invitation to attend dinner and music gatherings in large mansions was one of the main perks of being attached to a distinguished musician. For the pupil, the Ustad was like something you wore when you went out.

The old system of subservient discipleship in music, with the pupil bowing and scraping to his Ustad was now a dying institution – give or take a few rich, displaced Indians; rich by exploiting the native Black population of Africa and displaced by the turning of the worm. Originally rich because of their fathers' little small-town shops, but now richer because of their own hard work in Britain and their motels across the Atlantic.

But what use riches if the soul feels permanently displaced? Permanently out of place, at ease everywhere, yet at home nowhere. Roots, that's the answer. Find one's cultural roots. What roots? The folk songs of Gujarat or Rajahsthan? The money-lending traditions of their Banya-Marwari forefathers? No, find the kind of cultural roots that have been endorsed and made respectable by the West. Those are the best kind of roots. The desire to return to one's roots had to be compatible with all that was dear to, and revered by the host-culture: chicken tikka masala, poppadoms, balti, Kamasutra, sitar. And this same British host-culture had accorded "World Music" a status unmatched in its various countries of origin.

The Ustad had stationed himself in his pupil's grand mansion for the whole of his current British concert tour. And this was his only day off in an otherwise hectic schedule that would take him up and down the country. The Ustad felt happily frenzied and important at the very thought of it. And he was right to feel so. True enough, it had been designed to look like a hectic schedule, but in reality, it was a goodwill gesture on the part of his old and faithful following. They had raised the money somehow, and had booked large prestigious venues in different British cities. The concerts would, in fact, centre on various younger musicians showing off their wizardry on a variety of modern instruments while the Ustad was to come on at the very end, just for a few minutes as a very special "surprise."

There would be garlands and speeches. The Ustad himself would talk for about six minutes out of his total allotted playing time of fifteen. Then he would play a bit, and the "Wah wah's" and "ooh-aah's" would drown the sound of his instrument. The real stars, all those younger musicians who had just demonstrated the most amazing kinds of musical technique and youthful vigour, would then stand just by in a line, their eyes and heads lowered, some even quietly sobbing out of takalluf-ridden pretended-respect, and then, one by one they would all come up to him and touch his feet.

The younger musicians would apologise for their own impertinence – in a manner borrowed from Lucknow – the impertinence of playing at the same concert as someone as Great as himself. There would be masses of crawling and feet touching and ear-tugging. It was customary to tug at one's ear every time the name of any great musician came up – living or dead. The Ustad would pat the heads of the younger musicians and wish them a long life. Even if they weren't officially his pupils, in that one moment of feet-touching, they would take on the submissive pupil-persona.

The Ustad loved this part of the evening best. It was his great moment. This ritualised meek-and-submissive routine would have to be fitted in somewhere between the ambassadorial garlands, speeches and the Ustad himself playing a few notes from one of his ancestors' special antiquated compositions. It was a nail-biting moment for concert organisers. One could never accurately calculate the time factor on such things. And if the venue happened to be one of those characterless, clinically sanitised concert halls set inside those large, ugly, grey, so-called arts complexes, then at exactly 10.45 pm various uniformed personnel, with about as much charm as the average Gestapo recruit and a zero understanding of the crawling, ear-tugging and feet-touching ceremony, would start appearing at the doors. Lights would be switched on, buzzers would start buzzing, bells would start ringing, and wristwatches would be pointed at threateningly.

Yes, it was the concert organisers' worst nightmare. An Ustad in full flow on the one hand, and the Gestapo pointing to the clock on the other, was the worst thing that could happen to an already frazzled stage manager. Not that any of this mattered to the Ustad. Time was meaningless to him – unless it was his own time. Everybody else was supposed to have time in unlimited quantities.

Just one day off in a hectic schedule, and even then no peace, he thought. My only day off and even today some film woman wants to come and see me.

Strange though it may seem, in his long and distinguished career, he had never once been approached with a film proposal. Most producers just assumed he was too big and too grand to just turn up and record the background score for a mere film. And true enough, at one time he would have been insulted and horrified at such a proposal. But times had changed. He badly needed a comeback of sorts. Something that would show those younger musicians just what he was capable of. Sure, they crawled to him in public, but he knew exactly what they said behind his back. He wasn't fooled for a minute. And quite suddenly, without even knowing what it exactly entailed, the Grandson-Ronson Ustad felt quite keen on this new offer.

He decided to be extra charming to this woman. Should he wear his usual kurta-pyjama, or would it be better to appear relaxed in normal western clothes? He opted for the Indian look – he was usually more comfortable that way, and anyway, if she wanted to talk to him about a major film assignment involving an Ustad, he may as well exude the Ustad magic now, and get into the role. Whatever she might want, he never for a moment doubted his ability to deliver. He had complete confidence in his own musical ability – and quite rightly so. Music was his life.

He had performed all over the world and had a larger number of recordings than any other classical musician of any nationality. He was respected for his abilities both in India and in the West. But now, his concerts were more symbolic rather then the stunning feats of dexterity and musicality that they had once been. Most people attended out of a sense of nostalgia for the Great Ustad of yesteryear – he who could make the earth move with one single note. Although nowadays, his accompanying young percussionists had more of a following than he did, and moved the earth in different ways for their female groupies, it was always officially understood by all concerned that the Ustad was the Big Star and that it was for his benefit that the women had turned out in full force. Backstage, after a major performance, the same understanding applied. Even though the women battled with each other to get close to some of the other younger, accompanying musicians, the Ustad believed they were there only to get a good look at HIM. Most of his accompanists were shrewd enough to let him go on believing this. They needed him too. They needed the magic of his name. They needed to ride on the outdated myth of his fame. They needed concert bookings in exotic locations.

He was meticulously superstitious – never agreed to a concert date unless the numerology was right and never took a major step without first consulting the family astrologer. He was hugely suspicious of other musicians and even of their relatives and fans offering him anything to eat or drink. Much as he liked his food, and much as he adored going to dinner-parties, he was always ultra cautious. Somehow, he always managed to get someone else to taste it first.

He lived in perpetual fear of being poisoned in his own country. It must be understood that this imaginary "poison" was not of the kind that would kill, but more specifically, of a kind that would maim his hands – his wrists and his fingers, vital to playing that instrument, and he would never be able to play again. When he had confided his fears to a close friend in America, he was informed he could always insure his hands for an enormous sum. He liked the idea, but never got round to doing anything about it. He completely failed to grasp the ideology behind insurance. If his hands could be insured for sixty million dollars, then why couldn't someone just give him that amount right now, as a tribute to his genius? Why would his hands have to be maimed to earn their true worth? In any case, when travelling in the West, he usually relaxed his food-tasting rules. Somehow, he had figured out that Westerners and foreigners didn't go in for that sort of thing. He classified them as scientific. "They have science instead of God, Thank God!"

24
KEBABS AND BONES

The Ustad was getting nervous. She would be here any moment, and that useless pupil-host of his had disappeared again. The Ustad had specifically ordered his student to be present for the film meeting, because he knew these British-Indian film and TV types only spoke English, and they spoke it so fast and in such an accent that he could barely make out the words. On such occasions he could do little more than say "No problem... no problem." His own English was reasonable, but he had great difficulty with regional accents. Oh, where was that stupid fellow? Why did he always disappear when he was most needed? The Ustad was still fretting when a silky, honey-coated female voice, from just somewhere behind him announced:

"Adaab-arz karti hoon Khan Sahib."

He whizzed around to find a shabby-looking young woman in torn, faded jeans and bleached hair, file-and-phone-in-hand. Could that have been her own voice?

She continued in flawless Urdu:

"I apologise for disturbing you. It is truly noble of you to agree to share an hour of your priceless time with me, a mere slave. But you could transform this slave into the luckiest woman on earth with just a few vibrations from a single sitar string. Dare I hope for such an eventuality? Will the sky ever come down and touch the dust of the earth?"

Time stood still. The Ustad had never been addressed in this fashion. This could be Tameezan the Courtesan herself. This is how Tameezan would've spoken to his own grandfather. But this was no Tameezan. This was a most definitely European-looking woman in an old pair of jeans. No bangles, no hair ornaments, no henna on her hands. Yet she had all the beguiling grace and self-effacing charm of a nineteenth century courtesan. This woman was the answer to all his prayers. He resolved there and then, whatever she wanted, he would do. He would abandon his sitar and take up the tabla if she so wished. The Ustad felt light as a bird and wished his wretched Gujarati-speaking pupil would remain absent for a few hours more. Who needs him? Two is company, three is a... well, who needs bones in the middle of a kebab?

25
TOUCH ME NOT

Robert Kasoga was the brightest boy in his school. School? Well, it was really only a gathering of ragged children under a shady tree presided over by an elderly Indian gentleman whose only teaching qualification was his adept use of the cane. Although Robert's father could not afford to send him to a proper school in town, by some miraculous process known only to the cosmic forces, Robert managed every year to top the national lists in almost every subject. If Robert had been an Indian, then no doubt, some kind of private scholarship scheme would've seen to his higher education. But he was Black, and Asian businessmen who frequently funded scholarships in memories of their grand ancestors, would never have dreamed of awarding it to a lowly Black. Can't let these guys get too educated. Gives them ideas above their station. It was best if everyone knew his place otherwise the world would just collapse. Kalyug! Look at that other chap... Solomon... or Simon, whatever he was called – just because he managed to get through secondary school because of his wretched mother's immoral work in the night, now he'd become Union Leader of Domestic Servants. Now there was a minimum wage demand and every Sunday off. Outrageous! Why do they need Sundays off? What else do they have to do with their lives? Surely their only job is to serve us? If you gave them Sundays off it invariably meant hangovers on Monday mornings.

So Robert remained at the village school under the shady tree, in the small Western province. Robert's father had a part-time job repairing radios and gramophones at the Mohanji & Sons General Store. Mohanji had taken him on, on the condition that he would gradually teach all his repair skills to the still-young Mohanji sons. Fully aware that passing on knowledge in this way would result in his own eventual redundancy Mr Kasoga, nevertheless, agreed to Mohanji's atrocious condition. At least it was a job. And it brought in a small, regular wage that just about covered the family's minimum cash needs. At least he could go on paying Robert's school-fees – a small amount, but a princely sum for the poor Kasogas. Apart from the paltry wages, Mr Kasoga also had a small plot of land attached to their mud house, where his two wives tended to the peas, beans, potatoes and yams. This provided the family with its staple diet. At least they didn't have to buy much food – apart from the very occasional chicken and the twice a week maize-meal to make porridge. Occasionally, the two wives would quarrel, but more often than not, they would both gang up against their husband.

So when Mr Kasoga died suddenly and tragically, there was no other option but for Robert to give up school and find a job. But that didn't stop him from carrying on with his studies, all by himself in the evenings, under the one and only lamp post in the village. Robert would just sit there reading – reading anything he could get his hands on, even a month-old newspaper. It was a common sight for villagers to see Robert sitting under the lamp late into the silent night, punctuated only by the rhapsody of fluttering moths, all vying with one another to be the first to be consumed by the light. Robert knew that that was just one kind of light – the kind at which moths throw themselves. But then there was enlightenment, which was a different thing altogether and initially, books and reading materials were essential to get the ball rolling in that direction.

There was no question of compensation for Mr Kasoga's death. Mr Mohanji maintained that life and death were in the hands of God, and the Morality Committee backed him on this indisputable truth. It was easy. All you had to do was bring God into the argument, somehow, and then you could always have the last word.

No human being could be held responsible for another human being's death. After all, hadn't Mr Kasoga died on the spot when a badly placed cardboard box in the over-loaded, over-crowded shop, containing the very latest stereo equipment had fallen on his head? Even so, in a mood of God-fearing generosity, Mr Mohanji offered to pay the funeral expenses and the balance of the monthly salary. Strictly speaking, he shouldn't have had to do this. After all, Mr Kasoga was in breach of contract. He should have worked the whole of the month, but had died during the third week, so strictly speaking, it should only have been three weeks wages, but Mr. Mohanji, out of the goodness of his heart, was paying the family for the full month. "His generosity is an example to us all," pronounced his friends in the Morality Committee.

All the Muhindi community in the town agreed that Mr Mohanji had been most compassionate in sorting out the Kasoga affair – all except Mrs Henara, that is. But then she always had to be different. Since she always felt a cut above everybody else, she could never subscribe to the majority view on anything. Majority meant plebs. Plebs were common. She was special.

On hearing the news of the death, Mrs Henara jumped into her little Fiat and drove at top speed to the Kasoga household, twenty miles away. She ordered both the wives, and Robert, to take legal action against Mr Mohanji. She didn't say how they could go about it, or offer to pay for any of it. Nor did she suggest the name of a lawyer friend. She merely stated what ought to happen, cooed at the babies for a bit, and then swept away in her pastel chiffons leaving a trail of expensive French scent behind her. They had offered her a cup of tea, but she declined. How could she drink from their cups?

Now that his father was dead and there was no hope of going to school, domestic service would've been the only career open to Robert. He was still only 15, much too young to get a clerical job. And the family desperately needed money. But Robert winced at the thought of being at the beck and call of the likes of Mrs Henara, and only people of her class employed servants at realistic wages and offered decent accommodation in the grounds of their luxurious houses.

It was out of the question. He could never deal with her sort of people on a day-to-day basis. And the Dukavallas? No way! His father had met his tragic death while serving the Dukavallas. They seldom employed servants anyway, because their daughters had to be trained in the domestic arts in preparation for marriage. Besides, they had huge hang-ups about Blacks not being allowed to touch this and not being allowed to step there. He had to find the kind of work that would keep him as far away from these people as possible – preferably well outside of their homes.

There was only one thing for it: clean their shit. That way they never let you come near them – not in a million years! Even your shadow was not allowed to fall on them – and that suited Robert just fine.

26
PEARLS AND DIAMONDS

Destiny has no respect for geography. Places separated by thousands of miles and people scattered through time-spans of hundreds of years, can sometimes become inextricably linked by the script of destiny.

And that was exactly what happened. A group of professional women – those of the oldest profession in the world – made their way from the small kingdom of poetry (otherwise known as the largest diamond in the crown of Takaluff) to the shores of Britain. Here, they feigned various uneasy alliances with groups of dispossessed, but now even richer men, who had made their way to these same shores from the country that was the Pearl of Africa's Crown. This meeting of the former dwellers of Pearls and Diamonds, could only have been arranged by destiny. If destiny had not intervened, never in a million years could the courtesans of Lucknow have ever found themselves in London, in the same bed as the Dukavallas of small-town Pearl.

The courtesans were making history. Or history was making them. Their mothers and grandmothers may have been domni's – singing and dancing entertainers, but their daughters and granddaughters were determined to up-grade the family profession. They no longer had clients – they had "friends". They no longer charged per session with the odd gift of valuable jewellery for special occasions. Now, they insisted on having the deeds of their Knights-bridge and Mayfair houses made out in their names. They insisted on private school fees for their many children.

India was partitioned in 1947, and the Muslim State of Pakistan created. Everybody knows that. Everybody knows that massive numbers of people lost their homes and moved across the new border, enduring the greatest hard-ships. It was one of the largest mass displacements of humankind. Against a backdrop of mindless violence and bloodshed, Muslims fled to the new country – Pakistan, while Hindus who found themselves on the Pakistani side of the border, fled to India. A significant group of professionals, mostly teachers and doctors set off for Africa. Everybody knows that.

But what nobody knows is that in 1948, or thereabouts, another mass immigration took place – not across the Indo-Pak border, but across all the seven seas, into Britain. The immigrants were all women, all stowaways, and all descendants of courtesans made stateless by the disbanding of India's various lesser rulers.

Saloni was one such woman – last in a matrilineal stream of renowned courtesans. And like all the other women, she hoped and prayed for a fresh start. She'd heard that in England, as long as you were prepared to work hard, there was lots of money to be made. And best of all, nobody moralised about your dubious origins. The British were not nosey in that respect. But it's difficult to teach an old dog new tricks, and soon, just like all the others, she too was firmly established in the old family business. Saloni remained a courtesan, but in England, they were always called "Socialites". Beautiful women – thirty or forty-something – offering all the usual services plus a vital added ingredient – Orientalist exotica – a touch of Eastern Promise, straight from the Kamasutra. The women imagined that this exotic quality would be in huge demand amidst the newly-returned Raj Brits. But it didn't quite work like that. Instead, the courtesans-turned-socialites found themselves doing rather well with the newly mobile Asian nobility – the international jet-set who whizzed around between the south of France and Belgravia. Ordinary Asian communities complete with Asian corner shops were as yet unknown in Britain, while Indian call girls were virtually unheard of.

For the chiffon-sari-clad socialites, life was one hectic round of parties and dinners. Liaisons and associations, understandings and misunderstandings with gentlemen of means, and regular cheques from regular clients. Tea at Fortnum's. Lunch at the Ritz. Harrods in the afternoon. They no longer had to sing or dance. They just had to turn up at the right parties and make sparkling conversation. And then? Well it all depended on who you met, how fat his wallet, and how far he intended to go. Different levels of attachment carried different rates. It was a lot of money when converted to Indian rupees – something the women couldn't help doing in the early days.

But their biggest compensation came in the certain knowledge that theirs would be the last generation of professional courtesans. Their daughters would not have to suffer the indignities of massaging the male ego. Their daughters would be sent to the finest institutions and educated to the highest standards. Then they would marry well – or perhaps not marry at all. Who needs men? Your grandmothers have crawled to men for hundreds of years. Now you're free. Just make something of yourself, and stand on your own two feet. Never lie down for a man if you don't want to. And money? There were more interesting ways to earn money – more fulfilling ways.

So a new generation of women emerged. For some inexplicable reason, these stowaway-illegal-immigrant courtesans only ever gave birth to daughters. That would've been considered excellent news in the traditional courtesan set-up back home – a daughter to carry on the mother's business. But now, there was no question of that. Their mothers had not suffered those perilous boat journeys for nothing. Lucky daughters of plucky mothers. They excelled in everything they touched. They became lecturers, painters, writers, teachers, doctors, film-makers. They were sent to boarding schools right from the start. They had to be kept as far away as possible from their mothers' real lives and their real livelihood – the one that paid the school fees.

It was imperative the daughters remain pure as driven snow, for that was their strength. Their purity and chastity would bring them the pride their mothers and grandmothers had been denied. Most of these girls were sent to school in England, but a few were also sent away to equally good schools in the British-built hill stations of the old homeland – the further, the better. After all, the object of this whole exercise was to keep the daughters from being splashed with the muck of their mothers' seedy lives.

In keeping with the stowaway-courtesan tradition, Saloni sent her only daughter Seema to an exclusive girls' school on the Himalayan Slopes. Seema was exceptionally bright and was definitely showing an aptitude for chemistry and biology. But school holidays were always a problem. Saloni didn't really want Seema in London. Instead, she paid for her daughter to travel in Europe, or America – or wherever she could stay with friends – respectable, classy, wealthy friends.

On one such trip, Seema fell in love with a young medical student. And then she deliberately picked a university in his town, to read Biology and to be near him. Seema assumed she would join her mother in London once her studies were over, but Saloni wouldn't hear of it. She threw her hands up in horror and insisted that the girl find something to do somewhere else: "Go to Paris. Or New York. There's nothing in London for you."

"But what would I do in Paris? Why can't I stay in London with you? I really want to teach. I could teach in a school and...."

"No, I don't want you living in London. This is no place for a young woman."

"Why can't I go to my father? You said you'd tell me about him some day. Who was he?"

"A gutless bastard. I don't want to talk about him."

What else could Saloni say? The identity of her daughter's father was neither here nor there. He was probably languishing somewhere in the heat and dust of the newly independent homeland. He'd meant nothing to her. Just another client, and a slight mistake in calculations on her part.

But Seema always asked questions – too many questions – questions that could never be answered. And these days, her mother seemed to live on some remote planet of her own – always in a daze, and vague in the extreme. They only ever talked on the telephone, or occasionally, Saloni would call on Seema – in Scotland, or somewhere in Yorkshire, or wherever Seema had deposited herself since she was not allowed to come home.

Then one day there was a call from one of her mother's friends. Saloni's body had been found splattered on a pavement outside a big hotel. She had thrown herself, from the eleventh floor it was said, but it could have been foul play. She could've been pushed. There was this sinister character who was supposed to be her drugs supplier. Some said he was also her pimp. It seemed they'd had a fight, and then that same night... maybe he had pushed her?

Seema was dazed with shock. None of it made any sense. Pimp, drugs, her mother in a hotel? Corpse splattered... drugs?

Devastated by the death of her only relative, Seema panicked and decided to get married. She'd already got a good degree, and in time, inherited all her mother's money. She was horrified at just how much there was. She knew they were very well off, but she had no idea her mother had stashed away so much – so many sound investments. A huge house in Belgravia, stocks, shares, jewellery....

Her young medic boyfriend had recently been cooling off a bit, so she deliberately told him all about her inheritance, in great detail, hoping he wouldn't have heard the rumours about pimps and drugs. It did the trick, and suddenly, he was quite keen on her, all over again. She knew exactly why. But she wanted him. She had no one else.

He was offered the post of surgeon at a brand new hospital in a small country somewhere in British East Africa, and Seema was thrilled at the prospect of at last being able to have a permanent home somewhere on this earth. She had spent her entire childhood being passed around like a parcel from house to house, country to country.

And Africa was indeed Seema's making. Real freedom and security at last. True, her marriage went sour within the first few years, and it ended with her booting the surgeon out, but not before he'd squandered away most of her inheritance on drink and his many mistresses. Still, she was glad she had held on to her mother's house in London, and the rent money from that house was forming a nice nest-egg in England if she ever needed to leave Africa. But why would she want to leave Africa, her first proper home? Here, in small town Pearl, she was a somebody, just as her mother had wanted her to be. She was a big fish in a small pond. Here she could espouse theories of the kind that couldn't be disputed. Her maths and intelligence theory had taken shape right here, in this equatorial paradise. Here, she was perceived as someone with class – and what's more, nobody had any inkling of the family history.

Back in England, the Indian settler community was growing at an alarming rate. Connections were being formed, names were being mentioned and whispered, and remembered and recognised: "Wasn't that the same Saloni from Lucknow who came to Delhi and then operated out of the bazaar behind the shoe-market? Didn't she then disappear overnight? It's possible she might have wound up in London. And that hotel incident? Was it suicide or murder?"

Twenty years on, in England, in India and even in Pakistan, people were still whispering about her mother, but not in dear little Pearl.

The seedy past was well and truly over in the anonymity of small town Africa. Pearlite Indians, especially the trader-Dukavalla types, had been in Africa for at least two generations, and were not very up-to-date on Indian courtesan-socialite gossip. Seema Henara could relax and enjoy all that Pearl had to offer. A job with many perks, a beautiful house and a child of her own, to say nothing of a full staff of servants, including a special mosquito servant. But most important of all, she could feel superior to the less educated Dukavallas. Yes, she was glad she didn't live in England. She was glad her mother had never wanted her to live there. Where in England could you have this sort of life, by being a mere teacher?

27
GOD'S HUMBLE SERVANT

Thanks to her flawless Urdu, the Producer and the Ustad were getting on famously: "Ustad-ji," she used the traditional "ji" for added respect, "You'll do it? I can't say how grateful I am – how can I ever thank you?"

"No, no, not at all beti," he had, in just one meeting, decided to adopt her. "Very good of you to come to me. It will be a pleasure. I am a mere servant of Allah, and my duty is to serve, through music, that is why I was given this gift. That is what music is all about. It is given to you so that you may use it to soothe and heal other aching hearts. It's not for yourself, it's for others. Don't praise me, praise Allah!"

Hmmm, he says nice things, but he never uses ten words when a hundred will do. She carried on crawling: "It's absolutely thrilling. Just think, you'll be playing for your own Grandfather – isn't that just great?"

On her mention of the Grand Ustad, she had blasphemously forgotten to add on the "Lighter Up" title. Even so, on hearing the name of his esteemed ancestor, the Ustad quickly held both his ear lobes and ceremoniously tugged at them. She was mystified by the gesture. Her SOAS Urdu course had not touched on this at all, but she decided to do the same, just to appear in the know:

"Just imagine Ustad-ji, the legendary Lighter Upper of the Universe, the Grand Ustad, will come alive through your fingers. Every time you vibrate a string, he will breathe... aah... wonderful!"

"Truly, truly wonderful. And I give you my word you'll get the very best from me. Things that have never ever been heard or recorded. My distinguished grandfather – the Lighter Up of the Universe – (quick ear-tug again), Allah rest his noble and refined soul, refused point-blank to be recorded. He just said NO! So, you see, it'll be a first – yes, yes I promise you that..." he carried on with promises for quite a while, expansive and generous.

Somehow, it's so much easier to be generous in Urdu, the Producer noted to herself with some satisfaction. If this conversation had taken place in English, then everything would've been much tighter and meaner, and somehow doled out more resentfully. That usually happened to languages when they became languages of commerce and technology.

"Oh, Ustad-ji! I can't believe my luck. A thousand thanks again to that brilliant World's Number One Composer who made it possible. 1 wouldn't even have known how to find you. How can a worm touch the moon? Where you, and where I? Thanks to him that you even agreed to see me, thank you, thank you...."

The slightly salted butter was being laid on thicker and thicker.

"Yes, he's a brilliant kid! What a wonderful human being! Do you know how many hardships he had to go through to make it as a musician? And look at him now! Still, Allah gives to those he wants to give. What I really like about the Composer is however modern his other stuff, when he wants something pure and classical, then he comes straight to me. If he wants a proper sitar solo, then he'll go to a proper sitar player. May Allah let him prosper even more. Do you know he was composing tunes at the age of eight? Yes, eight! I first met him when he was 15. I met him through a very well known temple singer – have you heard of Kanhayya Lal?"

"No, can't say I have...."

She wasn't too surprised that the Ustad could be so gushingly praise laden for the Composer. The Composer had no rival family "musical gharana" behind him. He was a one-man, self-made show. No competition. No question of great musical families colliding with each other. He was no threat. On the contrary, he was an excellent contact for the Ustad and brought him much lucrative work.

"Ustad-ji, I want to thank you once again for taking everything so well. You are indeed a broad-minded man. After all, I am telling the story of your own Grandfather, and there's all sorts of... well you know, all kinds of personal details... some real, some made-up. It's so good of you to not quibble about anything. I'm so grateful," she said as meekly as possible.

"It's your story, and you have every right to tell it as it appears to you. Just because I'm playing the sitar for you, doesn't mean I'm officially endorsing the story. After all, you're just telling a story about a story. The Composer gave me a quick summary of your script. You know I don't read much English, but he explained the plot to me, and I can't say I object. Everybody knows Tameezan was besotted by my Grandfather. Who wasn't? So were tens of thousands of young women like her. It's perfectly natural. But he, he never laid a finger on anyone. He was a pious, God-fearing man. Only lived for his music. He could have had several wives, but he only ever had the one, my grandmother. She was his main inspiration. She was everything to him. When they were young, she used to sit at his feet while he did his practice. And do you know, on the very rare occasion when he hit a false note she yelled at him. Yes! His meek, obedient purdah-ridden wife actually shouted the choicest rude words in Urdu if he messed up on his sitar. She was the only person who ever scolded him. That's the sort of woman she was. He was devoted to her. Her gajjar ka halwa was as legendary as his music. With a wife like that who needs courtesans? Clean as a whistle... an exceptional man – you wouldn't get that these days. I should know. Women throw themselves at your feet when you are a famous musician – ho! Don't I know it? I've been at the receiving end of that non-stop – even now – even with my grey hair..." he broke into an uncontrollable, self-congratulatory laughter and winked at her.

She laughed with him. She was perfectly aware of the trail of broken hearts he'd left behind his rapidly advancing footsteps. They all did this. They all emerged clean as anything with the ultimate defence: "Well what can I do if women keep falling in love with me? Is it my fault? A fly can fall in love with a bull... so what?"

"But Ustad-ji, it was that big night wasn't it? It was on that occasion of the famous Nawab's party, to celebrate the birth of his first son? Wasn't that the same night when Tameezan sat singing a ghazal, and then your Grandfather came in, and then he just...."

"Something like that... yes, that was an important night. There is so much evil in this world. People will do anything. Still, never mind, it's all in the past. The main thing is he never ever expressed an interest in Tameezan and that is what pissed her off... and that I think, your script expresses very well...." The Ustad was clearly holding something back.

"You think she did it? I mean what did she do? How exactly did she...?"

"Oh come, come! You hired me for the sitar. If you wanted a script consultant, you should have come to me before writing the script...."

He laughed again. "No, no, you just tell it like you want. My family secrets cannot be revealed. I'm saying as much in every press interview. I am only a musician, Servant of Allah, and as long as you choose authentic music for your film, I'm happy to play it for you. I'm telling everyone I have nothing to do with the script. After all, the story is not about my grandfather – it is about a British television crew making a documentary on Tameezan the

Courtesan. And we all know how often British TV gets things completely wrong... thee-hee, ha ha ha!"

He laughed heartily. "Are you saying my version is completely wrong then?" The Producer felt put down by his gleeful dismissal of British TV output, her sacred altar of art and creation.

"I'm saying nothing of the sort. Your version is just a version. It's quite feasible, but it doesn't have to be true. Your story is just one attempt at explaining something – but there are a lot of other truths. Others would tell the same story a different way – different emphasis – why do you worry? You tell it like you want to tell it. Take it from me – in this life if you want to do something, you can't start worrying about how it will be received by others – most people are so ignorant anyway – I should know!"

She found herself swelling with respect and admiration for the man who called himself a slave of Allah. A sort of ambassador appointed by God to spread the word through music. Yet, such humility, such eloquence, such intelligence, such broad-mindedness, such forgiveness. Yes, here surely was a true man of God.

Still, it's not entirely unknown in human history for promising beginnings to turn sour, particularly when human beings build pedestals of such unrealistic proportions that they can only come crashing down. And the heroes they place on these pedestals often fall and shatter beyond all repair. She knew all this. But for the time being she chose deliberately to keep her rose-tinted glasses on. This was getting exciting. Things were beginning to happen. Exuberance is a dangerous thing – it forces you to see only what you want to see.

28
FIRST, THERE WAS SOUND

"Sound. That's the crux. Sound can make or break a film. I always think of the sound first. First I play out the sound-track in my head for every scene – I can actually hear the final mix – only then I start to worry about what we'll show and how we'll show it. We have to get the sound right. Sound is all. The whole universe is based on sound... listen hard and you'll hear the echoes of the Big Bang. Even in the Bible – first there was the word. Words are sound. Sound is vibration. Sound is the food of the mystic."

The Producer's pompous eulogy on the virtues of sound was eagerly received by those present: the thoroughly modern God's Servant Ustad, the World's Number One Composer, and Ronnie the PA. The PA just hung on her every word, feeling enormously privileged at being allowed to be present at such a vital, creative session.

"So, let's just concentrate on that final scene. The general theme music for the rest of the film will grow out from that, I hope. Now, a medley of sounds to establish the fact that the evening's entertainment has been in progress for a while. Lesser musicians playing sarangi, sarod, whatever. Then, Tameezan the Courtesan with her landmark ghazal. Then finally, the Grand Ustad, the Lighter Upper of the Universe – with all due respect – taking centre stage with his own special composition, but we all know he doesn't get to play it, so our real finale is the ghazal, THE ghazal, right?"

Every time the Grand Ustad was mentioned, everyone, including the grandson Ustad, tugged at their right ear. PA followed suit. He didn't understand why, but they were all doing it, so he'd better do the same. He must ask the Producer about this peculiar practice, later, alone, in private. It wouldn't do to appear stupid in the presence of such distinguished people.

"Don't worry about the ghazal at all," chimed in the World's Number One Composer breezy as ever, baby-faced, bright, and annoyingly over-confident: "I know exactly what to do about that. As soon as I'm back in Bombay I'm going to talk to all my poet friends. We'll get lots of different ones and then choose the best. Leave it to me."

The Producer was irked. How presumptuous! They hadn't even discussed the scene and here he was, claiming to know exactly what to do. She hated his self-assured manner. She liked things to be difficult and complicated, requiring much discussion and deliberation – brainstorming, she called it. She had hoped they would both pace up and down for several nights, before the muse finally descended and suggested the correct ghazal formula.

"Well, just wait a minute," she began as politely as possible. "It's not as simple as that. This ghazal is crucial, the high-point of the entire film. And it's while she's singing this ghazal that her beloved wretched Grand Ustad enters…" she broke off uneasily, suddenly aware of the presence of a real-life descendant of the notorious Grand Ustad.

The lesser Ustad gave her a hateful look, but then remembering how much she loved his music and how she always flattered him in the best Urdu, he decided to soften up a bit:

"Please, do go on. Don't mind me. It's not a problem, really. Everyone knows Tameezan Bai was hopelessly in love with my grandfather. If I minded about that sort of thing, would I have agreed to do all his solos for you?"

Yes you would, you slime-ball, she thought. In India, it would take you ten years to earn what I'm paying you for a single assignment.

The Producer resumed her Boss mode: "As I was saying, there's a mood of expectancy, even apprehension. The ghazal has to capture all those years of pining and longing for him, but it also has to have a mood of exuberance – the joy of seeing him for the very first time. And then, that precise moment when she spots him, and their eyes meet – that has to be built into the ghazal – music and lyrics. It's not easy, I know, but you see you can…."

"Yes, yes," said the Composer impatiently. "I've read the script you know. You don't have to go into it again and again. I tell you, I know what to do. It's easy!"

The PA had been following these exchanges with deep interest, almost open-mouthed. So this is how it was done. Creative people just sat together in a room, and sipped tea and smoked cigarettes, fought a bit, and out of that grew masterpieces. He couldn't wait for the ghazal to be ready. He couldn't wait to be able to think "That's the one – I was there at its inception." Suddenly he felt he ought to have an input in the creative process:

"But what style will it be? Not too classical I hope? It must be in easy Urdu so that everybody can understand,"

The Ustad shot him a poisonous look and then assumed an expression of aloof superiority. "The ghazal can only be within its context – the context of that time. The language of that period and authentic instruments of the kind that would have been used for courtesans. Just a bit of sarangi, constant, subdued, tabla and a tanpura. And maybe a little light ghungroo, as she taps her foot to keep time – not dance-bells, but pa-zeb, payal, you know, tinkling softly. That's all! Nothing electric. No modern sounds. Tameezan Bai's poetry was renowned for its rich language and elaborate use of the Persian idiom. Her metaphors have been used and re-used endlessly. She was a most talented poetess. And she was in love with my grandfather – he who lit up the whole Universe."

As the great man was mentioned, various ears were hastily tugged at again.

If the Composer was at all nonplussed by the Ustad's pronouncement on the ghazal, he didn't show it. Not that he was planning to add any modern electronic sounds, but that sort of thing was his business. He was the Composer. The Ustad had merely been hired to play the sitar solos. How dare he appoint himself the authority on THE ghazal! That was the Composer's domain. But suppressing his resentment in true takalluf fashion, he spoke with forced meekness and servility:

"Yes Ustad-ji, absolutely, kya baat hai, wah! Bohat khub! I couldn't agree more."

The Producer added her usual slightly salted butter in textbook Urdu: "Right on Ustad-ji! Who would know better than you? We're so fortunate to have you working with us," and with that, she almost pulled at her ear-lobes, before remembering, just in the nick of time, that that was a gesture used as a mark of respect only for those distinguished artistes – dead or alive – when they were not actually physically standing before you. So she just pretended to scratch her ear instead. The PA, who had been about to follow suit in the aborted ear-tugging exercise, also scratched his ears instead, and was now even more confused and mystified by the whole ceremony.

Both the Producer and the Composer had been quick to side with the Ustad. The Composer was always very good at sucking up to prima donna ustads. As for the Producer, she always sided with whichever camp promoted authenticity and purity. Purity of language. Purity of music. Purity of sound. For sound was all. Film was sound. Sound was film.

29
LITERARY MASTURBATION

"Hi! It's me. What's up? Where the hell are you these days?" Ash sounded relieved to have got her for once, instead of the usual answering machine.

"Oh, busy, busy, you know..." Sonia replied guardedly.

"But whatyya doing? I called and called, even late at night. You're always out!"

"Hey, what's this? You're not my husband you know!"

"Oh come on! We used to speak at least once a day, and you've hardly spoken since that mysterious early morning meeting. So, what happened? What did he want? Who is he?"

"Oh, nothing much. Just some other Ugandan Asian made good. He wanted me to write a speech for him to give at some big reunion event, you know, when they all get together and brag about how well they've done for themselves in Mother Britain."

"You do that? You write speeches? I didn't know...."

"How many times have I told you, you can't know everything about a person? Why don't you ever listen to me? Of course I write speeches, in fact you know that phrase supposedly coined by the Prime Minister that's caught on so well? Oh, never mind, I shouldn't tell. Ghost writers don't tell tales..." Sonia paused dramatically.

"There you go again! All deliberately mysterious. Anyway, what else have you been up to?"

"This and that, nothing much. Research, you know, just research for my next book. What about you? Still stuck on the same script?"

"Yes, sort of. But it's beginning to take shape. I wish I'd chosen a subject I really knew about. It's so hard to write about another culture, especially in another century. Still, I'll get there, eventually, I'm sure...."

"Ash, you just have to keep at it. Just stop talking about it and start doing it. Of course it's much easier if you pick something you know about. But if you always insist on writing other people's experiences, second-hand, then you'll always be stuck."

"Objectivity is important. You can't be too deep into something. I'm like an onlooker, impartial, uninvolved...."

"Then where's the passion?" she almost screamed. "What about love? How can it be a labour of love if you're not wrapped up in it?"

"And you? Are you wrapped up in all those boring Big Dinner speeches you write? Where's the passion in that?"

They were headed dangerously close to a fight. For reasons of her own, she had kept her distance over the past few weeks. She didn't want him to know too much about her work. It might make him feel hopelessly inadequate again.

"Come on Ash. Let's stop this work talk. Let's talk about sex. Anything interesting on that front lately?"

"No, but I think I'm close to inventing the sort of woman I could fall in love with. I'll make her, and then I'll fall in love with her."

"And then you'll fall OUT of love and find another excuse to abandon the script. Grow up Ash! You can't thrive on literary masturbation forever!"

30
SOLO HONEYMOON

"Oh thanks, Ronnie, I really appreciate it. Thanks for staying so late – we've covered a lot. Anything else?" she asked, truly grateful that the PA had cancelled various family engagements to discuss schedules and logistics with her, late into the night.

"No, darling. That's it, I think."

Ever since he'd become the PA, he had allowed the word "darling" to appear constantly and frequently in his speech. In showbiz, you addressed everyone as "Darling" – men and women. "I'm so excited about this film. It's going to be the best. Such a clever script darling. It's great working with you."

"Well, let's hope it stays that way. It's not unusual in this business for people to fall out after shooting a roll or two," the Producer cautioned in over-wise tones.

"Oh Darling! Never! I can't imagine us falling out.".

"Anyway, good of you to stay so late. What were you meant to be doing this evening?"

"Nothing much. I had an appointment with my CI."

"What's a CI?"

"A Colonic Irrigationist. You should try it darling. You'll feel wonderful."

"No thank you. It was called an enema when I was a kid, and unlike you, I don't relish the thought of pipes and tubes up my rear end. In fact I don't like being penetrated at all, whichever way."

"Darling, how wonderfully eccentric of you," the PA squealed with relish, clearly delighted at being privileged enough to be discussing penetrative intimacies with one so talented and so bitchy.

"Anyway after my CI, I was supposed to go on to the Cafe Poser to meet some friends of the Lizard, you know. I'm not really allowed my own friends. You're the only friend I've got. She tolerates that because it's work, but I know she's really insecure about you. Specially if we have late night chats on the phone."

The PA's wife was always referred to as the Lizard, owing to her peculiar skin-tone – a sort of pale-biscuit colour with an orange under-tone, not unlike that of the household gecko.

"Oh but that's ridiculous! How can she be jealous? It's strictly business. What am I to do? So many bloody egos to cope with. And we have yet to meet the Actress, but she's probably a new born babe in ego terms, compared to the Ustad. What a pratt!"

"Oh, yes, darling. The Ustad. He's such a pain, but he's sexy. Do you think he fancies me?"

"They only fancy themselves, these Ustad types. He probably winks at you and smiles a lot, but that's because you do all his fetching and carrying. Don't be taken in by that. And for goodness sake, don't go falling in love with him. I have enough tantrums on my plate."

The PA carried on dreamily: "He has such a lovely voice. Why are musicians called Ustad?"

"It's just a term of respect. It means teacher. But nowadays they award it to themselves as a sort of title. If they're Muslim they call themselves "Ustad", if Hindu, then "Pandit". Same thing. In the old days, only your elders could officially give you the title, and even then, you wouldn't have dreamed of using it if your own teacher was still alive somewhere in the world, leave alone present in the same room. But nowadays they become Ustads at the age of nineteen, and call themselves the world's greatest spoon-player or whatever."

"Oh I adore it when you talk like that. You're so bitchy darling. You love their music, but you hate them."

"Don't get carried way, darling" – she said the 'darling' forcefully. "I don't hate anyone. I just see right through them. They're so bloody obvious."

"Yes, but so talented with it. I don't understand much about it, but every time the Ustad plays his sitar or sings a bit I just get transported with ecstasy… ahh… ooh, darling, the earth just moves!"

"Yes, well, just make sure that's the only kind of earth-moving you get for the time being. No hanky-panky… I mean it!" She was clearly issuing an order.

"Oh darling! What a scream! There's my wife jealous of you. And here you are, positively forbidding me from doings with the Ustad. What a hoot!"

"Look, stop being silly. I'm just advising you, as a friend. You never know where these guys have been. They travel a lot, meet a lot of people… you know what I mean?"

"Yes, thanks for the advice darling. Too bad you don't follow it yourself. The Composer travels even more than the Ustad, but that doesn't seem to deter you."

"That's different. He's in love with me."

"Oh yes? Really?" Although the PA had tried not to sound too sarcastic, she didn't like the way the conversation was headed, so she switched into her theoretical mode:

"Yes, well, there you have it. Love's like that you know. It just is. It can't be turned on and turned off at will. It's not his fault he's in love with me. He just is."

"And you? What about you? Why are you stringing him along, darling?"

"I'm not stringing him along. I don't love him, and he knows it. I've told him. And that's why he wants me. I don't really mind too much. He's good in bed. Such rhythm! That's the good thing about musicians."

"But you just said you hate being penetrated," the PA squealed at this rare opportunity to point out a contradiction.

They both laughed companionably, PA thoroughly enjoying these snippets of her sex life, and now determined to stay with the subject: "Hmm... I see. It's going to get deliciously complicated darling. Everybody's going to be so jealous of you. The Groupie is already giving you daggers.... I can't wait to see what happens when the Actress arrives. They'll both scratch each other's eyes out, and then fall dead when they realise it's you he wants. I can't wait! Oh, darling, isn't it wonderful?"

Ronnie the PA was really getting too sharp these days. She decided it must be the result of her influence.

"Everybody, so jealous of you..." he was clearly wallowing in his delight.

And especially you, she thought. What wouldn't YOU give to sample the Composer's innate sense of rhythm, first hand?

"Yes I love that part of it," she replied, cool as a cucumber. "I love watching their faces gripped with uncertainty. There's nothing I enjoy more than the sight of an insecure woman – never sure of her man. Suspicious. Watchful. Do they ever realise that their faces can be read as easily as *The Sun* headlines? And Groupie too. Poor woman. All those years of facials and manicures and rolling paratthas and then having to eat them all by herself. And now all that excess weight to shed as well. Poor, fat thing!"

They both laughed again. Work was clearly over. They were sliding into a gossip session. The scene was clearly set for secrets to be disclosed, and giggled over.

"Come on, I'll buy you a pizza. Forget your wife's boring friends at the Cafe Whatever!"

"Oh yes please, darling! I'd much rather be with you. I'll just phone the Lizard and tell her we're running late."

It was late and they were both starving. They gobbled down their pizzas and then sat back, sipping mineral water. His CI had advised him to drink plenty of water.

"Oh, I'm bloated! I don't know how I'll drive home," he groaned.

"Don't go home. Come back with me. You can have the Futon."

"Oh she'll be furious! Oh I couldn't do that to the Lizard!"

"Let her be furious. Why do you care? You're just staying at my place because you're tired. Just tell her that. Tell her it's not what she thinks."

"Oh she'll never believe me darling, you don't know her."

"Oh well, you're welcome to come and stay if you want to. We have an early start tomorrow. It would cut down your travel time. But if you're scared of your wife, well then that's another matter." She was determined to stir things up.

"I'm not scared of her… I just don't want a scene," the PA protested, clearly weakening.

"What's the point, especially when there's nothing in it?"

"Exactly! There's nothing in it, but you're still petrified into obedience. She knows we're friends and that you confide in me. That's what drives her mad with jealousy. I think she would prefer it if we were lovers. That way she could at least play the wounded, victim-wife. She would know how to cope with that. But how to cope with a husband whose closest friend is a woman?"

"Yes, darling. She thinks the wife should be the closest friend."

"That's the last thing a wife should be. Wives should be wives and friends should be friends. The same goes for husbands. I can't understand how couples who start off being friends then end up marrying one another? Such degradation. How can you take something as noble as friendship and turn it into a practical, physical man-woman relationship that consists of procreating and going to Tesco's together? Anyway, it never works, we know that."

"Yes darling." He wasn't going to contradict her. And sure enough, he and his wife had at one time been good friends. For some mysterious reason, couples who had just been lovers seemed to have better marriages than those who had once been friends, and couples who hadn't even bothered with a courtship but had been introduced by their parents and then sanctioned by astrologers, seemed to fare best of all. Zero expectations.

"You see marriage isn't about friendship," the Producer proclaimed importantly. "It's a practical down-to-earth, domestic arrangement. Of course, you have to like and respect one another. A little bit of sexual chemistry also helps. Beyond that, nothing! There's no need to try and be friends as well. You do that with other people. That's what real friends are for."

"But you never married, darling. How come you're such an expert?" again, he did his best to avoid any hint of sarcasm.

"Well I was married, once, very briefly. It was a huge mistake. He was my best friend. We should have just remained friends instead of trying to play housey-housey."

"Gosh, how exciting! Who was he? When were you married?"

"Oh a long time ago. It lasted three days. In the end I went on honeymoon – on my own."

"No! How dreadful for you darling."

"Not at all. It was all set up and booked, so I just chucked out his ticket and decided to put mine to good use. I had a lovely solo honeymoon in Bali."

"Oh no! Poor darling, you're too much!"

"It was quite fun, actually. I made loads of new friends. When you chat up strangers and tell them you're on honeymoon all by yourself, everyone wants to get to know you better. And, then I came face to face with my husband of three days! He'd also turned up for a solo honeymoon. We're so alike. We just collapsed in stitches and became very good friends once again. We'd talk for ages, just like the old days, and then go our own separate ways at bedtime. It was wonderful! But the next time I met him, it was in Rome. In a hotel elevator. We were stuck for over half an hour... and well... there was nothing else to do. So we became lovers. Since then, we've met regularly."

"When?"

"It's never a case of WHEN – it's more a case of WHICH city, and most important, which BED..."

"Darling! How original!" cooed the PA. "Anyway, what does he do?"

"Oh, he just travels a lot...."

31

MARITAL BLISS – 3 DAYS EXACTLY

To be single – and to successfully remain single – you have to have reasons. That's the way it is for single people. Nobody would dream of challenging a married person for choosing to be married, nor would anyone dream of cross-questioning them in the hope of catching them out on some ridiculously inconsistent stance. Nobody would ever feel the need to point out to them the inconsistencies and contradictions inherent in the married state. But for single people, life is one long agony of justification. Don't you get lonely? Aren't you afraid of old age? Don't you want children? Why are you against marriage?

Just show me one person who is against marriage! The question isn't one of marriage. It's a question of marriage to whom? And for what reason... exactly?

But sooner or later the quizzing and arguing gets to you, and in a fit of panic, you grab the nearest half-decent partner you can lay your hands on. Twenty-nine is the usual age for this kind of panic to set in. It's something to do with the cycle of Saturn – the Responsibility Planet. Saturn takes between twenty-eight and twenty-nine years to complete an orbit and return to the place it occupied at the moment of your birth. From here, Saturn beckons that you face up to your responsibilities – do the grown up stuff. For this reason, at twenty-nine something one feels on the shelf. If one could just lie low and wake up to find that two or three years had somehow, miraculously whizzed past, then Saturn would have moved on and the panic would be over.

But life doesn't allow you to go under your duvet and stay there for two or three years. And if you're nearing that dangerous twenty-nine something, then those unrelenting inquisitions on your state of single-hood can finally push you over the brink and make you want to be one-half of that entity called a couple. Only later, much later, does one realise that those well-meaning sermons had come from unhappily married people, resentful of one's independence and jealous of that rarest of commodities known to man – Peace of Mind. I say this realisation comes much later, because generally speaking it does. Only in my case, because I happen to be of above average intelligence, it came in three days.

And so it came to pass... I married the World's Number One Composer. And the marriage lasted exactly three days.

32
SUGAR & SPICE &...

My mother keeps going on about my school report. I got three-and-a-half marks out of a possible hundred for maths. And that too because I just guessed the speed of the train. I'm in a deep depression again – not because of the maths, I don't care about that – but now that term's ended, I have no legitimate excuse to hang around the Mohanji shop. No little boyfriends, no Widow, no songs.

My mother goes there sometimes to buy spices. The chilly-pounding should be completed any day now. I hope we need red chilly-powder. That's my only hope now. I hope she takes me with her, so I can gaze at the Widow on her sewing machine while my mother negotiates the price with Mohanji. Will there be time to take a quick peek in those wonderful toilets? But I don't know when the next visit will be. How can I find out? Do we need to buy spices soon? Are we running low? The kitchen is out of bounds to me. But I have to find out somehow....

Everybody rests in the afternoon. Grown ups always say life is too short and then they spend most of it sleeping. The house is dead quiet and I'm bored. I'm also a bit anxious to fix up the next visit to the shop.

I tip toe into the kitchen. It's a room I don't know too well. I'm never allowed in it. Not sure where to start looking. There's a small larder attached to the kitchen. It's a bewildering place. Rows and rows of tins and containers. Sacks of flour, brown for roti and white for cakes. And huge sacks of rice, lots of it. Needle-fine for daily consumption, fat and round for puddings. But where do they keep the spices? I've climbed up a lot of trees. Shelves are much easier. If my plan works and I manage to find and dispose of the spices, we could be going to Mohanji & Sons General Store pretty soon. Yippie!

A pair of antennae perform a menacing circular dance from a crack in the wood. That's got to be a cockroach. My least favourite creature. No, I'll tell the truth, I'm petrified of them. That's the trouble with a childhood full of creepy-crawlies. The only way to cope is to make them all God and pretend they can only do you good. I've managed this with mosquitoes and even spiders. But cockroaches, no! However hard I try, I cannot attribute that same Divinity to cockroaches.

But I have to go on. This is an important mission requiring courage and determination. If I fail, I might have a to face an indefinite period of uncertainty about my next visit to the shop. And patience is not one of my virtues. My mother often says that when God was doling out patience by the bucketfuls, I somehow went missing from the queue.

Be brave. Go on. Leave the shelves for a bit. Maybe the cockroach will go away. Send it a mind signal: I'm a friend. I haven't come for you. I've come to check out the spices. Look away for a bit to prove your good intent. Look the other way, please Mr Cockroach. Go back into the crack... please....

A built-in concrete surface in the larder. Very useful for standing bowls of various things. Yoghurt cooling and setting in a bowl of earthenware. In Swahili they call it Maziwa Lala – Sleeping milk. Even the milk needs to sleep on these hot afternoons, I muse. Bread-dough rising in a stainless-steel container. Prod it. Wonderful spongy texture. I could play with it all day, but I have more important things to accomplish. And then, wow! What a discovery! A wonderful diversion! Spice-hunt momentarily forgotten as attention is taken up with a whole bowl of raw cashews... now there's a welcome sight. Spice hunt transforms into successful treasure hunt. What a lucky find! That's my other gripe at present. That's the other reason I'm depressed. I'm just not allowed enough nuts and raisins and things like that. My mother hates fat kids, especially girls.

No moment like the present. Go for it now. As big a handful as possible, straight into the mouth, yummm... aahhh! Yuck! What?? Help... Oh no!

Peeled garlic cloves. There's no justice in this world. Help me someone! Spit out quick! Where's the kitchen sink? Oh hell! Why don't grown-ups or their servants ever label anything? I may have failed miserably at maths but I could read better than most other children – maybe that's why nothing's been labelled. Just in case I find something that says "Pear Drops." Unless you've chewed thirteen raw garlic cloves all at once in the hope that they were cashews, you won't fully appreciate my distress. Horrible raw garlic taste in my mouth but determined to pursue my spice investigation. A quick dab of yoghurt from the earthenware pot to neutralise the pungent garlic flavour.

Then back to the hunt. Rows and rows of glass jars, and at last, after encountering various mysterious seed-like substances resembling insects, I find a set of identical containers. We're getting warmer now. Yellow, red and brown powders. I bring them down one by one and proceed to empty them into the back garden. I start with the browns. It works. Then the yellow. Not much luck this time. A large amount of it spills onto my white dress. Drat! Never mind. Move on to the red. It's sticking a bit because of my sticky yoghurt-fingers, so I shake the metal container up and down, to loosen the power. A large cloud of reddish-pink settles on my hand. I sneeze, then rub my eyes. Half a second later, I hear myself screaming. And that's how they found me – reeking of garlic, howling open-mouthed, exhaling garlic fumes everywhere. Sleeping milk in my hair, and face and dress covered in red and yellow, eyes stinging, wailing my head off.

"What yah doin' missy-baba?" yells Cook. "Covered in spice and maziwa lala! Yah tryin' be tandoori chicken or what?"

Mission failed. But at least it solved one small mystery. A small step forward. Now I knew about the basic ingredients for tandoori chicken.

33
THE CURSE

Although she looked like a born-Widow, The Widow hadn't really always been a widow. There was a time when she had actually been married. I was only five at the time, but I remember the days of the Widow's wedding very well – several days of festivities until she was married off to the young drunk, so that Mohanji could buy cut-price bicycle parts for his shop.

I remember it well because it was my first proper wedding attendance. I was allowed at all the ceremonies. No longer a messy toddler, I was able to go independently from room to room to backyard – that's where it was all happening. Grown ups are so secretive with another about cooking. They reveal a little bit, but they never tell all. They always leave out one or two small, but vital ingredients. And if I butt in, I'm asked to shut up. Anyway, I'm still only five – who would believe me? I swear I saw the old hag add two whole mashed potatoes to the gulab jamun mixture. And I saw another Masi surreptitiously add sugar to the zaffron, but she called it "kesar":

"Makes more colour, uses less, so expensive, too much bad for your heart," she had muttered under her breath, but who'd believe me?

Onions were being chopped in the courtyard for days in advance. Damn these modern food processors spelling death to the sociable onion chopping ceremony. I had always wondered why everything began with onions having to be chopped. I had never been able to figure out how chopped onions ended up looking like golden-red curry. What was the connection? All was about to be revealed.

I remember the wedding very well, because it was the first time in my life I had been allowed to have mehndi – henna – on my palms, just like a real grown up, and for once, my mother didn't object. She welcomed the rare opportunity of both my hands being out of action for a good four hours or so, waiting for the orange-red tint to take. The dye should have lasted a good two weeks, but sadly for me, it faded within a couple of days – all because I rather foolishly offered to help shape some dry lentil cakes – called "vardis" – because I thought it would be fun. I was never allowed in the kitchen at home, so here was a God-sent opportunity to play "cookey." But I got bored after the first three I'd shaped, rather badly. "What's this? They're supposed to be round-circle – not like map of India," the lady-in-charge of the vardi-shaping ritual barked at me, because she believed it was never too early for little girls to learn lady-like things. The sticky lentil paste gradually scraped away the beautiful orange-red of my palms, and turned them a dirty yellow. But all in all, these courtyard culinary preparations went a long way towards answering certain vital questions, thanks to the open courtyard system of communal cooking for special occasions: How could so many different, un-appealing, raw ingredients end up being so edible? How did a sack of loose powdery flour end up in hundreds of puris? Special ways of stirring – a twist of this, a pinch of that – the secret ingredient – I saw it all. Not many five-year olds in the civilised western world of Kenwood and Magi-mixes and enclosed kitchens, could ever boast of having seen the birth of a samosa. I watched fascinated, as strips of pastry were deftly transformed into equilateral triangles, filled and fried in boiling karahis of oil. Equilateral...? How did I know such words? Maybe my maths wasn't so bad after all. Maybe I just decided to be bad at maths to annoy my mother.

The young drunk's family and close friends arrived eight days before the wedding and took over the entire house. The Widow-Bride's own family were forced to sleep in the courtyard on mattresses spread out amidst the various cooking utensils and trays of goodies – some ready, some not so ready. There were several huge round trays of freshly made laddoos, put out to dry and set. I was secretly quite envious of my Mohanji boyfriends. Imagine sleeping next to a tray of laddoos – some people have all the luck. Or maybe not.

During the eight days leading up to the wedding day, the Mohanji family had forty extra people to feed, accommodate and entertain. The men sat around drinking endless cups of tea and requiring numerous snacks every time a cup of tea was served. They mostly talked about the difficulties of doing business with the Blacks. These "kalias" – Blackies – just couldn't be trusted. You had to be so careful. The Dukavalla Indians seemed to live with the constant dread that some day, these not-to-be-trusted Black chaps would be in charge of everything. They would prophesy – quite inaccurately – that that would be the day the Asians would all just quietly go back to India, taking with them all their belongings, all their savings, all their daughters, hymens intact. One day they would all get completely fed up with Black & White immorality and shamelessness and return to Mother India's bosom for good! Where would the Blacks be then, eh? Every discussion on the subject ended with that vital question, after which every man just shook his head in a gesture of hopelessness and despair, coupled with a triumphant facial expression of "serves them right – let them learn to do without us!"

The women who had come as guests with the drunk bridegroom's party, by tradition, were not expected to join the team of cooks' helpers out in the courtyard. They just sat around in shiny saris, bedecked in gold jewellery, reminiscing about their own weddings. In the evenings, the Mohanji boys would entertain their sister's future family with their own adaptations of various Indian films – songs, dances, fights, memorable dialogues. Mohanji Boy No. 4 did a particularly good Akbar The Great based on Prithviraj Kapoor.

The young drunk also had various younger brothers – a whole batch of them – cheeky streetwise kids, perfect rascals compared to Mohanji's well behaved, obedient sons. But then the young drunk's brothers were in a special privileged position – they were the bridegroom's brothers, and as such they could behave like they owned the place. They all wore skin-tight drain-pipe trousers with shiny pointed-toe shoes. They all carried combs in their tight bum-pockets. They combed their hair, on average, every two minutes.

One of these boys took me aside in conspiratorial fashion and let me in on a big secret. An important mission, he called it. He told me that it was an old tradition in their family that whenever one went over to wed a bride, something precious had to be stolen from her house. This was a sacrosanct ritual, and if it weren't properly executed, then bad luck would fall on both families for many years to come.

I was enlisted as his accomplice. My job was to divert the Mohanji side so that the drunk's side could proceed with the ritual theft of a transistor radio. A portable radio such as this was a rare and precious commodity in those days. The Mohanji boys had served a massive penance to jointly own such a device. They had, all nine of them, relinquished their pocket-money for a whole six months, at the end of which Mohanji had agreed to make the purchase. And then only on the condition that they listen to the words of Indian film songs properly and endeavour to bring more authenticity to their Sunday evening Indian-film re-enactments.

So when tight-pants-Bryl-cream comb-in-hand took me aside and whispered his plan, I was caught in one of life's earliest moral dilemmas. I knew how the Mohanji boys had suffered for that radio. But if I didn't cooperate with the Elvis look-alike, how could I carry the burden of a curse on both families for several generations? And it was not entirely unlikely that some evil would fall on me as well. A curse is a big word for a six-year old. A curse suggests witch doctors, and dolls with pins, and a floor covered in fresh chicken blood and feathers... all frightful things, conjuring up frightful images in a hyperactive mind.

So I accepted the assignment. I created the necessary diversion by pretending to hurt myself followed by a noisy tantrum in the middle of the floor. All my Mohanji boys gathered around me in a rugby-style scrum to try and cheer me up, while tight-pants-freshly-combed-bryl-cream-hair, proceeded to swipe the radio.

But then I had a pang of conscience, or you might call it a devilish desire to make trouble just to watch the fun. Anyway, I was bursting to tell. I whispered to the scrum bending over me: "Quick! Look! He's going to take it! Quick, save the radio!"

An enormous scuffle followed and the prized radio was successfully reclaimed by the Mohanjis. But to this day, I go on blaming myself for the way things turned out. When some months after this incident I learnt that the daughter had returned to live with her family and her husband had died of drink, I was convinced this was the curse playing out. There was no doubt in my mind that my refusal to aid and abet the would-be thieves of the radio had resulted in some massive curse and the poor girl had become a Widow. It was all my fault. Yet, just two years after every imaginable misfortune had befallen her, the Widow was able to issue an invitation to feed nine virgins. How could this be? Everything that could have gone wrong in her life had already gone wrong. What could've suddenly gone right? How could she be in a position to do a deal with God? What could God ever have done for her?

34
LOVE LETTERS IN PHYSICS

What's he up to? Why the sudden interest in me? My Uncle usually does nothing except heaps of marking and going off to play tennis. He's never ever had time to talk to me. Just ignores me most of the time. So imagine my puzzlement when all of a sudden he offers to take me for a long walk.

I'm suspicious. It's probably going to be yet another lecture about my maths result. My mother has asked him to have a serious talk with me. What sort of civilization subjects its children to maths and split infinitives in Latin at the tender age of eight? We are Indian. Why should we have to struggle with Latin? Do European children struggle with Sanskrit? When I grow up I will secretly study Sanskrit and shock them all. I will speak only in Sanskrit. I have no idea how it sounds or how I would go about learning it, but I know there is a language called Sanskrit, which is a sort of Indian Latin. And there are oodles of delicious sounding songs in Sanskrit. I know because I've heard them in the Temple. They call them prayers, but I call them songs. I turn everything into song. That's the only way I can cope with living in World – this otherwise senseless Duniya.

I'm hoping my Uncle has forgotten all about our walk. But no such luck. At five sharp he finds me in the garden:

"Come on baby-jaan, let's go," he beckons in suitably avuncular tones.

I trail along reluctantly, aimlessly kicking a small stone along the way. Wonder when the lecture will start?

"You must miss your young Mohanji boy-friends. Are you looking forward to term-time again?"

This I had most definitely not expected. How could my Uncle, of all people, feel for my loneliness? Maybe he was human after all.

"If you like, I'll have a word with your mother. Maybe once in a while you should be allowed to go there for an afternoon. I'm sure you want to see your little friends."

His gentle, conciliatory tone disarmed me completely. I quite forgot to produce the usual sulky expression I reserved for my Uncle and others like him.

"Oh yes! Please! Please talk to her. I'm so bored these days. It would be so nice to be allowed to go to the shop. Do you think you can tell her soon, please Uncle, please?"

"I'll do my best. But you'll also have to do something for me which will be our secret."

"What? What? I'll do anything! I love secrets!"

"Listen, I'll give you something – a piece of paper – and you pass it on quietly to the Widow, when nobody's looking, OK? And then she'll give you another piece of paper, which you bring straight back to me, right?"

"Sure! Easy-peasy! No problem. Yippie Yah Yah!" I see no need to disguise my thrill at being singled out for this secret mission, but it would have been uncharacteristic to show no curiosity, so I add: "What's in the piece of paper?"

"I'm helping her to study. Poor woman, she just cooks and sews all day. She wants to learn maths and physics and I'm helping her. I'll be sending her some lessons, and you'll be delivering them safely to her. I hope you realise this is a really important task. You're helping improve someone's mind. If you get found out, then it will have to stop. She'll never be able to do anything else with her life. And you'll be to blame. Education is her only hope. Those sort of women need an education."

"What sort of women?"

"Poor unfortunate souls. Married off early to unsuitable types, then widowed. Then just exploited in their greedy fathers' shops. She wants to study science but nobody will let her. You know Mohanji hates spending money. So I'm tutoring her, privately."

"Oh Uncle, you're so kind and so clever! Will you tutor me privately in Sanskrit?"

"Sanskrit? What ever for? What are you going to do with Sanskrit? Anyway, I don't know a single word. I could teach you more science when you're older. At least with science one can get a good teaching job."

"Oh, OK then, science. Anything – just anything, as long as it's in secret. I want to surprise mummy. She thinks I'm stupid because I can't do maths."

"Yes, OK, but for now just concentrate on your school work and then we'll see, when you are older. But meanwhile, remember our secret?"

"Yes, I'm so excited. When should I go? I mean when is her first lesson due?"

"It's not her first lesson. I've been teaching her for a while. But now her studies may be abruptly interrupted since that mean Mohanji might fire the

Bhangi. I used to send her lessons through the Bhangi, you know, the one who also washes the school toilets."

"He's fired? They've fired the Bhangi? So have they got another one?"

"How would I know? I don't concern myself with their affairs. I'm only interested in helping the Widow to make something of herself so she can get out of her wicked father's clutches."

The wicked father theme fails to register. I have other, more important things on my mind. I'm preoccupied at the thought of a Bhangi-less Mohanji toilet:

"If they haven't got another Bhangi, then the shit must be really piling up. Oh Uncle! I'll have to go as soon as possible. Can you arrange it quick? I must take a look!"

"Whatever are you babbling on about? I only want you to go and play with your friends as normal, and when nobody is looking, go onto the verandah where she sews and give her my letter… I mean lesson."

"Yes, all right. I said, OK," I'm squealing with delight now, "But when, please WHEN?"

"Soon, I'll arrange it soon."

God works in mysterious ways. Of all the people in the world, I never imagined my cool and aloof Uncle would come to the rescue and intervene to legitimise my Mohanji shop visits.

During those school holidays I took numerous pieces of paper and slipped them to the Widow as instructed. But she never gave me anything to take back to him. Every time I returned from the shop my Uncle would be waiting for me expectantly, and every time I shook my head, he looked like a schoolboy who'd had his last ten-cent piece taken away from him.

I felt very sorry for him.

"Don't worry Uncle. Maybe she hasn't had time to do her homework yet. Give her time. I'm sure she will work on it and then send you something to mark. She has so much to do. And homework isn't that important if you're not properly in school," I say importantly, with the wise air of one who knew the downside of having non-stop, compulsory homework.

"Does she ever say anything?" he asks of me, tentatively.

"No, I just give her the paper and she quickly sticks it down her blouse and then carries on sewing. She doesn't even look at me."

"Does she read it? Have you ever seen her reading any of it?"

"Er… no, not really. I suppose she reads it later on. Oh, sometimes she goes straight to the toilets at the back. That's where she reads it I guess. Yes, that must be it! How can she read it in front of everyone? It's a secret. isn't it? Nobody is supposed to know she's having physics lessons from you."

My Uncle looks utterly forlorn. He can be quite handsome when he's pining.

But what an idiot! Grown ups can be so stupid. Does he really think I deliver those pieces of paper without first reading them myself? But in a funny sort of way I feel really sorry for him. I don't know why grown ups fall in love, but I think it would be nice to have that love returned, sometimes at least.

So I resolve to start replying to my Uncle's love-letters to the Widow. Where's the harm? It will make him happy, and it will save her the trouble of finding the time to write to him. Yes, I'm growing up at last. At last I'm prepared to help someone else instead of only thinking of myself all the time. And so at the tender age of eight, I wrote my very first love letter... to my own Uncle!

35
THE SPECIAL MASSEUR

"It's great to have you on board Ronnie. You've already sorted out so many headaches for me, and we haven't even begun shooting yet. You're a brick!" The Producer is in an unusually generous mood.

True enough, Ronnie was worth his weight in gold when it came to tricky situations, and he was certainly not afraid of hard work. He had a wonderful manner with people and seemed to carry with him a sort of invisible soothing balm where other young men would've carried filofaxes and mobile phones. A few minutes of chatting to Ronnie and even the most irate, tight-hearted, pig-headed people, appeared visibly relaxed and at ease with the world. He would have made an excellent dentist.

"Oooh, I just love it darling." He made lavish use of the word darling, now that he was in showbiz. It was the buzz word to prove to everyone that you worked in films.

"I just love working with you, darling... I'm learning so much – all the mysteries of film making... it's magic," he enthused, not forgetting to use his special soothing balm. It was reserved for her as much as it was reserved for her Big Stars – Grandson Ustad, Number One Composer, and no doubt, very soon the Actress herself, already on her way from Bombay and due to land in London tomorrow.

The PA gushed on with the ego-enhancing balm: "Thank you so much darling for introducing me to films... you know I've always wanted...."

"Yes, yes... fine, no problem...." she butted in impatiently and then launched straight into a lecture. "I knew you would pick up the technicalities in no time at all. Most film people like to shroud their work in mystery – they like to make it look difficult so that they can feel important. There's really nothing to it. The most difficult skill in any profession is learning to deal with people, especially prima donnas. And that's where you take the biscuit! Such a natural. You may not know a piece of celluloid if it hit you in the back of your head, but you know how to take the most blown-up ego and massage it ever so tenderly, so that it doesn't collide with the even more inflated ego standing next to it."

"Yes, that's why I hired you," she thought to herself. Film technicians are two a penny, but where else would I find an integrated all-built-in, fully portable ego-soothing machine like you?"

"How do you do it, Ronnie?" she asked.

"Oh, I just like people. If they think they're more important than anyone else, then there's no harm in letting them think that. Honestly, what difference does it make? The main thing is to know how to manage and control their ego. Feed their ego so that it works for you. Forget your own ego – make someone else's inflated ego work for you. Remember how you had the Ustad eating out of your hand? And all for just a few words of submission in your beautiful Urdu? You must teach me Urdu when all this is over. I'm already getting better at it."

"Yes, I'm glad I managed to crawl to the Ustad – that was excellent advice Ronnie. If I didn't already have parents, he'd want to adopt me. He's so much older, yet treats me like royalty. Still refers to me as "Aap". Even says special prayers so that I might find a husband worthy of me. What an ass!"

"Yes, but a lovable one and so talented with it. What a voice! I find him quite sexy."

The Producer changed the subject abruptly.

"Now, remember Ronnie, you're picking her up at Heathrow at nine sharp, and driving her straight to her hotel, OK? Play it by ear – if she wants to rest, make yourself scarce. If she looks like she needs to chat, then stay and talk to her. Have lunch. Keep her amused and I'll be there at four."

"You're so considerate, so thoughtful, darling. I always thought directors were monsters. But you're so motherly...."

She genuinely liked the PA, but at times got fed up with his unending flattery. Why did he have to be such a fan? Why did he always behave like the founding member of everybody's fan-club? No doubt, he was going to crawl all over the Actress as well. The Producer felt a tinge of jealousy. Ronnie was hers. She'd found him, and she'd hired him. And he should never forget that. He'd better remain loyal to her. She had deliberately assigned him to pick up the actress rather than go to the airport herself. She knew he would provide vital information on how best to handle the woman for her first meeting.

Although she had some difficulty admitting it to herself, the Producer was more than a little nervous about meeting the Actress. The clue to the whole mystery lay somewhere near this woman – the woman Mr Moneybags had targeted for some elaborate revenge plan.

So how should she behave towards the Actress? Normal, neutral, professional – or be a bit nosy and try to find out what was going on? No, that might blow the whole scheme and then she'd never get to make her precious film with its even more precious original music.

No, the best plan was to let star-struck PA do all the nosing and digging, and for her to appear the cool and aloof, even slightly absent-minded, pre-menopausal, professional arty-farty film-director boss.

The film was important, but she also had to get to the bottom of Moneybags's plans. This was vital. Otherwise the project could be in jeopardy. As it was, it felt like groping in the dark for the proverbial needle in the haystack stuff. Sure, she was going through all the motions and work was proceeding fine, but she had this unavoidable feeling of standing on the edge of some dangerous cliff. She took out a little notebook and wrote:

"There's nothing wrong with cliffs, as long as you have some idea of the drop. You have to know what's at stake. Life is always a curious mixture of gains and losses. But the secret of success is learning to identify which is which."

36
THE EGO HAS LANDED!

The PA had had one of the best days of his life. He had spent the best part of it semi-sprawled on the Actress's big bed, pyjama-party fashion – just like old friends.

Here she was – a real Indian film actress, a star – and all she wanted was to chat, and chat and chat to him. This was the closest thing to heaven. He offered, half-heartedly, to leave her to rest several times, but she wouldn't let him go. She wanted to know all about everything, and she wanted to fill him in on all the Bombay gossip. Real life stories about famous people. Off-the-record scandals about abortions and mistresses. Rivalries, jealousies, off-the-sets arguments, drugs, guns, mafia dons. But in true PA fashion, he was efficient enough to tear himself away from her chatter for about a quarter of an hour to phone the producer, as promised, to fill her in on her leading star.

"Oh darling, she's just wonderful. Soooo beautiful. A bit fat, but I'm sure she'll lose some of that weight if you want her to."

"Nonsense! I don't want her to lose any weight. She's playing an intelligent 19th century Lucknow courtesan, not a 20th century bimbo anorexic. The courtesans were loved for their lumps and their bumps and their big bosoms."

"Oh, really? Then she's just the right shape, darling. But will she look OK dancing?"

"I've already planned a real dancer substitute for the difficult bits. Most Bombay bimbos can't do the pure stuff to save their lives. Anyway, enough of that. What's she actually like?"

"Oooh! So sweet! Very friendly, very chatty. You'll never believe what she's told me about the Kumar. You know, that one… yes, the same. Anyway, it seems…."

"I don't give a fuck about any of the Kumar's right now. Just give me a quick rundown on her. How's her Urdu?"

"Non-existent. But she knows a few phrases. She only speaks poor English, with a sort of heavy Indian accent…."

"Never mind the accent – how's her actual English?"

"Pretty bad."

"So what language does she speak?"

"Only English, really."

"Christ! OK, make a quick note for later. Call up an Urdu academy or anywhere else you can find, and track down the best language teacher. Arrange a meeting for me. Oh God! And I thought we would just need elocution and deportment. OK, what else?"

"Oh, where am I going to find an Urdu teaching place? Wouldn't it have been easier to get her tutored in India?"

"Yes of course it would have been miles easier, but Moneybags wants everything done here..." she stopped, guiltily.

"Moneybags? What Moneybags?" he asked, genuinely puzzled.

"Oh, never mind." Drat, this was impossible! Sooner or later she'd have to confide in someone, but she needed more facts first. She changed the subject.

"Who speaks Urdu properly in India anyway? She may as well train in London. More chance of acquiring an antiquated Lucknow accent with a tutor in Tooting. Oh, come on, quick, give me the rest of it. What sort of personality?"

"Very sweet. Lovely eyes. Designer nightwear. Good taste. Gorgeous hair, lots of it, very fair skin... beautiful hands, long nails, lovely purple nail polish. and oh, arrived in Armani jeans, Gucci shoes... and...."

"I said personality, not whether she wore Gucci or Poochi," she interrupted impatiently.

"Oh, nice. Very chatty. Thrilled about the new part. Said she loved your script."

"I'm surprised she could read it, huh!"

"She loves reading. Lots of romantic novels. Grew up on Mills and Boon. Loves Barbara Cartland and Jackie Collins."

"Forget her impressive reading list! I'm more worried about getting her to speak properly. Anyway, I'll be over in a while. Keep her chatting. Get her to talk about her own love life instead of gossiping about this Kumar and that Kapoor."

"Hey, are you really interested in her love life? Darling you're such a snoop! She lives with this writer chap...."

"No not him, find out about before that. All her men. Was she ever married? Was one of them much older... any connection with East Africa? That sort of thing."

"Why, why do you want to know?"

"I don't want to know… I'm just saying find out whatever you can in a chummy sort of way. She seems to have opened up to you. It would be useful to know about her previous men."

"OK, I'll do my best… but I feel you're holding something back from me. How can I help you unless you tell me what's up?"

"That's exactly what I said to Moneyba… oh, never mind. There's nothing to hold back. Oh, Ronnie, I don't know what to say. When the time comes I'll tell you whatever I know, but not now. I don't want to say the wrong thing… you get me? It's for your own protection."

"Yes, OK," he said dejectedly, and then cheered up immediately at the thought of going back to the Actress's room for more gossip. He couldn't believe he was actually being paid for this work!

37
SOUND WITHOUT PICTURES

Marriage before her eighteenth birthday, and it had started to turn sour within the first few weeks. It wasn't even as though he didn't love her – quite the opposite – and she too was besotted with him. But they just never saw one another often enough to indulge in activities pertaining to mutual besotation. Money was tight, and they hardly ever went out.

They had already been through so much together. And it was still less than two years since the hastily arranged marriage when they'd arrived in Britain on a foggy November night, and when she'd had imagined that their troubles were finally at an end. But their troubles were just beginning. What had already happened was nothing compared to what was still in store. He worked day and night. He had to. She liked nice things. She had to have them. She was special. She was film star material. A film star still waiting to be discovered. Even in those days, her bill for two simple items of lingerie would not be less than a hundred and eighty pounds. And all for what? What's the point of sitting around in sexy lingerie when there's no one to look at you?

He was always at work. At six in the morning he did a cleaning shift, in the afternoon, a factory shift, and most nights he worked as a security guard. At weekends he drove a minicab. Eventually, he set up his own mini-cab company. Things were looking up a bit financially, but he was still always at work. She grew restless. All dressed up and nowhere to go. She spent all his hard-earned money on clothes and make-up but her film-star qualities had yet to be noticed, leave alone acknowledged by anyone. She decided to pose for some men's magazine specialising in Asian "babes." They paid quite well, but didn't call her often enough. They always wanted new faces. Once their readers had seen all there was to see, that was it. They wanted a new face, or more appropriately, a new pussy.

It was around this time that she first met Mamta. Mamta and she had posed as pretend-lesbians for one of these magazines playing out the ultimate masculine fantasy. There was nothing a heterosexual man liked more than to see two women lolling about on dry-clean-only silk sheets, pretending to turn each other on, with his good self sandwiched somewhere in between.

On that shoot, each had been weary of the other, not only in that neither woman was really a lesbian and keen to make that fact clear, but also in terms of each trying to appear sexier and more alluring than the other. But professional jealousy turned to girlie camaraderie as the double-ended vibrator kept slipping into the wrong places and going off at the wrong time, throwing both girls into fits of hysterical laughter.

After the vibrator incident they became close friends. In between shots, they drank long coffees and smoked long cigarettes and compared dreams. They both wanted to be film stars, and disinfected vibrators were just a necessary interim step on the road to fame and success. Mamta had a flat in Kensington where the two girls started spending more and more time together. She liked Mamta's flat because it was in Kensington. Kensington was nicer than Kensal Green. She could never bring herself to say Kensal Green – she referred to it as K.G. hoping that someone might think it was an approximated abbreviation for Knightsbridge. Gradually, most of her things wound up at Mamta's place. In the end she was usually to be found here, especially at the weekends, while her husband was busy driving his cabs for people who were too drunk to drive themselves.

It was widely rumoured the two girls had set themselves up in the business, doing a roaring trade in helping sexually frustrated Asian men live out their fantasies. Her husband ignored the rumours. He was just relieved she'd found a friend to fill her empty hours, and a non-threatening female friend at that.

The girls spent their mornings sleeping, afternoons shopping, and evenings working. Work involved gate crashing a lot of high society parties and dinners and distributing calling cards to anyone who looked even remotely wealthy and influential.

Then came the Dream Merchant. He said he was a Bombay film producer on the look out for new faces and new possibilities. And within three weeks of meeting him at a private ghazal recital in the dingy basement of a Euston hotel, they were in the Business Class cabin of an aircraft headed for Bombay.

There's no doubt about the fact that the plane itself was headed for Bombay, but the girls were off-loaded in the Gulf, and the rest is history.

That was the last time she saw Mamta. God knows what became of Mamta, but she herself managed to escape, thanks to a kindly Pakistani man who offered to pay for her one-way fare to India if she carried a precious parcel for him. Just video tapes, supposedly on various Islamic subjects. Architectural programmes about mosques – a full pictorial guide to the Hajj. "Difficult to get this sort of stuff in India. Poor Indian Muslims. They never get to see this sort of thing. You'll be doing my religion a big favour," he had said.

The one and only primitive video cassette player at Bombay airport customs suffered from clogged heads. The fast-forward button was broken. No pictures, but the sound was clearly audible – crisp commentary in high-flown Urdu. The wonders of Samarkand and Bokhara. Glorious sunsets in Medina. The call to prayer. Very special presents for her Muslim friends, she informed the customs' official. He was a reasonable sort of man – most unusually for an Indian bureaucrat. Afraid of causing yet another Hindu-Muslim incident, he quickly checked all six tapes, sound only of course, and gave them back to her.

The noise, heat and chaos of Bombay made no impact on her. Although it was her very first visit to India, she was quite content to sit back in the taxi and think of nothing in particular. The clearly visible and desperate poverty that lined both sides of the road leading from the airport to the city had no meaning for her. How people lived or what their destinies brought them was of no concern to her. She was here to become a film star. And this was the right city for that. For her, the very fact that she'd escaped her potential fate as a sex slave in Bahrain, and had then managed to get herself to Bombay, was proof enough that she was cut out for better things.

The precious cargo she had carried to Bombay was received eagerly at its destination. He seemed a decent sort of man. He said he dealt with religious literature, publishing thin booklets on various Islamic subjects, and occasionally buying in educational videos for copying and distribution. The Hajj video was particularly eagerly awaited amongst all his rental outlets. Sound only, of course. The pictures were a different matter, but it was safe to assume they would match the commentary. How could you have a commentary about the Hajj laid over folds of silk sheets…?

He offered her a cup of sickly sweet tea, and then without her even asking for help or guidance, he launched straight into a speech:

"Here, he might be able to help you," he said pointing a scrap of paper in her direction. "He's a brilliant writer – and poet. But this big bad world wasn't prepared to recognise him for that, or let him make a living out of it. At least the Cinema – although ruled by Shaitaan – at least the cinema lets him make a decent living. Over twenty films. So many brilliant stories. Where would they all go if they didn't get made into films? But don't expect too much. It's a horrible business. Much competition. Lots of bad people around. Be careful. But if you can work hard and Allah is willing, who knows, you might make it. Even in an evil business like cinema, you need Allah's will on your side, otherwise, just forget it!"

She hadn't expected this religious man to approve of her film-star dreams. Still, she took his personal blessing as a sign from God. She was clearly destined for something big.

38
NIPPED IN THE BUD

"Any Other Business?" asked Mr Mohanji, Chairman of the Small Town Indian Morality Committee. They'd just dealt with all the routine stuff – the new African government's insistence on racial integration, particularly for the young, and the ever-threatening eventuality of forced Afro-Indian marriages. For some strange reason the Mohanji tribe of dukavallas always imagined that their daughters would be dragged away by force and married off to Black men. It never entered anyone's head that one of their daughters might actually fall in love with someone, who might just happen to be Black rather than Asian. And it was even more unlikely that one of the Asian sons would fall in love with a Black girl. After all, Indian boys always liked fair-skinned girls – the whiter the better. That's how they'd been brought up. So this new forced integration threat seemed only to apply to virginal daughters. That was the reasoning, anyway.

And then there was the matter of that wretched sex education film. All the schools had jointly arranged a special viewing at the big cinema and attendance was compulsory for all over-twelve's. Mohanji and his Morality Committee colleagues had taken a firm stance against any such dirty film.

"Chhee-chhee! Hey Ram! Kalyug!" they claimed.

So what if the school itself had organised the screening? Those whites were pretty shameless anyway, and now these snooty European area Asian teachers also seemed to have forgotten their noble heritage in favour of frank and open sex education for children of both sexes. Mohanji's Committee had petitioned the schools and insisted that the film was first shown to them, and to give them the right to decide whether or not their daughters would be permitted to attend. The petition had been successful.

"Any Other Business?" Mohanji asked again. One of the other men cleared his throat tentatively and started to speak, but he seemed to be having real difficulty in getting started. He was a rival Dukavalla from the other side of the Square but his business was not as successful as Mohanji's, so Mohanji could afford the benevolence of coaxing him to speak. "Come on Bhai, what is it?"

"Well, you know these Bhangi people – you know toilet cleaners – shouldn't they go directly to the backyard? I mean, no business to go anywhere near house or shop, right?" the competitor Dukavalla finally began, cautiously.

"Yes, yes, so what? What are you trying to say?"

"Well I've seen the Bhangi hang around your shop verandah. What's his business there? Why is he contaminating your shop?"

"What do you mean?" Mohanji raised his voice, uncharacteristically. "He never comes near the front of the shop. And even if he did, why shouldn't he be allowed to buy himself a drink after all his work? We observe all the rules of untouchability. We don't take money directly from the Bhangi. We don't touch his soiled coins. He's asked to drop his money into a bucket of water. We pick it up later and purify it properly. What's your problem anyway?"

"No, no I didn't mean that. I didn't mean he hangs around as a customer. I've seen him, from across the square, loitering on the verandah, chatting...."

"Chatting? Chatting to whom? Who would chat to a Bhangi, hey?"

"Well, your daughter, you know – that poor unfortunate Widow-Bechari. I saw her looking at him and smiling. She was on her sewing machine and he was clearly looking in her direction."

"Why shouldn't he? God has given him eyes to look, no? Just because he looked at my daughter, so what?"

"Yes but she didn't have to smile at him. It gives those fellows the wrong idea."

"No, you've got it all wrong. I'm sure it's nothing to do with my daughter. It's that good-for-nothing girl – you know, Mrs Henara's out-of-control daughter, the Brat. She's always nosing around the Bhangi. And she's always playing on the verandah. He was probably just chatting to her."

"Why would an eight-year old want to chat with a Bhangi?"

"You never know with these progressive types. Their mothers are too busy with so-called careers to worry about what their children might be up to. She just gets off her school bus and comes straight to our shop to wait for her driver. I gave permission for that. Mrs Henara wanted her to wait here rather than mess around all over the Square. How was I to know the child would start flirting with the kaalia Bhangi?"

"I wasn't talking about the child. I was talking about your Bechari Widow daughter."

The rest of the committee fidgeted nervously as they felt the accusation sink into Mohanji's unbelieving mind.

"Say it straight! Why don't you just come out with it?" Mohanji's voice was breaking.

"There's nothing to say. Just that these sort of things should be nipped in the bud. Today it may be just a smile. Tomorrow they'll start talking, and then meeting, and then who knows?"

"Go and wash your mouth out you filthy money-lender," roared Mohanji. "Accusing my poor daughter of having doings with a Bhangi! Who the hell do you think you are? As Chairman I would like to propose your expulsion from this Committee with immediate effect. Can we have a show of hands please," he turned to the others.

They sat motionless, their eyes lowered. Mohanji took their silence to mean they were on his enemy's side.

"OK, fine. Do what you like. I resign from this Committee. Either him or me! I tell you, I'm out. How can I sit here after listening to such... such..." he broke down.

"No, wait, wait," one of the others finally spoke up. "Sorry Mohanji-Bhai, but he does have a point. There may be nothing in it, but surely it's worth checking out, just for our own satisfaction? You know this sort of thing affects all of us. If one girl gets away with it, then all the others will demand the right to get friendly with Black men. And please understand, it's not just that he's Black – the man is actually a Bhangi. In India that's like being untouchable. We have to keep up these old Indian traditions. If we don't, then who will?"

He was clearly the diplomatic one. Mohanji and his rival both calmed down, deep in thought.

"All right," said Mohanji, after some thought. "I'll look into it. This guy who just sweeps up shit, how dare he even look at my daughter? I'll tackle him about it. But if your accusations are wrong, I demand an apology, in public. Just as you have accused me before all these people, you will eat your words and apologise to me in front of all of them. You will also make your apologies to my daughter – through me – for having such filthy thoughts about her."

It didn't occur to anyone that the Bhangi might also need an apology. And not in their wildest dreams could they have imagined that the same Bhangi would soon be deciding their fate... and the fate of all their little shops!

39
THE HEART IS HINDUSTANI

Mrs Henara was dogged by a perpetual sense of unease. Nothing was quite as it should be. At one time, she'd thought she would have years and years to figure things out and put them right. But the fast footsteps of time were getting louder. A teeny-weeny thing in a pink shawl was already sporting limbs that could reach almost everywhere. She winced at the memory of the spice shelf in the larder. And now this long-legged, fast-growing creature was sporting a fascination for multi-limbed gods. Time was moving unstoppably too fast.

Mrs Henara's on-going unease was nothing new. She'd had it ever since she'd first disobeyed her mother. In their all too brief holiday meetings, the one and only instruction that Saloni the Stowaway had ever spelled out to her had been: "Whatever you do, don't ever marry a Muslim."

A strange thing for a Muslim mother to say.

"You'll be miserable if you do – dogs, all of them! Find yourself a nice Angrez. A cultured White man – they're much better at being hen-pecked. And if you must marry an Asian then make sure he's not Muslim. Check inside his pants if you have to…."

But Seema Henara had gone and done the opposite, not out of spite for her mother, but because she had happened to fall in love with a Muslim surgeon. She was convinced her marriage had failed because her mother's soul had not blessed the union. Deep in her heart, Mrs Henara entertained a cherished fantasy – but since she had no daughter of marriageable age, it could only ever remain a fantasy – safe from any danger of implementation. But that never stopped her mouthing off about it:

"What's all this Bhangi Bhangi talk? Is that the way to talk about a human being who does an honest day's work?"

She was addressing a small group of people gathered at one corner of the Market Square on a Saturday morning. An assortment of people going about their Saturday morning tasks had paused momentarily to have a gossip about the Morality Committee and its ultimatum to Mohanji over the business of the Widow and the Bhangi.

"Stop saying Bhangi – his name is Robert," she said in a high moral voice. "And he's the brightest thing this side of the Equator. So what if he couldn't go on studying? If I had a grown up daughter, I can think of no one more suitable than Robert for a son-in-law. Hard working, good-looking, honest, intelligent, loyal...."

A chorus of disapproving "Hai-hai's" and "Ram-ram's" and "Tauba-tauba's" rose from the open-mouthed assembly. She raised her hand in parliamentary fashion:

"Just hear me out, tell me, what's wrong with him? That he is poor? Ha! Many of your ancestors were poor." She fixed her parliamentary gaze on two of the women who were now Dukavalla wives, but their fathers had originally been street vendors of roasted peanuts and ice cream.

"No, that's not it, is it? None of you will say it out loud. What you don't like is that he is Black! That's it. Just because he's Black he's not good enough for your daughters! Just who do you think you are? You live in their country and then go "chhee-chee" at the colour of their skin."

One of the men, an exceptionally white-skinned Kashmiri-Punjabi garage mechanic, spoke up:

"No problem Mrs Henara. If you like him, then marry your daughter to him when she grows up. No need to tell us what we should be doing. And if you're that concerned about his education, then you pay for him to go to school – he doesn't have to be your son-in-law for you to help him. Yes, you go and do it – send him to school, make him a big, big minister, then who'll clean our shit?"

"That's it – that's just it! Don't you see how unreasonable you're all being? You make someone clean your shit and then you call them unclean. I hate these Indian double standards!"

At times like these, she chose to be an outsider. When she referred to "these Indians" it was implied that she was another kind of Indian, an altogether more upright one, a more cultured one, a more tolerant one – the exceptional Indian-Muslim enlightened Indian who went from temple to Gurudwara and Bhajjan to Evensong just to prove how broad-minded she was.

"Never mind the shit-sweeper," one of the other women spoke up. "What about that Widow? Is it right for widows to remarry? I ask you, where would society be if every widow demanded the right to re-marry? What would become of our daughters? Who'd want them? There's hardly enough young men to go around as it is…." She stopped suddenly, remembering the identity of the young man in question.

"What are you objecting to exactly?" Mrs Henara was keen to cash in on the contradiction. "The fact that the Widow might remarry or the fact that she might marry a person you call the Kaalia Bhangi – Black Shit sweeper? What's your problem exactly? It's not as though you've reserved him for your own daughter, is it? What is this mean-heartedness? I just don't get it…!"

She shook her head in a gesture of helpless exasperation, turned on her heels and marched away assuming the pose of the world's one and only champion of Black human rights.

Soon after this Saturday morning debate, the Haq family threw one of the grandest parties in the history of the town, to celebrate their daughter's sixteenth birthday as well as pat her on the back for a terrific Senior Cambridge exam result. The town's only hairdresser and beautician almost died of fatigue, make up counters at the one and only Pharmacy were stripped of stocks, and tailors worked round the clock as outfits were elaborately planned and executed. That most memorable party of all time was to turn into a vital milestone. Afterwards things were referred to as happening either before, or after the posh Haq party. Cars drew up one by one in the Haq's semi-circular, gravel covered drive. Multi-coloured fairy lights lit up the entire garden. Every leaf on every branch in every tree twinkled with star-shaped lights. A band played on the verandah, and just as the orchestra struck the popular tune of "Mera juta hai Japani, yeh patloon Inglistani…" (loved by the Pearlite Asians for its crucial message that one's attire could be from anywhere, but one's heart was essentially Hindustani), Mrs Henara arrived, bang on cue, wearing a proper African basuti, made out of local cotton in a gaudy floral pattern, complete with matching head-dress and bum-wrap. Most unprofessionally, even the band stopped for a split second. Everyone turned round, almost at once, and a full thirty-second silence followed: bangles stopped jangling, long earrings stopped swaying, silks and satins no longer rustled in the evening breeze and even the insects seemed to fall into a stunned silence. It was as though the Universe itself had been stilled for a moment.

What was she doing in African dress? What's she trying to prove? What a stupid show-off woman!

But worse was to come. Fast on her heels, and looking completely dazed and bewildered, was Robert the poor shit-sweeper Bhangi in a brand new suit.

"Well, hello" she cooed at the stunned crowd, and then walked straight to Mrs Haq, who was a tubby five-foot-nothing whose six-inch stilettos kept sinking into the soft lawn. The much taller Mrs Henara bent down pretending to kiss her on the cheek. Mrs Henara had the self-assured manner of one who had just walked into a party with a famous and much sought after celebrity.

"You said bring anyone you like... so here we are, I have a surprise. Robert agreed to come, isn't that nice of him? Come here Robert, do you know Mrs Haq?"

Robert's expression conveyed he would rather be in a torture chamber, but he was too much of a gentleman. He stepped forward awkwardly, put his hand out, then took it back realising they'd deemed him untouchable. and in a mumbled sort of way just managed to say, "Hello, very nice garden...."

Robert hadn't seen too many manicured gardens. His job demanded that he go straight to the backs of houses – or at least those houses that didn't have flushing indoor lavatories. That would most certainly not include the Haq's house. But Mrs Haq knew exactly who he was and she shifted from foot to foot on the uncomfortable high-heels that seemed determined to transport her to the very core of the earth, while at the same time she tried to make urgent signs to one of her own servants to fetch a separate glass for Robert – don't bring that tray of drinks round yet..., no, no, no please... too late....

An over efficient servant had already appeared with a tray for Mrs Henara and Robert. He was simply following instructions. He had been told to accost all new arrivals with a multiple choice of drinks arranged on a large, circular, silver tray. And if they didn't want wine or Fanta or Coke, then they could make their way to the bar at the far end of the lawn, where another servant would fix them with any drink of their choice.

Robert had the good sense to say "No thank-you," thus avoiding a major untouchability incident. Any mixing up of crockery in this way would've meant no one would ever eat or drink in the Haq household again – well, not until all the crocks and glasses had been replaced.

The Haq servant gave him a poisonous look. He didn't mind waiting on Muhindis and Muzungus – Indians and Europeans – but he was pissed off in the extreme at having to be servile to one of his own colour. And it wasn't even as though Robert was some Church person, or an office worker. Everyone knew what Robert did for a living, and the Haq servant, who considered his job as butler in the luxurious Haq household a source of never-ending pride, squirmed at the indignity of having to serve drinks out of a silver tray to a mere shit sweeper. He sniffed the air and made a face that implied he had just caught a whiff of bodies of sinners rotting in hell fire.

But if the stuck-up Haq butler thought he was being subjected to the stench of hell's burning bodies, then Robert's own predicament having been subjected to the devious Mrs Henara's treachery, closely resembled the burning body itself, consumed by the flames rising from the pits of hell. This... just this, this one single incident is enough... this was a crime more heinous than racism itself. This was the crime of tokenism, and it wouldn't go unpunished.

40
ST. SEEMA

Robert Kasoga had great difficulty trying to figure out just how he'd allowed himself to fall into such a cruel trap. Mrs Seema Henara was really the worst kind of Muhindi. At least the others despised him for his lowly Bhangi status and his Black skin and said as much, but she just used him to make herself appear more liberated and broad-minded. An altogether different kind of Muhindi – the worst kind of Muhindi.

He knew she cared nothing for him. If she had really cared for his feelings she would not have subjected him to that humiliating fiasco at the Haq's.

He hadn't forgotten her speeches when his father had suddenly and tragically died after the Sanyo box in the Mohanji shop had fallen on his head. He hadn't forgotten how Mrs Henara had bullied him and his family to take legal action. He hadn't forgotten how she had not offered even a single cent towards legal costs. And he certainly hadn't forgotten how she had refused his mother's offering of a cup of tea – already prepared and laid before her using up the family's entire milk ration for the day. He knew she didn't want to put her lips to their crockery, so why the hell was she so keen to fuel rumours that she might have been putting her lips on various parts of his anatomy?

Yet Mohanji, the same mean-mouthed penny-pinching, tap water-selling Mohanji had at least forked out the funeral expenses, to say nothing of a full month's wages. The Dukavallas were at least predictable: openly bigoted and racist, but at least you knew where you stood with them.

Robert cursed himself for the thousandth time for not having been more alert to Mrs Henara's devious ways. He should have known. On that fateful day of the Haq party, as soon as Mrs Henara had casually said:

"Come over to the house Robert. I have some books for you," he should have known there and then that she certainly had some scheme designed to make her appear grand and controversial.

Robert the Bhangi had vowed to himself that he would keep away from the phoney do-gooding Mrs Henara. He had turned down her offer to work in her garden. He had turned down her offer of free tuition in Biology. But an offer of free books was too much to resist. Old school textbooks and some other unwanted books of her brother's, she'd said. So he had gone to her house, and if she was just going to be throwing them away then why not? It was no obligation – no big favour. Giving him some old books would not automatically entitle her to a sainthood, white sari and all. He would just take the books away and study them by himself. He would have nothing more to do with her. No lessons, no sermons, no mind-improving schemes aimed at his betterment.

Poor Robert, only just turned eighteen and still so green in the ways of the world, now that we've established, beyond a doubt, that even small town Pearl was part of this big bad world.

"Have you eaten anything?" she had demanded to know as soon as he arrived.

"No? Not yet? Then have something now. Here, come this way."

She'd shown him into the kitchen and sat him down at the servants' table and fed him some leftovers using the servants' crockery. He should have walked out there and then, but he was very hungry. And she did have a lot of good books to give him, so it was in his interests to act meek and mild and grateful.

When he'd finished eating, she announced she'd bought him some new clothes. He should have known then! But he had chosen to ignore that little voice in his head – only a little voice, drowned by the delighted squeals of his greedy side. There was no denying that he was thrilled at the prospect of new clothes. His one and only shirt was getting rather threadbare:

"Thank you, thank you. There was no need really. You can always me give your brother's old clothes, I don't mind. There's no need to buy new clothes for me. You are very kind, Mrs Henara," he had crawled with grateful glee.

"Not at all dear boy. Now listen to me. Can you please, please do me a big favour? My tiresome brother is always so busy. He refuses to take me to that new technology exhibition – you know, that German one? It finishes to-morrow. You know I hate going alone. These awful Indians gossip so much. Just because I'm single, every man thinks I'm fair game. I would feel so much better if I had someone with me. It would be good for you too, good for your mind. They have all kinds of gadgets there. You know, there's a telephone on which you can see the person you're talking to… isn't that wonderful?"

Robert was always interested in anything that spelled progress. Even if that progress was never destined to figure in his life. This was a good chance to see something new – and tickets were ten shillings. He would never have been able to go on his own.

She'd left him browsing through the books and disappeared to get changed. When she emerged in full regalia, powdered and perfumed, he should have known then. It was clear as hell she was up to something. But politeness, coupled with that inexplicable servant-mentality of not questioning your betters, prevented him from remarking on her unusual appearance. He assumed she wanted to look smart for the exhibition, but what was an Indian woman doing dressed in traditional African clothes? He deliberately chose to dismiss the feeling of unease. Oh, what does it matter? The Henaras of this world are a law unto themselves. Even dignitaries of her own race cowered under her bullying tactics and never-ending theories supporting the bees in her bonnet. So who is he, a mere shit-sweeper, to ask her what the hell she was doing dressed in a basuti and matching head dress?

While she got her car out of its shaded parking space, Robert decided to cheer up at the prospect of being introduced to the technology of the future. He had assumed, rather foolishly, that he would be sitting in the back, but Mrs Henara positively pushed him into the front seat.

"I need to stop off somewhere first... briefly. You'll come won't you?" she asked casually.

"No, please. I'll just wait in the car – or I'll get out and wait in the street. I don't mind waiting...."

It was no use. His brilliant self-taught mind had already figured out the plot. There was nothing he could do now. She was single-mindedly accelerating past the neatly trimmed hibiscus hedges lining the hilly roads of the European area, heading towards the Haq mansion on a nearby hill. And what else could he have done? Had he asked for the car to be stopped, then how could he have stepped out with any kind of dignity, wearing the brand-new suit of her generosity and carrying in his arms the books she had so thoughtfully put aside for him? And so they'd arrived at the Haq party – Robert now uncomfortable in the extreme in his new suit, and Mrs Henara in her basuti wafting Chanel No 5 and brazenly showing off her new "escort"....

No, Robert no, no bitterness. This too will pass. Just put it down to experience. Grin and bear it. Your day will come....

41
MUTUAL DECEPTIONS

"One day, when I'm bikkaming rich and famas, you stop driving cab. We will live here, Bombay. Near water. You can be manager. All stars have manager...."

The Actress hated writing letters. But she never hated herself for not having the courage to officially end her sham of a marriage. She wrote regularly to the hard-working husband she had left behind in London. And this she did in spite of the fact that she had acquired a brand new lover in Bombay.

What else could she do? His wife and children lived several hundred miles away, so to all intents and purposes, he was single and available. She needed a place to stay and one half of his bed was good enough for her. He made her feel secure. But she still needed her cab-driver husband somewhere in the background. Nothing like having a ready and willing husband in some other far away country – just in case all else fails. She was the sort of woman who always had to have a partner – even if it was someone she hadn't seen for years.

In the early days he wrote back regularly:

"I thought you and Mamta were only going to India for a holiday. There is really no need to put up with all this hardship. If you find something to do and you can enjoy yourself that's fine, if not, what's the problem? You don't need to work. My business is doing OK now. We'll never be rich, but we could have our own house soon. I've seen a really nice two-bedroom place in Neasden. Going cheap. The guy wants a quick sale. What do you think?"

Neasden! How could anyone live in Neasden? Her London was Knightsbridge, Brompton Square, Kensington, Regent's Park, Hyde Park, Belgravia. How could any self-respecting person possibly live anywhere else in London? No, she didn't see herself in Neasden.

His next letter reassured her: "I'm not doing anything about the Neasden house yet. Perhaps you want to live a little closer to central London? There's a nice new conversion block going up in Cricklewood. I'm looking into it, but first, tell me what are your plans? When are you coming back?"

With every letter, he inched a little closer towards central London, but never quite close enough to Brompton Square. Whatever God-forsaken area he mentioned for their ideal dream house, it was never quite good enough for her. He would never understand her. What use a husband who doesn't share your dreams?

Then his letters stopped. She never bothered to try and figure it out. It suited her. Just as she was determined to become a film star, she was equally determined to avoid facing reality. It suited her that the marriage should wither away, rather than reach a definite end.

Then came the mild affair with the sleazy film journalist. He was useless in bed, the original one-minute wonder, but at least he got her a photo session in a major glossy gossip rag. Those scantily clad photos eventually bore fruit. At first, she was just the vamp. Then the vamp with the heart of gold – the one who gets to move her mouth to the title song of the film and then dies at the end.

And all through this, she continued writing to her husband-in-name only. But he had long stopped replying to her letters. Sometimes she wallowed in the anger that was welling up inside her: "How dare he forget me? Me, film star, he only cab driver?"

So when some years later she was handed a letter bearing a London postmark, she was, understandably, petrified. After all these years, why had her husband finally decided to write? Could it be he had met someone else and wanted to remarry? Oh no! He was her insurance policy, how dare he remarry?

She dreaded the thought of divorce. True she hadn't seen him for years, and yes, she had been the one to run away from him, but how dare he divorce her? She didn't like the idea of being a divorcee, especially since her clever film-writer boyfriend showed no signs of being ready to sign on the dotted line of a marriage contract. How could he? He was still officially married. He wanted to go on being married. He hadn't seen his wife for years either, but a wife was a useful thing to have. If any affair got too hot to handle one could always claim guilt for the wife and pretend to go back to her. It provided the perfect, most honourable excuse for switching mistresses. The writer needed his wife as much as the actress needed her husband. They were both the same sort of people really. That's why they had ended up together. Mutual deceptions.

Deception only takes root within deception. It is not possible to be deceived unless you yourself have a hidden agenda. Life has a funny way of evening out the score. If you were the sort of person who had a particular kind of emotional insecurity, then, more often than not, life arranged it so that you met another of the opposite sex, with exactly the same insecurities as your own.

Two people with matching insecurities were often the reality behind what was romantically termed the ideal couple. The struggling actress and the has-been writer certainly made an ideal couple. They both needed an active, work-related sexual entanglement in their lives, while at the same time maintaining a link with an absent spouse for reasons of emotional security.

She held the London post-marked letter in her trembling hands, and finally managed to tear open the envelope. She still couldn't bring herself to look at its contents. Just one sheet of paper, not even fully covered in print. No divorce papers. Nothing resembling a solicitor's official header. What on earth was this?

An offer to portray a 19th century Lucknow courtesan in a new British-Indian film. She thought she was dreaming. Little did she know that she was to be cast as the central character in someone else's dream....

42
JHATAK-MATTAK

"Hi! I hope you had a comfortable flight?" the Producer asked politely, in a manner not usually reserved for dealing with Indian film-star types.

"Oh ya. Grrreat!" purred the actress. She was lounging on her bed in a frilly nightdress, cleavage and all, quite unbothered by the male-PA's presence. The Producer noted with some regret that the nightdress, provocative and vulgar in the extreme, would nevertheless have looked quite fetching in the event of a hotel fire.

But the matter of the revealing nightdress was quickly eclipsed by the startling revelation that the Actress was an ardent practitioner of the "jhattka" – not really surprising, given the masses of voluminous, silky, reddish brown hair given to falling over her face approximately once every ten seconds or so. Jhattka was really only the Producer's code word for the world-famous "flick-back", but since the Producer has been to SOAS and prides herself on "thinking in Urdu," she prefers to think of it by an Indianised name.

Basically, no manual on the art of flirting would've been complete without detailed instructions on such a gambit. It's about wearing long hair in such a way that it has to be flicked back from the left eye as often as possible. Hair is an essential aid in the art of effective flirting. It has to be touched, twisted, coiled and every so often thrown back from the face with a flick, using the back of the hand. Needless to say, the manoeuvre results in masses of hair being temporarily – very temporarily – cleared off the face while at the same time, the head is subjected to a seemingly involuntary upward motion, emphasising the dimple of the chin (the clearest sign of a flirt). A head thus pointing heavenwards, albeit momentarily, has the added advantage of minimising any wrinkles or tell tale facial lines. The Producer seemed to remember vaguely, from her extensive perusal of Orientalist literature, that the women of the Ottoman harems had always preferred the woman-on-top position so as to be able to employ the coquettish jhattka as often as possible. Or was it the other way round? Surely, facial lines were less visible if you lay under....?

The Actress's harsh accent cut into her attempts to recall the harem technique:

"Oh, you arr so much young. I thought maybe you old-old with glasses. Oh soery, don't want to be rude, you know vott I mean, yaar?"

The Producer felt irritated by the harsh Indian accent, coming so fast on the heels of an extra hard jhattka. There was really no harm in speaking a foreign language incorrectly, but why did these empty-headed, frilly-nightie-jhattka types consider it below their dignity to speak in their own mother-tongue? She decided to get haughty and switched into Urdu, just to impress.

"I'm glad you've arrived safely. There's lot's to do. You know your first job is to learn to speak Urdu. We're arranging it. You'll get a few weeks' head start, then we begin shooting, but your Urdu lessons continue. Now, for the...."

"But I speaks Hindi very good yaar," the Actress interrupted in her sing-song English.

"No, not Hindi, I said Urdu," the Producer was chuffed at being able to use her favourite card. Then, in the first flush of a mild victory, she decided to soften a bit: "OK, fine, so why don't you speak to me in Hindi then?" she asked, fully aware of laying a trap.

"You von't understand my Hindi. I speak for fillum only. Can't speak ewery day. I like to speak the Engliss only. But if you giw me Hindi script, writtann in Engliss word, I vill read with parrfact accent."

"Ronnie," the Producer said, turning to the PA with an audible sigh, "Make a note to organise some English classes as well. We'll need it for interviews and things."

"I born in Africa, yaar, don't you know? Everybody speak the Engliss there, so my Engliss very good, nacharrally!"

"Africa?" The Producer was visibly taken aback. "So when did you go to India?"

"Not India straightavay. First came to UK. That's why also my Engliss good. I was only eighteen-ear. Stayed here von ear. Then vent to India. Lots of chance for me there. Became famas wery quick."

"Can you dance?"

"Oh ya! Af-koss."

"What kind? Bharata Natyam? Kathak? Odissi? Manipuri?" The Producer was clearly thrilled to see the Actress's uncomprehending expression.

"All kind. All mix. Nightclub dance, cabray specially. You must have seen. I also sing."

"No, I don't need you to sing. All that is under control. The best voices!"

"But I also sing gajjall if you want, no problem."

"No, I don't want," replied the Producer getting exasperated. Her magnum opus already looked set to be a flop. Moneybags might win after all.

"Wery nice script," continued the Actress. "Is make-up man good here? Must be. This is London after all! Vill they know how to make me look like typical tawwaiff?"

"Oh, darling, don't you worry about all that. It's all under control," sailed in the reassuring tones of Ronnie the PA. "Don't worry your head. That's for the rest of us to worry about. You just work on your Urdu and your voice and all that. We'll transform you. You'll be so sophisticated. Don't get me wrong. I don't mean you're not sophisticated now, but you know, everyone needs some polishing. There's a huge international press launch on the first shoot day. You'll be the centre of attention darling, just think!"

The Producer loved the PA's ability to paint a bright picture, no matter what the scenario. She resolved to be more charitable towards the actress.

OK, so she was a crass, crude-sounding, jarring-bad-Engliss-only speaking overweight C-grade bimbo film star from Bombay, but who knows, she might be transformed into something quite different? Remember caterpillars and butterflies? And since evil Mr Moneybags was clearly planning to punish this actress in some way, couldn't she, the Producer-Director turn the tables on him by turning the actress into an attractive, alluring, interesting and present-able specimen, with a perfectly polished multi-lingual personality and flaw-less Urdu to boot? And all this at his expense, quite literally! Why not? Teach the bastard a lesson! Whatever axe he was grinding, he had no right to play with a woman's life. She would transform this woman into a successful force in her own right. And a major film at the end of her transformation would add icing on the top. Real fame for the Actress and even more acclaim for the Producer-Director.

She addressed the Actress with renewed warmth: "Did you really like my script? What do you like best?"

"My role. So important. All me. But why you diddan't put ending? I vont to know vot happens."

"I deliberately haven't told any of the actors what happens next. I want a completely natural reaction. You'll see what I mean when the time comes."

"Wery mystery. I like mystery. Is there going to be murder?"

"Oh darling, you're impossible!" squealed the PA with delight, as usual coming to the Producer's rescue. "Come on, what are you planning to do this evening? Do you have any friends in town?"

"No, not any more, yaar. I use to. But don't know ver everyone is gone now yaar."

"Never mind darling. You'll soon make lots of friends. As soon as word gets round you're in town, they'll all be falling over each other in the hotel lobby to catch sight of you. Some friends are having a dinner party this evening. They'll die of shock when they see whom I've brought along. The Lizard will probably die too – that's my wife, by the way. She gets very jealous, so be careful darling. Anyway, be ready for eight. I've got to go now. I'll leave you two to it."

The Producer congratulated herself for the umpteenth time for having had the vision to hire this young man as her PA-Chamcha. Thanks to him, she had been saved the arduous task of keeping the boring Actress amused in London. He whizzed off blowing kisses to both of them.

A strange silence fell on the room. That usually happened to rooms when the PA departed. The Producer walked over to the bedside phone and ordered some tea. She then decided, unprofessionally, to sit at the foot of the bed, instead of the armchair. It was chummier. The actress relaxed and decided this producer woman wasn't, after all, as stuffy as she'd first imagined.

"You been in UK long?" the Actress asked, trying to get friendly.

"All my life, I'm British. English actually," replied the Producer, loving the sight of the Actress's open mouth and wondering how to start questioning her for details of Moneybags.

"But how you speak Urdu? I am so impressed."

"I like languages. I studied Urdu at University. And then I read some Hindi as well – I suppose you could call me an Indologist." She paused momentarily to enjoy the impact of the unknown word on the Actress, and then continued: "I read a lot – I have to... for vocabulary... I don't get enough conversation in Urdu. All my Indian and Pakistani friends like to speak in English only. They usually call me up if they want to know the meaning of some difficult Urdu word...."

She hoped the Actress would feel suitably chastised and hopelessly under accomplished, but the comment just seemed to go over her head. The Actress changed the subject:

"You married?" she asked.

"No, well... not really..." she began uncertainly, and then seizing this God-sent opportunity, she sent the question back: "And you? Married?"

"No, not properly. Boyfriend only – ve are wery close."

"So I take it you get lots of work in Bombay?" the Producer asked.

"Yes, I am big hit. They likes me there. Can't ewen go out without otograff. Hawe to sit in all day. So boring. Then your letter. I really believe in God. Do you believe in God?"

"I'm beginning to," the Producer replied cautiously.

They fell silent for a while. The Producer used the time to observe the Actress. Quite beautiful – even fragile. Definitely overweight, but delicate. An unusual combination. Good skin. Bright eyes. Deceptively broad, intellectual-looking forehead. Sensitive hands. Copper-coloured dyed hair and eyebrows to match.

"I'll need you to get that hair-dye out before we start shooting," she said bossily.

"Vy? You don't like? I can hawe vig, no?"

"No, that's not the point. I need jet black hair. Long. We'll add extensions of course, but grow it anyway. It has to be oiled, parted in the middle and twisted into one long plait."

"Oh no! I don't vont to look old fashioned like that. Nowadays in Indian fillums tawwaiffs can have modern hairs. Good styles...."

"I'm sorry, but you're playing a nineteenth century courtesan and you have to look the part. The figure's fine, but I might need you to put on just a little more weight. English chocolate will take care of that I suppose. My only problem is going to be matching your shots with the real dancer – she's quite a bit thinner. I can't get a fatter dancer."

"Vot? Why another dancer? I told you I vill dance," petulant jhattka followed.

"Er... no. It will take several years to train you in Lucknow-style kathak. It's just not worth it. There are lots of good dancers in London, only too grateful for the work. Let's not make life too difficult. You'll be busy enough with your Urdu tuition."

"If you don't like the vay I speak, why not get someone else for dubbing my lines, and let me dance myself? I don't want to miss dancing. I like wearing dance costume. Vill you have nice ones made?" Barbie-style jhattka followed.

"Yes, yes," the Producer was getting impatient with the Barbie-doll syndrome. "Don't worry, you'll get to wear them all. And there's going to be some exquisite jewellery. There will be lots and lots of close-ups, but you won't have to dance. Someone else will do it in the wide shots and back shots."

"OK, you are boss I suppose," she said dejectedly, but not before performing an extra-sulky jhattka.

The Producer started feeling sorry for her again.

"Look it's much better that you learn Urdu properly. That's something that will help you in your future career. It's a great opportunity to polish your voice and everything else. Take on a new persona. Develop new interests. If those wretched semi-literate Indian film journalists write you off as an unclassy Gujju-ben, here's your chance to show them what you're really made of. We are all right behind you. You'll emerge completely changed from this role. They'll all be forced to take you more seriously. All those Indian producers will be falling over one another to sign you on for their pseudo-historicals and those wretched so-called Muslim "Socials". And you'll be able to turn your nose up at all of them and opt for the theatre instead! Or just go to Hollywood. Show them all!"

"Why you are doing all this for me?" the Actress asked seriously, her face soft, her eyes misty. She seemed truly grateful. And that look of indebtedness made her even more beautiful. "If you vonted good Urdu vy you diddan't take someone else?"

The Producer stiffened, visibly. What was she to say? I had to take you because Moneybags made it the one and only condition of an otherwise blank cheque?

"Who else could I take? Can you name even one Indian actress aged between 22 and 39 who can do classical dance *and* speak Urdu properly? I may as well take a gori woman from here and stick a black-haired wig on her head."

"OK, not from India, but you could have good Urdu-speaking girl from Pakistan, no?"

"What! Are you serious? A Pakistani actress would need even more electrocution – as Moneybags would call it..." the Producer started giggling uncharacteristically in an off-guard moment.

"Who calls it? Money who?" the Actress asked, genuinely puzzled, but with enough presence of mind to enact an extra-hard jhattka.

The Producer came to suddenly: "Oh, just some friend of mine who has difficulty with long words...." Oops, that was close! Be on your guard, she reprimanded herself.

"I like people who speak long words. I vill be learning all that, yes? Because Courtesan is very vell educated and speaks beautiful. You vill make me like her, yes?" she asked warmly. "I vont to be just like Tameejjan," she said dreamily.

A gentler jhattka was employed again.

43
DOLLIES AND DOLLY MIXTURES

Mrs Mohanji was unique. She was a shopkeeper's wife who had never ever gone shopping. Quite possibly the only woman in the world never to have done so. Mohanji bought her whatever she needed. She appreciated his reasoning that if she was allowed to go shopping for herself she might be tempted to buy other things... things connected with greed rather than need.

She was a quiet, unassuming woman who rarely spoke in the presence of men. She adored her husband. He could do no wrong. OK, so he was a bit tight with money, so what? Hadn't he just managed to turn his small hand-cart soda-selling business into two successful shops? And in all the years they had been together, he had never so much as looked at another woman. He was respected in the community. He was Chairman of the Morality Committee. Others looked to him for moral guidance while the Temple Guru himself had said Mohanji was a very special soul – not like all the others.

She supported his every stance, and gave her full backing to all his cost-saving policies in the home. She was just fourteen at the time of their arranged marriage in India, after which he'd brought her back to Pearl, his birthplace. She had given birth every year, for ten years. At twenty-five she already looked middle-aged. Those early years were spent cooking, cleaning and looking after the children. But now the children were older, she didn't really have that much to do. She busied herself hand-embroidering bed linen. Endless pillow-cases with the word "Goodnight" monogrammed in different shades of rainbow-coloured threads. Bed linen fringed and knotted to make tassels along the edges. Crochet-borders, real home-made lace, food-covers made of net and edged with shiny glass beads. Most suitable time-consuming activities for one who no longer had the responsibility of running a household of twelve.

Ever since their Widow daughter had returned to live with them, Mrs Mohanji had relinquished the domestic throne in the belief that her unfortunate Bechari Widow daughter ought to be allowed to earn her keep. That way, the girl would feel better about still living in her father's house. Dignity. That was what life was all about. You could be stripped off everything you owned but dignity was not transferable. Either you had it, or you didn't. And Mrs Mohanji most certainly did, and intended her daughter to have the same.

Although uneducated in the usual sense of the word, and only able to offer a thumb print on the rare occasion that a signature was required, Mrs Mohanji nevertheless seemed to possess the greatest wisdom and sensitivity in terms of dissecting the many finer nuances of human nature. She knew that for a young married woman, there was nothing quite as demeaning as being returned to live in her father's house. It was shameful indeed that your in-law's had no further use for you. There was only one way to ease that shame. And that was to let the poor Widow take over the running of the household. Let her feel truly at home. Sure, Mrs Mohanji retained her supervisory role, but for all practical purposes, the Widow was the housewife in the Mohanji house-hold, leaving Mrs Mohanji with oodles of spare time. Time with which she did almost nothing except her elaborate weaving of threads – in some form or another, using this kind of needle or that kind of hook. And when she wasn't doing that, she performed various protracted, lengthy religious rituals. On certain days, when she observed a special fasting routine to ensure the continuance of a long and healthy life for Mr Mohanji, she spent most of her time in her so-called puja-ghar, a prayer-room. The room was really more of a small walk-in cupboard with shelves, just off the backyard – a small storage area for the shop, housing many canisters and jars of biscuits and sweets. She had reserved one shelf for herself, to display her many gods and all their associated props. Here she sat, day and night, praying, oozing clouds of fragrant fumes – a wonderful holy smell of incense and fresh flowers, quite overpowering at times, and more than sufficient to cover the less pleasant odours at the far side of the backyard.

Once a month or so, she would stand in the yard itself, head covered with the end of her sari, the hooded-look sari gently swaying in the evening breeze. She would look up at the sky, straining her needlework eyes to try and see something. And then, as soon as she spotted the new moon, or it was pointed out to her, she performed various rituals, consisting of drawing threads from the end of her sari, and catching the reflection of the new moon in a basin of water. Then she distributed sweets to whoever happened to be around. More often than not, it was usually the Henara Brat who was the first recipient of these auspicious offerings. Somehow, on new moon days, the Brat always managed to hang around in the early evening. God alone knows how she knew when the moon would appear – walking bloody ephemeris – but with her sharper eyesight she always managed to spot it first. And then she took the utmost delight in informing the poorer-sighted Mrs Mohanji that her God was safe and sound, and had appeared once again in the form of a barely visible, needle-thin crescent. It was customary to give the bearer of this happy news the largest share of the sweets. And Mrs Mohanji was never one to break with custom.

****

It's a new moon day, I know. I know all sorts of things. They call me a "shit-sniffing-Brat" who can't do maths but little do they know how much I know of things. I'm behind the shop as usual, but no Mrs Mohanji in the courtyard. I'm hoping my driver will be late. When his girlfriend is in a good mood, he's always late. Sometimes his flies aren't done up properly. That's how I know when his girl friend has been in a good mood. Somehow, his half-undone trousers and her moods are connected – I don't know exactly how – but I know that they just are.

But where's Mrs Mohanji? I really need to see her and tell her about the new moon. It's really important for her... well... it's kind of important for me as well. It's ages since I've had any sweets. My mother has funny theories about sugar and teeth, but then she has weird theories for everything. No other parents have those theories, and if it wasn't for the generosity of my Mohanji boyfriends and for Mrs Mohanji's Moon Good, I don't think I'd ever have known the taste of a real sweet. Pear Drops, Jelly Babies, Striped Peppermints, Dolly Mixtures, Smarties. Failing that, either Barfi, Laddoo or then, if I was really unlucky, just plain crystals of Shakkar.

Something feels not quite right today. The shop has closed early, and there's a menacing hush over the Mohanji household. There's no cooking in the yard, and I don't see the Mohanji boys anywhere. I'll just poke my head in the puja cupboard and see if she's doing her prayers in there. Nothing. Just various dolls dressed in shiny costumes, staring back at me, smilingly and silently. I like that one with the flute. He's really cute. If only he would come to life and play that flute, I would follow him to the other end of the world. If I heard that flute in the middle of the night, I swear I would jump out of bed and dance to his tune....

But he doesn't move. He just smiles at me. I know he's a boy, but sometimes he looks just like a girl. I crane my head to look at the shelves high up above the dolls-shelf. Rows and rows of jars of sweets. Extra supplies for the shop,

I guess. If she's not in here praying, then where is Mrs Mohanji? I'd better check up in the house. I cross the backyard, littered with furniture. How strange! What's all the furniture doing in the backyard? I weave my way through the piled up chairs and tables and mattresses. Sometimes I have to scramble over things. I pretend I'm mountain climbing and allow myself to fall from a table and land onto a soft mattress. What fun! I could just stay here and play this unusual bonus of a game, but I must find Mrs Mohanji first and tell her that her God is here. How can she do this to Him? Her God has shown Himself to her and she can't even be bothered to see this magnificent sight? Most unlike her!

The small Mohanji house at the back of the shop is packed with people. Well they're all women actually. They're all wearing white. Every single room and every single space is packed with women in white. The men are all gathered on the shop verandah. Hundreds of them. This is very strange. I don't actually recognise anyone... unless that's... could that be Mr Mohanji? He looks dreadful! What's that greyish fuzz on his face? Is he trying to grow a beard? I'm frightened of beards. No doubt he's growing a beard to make a saving on razors and shaving soap. What's the matter with him? Has he been crying?

I suddenly become aware of a disturbing sound of whining and moaning coming from the direction of the most crowded room of all, the Mohanjis' bedroom. I don't know what's up, but my stomach feels hollow. I peep into the bedroom. Mrs Mohanji is lying on the ground. Why on earth is she sleeping at this time? How can she sleep when her God is awake? And how can she lie so still while He smiles radiantly in the sky? And why is she on the floor? She is draped in white with fresh multi-coloured flowers all over her chest. Orange and red flowers. On her head is a shiny red cloth, matching the red and orange marks on her forehead. I've never seen anything so weird and wonderful before. Some kind of brand new ritual? I love rituals.

Should I just go and wake her up and tell her about the new moon? She might just want to get up and salute her Moon God. Will I get my sweets? But someone is already chasing me away from the room: "No children in here please – out with you!"

But there's a new moon, I promise, I'm not fibbing, I protest, already feeling the onset of depression at the possibility of being done out of my monthly sweet ration. But no, they won't let me go anywhere near Mrs Mohanji to inform her that her Moon God had appeared, right on cue. It wasn't fair.

Nothing was fair. Mrs Mohanji had been the only one to observe that ritual and now she was asleep. This may sound strange, but she looks like she might just sleep forever. Grown ups sleep far too much!

It's all down to me now. I can't leave the Moon God unsaluted. I have to do something, so I'm headed back to the puja cupboard. I stand before the smiling deities in their shiny-doll costumes trimmed with tinsel. Today, they gaze back at me differently. I realise now that I'd never really looked at them properly before, being more preoccupied with the sweet jars on the upper shelves and with receiving sweets from Mrs Mohanji. But now, it felt as though they were smiling directly at me. They had chosen me to be her successor. I am convinced I have inherited the Moon God ritual directly from Mrs Mohanji.

I feel a new sense of grown-up self-importance. I pick up the wide-bottomed basin that Mrs Mohanji uses for the ritual and fill it from the bathroom tap. I put it down on the ground carefully, but I'm not sure what's supposed to happen next. Should I be seeing the new moon inside the basin? No, how can that be? It's barely visible in the sky, how can I make the water catch its reflection? Was the reflection game some other ritual? Was that the ritual when she fasts for Mr Mohanji's health and catches the reflection of the full moon in the basin? No, no, she used to do that with a huge sieve... she used to say the moon must never be seen directly, but through a sieve... oh! I'm so confused now. I wish I'd paid more attention. I was only interested in sweets in those days, but now I'm growing up a bit, I really want to know how to do the ritual properly, step by step.

What else, what else? I have this overwhelming urge to do something, to perform some kind of ceremony, but what to do?

Threads! Remember the threads! Mrs Mohanji used to pick threads from the end of her sari. But I've only got this checked cotton frock – pretty difficult to find loose thread-ends. Damn my mother and her insistence on invisible hemming. Oh to hell with it! I'll just rip the hem. Good, that's it! Now I'll wave the threads in the air like Mrs Mohanji used to do.... Nine. There had to be nine strands of thread. That's funny... there's something else which needs nine of something....

What happens next? I have nine threads. Just look up at the new moon, perhaps. What to say? Mrs Mohanji used to mutter something under her breath, but I don't know the words. I wonder if I could make up a song instead? I'm good at making up songs. Would the Moon God mind a song instead of whatever words Mrs Mohanji used to recite? Worth a try. So I softly sing my made-up song, eyes closed. Then I look up, a little frightened, but the moon's still there. So God wasn't angry with me, otherwise He would've disappeared.

Good. So far, so good. Now we come to that part of the ritual that I know really well. I could've performed it straight away, but I wanted a bit of a build up, just to replicate that feeling of joyful anticipation when I used to wait for Mrs Mohanji to finish muttering her magic words and start giving out the sweets.

For this part of the ritual, I am extremely confident. And I'm going to do it out of one of those sweet jars on the top shelf. Lots of free furniture lying around in the courtyard, so climbing up is no problem. How thoughtful of people to leave so many items of furniture for me to stand on. It's difficult to hold onto the jar and climb down, but I've managed, somehow. I've climbed so many trees before now, so I'm a bit of an expert.

Dolly Mixtures. They'll do. Lots of lovely colours – some stripy little cushions and some miniature marbles in green, red and orange. I know Mohanji sells them one by one, separately, five cents each. It's quite a treat for me to have a whole jar to celebrate the New Moon.

A generous fistful of dolly mixtures straight into my mouth. Pretend Mrs Mohanji is putting them in my mouth, as she often used to. She used to call it "sweetening the mouth." And then one more fistful for Mrs Mohanji, but she's asleep so I'd better scoff them myself. And then one more for all the people whose mouths she would've sweetened. I would do the same, but I'm not allowed inside the house just now with all those weepy women. So I'll have to eat their share as well. And then another fistful, just for luck. And then another one to celebrate my first ever performance of a real religious ritual. Three more fistfuls in memory of Mrs Mohanji who would never ever be able to observe the ritual again. Sad, isn't it?

****

Mrs Henara had arrived at the Mohanji's to offer condolences. Well it would've seemed rude not to. It would've been downright mean to just send the driver to pick up the Brat as usual, without a word of acknowledgement about the sad news of Mrs Mohanji's sudden death. So she came herself, paid her respects to the corpse quickly, and then started looking for her daughter, eager to drag her away from this house of death and wailing as swiftly as possible. And more than just a little eager to get the Brat away before they lifted up the corpse and took it to the riverside ceremonial ground for cremation. No, that would never do. It would bring a thousand unanswerable questions from the Brat, and Mrs Henara had no patience for that sort of thing right now. She just had to get her away quickly. She'd never even have let her come here if she'd heard about the sudden death of Mrs Mohanji earlier. But the school bus had as usual stopped at the Market Square, and the Brat, seeing that the driver had not yet arrived, had jumped off and no doubt run straight across to the shop as usual.

But where was she right now? There was no sign of her anywhere. Mrs Henara didn't want to re-enter the house, having expressed her sympathies so explicitly and having already explained in great detail why she couldn't stay to see the body off. So she made her way to the backyard through the small side-door usually reserved for the Bhangi, leading to the area outside the dreaded family toilets. She covered her nose with a scented handkerchief and dared to venture where no professional-class Muhindi had ever ventured before. Only Bhangis went to this part of a dwelling. Or the shopkeeper classes for nature's calls. Where the hell was the Brat? She really must make some other arrangements for the half-hour between three-thirty and four pm. She'd had enough of her daughter hanging around this awful place and picking up terrible habits, to say nothing of her disgusting Gujarati-English accent. And contrary to Mrs Henara's hopes, the Mohanji boys' maths-ability had not rubbed off on her child, and neither had their tendency to parental obedience.

And then she spotted a small figure bending over in a familiar red-checked dress. Could that be her good-for-nothing child? It was most definitely her dress but it was hanging unevenly like the hem had just come undone. And the wearer of the dress was kneeling on the filthy, muddy ground outside the toilet area and vomiting, violently and uncontrollably.

"What's going on? What on earth happened? Stop it! This minute! Do you hear me..." she screeched, without a thought for the child's distress.

"I... I..." the brat was overcome by another huge surge of stomach contents headed upwards... "I was just... dolly... you know dolly mix...."

"What doll? Whose dolly?"

"No, not that kind of dolly... can I have some water please? Please, mummy, basin... basin on the ground... tap in the corner... please...."

"Shut up! You're not allowed to drink the filthy water here. Let's just clean you up under that tap and then we're going straight home!" She pulled the Brat to her feet.

"But the dolly mixtures... I have to tell Mr Mohanji, otherwise a whole jar will be missing and he'll blame the poor boys, and...."

"What is this dolly-dolly?"

Just then, the cupboard door on the other side of the backyard swung open with a gust of wind, and Mrs Henara spotted the various figurines in shiny costumes, representing holy deities in Mrs Mohanji's puja cupboard.

"Oh I see", she pronounced in an enlightened manner. "Dolls, yes, I see what you mean. Just looking at them made you sick, yes? Now, baby-jaan, listen! You should never say that in front of anyone. You heard me? It's OK to think it, but don't say it. I know they look silly, but they are Hindu gods and you must show respect. I know they make you puke, but still you should show...."

"No, no, no!" the Brat was screaming hysterically, her voice hoarse from vomiting, her spirit inconsolable against her mother's cruel remarks: "Please don't insult them. Don't call them silly, please. I wasn't sick because of them... you see mummy... the other kind of dolly, I mean dolly mix... oh, never mind... water... please...."

There's no experience in the world quite as alienating and isolating as being perpetually misunderstood by one's own mother.

44
GHEE SHAKKAR

The first recording was just two days away. The Composer himself would probably fly in just half an hour before the recording. In fact, if the recording studio had had a helicopter landing facility, then he would probably have touched down just as sound levels were being checked. But the Ustad arrived in London two days early for his recording, hoping to be snapped up for a private "mahfil" or two. But when no such invitation came, he felt at a loose end, and the Producer realised he would have to be kept amused somehow, otherwise he would be unbearably grumpy for the recording. All the Ustad's London-based students had done a vanishing act on hearing that he would be coming to London for a recording. No student was too keen to be stuck with the task of amusing the Ustad while he was trying to kill time. And so it fell to poor Ronnie, with his limited Urdu on the one hand, and his ever-suspicious Lizard wife on the other, to keep the temperamental Ustad amused and occupied. The PA didn't really mind, but the Ustad never seemed to carry any money. So the PA always had to pay for the taxis, and buy all the coffees, snacks, cigarettes and alcohol. All this he would reclaim on expenses, but it was still irritating that the Ustad always expected someone else to pay.

Although she had safely foisted him onto Ronnie-PA, the Producer decided she should at least join them for dinner on the first night. That way, the Ustad could whine on about the mysticism of music, and about all his legendary ancestors and feel he was being appreciated properly. Poor PA only knew Bombay film music, or the kind of western pop which often appears as Smash Hits Vol. 33.

In the absence of a dinner invitation at somebody's house, the Ustad's second best kind of evening out was to eat in an Indian restaurant so that he could boss the Indian Bihari or Bengali waiters around. And he could do so gleefully because music-minded or not, every Indian waiter was likely to have heard of him. Many of these restaurants would also, as a tribute to mark the celebrity visit, immediately play one of his sitar albums. This pleased him very much. Quite often he would let a spontaneous "Wah wah – what a thing!

Subhanallah" escape his lips as he admired one of his own embellishments on a particular note.

The Producer envied him for this. It must be a great feeling to be so moved by your own work. Whenever she sat and watched any of her own old documentaries, she felt suicidal. She always spotted mistakes. It was hugely embarrassing. Something always seemed wrong. It never came out as she had intended. It might have been acceptable to audiences, and even mildly successful at the time, but somehow for her, it was always a disaster. Too many bad memories. Long hours and sleepless nights. Rushing through the final weeks to deliver on time. Personality problems with performers and technicians. There was always some big problematic saga attached to each scene. Nothing was ever as straightforward or as painless as it looked in the final version. And yet this Ustad was able to enjoy and even pat himself on the back for something he had recorded over twenty years ago.

"That was really nice – I'm stuffed, I shouldn't have eaten so much," said the PA patting his small, flat stomach.

"I'd like a sweet," said the Ustad patting his rounded bulging stomach. "It helps to settle everything else. There's far too much propaganda against sugar and ghee in your country. There is nothing as pure as ghee. It is the best substance known to man. It is the secret of good health. My grandfather used to...."

"Let's ask for the menu," interrupted the Producer, afraid of yet another story about how his grandfather drank a small stainless steel bowl of warm, melted ghee first thing, on waking up each morning. Yughh!

The Ustad was handed a dessert menu. He stopped at the first item. "Ras Malai? No... these Bengali sweets are just milk, milk and milk. Now I remember my mother's carrot halwa. I wish I could describe the taste to you... it was like... just like Raag Kedar on a cold night."

The Ustad grew dewy-eyed at the memory of the halwa while the Producer tried to devise an on-the-spot theory about particular foods going well with certain raags.

"They don't normally serve carrot halwa in restaurants," said the practical PA. "How about gulab-jamun? Those are fried in ghee, aren't they? You like ghee...."

"They ought to be, but you westerners cook everything in oil. It's a joke!" snorted the Ustad. He finally settled for something sweet and sticky, and Producer and PA decided to move on to coffee. The Ustad only ever drank tea, but hated the way tea was made in England. What? Tea bags? For the Ustad, tea bags were the second worst invention after condoms. And whoever heard of adding cold, uncooked milk to a cup of tea? Milk should always be cooked in with the tea leaves. And it should boil furiously and simmer for ages until it took on a rich pinkish colour. The equivalent of four spoons of sugar per cup of tea should also be cooked in at the same time, along with a whole cardamom and a generous pinch of salt.

He was always teaching people to make what he called "proper" tea. The PA had already mastered the Ustad's tea recipe and had in typical efficient Ronnie-fashion, made sure that the recording studio kitchen was furnished with a small saucepan and a jar of cardamoms. He was most obliging in providing cups and cups of it – sometimes gaining access to the Ustad's hotel kitchen in order to do so. So, on this occasion he thought nothing of asking the waiter if he might be allowed into the kitchen in order to prepare the Ustad's special tea.

The restaurant staff had never had such a request. They were clearly reluctant to allow one of their customers into the kitchen (obviously for fear of what he might see), and a somewhat stiff and awkward debate ensued. The manager offered to make normal tea for the Ustad:

"We'll make it extra strong – just tell us how he'd like it. How many bags?"

"But that's not the point. It has nothing to do with the strength of the beverage. It's HOW it's prepared. Look I know how to do it. Why don't you just let me?" the PA persisted.

"Sorry, against regulations. No insurance if accident in the kitchen. Against hygiene rules..." the normal bureaucratic stuff followed.

"Oh, forget it," butted in the Producer. "Let's go to my place and make Ustad-ji's tea. We can sit and chat there. Cancel the coffee – we can have that at my place too."

The restaurant manager did not hide his disgust. Just because he couldn't provide tea to the Ustad's taste, they were cancelling the coffee as well. The Ustad cheered up at once, taking a great delight at the Manager's pissed-off expression, and thrilled at the prospect of being asked at the Producer's place. He loved visiting people's houses. He could park himself down for as long as he liked, and he would always be driven back to his hotel afterwards.

"Why not invite some of your other friends over, and we could all have a really nice chatty evening?" suggested the Ustad, clearly in the mood for a late night mahfil with him holding court on all aspects of music.

She considered his suggestion. Inviting other Indian music fans would clearly take some of the heat off her. She wouldn't have to work so hard at listening to him. Yes, it was a good idea. A late night tea party. But at such short notice? Who would be game? Unless…? Then an idea suddenly struck her. She reached for her mobile phone:

"Hello, are you doing anything right now?"

"Hi! No, not really, just watching TV. Why?"

"I've got some friends over – we're going back to my place for tea. Why don't you join us?"

"I'd love to but I don't think I can…."

"Well, you know we have this recording on Wednesday, and everybody's in town already – quite nice, to have some extra time to chat to them properly. I know you love music… I thought you might enjoy their company. Also, you'd be doing me a huge favour. I could do with having another woman around. It's all men."

"Oh, really? You mean they're already here for your recording? The musicians? Oh yes, I'll pop over. Right away. Thanks for asking me, I really appreciate it. See you soon – which is your turning – is it first or second left after the lights…?"

The Producer was pleased with herself. She had done that rather neatly. If the Groupie had somehow got the impression that the World's Number One Composer was also going to be there, then that was her problem. And if that knowledge made her move like lightning at 10.45 pm for a twenty minute drive to the Producer's place, then that too was of her own choosing. That was the trouble with these bloody groupies – blindly and hopelessly in love and refusing to wake up and smell the coffee. The Producer refused to feel anything even vaguely amounting to a sense of guilt.

45
A GIANT LEAP

I hate afternoons. The sun is so hot – much too hot to go and play in the garden. If I stepped out even for five minutes I swear you could boil an egg on my head. I can't wait for tea-time. That's when it cools down a bit and I can go out again. The house also gets livelier then. The grown ups start getting up from their afternoon rest. Why do they have to sleep so much? I often hear them say Life is short, life is too short. So why the hell do they sleep it away? My mother refuses to be disturbed during her siesta. I have no one to talk to. How can I ever develop my wonderfully clever theories if I can't discuss them with anyone? Why couldn't my mother have had more children? There should be a law forbidding people from having only one child.

I can't even have imaginary friends now. I used to be able to conjure up imaginary friends just like that, but I don't know how to do it now. I've lost the technique I think. Somehow, I just know they aren't real any more and that's no fun. It's awful when you get to know things. Sometimes I think it's better not to know too much. I think I must be growing up. What can I play all by myself? Treasure hunt again? There's nothing more to find. Still, I could tackle that special small chest she keeps locked, and snarls if I so much as look at it. Yes, that can be my project for this afternoon. This thought has already cheered me up a bit. The reason for my current bout of depression is that Man, whoever he is, has just landed on the moon, and I'm worried sick about Mrs Mohanji's Moon God. Will he be all right? Right now, this very afternoon, they're supposed to be walking all over the moon. How discourteous! I thought one wasn't supposed to walk all over the gods.

I wonder where Mrs Mohanji is now? Will she know about the Moon Walk? What will she think? Can she see the moon from where she is? What about my sweets? I miss those days very much, when every new moon she performed various mysterious rituals and then gave me lots of Dolly Mixtures. Dolly Mixtures? Oh no! The very mention pumps saliva into my mouth and brings on a queasy feeling. Sometimes she also gave me shiny little crystals of sugar – "sakker" she called it, but my mother says it's called "nabaat" or "misri." My mother always has a different name for things. As soon as I learn some new word from the Mohanji's, she immediately contradicts me and calls it something entirely different. Well, never mind, I may as well tackle that locked chest now. It's the last unexplored thing in my house. I need a key. How many possible places where a key could be hidden? I know the way my mother's mind works. That's the advantage of being a daughter. Only a daughter can know how a mother's mind works. She always thinks she uses the unlikeliest hiding places, but I know better. I'll try her sewing box. Sure enough, big bunch of keys nestling amongst crochet hooks, buttons and reels of cotton. Keys of all shapes and sizes. One of these has to fit. I begin a systematic process of elimination – it takes forever. After all this effort, I hope it doesn't turn out to be anything too boring like jewellery or double-knitting wool. But no, my labours have not been in vain. This is most interesting. Photographs. Who are these people? A very nice looking woman all dressed up with ornaments in her hair in a formal pose for a brown-and-white photo. Hand under chin. Zillions of shiny bangles on her wrist. How nice. But who is she? She looks a little bit like my mother, but only a little bit. And letters. Faded ink. Curling, yellowing edges. I love reading, and I adore letters. But most of all I love reading other people's letters.

Wait! It isn't a letter. It's some kind of stripy pattern in the middle of the page. There are two lines of intricate squiggles, then a wide space, then another two lines of squiggles. It looks so pretty. Maybe it's a code. That would be fun. I love deciphering codes. Detectives have to do that all the time. But this looks too complicated, so let me just quickly copy out a short sample. It takes forever and my copy looks nothing like the original

People are beginning to stir. I quickly replace everything, pocketing my crudely copied sample of two lines. My Uncle is my only hope. He owes me. I've kept his secret about the physics lessons for the Widow, so he can jolly well help me for a change.

I find him in the front garden after tea. He's preparing to go to his tennis club. He's in a big rush as usual. He's yelling at a servant who hasn't yet finished polishing his yellow VW Beetle. I approach him with some trepidation, holding out my piece of paper.

"Is this some sort of code, Uncle?"

"Er... what? I don't know. It looks just like drunken spiders to me," he says impatiently.

"Don't you want to know where I got it? I just copied a bit of it from something that was flying around the back garden. Must've come out of the rubbish. What is it?"

"Oh, how do I know? Just some doodle or something." He's so utterly unimaginative! I'm going to have to make it exciting for him, somehow.

"It's not in English, is it?" I ask, as though coaxing a toddler with a well-known story.

He surprises me by pausing to take a serious look at it: "No, you're right. It certainly isn't English. Some parts of it could almost be Urdu."

"Urdu? How is Urdu written?"

"Don't bother me now. I'll show you one day when I have time. But not a word to your mother. She'll kill me if she finds out. You know you are only supposed to speak in English?" he cautions me on a basic law at home and at school.

"Oh, I won't speak in Urdu, I promise. I just want to know how it's written. Do they have A B C and that sort of thing?"

"Yes, of course. But it's not really my subject, you know."

He drives off aggressively in his VW Beetle, making crunching noises over the gravel. I'm left holding the piece of paper. I must copy the original in neater handwriting and then pester him to teach me the Urdu alphabet. Then I can work on deciphering this coded message secretly. This can be my new hobby for now. That should take care of a few empty afternoons. I must also listen in extra hard when the grown ups speak Urdu. It might help with my urgent, brand new, all-important-top-secret, decoding project.

The decoded message might lead to a special treasure buried in the garden. Or it might be some sort of secret about the Moon God. But how would I know? It's been three whole days since I'd raised the subject of the Urdu alphabet with my Uncle and nothing's happened yet. Every time I approach him, he shoos me away. But fate waves its magic wand and of all the unlikely people in the world, the slimy hilltop Maulana comes to my rescue. He's in our garden one day with a servant, taking some cuttings for the mosque garden. In sheer desperation I ask:

"Mr Maulana, is there an alphabet in Urdu?"

"Yes of course there is, baby."

"How can I learn it?"

"You want to learn to read Urdu? Really? No harm in it, I suppose. It can only help you with Arabic and then maybe then you'll learn to read the Quran instead of playing in the sun all afternoon. I'll teach you a little Urdu if you also promise to read the Quran. But first I must ask your mother's permission," he announces pompously.

Sometimes he can sound so utterly reasonable, but then he has to go and spoil it all by dragging my mother into it. I'm not quite sure just what he said to my mother, but her reaction truly amazes me. I had expected to be smacked for even bringing up the subject, but my mother, it seems, has just given her consent for me to learn to read the Quran. Wait, wait, no, I protest. I didn't want the Ko... I wanted Urdu.

The Maulana winks at me in friendly fashion. It's clear he's one my side and my mother is going to be hoodwinked into thinking I'm attending Quran lessons when in fact I'll be learning Urdu. I don't really care about Urdu. I just want to decipher the secret message.

My first lesson is thrilling. The Maulana writes out all the letters of this funny new alphabet using my coloured crayons. They all seem to point the wrong way. They're written from the wrong side, but I'm not allowed to use my left hand. Very confusing. But the letters are quite pretty, and I love the writing. I trace over the characters again and again. I give each letter of the alphabet a secret code of my own so I can remember which is which. I know that the one that looks like a breast with a nipple in the middle is an "n" sound. I like drawing that one. We're supposed to join up the letters when we make words. My favourite breast one no longer looks like a breast. It's quite different now. It gets an "au" sound joined onto it. And the whole word spells the number nine. Nau. Eureka! I recognise my very first word from the secret coded document hidden in the chest. There's a word nine in it somewhere! How exciting – just one small word out of millions of words, but a giant leap for a little girl.

The Maulana has presumably reported my success to my mother: "See, you can learn quite fast when you put your mind to it, see?" she points out unnecessarily. How could she know I had an important and urgent code to break?

"If only you did the same for maths you'd be brilliant! See, your brain isn't that bad at all." My mother specialises in stating the obvious. "You're just lazy when you're not interested in something. Maths is important, believe me."

The number nine. Nau. Whatever that coded message is, the number nine figures in it somewhere. Determination can move mountains, and while curiosity may have killed many cats, it nevertheless transforms my arduous task of deciphering this difficult language into one of the most exciting, spell binding experiences of my early life.

In time, I had a whole line figured out. But that was only the second line in the two-line pattern. And it didn't yet make sense. I would have to work on the other line, and soon, I would have to open the chest again and copy out the rest of the lines. This shouldn't be too difficult. I'm more familiar with the shapes now, and I even know the meanings of most of the small words.

But the next time I launch "operation chest", as I now think of it, that piece of paper has disappeared! Oh no! I'm just left with two lines, the same two lines that I'd painstakingly copied out as a rather bad drawing one hot afternoon.

And all because I was depressed about Man strutting about on my Moon God. I decided this cryptic message had come from the Moon God himself. This was perhaps his way of telling me what he felt about Man walking all over him. I linked the two things in my mind and it became even more vital that I should decipher this message as fast as possible.

Years later I learnt that this sort of linkage was called synchronicity. Two apparently unrelated occurrences become part and parcel of the same process. Man lands on the Moon, and the Moon God sends me a message... in Urdu!

46
IN DEFENCE OF MUNGU

I think I mentioned my mother's special bubble-bursting technique. She did it that time when she heartlessly informed me that we lived in the World, and now she's done it again. Does she realise that her so-called truths are destroying me? Just as I'm at the height of my faith in the Moon God, and I'm convinced He exists and even sends me coded messages, she suddenly drops a bolt of lightning:

"We are Muslim, baby-jaan. Leave all these different gods alone...."

"But I don't have different gods," I protest. "Just the One... I believe in the One and Only Moon God. Mrs Mohanji's Moon God. The Moon is just One."

"Nonsense!" she smirks.

It's just not fair. My faith is only just beginning to comfort me against the atrocities in the big bad World, and she has to go and ruin it.

"Why can't I have the Moon God?" I ask defiantly.

"Because there's no such thing! Nobody lives on the moon. It's just a lump of rock. Didn't I let you stay up and watch Neil Armstrong and Apollo 11 and all that?"

"Yes, but just because they went there... it doesn't mean they really went there... it's like a film. It was on TV wasn't it? So it's a film! You're the one who always says films aren't real. Those were actors, pretending to do a trip to the moon... weren't they?"

I like this line of reasoning. I've just thought of it. If it wasn't a film, then why was it in black-and-white? Only films are in black-and-white. Real life is always in colour. Yes, that's it! If it had been real, it would surely have been in colour....

But suddenly, I'm not so sure. It's all too confusing. I want life to be simple again. I want my Moon God back.

"Baby, listen. There is just one God. He is bigger than the moon, so how can he live on it? He made everything, moon, stars, the world... everything. Just believe in Him and know that everything is from Him."

She's trying to pacify me. Perhaps she is afraid I'll give up the whole idea of God. I sense I have the upper hand – a temporary advantage.

"No mummy, no, you just believe in your one Big God and I'll believe in my Moon God. And they can both be friends. Yours may be bigger and stronger, but my God understands about children, and that's all I need at the moment. Maybe I'll switch gods when I grow up, but not now. One is allowed to change, isn't one?"

"How could I have given birth to this kaafir heathen?" she moans at my Uncle later that evening. He doesn't look up from his marking, but mutters something like, "Oh, let her believe whatever she wants... it's good to have faith, in whatever...."

"No, no I disagree completely! Children should be put straight about these things right from the start. I can't have her thinking this superstitious nonsense. It's bound to effect her whole development." She is shouting at my Uncle.

"So why didn't you teach her about Islam from the beginning? What is she supposed to do? You hang around temples and listen to bhajjans and then expect your daughter to believe in nothing but Islam," he retorts, looking up from his marking.

I'm thrilled. A real fight! They're fighting because of me. I'm out of it now. They'll just argue with each other and I'll listen in. I love listening in to grown up arguments. That's how I learn big words.

My mother doesn't like being attacked on her temple policy: "Don't be so cruel. How much can I do? I work. I earn my own living. I've raised her on my own – she's a handful as it is. Just keeping after her to do her school work is bad enough – how could I have started on religion as well? And then she hangs around that squalid shop all the time, and she picks up their ways and their beliefs. How can I stop her?"

"I wasn't getting at you my dear. Quite the opposite. You've set her a very good example by going to temples and feeding priests out of your special vegetarian kitchen and all that. It shows tolerance for other faiths. That's the way it should be. She'll be fine. Stop worrying. But you can't be all liberal, half-this half-that yourself, and then expect your daughter to be nothing but a scarfed-up Mehrunissa Muslim. What an absurd notion! And since when were you a practising Muslim? Why are you making such a big deal out of it? It's absurd."

That's the longest speech my Uncle's ever made in recent memory, and it's all because of me. But my mother refuses to buckle down:

"Everything is absurd to you because you have no faith... you don't understand...."

"I understand perfectly. And I'm glad I'm out of it." He adds in superior fashion: "It's all nonsense. Invented by man for man. If she is making her own gods then let her... in time, I'm sure her allegiances will shift from god to god, and then one day she'll realise the truth."

No, no, no, Uncle please, no! No more truths! Every time there's a truth then everything thing else becomes a lie. Everything gets blown to smithereens. Please let me delude myself. Leave me alone with my illusions. Please let me find my own unique combination of myth and God. I know what I want, I know who I like – I like Moses... well Charlton Heston actually, but most of all I like my Moon God. And what's more, I've nicknamed him "Mungu."

47
RAAGS & RHYTHM

The Producer, Ustad and PA-Ronnie have made themselves comfortable at Producer's flat. The Ustad's special tea has been prepared and served expertly by PA, complete with broad grin and over-fussy attitude, tea-towel tucked in his waist-band. The Producer is pleased with herself. She has succeeded in conning the Groupie to join them later, having conveyed the impression that the World's Number One Composer is also part of this intimate late night tea party. The Producer puts on a disc of thumris with an expression that implies thumris are really a bit too light for her, but she is afraid of alienating the musically uncultured PA. She thinks she has reached the perfect compromise – light enough for the classically uninitiated, yet tasteful enough for Big Maestro Ustad, direct decsendant and grandson of the Lighter Upper of the Universe.

PA: (*eagerly, on listening to first strains of thumri*) Oooh! I'd just love to get into Indian classical music properly.

USTAD: (*pontificates*) Nobody can get into it – you can't find it. It finds you. You've got the right kind of spirit – that spark, you know? One day it's sure to find you. It's probably found you already. You just haven't allowed it to manifest in your nature.

PA: (*All agog with new-found knowledge of having been discovered by music!*) Oooh! How do I do that? How do I allow it to manifest....?

USTAD: Sohbat – sohbat is important. The company you keep. You should always hang around with the right people. Hang on to their every word. Avoid uncultured people. Tolerate them, but don't let them eat up large amounts of your time. Always stay near people who inspire you, people who can teach you things.

PA: But I always feel quite inspired after a gossipy session with my close friends.

USTAD: There's nothing wrong with gossip. It has to be the right kind of gossip.

PRODUCER: (*refusing to take any of this seriously, but joining in the fun anyway*) What's the right kind of gossip?

USTAD: You know what I mean. One should always talk about things that matter.

PRODUCER: Matter to whom?

USTAD: (*getting irritated with her*) This is outrageous! It's impossible to instruct you practical-thinking western-types. Why must you always rationalise everything? Why dissect every statement? Why can't you simply accept what I say?

PA: (*Hastily, anxious to avoid a row and more than a little anxious to pick up some wisdom from the Ustad*) Please, Ustad-ji, I'd like to know more about music and how it has found me. When do I get it?

USTAD: Yes, music. Now music is a truly amazing phenomenon. People think they've got music. But nobody's really got it. It doesn't belong to anyone – it's just there – it's in the ether. All that the musician has to do is to catch it, and convey it to those who cannot catch it for themselves.

PRODUCER: (*impressed*) That's rather neat. I like the way you put that.

PA: Please go on Ustad-ji....

(*He's eager for more knowledge but the conversation is interrupted by the sound of the doorbell. Producer gets up eagerly, thrilled by the prospect of the look on Groupie's face, when Groupie realises that the Composer is not present. The Groupie rushes in with a big hug and kiss for the Producer, wafting Giorgio all over the small, smoke-filled flat. She is dressed as if for a very special occasion. The Producer looks impressed. How has this woman managed to tart up in what can't have been more than 15 minutes?*

The Groupie enters the small living room eagerly, and it dawns on her she's been duped by the cunning, scheming Producer. Her disappointment is blatantly obvious to all present):

GROUPIE: (*casually, carefree manner*) Isn't the World's Number One Composer here yet?

PRODUCER: (*more than a little eager to enlighten her*) Oh no... he'll probably fly in just as we're doing sound checks on Wednesday.

(*The Groupie feels trapped. There's nothing she can do, and having often referred to herself as a music lover, and always having pretended to have been a genuine fan of the Ustad rather than of his younger accompanists, she forces an enthusiastic greeting towards him. He is clearly delighted. How nice of her to have come out so late at night, just to pay her respects to him. What a nice girl. Always came to concerts as well. And always appeared backstage to pay homage. A really valuable ally*).

USTAD: (*assuming the role of host*) Please sit down. Sit near me. I was just instructing our young friend here on the basic mysteries of music.

GROUPIE: (*With forced interest in her voice*) Oh, how very interesting....

USTAD: (*Turning to PA*) Now, see young man. See this beautiful woman who knows all about it. It found her, you know. Years ago, she came under its spell. And she's been addicted ever since.

PRODUCER: Music – he means music, of course. (*Clearly prepared to be charitable to Groupie, having dealt her such a devastating blow, and now quite pleased that she was here to divert the Ustad's attention, leaving her own brain-space free for worrying about the finer details of her Courtesan script. Everyone knows the Groupie's real addiction is musicians, not music.*)

GROUPIE: Oh, I just love music, it's all I need to survive. I could go without food for days, but not without music.

PRODUCER: (*meaningfully*) Yes, quite....

USTAD: (*with the air of one making a final winding up statement in a debate*) I could never go without food. Astakhfirullah! You should never say that. Food and music are not substitutes for each other. You devalue them both by putting them alongside one another like that. Each is necessary. Food for the body, music for the soul.

GROUPIE: (*smugly*) My soul is obviously more demanding than my body.

(*The Producer raises her eyes heavenwards, then quickly resumes her mind games with her cherished courtesan script*).

PA: (*Pleadingly, and keen to pursue knowledge*) Ustad-ji please sing for us. Can you please explain all the different things to me – what is a raag exactly? After all, it's the same seven notes in music – I know that much – so how does it all become so different?

(*The Ustad loves this sort of question. It gives him a perfect opportunity to hold court for hours on end*).

USTAD: (*in the manner of a lecturer*) You're right, my boy, – it's the same seven notes – the same alphabet. But different musical traditions employ different vocabularies. Then on top of that there are different ways of playing the same set of notes – different styles. A raag is very simply just a melodic framework – a sort of scale, strictly defined. The same selected notes are then improvised in different ways. The skill of a real musician is tested on his ability to improvise in original and interesting ways – but without ever venturing outside of the confines of the melodic structure... the raag....

PA: (*looking enlightened and impressed*) Oh, I see. How interesting. I never knew that. Please sing me a line of a raag.

USTAD: Here you are, here's a Bhairavi for you. (*He recites a short excerpt, ascending and descending notes, flawlessly demonstrating the essence of that famous raag.*)

PA: Oooh! That's lovely, it reminds me of a song from an Indian film.

USTAD: (*waving his hand dismissively at the mention of the film, and resuming lecture*) Look, you must remember this: film music, even when it's classically based, is usually a very watered-down version of the original thing. It's quite good as a first introduction, but you must listen to the real thing to gain a true understanding of our music.

PA: I've tried to. She (*pointing to the Producer*) has even dragged me off to a concert once or twice. But I find it takes so long to get started. I start to fall asleep. I wake up a bit when the tabla comes in and it starts to become more tuneful, then it goes all haywire again. It would be so much easier if they had words.

USTAD: (*really enjoying himself now*) You must understand that it is rigidly structured. When you say it's slow to take off, what you must realise is that the beginning of a raag – it's exploration phase – the "Alaap" – is the most important thing.

PRODUCER: (*eagerly jumping in to unnecessarily clarify the Ustad's point*) Oh yes, the "Alaap" is the same as foreplay in sex. If you didn't bother with foreplay and went straight for an orgasm, it would still happen, but it wouldn't be as satisfying. You need to get into the mood slowly... anticipation, you know...?

(*The Ustad looks shocked. He's not used to discussing sex in this kind of detached way with women. But he decides she had really drawn a very valid comparison. The more he thought about it, the more he liked it. Why hadn't he thought of that?*)

USTAD: (*Daringly, and determined to prove he is broad-minded*) Yes, you are absolutely right. That is exactly what the musician is doing. He's getting you into the mood. He's creating an atmosphere. He's exploring the notes, little by little – bringing in new notes, developing earlier ones. It is the equivalent of a very first sexual advance.

(*Groupie sits quietly. She's uneasy. She, more than anyone else in the room, appreciates the similarities between music and sex. Just like Producer to bring it up in that cold, detached matter-of-fact way, when she had hugged it to herself like her own special secret for years. She doesn't like sex entering into the conversation – she suspects another trap.*)

GROUPIE: I can't stay too late. I must leave after this coffee. I'm expecting a call. I only popped in for half an hour.

USTAD: (*clearly dismayed, and afraid of a shrinking audience*) Oh no! You can't possibly leave now that we're really getting into it. Make your call from here. Tell who ever it is to call you here. Come on, sit!

GROUPIE: (*helplessly*) Oh... OK, just another ten minutes, perhaps.

(*She's furious. Everybody has always used her. She doesn't mind being used by men – she needs that, at least she sometimes gets something in return, but what could the Producer ever give her? But she decides it's necessary to remain close to the woman now, just for advance information on the Composer's comings and goings.*)

USTAD: Now, what was I saying? It's very much like sex, but that's not all. That's just one obvious comparison. It's much beyond that. It's about feeling – you have to feel it. Don't just hear it – don't just listen to it – feel it. Don't listen with your ears, listen with your heart. Don't try to analyse it – just let it wash over you – go with it. See where it takes you....

PRODUCER: Just like sex! (*Butting in, refusing to give up the sex theme.*)

PA: (*Seriously*) So what happens after the Alaap? (*He's determined to pursue his education at the knees of the world famous Ustad.*)

USTAD: Well there is different terminology for instruments and voice, but basically, you start a mid-tempo, rhythmic section. The melody begins to take shape. The form starts to emerge.

PRODUCER: Heavy petting. (*She says, helpfully.*) Things start to hot up. You could even have penetration with slow thrusting in this section... or should that only happen when the tabla comes in?

(*She says all this in English only, for the PA's benefit and out of fear of offending the Ustad with too much sex talk. The PA giggles.*)

USTAD: What, tell me what's going on?

GROUPIE: (*Obligingly*) Oh, she's pursuing the sex theme again.

USTAD: Oh, very good! To what stage do you compare the medium tempo? ...(*fits of giggles from PA and Producer*) ...No, no, I'd like to know, really. I like your theory. Don't be embarrassed. I'm a man of the world. I'd like to know which stage we've got to....

PRODUCER: (*haltingly in Urdu, attempting to avoid any blunt references*): Well, you know, things begin to take shape. They progress – move forward, start getting into some kind of rhythm...."

USTAD: (*Triumphantly*) No, wrong! Completely wrong! THIS is the real foreplay – the mid-tempo. The "Alaap" was merely the wooing – and touching. At that stage they still had their clothes on. Now they've taken their clothes off and things are getting underway. You see, I DO know what you're talking about. I'm very modern!

GROUPIE: I think this is silly. (*clearly embarrassed*) One could compare a raag structure to so many different things....

PRODUCER: Like what?

GROUPIE: Oh you know – like reading a book: Introduction, Conclusion, all that sort of thing.

PRODUCER: Oh yes! Prologues and epilogues. For me the epilogue is usually a cigarette.

(*They all laugh out loud at this bit of personal self-revelation, and the Ustad grows surprisingly animated, forgetting his usual dignified image.*)

USTAD: It's better for you than drinking water. You should never drink water straight after. It gives you stiff joints in later life. My grandfather used to say that. I always have some sweets by my bedside.

PA: I always have condoms by my bedside. (*Determined to reveal something about himself too. Thankfully, he doesn't go on to reveal his preference for members of his own sex.*)

USTAD: Condoms are a disgrace to mankind – like firing blanks – what's the point?

PRODUCER: (*turning to Groupie sweetly*) What about you? What do you like straight after?

GROUPIE: (*giggling and blushing*) I really must go now. Thanks for the coffee. When's your recording, Wednesday, did you say?

PRODUCER: Yes.

GROUPIE: Can I come and watch? I love being at recordings.

PRODUCER: Well, I'm not sure. You'll find it very boring. And we'll all be so flustered.

(*She definitely doesn't want Groupie around. It would put Composer in a super-evasive mood. He'd keep disappearing to avoid Groupie, and then SHE would never be able to find him either.*)

GROUPIE: Oh, I don't mind. It's fun. What exactly are you recording?

PRODUCER: Oh just some sitar solos and a couple of orchestral pieces for in between....

GROUPIE: I'd like to be there. Which studio is it?

(*Producer and PA exchange helpless looks. Producer finally mumbles the name of a studio in North London, quite close to Groupie's large mansion.*)

GROUPIE: (*Excitedly*) Oh great! Come and have lunch afterwards.

PRODUCER: (*Icily*) We'll probably work right through lunch.

GROUPIE: (*Persistently*) Do you want me to bring a packed lunch for all of you? How many will you be?

PRODUCER: (*feeling really trapped*) It's so sweet of you, but I don't want to put you to any trouble. We'll manage with sandwiches. Really, don't worry.

GROUPIE: (*indignantly*) You can't feed this Great Ustad sandwiches! No, I'll bring some proper food in a large tiffin carrier. Do you like paratthas Ustad-ji?

This woman was impossible! It was one thing to have given her the wrong studio, but even Producer's heartless nature could not withstand the thought of the poor wretched woman turning up with a hot lunch at the wrong studio. That would have been downright mean. While she hesitates for words, the Ustad has already decided. If it was a contest between English sandwiches and proper home-cooked paratthas, no prizes for guessing which way the Ustad's vote would go!

USTAD: (*affectionately to the Groupie*) Oh yes! That's wonderful. Just like India! I always have my food sent from home if I'm in a studio. That's what I like about you. You've lived here for so many years, but you maintain our ways and our traditions. You're from Ceylon aren't you? Same culture as India. It's most kind of you. May you live a hundred years! Your delicious food would be most welcome.

PRODUCER: (*suppressing an uncontrollable urge to add weed-killer to the Ustad's tea – but not before the recording is safely in the can.*) Well, ring me first just to confirm the studio. Sometimes these things change you know....

The Producer wants to keep her options open. Part of her feels really irritated with the absent Composer. Why couldn't he fend for himself? Why did she always have to help him to avoid Groupie?

To hell with it! She decided she would allow Groupie, complete with tiffin carrier, to attend her recording session. Sod the Composer and his Groupie-avoidance tactics!

****

The Groupie drove back home with mixed feelings. Within moments of entering the Producer's flat she realised she'd been duped. And as she continued to sit in the Producer's smoke-filled flat listening to all their senseless rude talk of foreplay and Alaaps, her disappointment grew more intense. If only the Composer had been there too. Then the others could talk about sex to their heart's content, and she would just exchange meaningful glances with him.

He had, once or twice, made mad passionate love to her. The memory still brought a smile to her face. So what if it hadn't happened since? The fact that it had happened at all was something for which to be eternally grateful. How many women in this world could boast of even one night of passion with the man of their dreams? For many, it only remained a dream. For her, the dream had turned into reality, once, then twice... and there was always hope it might happen again....

She cheered up a bit and started planning the menu for next Wednesday's portable lunch.

48
INSPIRED BY A DISHWASHER

"Hello?"

"Hi, Ash it's me. How you doing? Long time no speak?" Sonia sounded light and carefree. Ash felt his heart tighten in sheer resentment. He too would have to appear creative and fulfilled.

"How ARE you Ashy-Pashy?" she asked again.

"Not bad. I worked quite well today, but I'm slightly stuck on a script...."

"Not again! Which one...?"

"A brand new one... this one just started coming by itself, thanks to your Zarine woman, perhaps. I don't see a direct connection but somehow... it's just flowing."

"So what's the problem? Why are you stuck then?" Sonia challenged.

"Not stuck stuck, just a bit delayed let's say. I find myself feeling very sorry for one of my characters. I mean, I created her, but now she's so real, every time I write about her, I start crying. I think I've really fallen for her badly... what should I do?"

"Oh don't be so silly! You can't fall in love with one of your own characters... come on man, cheer up. She's not real."

"She's real to me... I just wish I could meet someone like her. And she's such a good cook. That's just what I need, a sexy mother-figure to cook for me...."

"Oh you poor sod... OK, I can take a hint. I'm really busy tomorrow, but do you fancy a late supper? Come over and I'll cook you something...."

"No, no... that's not what I meant... thanks anyway... I'm in love... I couldn't really eat anything...."

"Oh my poor Ash-with-a-pash! You need to meet someone real. I've got this really nice Ghanaian friend... I think I should introduce you... get away from your computer for a bit... meet real women...."

"Can I tell you about my new script?"

"No, no, don't! You mustn't talk too much when you're writing – takes the steam out of things. Makes you tired. In fact you should only talk to me about things that are causing a problem or blockage. Don't give away something if you're happy with it. What's the point? Why tell me?"

"Don't you want to know?"

"No... I mean yes... but all in good time. When you've got something completed then I'll read it properly, OK? Don't give me too much now. When do you think you'll finish?" She tried her best to sound enthusiastic knowing fully well that Ash never ever finished anything.

"Oh, I don't know. At this rate it could go on forever...."

Yes, thought Sonia. I know you can go on forever... we've all been there before. You base every single one of your characters on the little snippets of gossip I give you freely. All your characters are my people. Weird people I've encountered and I've cultivated. And then I've generously told you all about them. And the next thing I know, they're sitting in some unfinished film script... oh Ash! When will you learn? Why the hell don't you ever get out and do your own research? Do you really think I don't recognise my own pompous, opinionated views of those people who have inspired your fictitious characters? Do you really think fiction is really only about thinly disguised fact? Oh come on, Ash! Write something of your own – something that comes from deep down inside you. Why annex my reality into your fiction?

But of one thing, Sonia was particularly glad. She had never ever given him the slightest bit of information about her own ex-husband's weird and wonderful background... not an iota of information. Here was a story that clearly proved that fact was indeed stranger than fiction. You couldn't make it up if you tried. That was a story she was saving for herself. Not that she would sink so low as to write fiction, but because she wanted to use that model as a case-history in one of her future books on cultural hybridity and racism in British colonial East Africa....

"Listen Ash. Can you do me a huge favour? The dishwasher's fucked up again... and...."

"You want me to come over and wash up for you?" he asked helpfully.

"No! How can you even think that? Listen, I've booked a plumber for Wednesday next – it's the only day I could get him before Christmas. Please, would you mind bringing your work here? I can't be here you see... there's something I can't get out of...."

"It's really difficult... I don't know. Unless I'm in my own room, on my own computer, I can never...."

"Oh, come on Ash! You have a laptop don't you? And let me tell you something else. Sometimes, being in a different place can do wonders, believe me. Who knows what fresh inspiration might come from being in my place... you never know...."

Yes, you never know!

49
BALD HEADS AND BEARDS

How dare he? How dare he call my hero "Mozis-Shozis"? The Temple Priest and Mr Mohanji's personal Guru can be so heartless. And on top of all that he is bald as well. I'm afraid of bald-headed men. Maybe I should just turn back and run....

I thought holy people had to be all sweet and gentle with a twinkle in the eyes. Like paintings of Jesus. But not so this Guru. He thinks little children should not be too interested in God. It was dangerous. It meant they were thinking too much. And this was no age to think. This was the age to be unquestioningly obedient to your parents and to protect them from shame and disgrace.

I resolved there and then to leave the Guru well alone from now on and instead, try asking my question to the Maulana in the hilltop mosque. He had been extremely helpful in teaching me the Urdu alphabet, even though he'd done that hoping he could then have the pleasure of teaching me the Quran. He's always going on about the Quran being the only book one needs to read, but who knows, he might know something about the Moon God as well? But I can't risk it. He can be just as frightening as the Temple Guru, in fact more so, because he has a beard. And I'm even more frightened of beards than I am of bald-heads.

I don't understand this fear. Why does an absence of hair on the head petrify me, yet an abundance of hair on the face and chin make me want to shit in my pants? But the Maulana's beard wasn't the only reason I was scared of him. He was inclined to touch me more than necessary. I didn't like being touched like that. Once, I complained about it to my mother and when she promptly took it up with him, he informed her that her spoilt daughter was possessed with an evil spirit and that an exorcism was in order for which he would charge only twenty-five shillings. My Urdu alphabet lessons came to an abrupt end after that episode.

No, I couldn't go back there. Not on my own, no way! I felt hopelessly lost between a lusty Maulana and a spooky Guru, and in my state of hopeless despair would've turned and run there and then, had it not been for a honey-coated, soft, silky voice gently reaching out to me....

I recognised the face of the special singer who was visiting from India, the man who had just been singing those beautiful temple songs that always made my mother feel superior to everyone else.

It all began because my mother said shut up for a bit and you might hear God. I kept very quiet, but God said nothing. So I went to ask the Guru, but when he said rude things about my Moses from the Ten Condiments, I was about to turn and run when the singer's voice held me spellbound:

"Come here, come here little girl. What's your name?"

"They call me The Brat – I have a real name but nobody uses it... will you be able to answer my question...?"

I didn't like the way the Guru was glaring at me, but in the singer's reassuring presence, my courage won hands down over any imagined fear of His Bald Holiness the Spook. The singer's face was so kind and soft. There was a glow of light just in the middle of his forehead. I'd heard people say he was about thirty, but to me he looked exactly my age. How could he be thirty? Thirty was very old, surely? Old people were thirty and forty and things like that. No, to me he looked exactly eight years and some months, just like me.

The singer turned to the temple spook: "Guru-ji, I beg your pardon, but children should not be discouraged from asking vital questions. Try to answer her. It is good to see a child so young already so interested in God. If they're turned away at this early stage, they may never ever return...."

He spoke in Gujarati, and I understood every word. He obviously didn't think I could understand Gujarati otherwise he would never have dared contradict His Bald Holiness in that candid fashion in the presence of a minor.

"Arr-re Kanhaiyya, you don't know her. Question-shwestion nothing. She just likes hanging around where she's not wanted. She's not even from amongst us. They are Muslims. Her mother likes listening to bhajjans, so they come here, and I never stop them. This is God's house after all, and everyone is welcome. And then the Muslims in our town are so reasonable, completely in line with our Panchayat. The town Maulana is an excellent fellow – most spiritual – always agrees with our Morality Committee rules. We're all Indians you know, same culture, bhai-bhai, we can all get on."

Kanhayya the Singer looked taken aback. "Is it true?" He spoke to me in English. "Is your family Muslim?" he quizzed.

"So what?" I felt trapped. I hadn't foreseen this obstacle. Families are too tedious. Just because they are of some religion or the other, you have to be that too. I embarked on my well thought-out line of argument:

"Just because my mother is a Muslim, doesn't mean I am – nobody asked me if I wanted to be a Muslim. Anyway, it doesn't count because I have a special God of my own, but you might know him because he was Mrs Mohanji's God as well. He lives in the moon. Do you know how to make him talk?"

The Singer squatted down and looked into my eyes. His whole face smiled, but he said nothing. I stood spellbound by his beauty. How could a man be so beautiful? He placed his right hand on my head, and he might have been about to speak, but there was this uncomfortably familiar panicky voice, gradually getting closer, and with it, a clear whiff of Chanel No. 5... oh no!

"Oh you silly girl! There you are! I've been looking for you everywhere!"

My mother has a habit of materialising out of thin air when she is least wanted.

"Why are you bothering these nice gentleman...? Then she ignores me completely and gushes forth to Kanhaiyya about his singing – what was that word... and what was that other line... and is that the same as...? She's using long big Indian names and Hindi words to impress Kanhayya Lal. She'll never stop at this rate, and then he'll be gone. Back to India. And I'll never get my question in... my whole life has been a series of unasked questions and unsolved puzzles.

"Mummy, please... I need to ask the singer something...." I try in vain.

I have been told on numerous occasions to not interrupt grown-up conversations, but for once I feel I have the right. My need is really urgent. This singer person at least looked like he'd taken my question seriously, and I love the light shining on his forehead. He was my only hope in a big world of unanswered questions.

I have to see him again. I must find a way of seeing him again. My mother ignores my pleas and goes on talking to him....

"Yes... yes, of course. When? When are you leaving...? Not for a while...? Oh, in that case please come to dinner. I assure you I run a fully separate vegetarian kitchen, ask Guru-ji. He has come to lunch many times. I am the only Muslim woman who is allowed to cook for high-caste Hindus. Even my cook isn't allowed into the kitchen that day. I do everything myself. All the pots and pans and spoons are separate for pure vegetarian food, believe me...."

I'm thrilled. I hope he accepts. My mother is obviously keen to sit him down to sing just for her, but at least I'll get another chance to ask him my question properly. I'm sure he knows something about my Moon God. All that remains to be done now is to cautiously work out some elaborate strategy to aid my negotiations about being allowed to stay up for the dinner and song event. I know I'll manage it somehow. The Moon God may not talk to me but somehow He always arranges things in my favour these days. Meanwhile, I'd better be on my best behaviour.

50
SAFARI

People whiz around at an alarming rate these days. Vast distances are undertaken and covered with the same ease as popping out to the corner shop to get a newspaper. I was in Beijing last week you know? I'm off to Canada at the weekend. Back next week. Then I have a three-day seminar in Venice. Then onto Delhi for a documentary film festival, and I'm back on Friday for the Stockholm weekend....

It can't be good for you. There was a time when a journey was an event, a major episode in one's life. Weeks of preparation, followed by days of stomach-butterflies and sleepless nights on the final countdown.

And in those days each place looked so different. Even going from the Small Town to the Big Town in Pearl was a massive adventure. Everything was different. Different food. Different shops. Different colour street lights. New traffic signs. And if you were going to the big neighbouring country? Well, then, that was the trip of a lifetime! That's when foreign countries were really foreign and when travel broadened the mind. Nothing particularly mind broadening these days. The same high street names everywhere. The same credit card signs and the same Italian food from Alaska to Turkmenistan.

Pearl was different. Even the shortest trip in Pearl was a major event. It was called a safari – travel in the old-fashioned sense of the world.

Friends would cook all kinds of delicacies for your five-tiered tiffin carrier. Dry home-made snacks for the road, or train. Special bottles for carrying drinking water. Bedding. Blankets. A small saucepan for heating the baby's milk. A camping stove. Thermos flasks of tea. As a nerve-jangler, packing for a safari was second only to moving house.

It was an established tradition in Pearl that as soon as the intent to visit friends or relatives in another town was announced, friends and neighbours rallied around the would-be travellers and began fussing. Those not lucky enough to take such trips for themselves, thrived on the excitement generated by other people's travel preparations.

When? Where? How? These were essential questions. Tattered maps were found and laid out and studied by all and sundry. Was that the best route?

Shouldn't they be going past that village, rather than cutting directly across to...? No, but Mrs Patel said she heard they were trying that other road because there's a nice farm on the way. But then they're missing the best scenery in the eastern province. Such a shame. Should we go and tell them? Yes, let's. And so it transpired that while you were in a complete panic, gathering up goods and chattels for early packing – for everyone always packed at least a month in advance – small groups of well-meaning people would turn up at your already chaotic, half-packed-house to offer advice on the best route. Or to offer to loan you their extra blankets – or to just sit around and chat while you panicked, packing lists in hand. They came for the buzz factor, and it would've been mean to not let them share in your pre-travel nerves.

Then the luncheons and dinners began in the final week before departure. If you were travelling in a week's time, then you couldn't be expected to have decent meals at home. Everything would've been packed away. It wasn't done to leave boxes full of food supplies behind – the servants were sure to steal while you were away. So everything was locked up and the last week was spent going from house to house, lunch here, dinner there.

The lunches and dinners were vital occasions on which to bid the travellers goodbye properly, and even for a two-week trip, good-byes were said as though they were the last farewell. Who was to say they would come back safely? Best to be prepared. Apologies were made tearfully and past mistakes – real or imagined – were dramatically forgiven in the spirit of pretended assumption that the next meeting would take place in God's house, somewhere up there.... The return of travellers was an even more exciting affair. The lunches and dinners continued. Of course, they'd only just got back home, so the kitchen wouldn't be fully operational just yet. Newly returned travellers continued to lunch and dine at the houses of their friends.

Again, these lunch and dinner gatherings provided a perfect platform for the most vital Pearlite ritual: to glean as much information as possible about everything that happened on the journey, every single little adventure, and a full account of the current situation in the place just visited. Even children were allowed to stay up and listen to the travellers' tales. It was said to broaden their minds.

Even the smallest, seemingly most insignificant journey was accorded the status of a round-the-world tour, so just try and imagine the consternation caused by Mrs Haq's announcement that she was going to London for a month! And that wasn't all. She was also taking Shireen, her sixteen-year old daughter, for a holiday.

Sixteen-year olds and sixty-year olds alike turned green with envy. To be able to visit London at such a young age! Some people have all the luck. She'll come back so smart, and so fair, and so marriageable. People were supposed to look fair-skinned when they came back from England. They were called "England-returned." Mrs Haq and her young daughter were, shortly, to be England-returned. A prestigious title for them, and a great honour for the small town. When they returned, everyone in the Small Town would be an expert on England, because their town would have someone who'd actually been there.

Only Mrs Henara stood slightly aloof from all the mania, but then she would, wouldn't she? Things had been tense between the two women, to say the least, ever since Mrs Henara had decided to take the Bhangi to the Haq party. And what's more, it was no big novelty for her. She had already been to England many times as a little girl, but nobody was supposed to know about that, so she couldn't brag about it. Splattered body on pavement and talk of drugs and pimps... and she hadn't forgotten how her mother always kept her as far away from herself as possible. A mother who didn't want you for the school holidays was not a mother one bragged about, even if it meant doing oneself out of the enhanced status that would come with being known as a well-seasoned traveller who was many times "England Returned." So she just stood aside and smiled in a condescending way at the others when they excitedly twittered away about Mrs Haq's forthcoming trip. It was the main topic of conversation everywhere you went. Even the aloof Mrs Henara had to acknowledge the upcoming event sometimes. Occasionally she made superior comments like, "Well, there's no question of blankets or cooking pots. You can't take those on a plane....

Plane? Aeroplane? They hadn't even thought about that! Everyone had been so excited about England and the prospect of having two England-returned females in their midst, they had completely forgotten that Mrs Haq and daughter were to travel by plane. Oh God! Better get those lunch invitations in quickly and say good-bye properly. Lesser chance of safe return if they're going by plane. Oh God, look after them please.

Air travel was still something of a rarity. It was extremely unusual to have someone within your own circle of friends who had actually flown.

In keeping with the town tradition, Mrs Henara also finally extended the usual come-to-lunch-or-dinner-or-both-invitation to the Haqs. It must be stressed that irrespective of the actual number of travellers, the entire family plus close relations had to be invited on such occasions. So she telephoned Mrs Haq and issued the invitation. Mrs Haq politely declined on the grounds that all their days, up to departure, were fully booked up.

"So kind, no thank you," Mrs Haq had said coldly, but Mrs Henara had taken that to mean: "No, I don't want to eat at the same table as a Bhangi – for all we know, he's probably moved in with you by now!"

Mrs Henara was enraged: So that's how she wants to play it. Fine. Don't think I don't know why she's going to England. I knew straightaway after that party. One look at the girl's face, and I knew everything! I can tell by the way they walk! Brilliant exam result, ha! What about that other result? The result of her doings with the Hindu boy? Disgusting! Muslim girl, Hindu boy – completely shameless! And of course she'll take the daughter on holiday – all the way to England, and do what has to be done. They can't take that risk here or in the Big Town. Doctors are the worst kind of gossip. I should know. I was married to one.

51
A SUITCASE ELOPES

I completely fail to see what all the fuss is about. OK, so they're going to England – whatever that is, wherever that is. Who cares? How can anyone in their right senses ever want to be anywhere else but Pearl? How could you once know this paradise and then consciously choose to visit some other place? Beats me. But then nothing that grown ups do ever makes any sense to me these days. Especially my mother. Bitching and bitching about Mrs Haq, and then inviting her to dinner – hoping she won't be able to come.

Three days to go to the Haq departure for England. Just two travellers, and forty-nine people preparing to see them off. They all want the novelty of waving to someone on a plane. I must admit I'd quite like to go and do that as well – something new to do, but I really refuse to feel excited for them. Imagine leaving Pearl for a whole month to go to England!

All kinds of things will be happening in Pearl and they'll miss them all. The crickets will be singing. The fireflies have special dances this time of the year. And there's another chilly-pounding day coming up. How can people not care about missing these things? I would be inconsolable if I ever had to leave Pearl even for a day – well how could I leave my Mohanji boys behind?

Just three days to go to the Haq departure and something mysterious is afoot. I've just been shooed away from the drawing room. My mother is in there, talking to the Haq daughter in hushed tones. The Haq daughter! She's never been here before. She is beautiful. And so clever. They had a big party when she passed her exams. I wasn't allowed to go. It was grown-ups and her friends only. My mother went I know, but every time I mention that party everybody looks the other way. I wonder why?

I'm going to position myself outside, at the drawing room window, and listen in. Wish they would speak louder.

They're talking in Urdu. Everybody thinks I don't understand Urdu. Wouldn't they just die if they knew I'd even learnt to read it!

The Haq daughter says she's going to leave her suitcase here in advance.

Tonight. And then my Ayah is to be given the evening off. And my mother is going to ask Mrs Haq for a special favour, to let the daughter baby-sit me. Hey, I don't need a baby sitter! I'm not a baby! But I'd best keep my mouth shut and listen hard....

So that's their plan! He's going to come for her in the night, at our house, and then they're going to run away together. My mother's feeling all holy and virtuous at the thought of uniting two lovers. But won't Mrs Haq just go mad with fury? Of course she will, but I know my mother. She'll just say – "I wasn't home. How was I to know what she was going to do?" And me? What about me? I have a dreadful feeling I'll get blamed for everything in some way. After all, she's pretending to be my baby-sitter. I'm sure I'll be dragged in... should I tell... blow her cover? Maybe not... then again, maybe I could just write a short anonymous note to Mr and Mrs Haq and warn mthem... but how to send it to their house? Should I telephone, disguise my voice, something like that...?

I had to do something. I couldn't just stand back and watch such wicked-ness, especially with me being used as a decoy. If they want to use me then they should ask my permission. Then maybe I would co-operate. I did a deal with myself. If my mother told me the truth about what was afoot, then I'd help her. If not, well... she leaves me no option....

My mother loves championing causes. Only yesterday she was bitching about Muslim girls and Hindu boys, and today she's helping this tearful Haq girl to make plans to run away with her Hindu boyfriend. I heard it all, every word, in Urdu:

"Oh aunty, I tell you, she just wants to take me to London for a diversion. It's a bribe. She thinks I'll forget him after a month in London. I can't live without him, I'll die, I promise I'll die. I'll kill myself. I'll throw myself from the plane...."

"Now, now, don't take on so. Look, I agree it's barbaric. Forcing girls in this day and age. Where do they think they are? Pakistan? You've come to the right place for help, my dear. Just don't worry at all. Everything will be OK. Just trust me."

My mother's enjoying being a woman with a cause.

"Stop whimpering! Now listen. I'll call your mother now, and I'll crawl to her for help. Urgent. Big Dinner Party at Europeans. Have to go. My brother also has to go. Ayah sick. Please, please send young Shireen to sit with my Brat...."

"What if she says no? What if she offers to come herself...?" the Haq daughter Shireen obviously doesn't know my mother, or she would have known that my mother has an answer for everything.

"Rubbish! Just three days before travelling to England? So much packing. How can she leave the house? She'll agree to send you. Her chance to make it up to me. She misses my friendship, I know. Just leave it to me, I'll sort it out. I hate to see young lovers separated. Everything will be just fine!"

No, mummy, no. It won't be OK. I'll tell. I'll tell everything. That'll teach you to shoo me away every time I try and develop a metaphor.

"Hello? Hello... is that Mrs Haq?" I finally plucked up courage for the vital phone call.

"Yes, speaking... who is that?" Mrs Haq squeaked.

"It's me...."

"Me who?"

"Me who knows something that you should know...."

"Yes, but who is it? What's your name? You sound just like a child, hello, hello?"

"She's going to run away. Don't let her go anywhere... please... I don't want to be involved. Then you'll all say it was my fault. It's not fair."

"Who is this? What are you talking about? Who is going to run away?"

I have to put the phone down. My mother has just entered the room.

"How many times have I told you not to use the phone without my permission? Who was that?"

"It was a call for me...."

"I didn't hear it ring... who was it, anyway?"

"My friend, younger Mohanji number nine...."

"I thought they weren't allowed to use the shop phone – I bet his father wasn't looking. Doesn't he keep it padlocked?"

"Yes, but they unlock it for important calls...."

"Was this important? What did he want?"

"Oh just to see if I was coming to play. Can't I go there tonight when you go to your dinner. I mean, can't I go and stay there instead of having a baby sitter here...?"

It was too late. Speech is a funny thing. It doesn't rewind. Once said, it's said.

"You want to go and stay there? What a joke! Where would you sleep? In their bathroom? They all sleep ten to a room as it is...." She laughs a cruel laugh. But I don't mind. I laugh with her, through sheer relief, because she's missed the boat.

No, I laughed too soon. My mother never misses boats:

"What did you say? When I go to dinner? What dinner? How do you know about any dinner? How do you know about a baby-sitter? What have you heard? Have you been listening at doors again? Tell me now!" She's yelling at me. She hasn't done that in a while. It had to happen sometime this week. It's long overdue.

My normal gumption deserts me in moments such as these. I just break down and cry and confess. And I pay a high price for the folly of owning up. Honesty is definitely not the best policy on such occasions. I'm locked in my room – every comfort provided, including two whole shiny pieces from the Black Magic chocolate tin she keeps hidden, but I'm still locked in. For her to actually give me chocolates it must be important! I'm told it's just for tonight. She promises me it won't happen again:

"Just one night, baby. I can't take any risks. This is very important. I can't have you messing anything up."

"But I won't mummy, I won't, I promise! Now I know what's going on, I'll help you, I promise. I won't mess it up. Please can I stay and watch them leaving?"

But the answer is a big NO and then I hear her turning the key on the outside. So that's what prison felt like. A locked room, and the rare sight of two whole pieces of chocolate. Now I knew.

Some hours later, I stand with my nose pressed to the window. It's dark outside. Luckily my bedroom window has a good view of the drive at the front of the house. I wonder when he'll come. Have they arranged a time? Will he be able to find our house? If she hadn't double-locked my windows I could have got out and hidden in the back of their car and run away with them. That would serve her right for imprisoning me.

I've just invented a new game called Prisoner. The baddies have locked me up and escape is impossible. But they're planning to overthrow the government and I know all about their plans. And according to the rules of my new game, sitting tight on sensitive information is much better than squealing. There are long term advantages to be gained from keeping my mouth shut. It's funny, but some things are more valuable when they're unsaid. I'm getting bored with this game. I'm sleepy.

I get into bed and fall asleep immediately. I'm woken up – I don't know how much later, by the sound of an engine. I jump out of bed and run to the window. But all I can see are flashing headlights. And somewhere in our house, I hear a door closing. Then the car drives away.

****

The atmosphere at the palatial Haq mansion on the following day was one very closely resembling that of a funeral. True to traditional Pearl ritual, on hearing about the death of someone, you dressed in white or black, depending on whether you were Hindu or Muslim, and at once went to their house to offer condolences. You didn't talk much, but you sat on the floor with all the others and wept when they wept. The men were in one large room, the women in another. In Pearl, communal grief rituals were even more important than inter-faith religious rituals.

Mrs Henara arrived and walked straight to Mrs Haq, Bhangi-Party tension momentarily forgotten, and gave her a big hug:

"Now, now, it's awful. I'm so sorry. Still, qismat, you know, what can you do? Children, these days... don't cry, perhaps it's for the best... think of all that dowry you've been saved, to say nothing of the expense of a real wedding...."

"What dowry? What are you saying?" Mrs Haq was hysterical. "She's taken all her jewellery... ALL, do you hear? That useless fellow will probably just sell it and then leave her, and she'll be back here, you just wait and see...." She broke down uncontrollably again.

Mrs Henara was really enjoying herself: "Now, now, what's the point in taking on so? Let them be – wish them all. I'm sure everything will work out in the end," she said with undisguised relish, while at the same thinking: Serves you right you hawk-faced Pakistani bitch! Saying all those foul things just because I happen to feel motherly towards poor Robert the Bhangi. Just because I treated him to an outing... you started to make out like he was my toy-boy! Serves you fucking well right. Moralise about me, and now see, your own goody-goody Muslim daughter has run away with a Hindu! Bully for her!

Mrs Haq had recovered from her hysteria, which had now given way to remorse and regret and the inevitable parental guilt that unfailingly follows such mishaps:

"Oh Mrs Henara, oh... Seema!" First names now, eh?

"If only, if only, I had let her go to your house and baby-sit, then none of this would have happened! Oh why was I so mean-minded? It's all my fault,

God is punishing me! You even asked for my help and I said NO! How could I? If only, if only… Oh forgive me, forgive me, my sister!" (Sisters now, eh?)

Poor portly little five-foot-nothing Mrs Haq! She honestly believed that if her daughter had been allowed to go and baby sit at the Henara's, then lover-boy would've never dared to turn up there. How was Mrs Haq to know that Lover Boy had indeed stopped off at the Henara's, just to pick up the previously deposited suitcase? That way, Shireen could safely slip away through the back door of her own house, minus any luggage. And if intercepted on her way out, she could just pretend she was in the kitchen for a snack. Mastermind Mrs Henara had worked out every detail.

Mrs Henara's part in the affair remained concealed. After all, she had only allowed a suitcase to be left at her place. And late at night, some unknown young man had come and picked up the suitcase. What was it to do with her? If Shireen ran away, she ran away from her own house, right under her mother's nose!

How could anyone hold Mrs Henara responsible?

Well, there was one person who knew that Mrs Henara was almost wholly responsible for the scheme. But nobody would've believed her. She was just a kid. But Mrs Henara knew that the Brat knew, and without saying as much, the Brat threatened to play this card every time the going got rough. But actually, things were getting pretty good these days. Remember that game about creating long-term advantages out of unsaid things?

Ever since that fateful night of the eloped suitcase, Mrs Henara had been exceptionally kind and gentle to her one and only child and had even most readily agreed to allow the Brat to stay up for the temple singer Kanhayya Lal's upcoming dinner and song event.

52
MOSQUITOES AND MASTERS

My mother has been in a tizz since early morning. She is preparing a special dinner for the temple singer, with her own hands. The kitchen is always out of bounds to me anyway, but today, nobody is allowed in, not even cook. My mother says everything has to be very pure and very clean.

"Why is the cook not pure and clean?" I ask in vain, knowing I won't get anything even remotely amounting to an answer.

"Doesn't she cook for us everyday, and we eat it, so why is that unclean? Why can't she cook for Kanhayya Lal as well?"

I'm shooed away as usual. Black hands cannot cook this kind of pure meal for a Brahman temple singer….

"But *you're* not Brahman," I protest lamely knowing fully well she's going to say, "But I'm Indian," meaning she's one up on Black. Being Indian, even Indian Muslim, meant being one degree better than Black – at least in the temple scheme of things.

She had a special bath, after which she went straight into the kitchen. She called it a purifying bath. If she was already Indian why did she need purifying? She usually has a bath in the evening, before going to bed. So why have another one now? Life is already too complicated – the capacity of human grown ups to make children miserable when there's already so much untold misery in World, never ceases to amaze me.

I could have sunk into another deep depression, as is my wont, had it not been for the joyful anticipation of the great Kanhayya Lal himself coming to our house this very evening. And what's more, I'm being allowed to stay up to hear him sing. On the whole, my mother has been jolly decent since the elopement of the suitcase. She's even agreed to my asking the singer a couple of questions, but "No mouthing off your own opinions – just ask respectfully, and then pay attention when he answers," I am briefed by her.

Later that day, my jaw drops towards my shoes as they all get out of various cars. Hey, what's this? It's not just going to be a quiet dinner and song and lots of questions from me. There's a whole entourage of people, including the Guru. My heart sinks. How can I ask anything with His Spooky Holiness the Bald right there, piercing me with his black eyes? Oh no! It's not fair.

My mother has changed into a white silk sari with a red border. I manage to grab her briefly before she steps out to greet the arrivals.

"So many people mummy, why?"

"Why not? It's a special occasion. It would be selfish to keep the singer all to myself. Other people like his songs too."

She's trying to make out like she's all noble and selfless, but what she wants is to appear more intelligent and more appreciative of the bhajjans and she couldn't do that unless there were other people present to whom she could feel superior. She has even invited Mohanji, who, given the devotional nature of the proceedings, has made an exception to his life-long rule of not socialising with the European area snooties.

My mother covers her head with the end of her white sari and bends down to touch the singer's feet, as a mark of respect. And then she spoils it all by pontificating:

"I don't ever have to touch anyone's feet – not on grounds of holiness or any other grounds –but for musicians, I make an exception of my own accord."

Nothing she does ever makes much sense to me. When really pushed to explain herself she says cryptically, "Well, you see, I'm a teacher. And all musicians are also teachers, only they're bigger teachers, even if they don't teach. By performing music they become teachers. Any one who practises music preaches God's word...."

So why the hell didn't she become a music teacher? Then everybody would be touching her feet. I'm sure she'd love that! But she says her mother would've never heard of it. She says she was expressly forbidden from studying music or dance. It had to be maths, or law or science. I'm intrigued. Normally, she hardly ever speaks about her mother.

My joy knew no bounds when Kanhayya Lal, ignoring all the grown ups fussing around him after the recital, came straight over to me and said: "Child, aren't you going to show me around your lovely garden?"

My mother loses no time in an attempted thwart: "Er... no... it's dark, you won't be able to see very much... well, there will be mosquitoes," she does her best to pour cold water over the plans.

But no, this time she can't stop me. The great Singer himself has requested to be shown around the garden, and he has singled me out for the privilege. I take him by the hand and start leading him out hurriedly, fearful that my mother might yet get her way. But to my utmost delight, I can hear Kanhayya Lal saying to her in beautiful poetic Hindi:

"Sister, even the mosquitoes have to be given a chance. They too are God's creatures and they're entitled to their daily crust. Let's see what they make of my blood. Will they like it, or will they reject it? You have all honoured me so greatly. Now let me be judged by your mosquitoes... let's see what they have to say in the matter."

I'm already in love with Kanhayya Lal, just for those clever comments about the mosquitoes. That's exactly what I think, but nobody ever listens to me. But when Kanhayya Lal says it, they go "Wah, wah!"

But the mosquito comment is nothing – the best has yet to come. All my mother's purity and purification rituals – her pure Muslim-Brahman kitchen, her separate vegetarian pots and pans – everything turns to dust as Kanhayya Lal insists on sharing a plate of maize-meal porridge with our servants, whose cooking pots are bubbling away cheerfully outside the servants' quarters in the back-garden. He sits down on the floor with them and eats an ample portion, praising it for its simplicity of taste and richness of nutrients. Zero fat. No sugar. No salt. Prepared and served with love – their one and only meal of the day. And then he leaves a ten shilling note on his empty plate. The horrified servants try to protest, but he says it's against his religion to eat anything he has not paid for.

That's done it for me. I'm in love. I spend the rest of the night in deep thought. I can't sleep a wink. I wonder if he'll wait for me until I grow up? It's not like he's a Catholic priest or something. Singers are allowed to marry, aren't they?

And sure enough we were married. But that was many years and many hardships later. And it was no ordinary marriage – in fact it wasn't a marriage at all in that sense of the word. It was something beyond that....

53
MUSIC, PURE MUSIC

Ronnie the PA has picked up the Ustad in a mini-cab to take him to the recording session. But it's a frustrating ride. It's raining heavily and the taxi hardly moves. The Ustad is smoking and the windows have steamed up. PA senses that Ustad is in a foul mood and decides some light conversation would be in order.

"It takes ages to move around London – unless of course you're prepared to go on the tube," says the PA, apologetically.

"I hate the very idea", declared the Ustad. "I don't care how long it takes to get anywhere, I'd rather be over the ground than under it. When I die, I'll have to lie under the ground anyway. I associate underground with death," he continued morosely.

The PA sighed.

They had been stuck in the same spot for over fifteen minutes. A sex shop on the left displayed a few sad-looking, crumpled items of frilly under-wear. The Ustad shook his head sadly:

"Westerners think sex is all about funny underwear. How sad! In the West everything is about quantity – never about quality. Good sex isn't about how often you do it – it's about how long it lasts."

PA sighed again. It was going to be one of those days, when everything western was wrong and everything eastern was right and noble, honourable and wise. Predictably, the Ustad unnecessarily spoke out at some female passer-by:

"Just look at that skirt. What does it leave to the imagination, eh? Those legs covered in blue veins. And that blouse that won't even button up. How ugly she looks – tauba, tauba…. Just look at her baggy eyes!"

"With all due respect sir, she's a working woman," their Pakistani cab driver chimed in unnecessarily, determined to prove that he valued hard work, no matter what.

The Ustad froze with anger. How dare a mere driver, and a Pakistani at that, just butt into a private conversation?

"Just what do you mean…?" the Ustad began sternly, but the PA had already sprung into action: "Please gentlemen, let's not have an argument over a woman we don't even know." He remembered how tiresome the Ustad could be if he was in a bad mood for a recording. They would have endless tantrums and false notes and re-takes.

The traffic moved slowly – another few feet in ten minutes. An uneasy silence followed. It was difficult to introduce another topic of conversation with the icy atmosphere that had formed between the driver and the Ustad.

"I've been listening to some of your older recordings," said the ever-diplomatic PA chattily. "They're beautiful. I wish I understood classical music properly…."

Ustad cheered up a bit and launched into a lecture about the pros and cons of live recordings, glad to have a subject on which the cab driver could not butt in.

They arrived in the studio reception area and found the Producer pacing up and down, while trying to make three different calls at the same time. As soon as she saw them she squealed in panic:

"Where on earth have you guys been? I've been waiting ages. The sound guys are threatening to go to lunch. What happened? You'd better have a jolly good reason. Hey, you haven't been doing the rounds of the naughty shops, have you?"

In her panic she had completely forgotten about politeness to the Ustad… too late now.

"It was the traffic darling… honestly…" started the PA by way of explanation.

"Oh come on – not that one again! You know the traffic's bad when it rains, you should have just set out earlier!"

"I demand an apology," said the Ustad.

"An apology from ME? You want ME to apologise because YOU'RE late?" screamed the Producer with unconcealed sarcasm.

Their relationship had been deteriorating since they'd started working together. She wanted to avoid unnecessary edits and fade-downs. She would repeatedly ask for a specific duration on a raag. He would say it's impossible, and carry on playing until it suited him. She wanted definite endings on particular pieces, while he would play for a whole thirty minutes instead of the requested one minute and twenty seconds….

He looked enraged. "Yes, you heard right! I demand an apology this minute from you! And I implore you to hold your tongue in future!"

"I'm really sorry, I've been so worried. I thought, maybe, you got the dates mixed up, or something."

"I never get dates mixed up," Ustad said coolly. "I've been recording and performing since before you were born."

"Come on everyone, let's get to work," said peace-making PA.

They were headed down a long corridor towards their studio when a junior member of the studio staff came running up behind them.

"Someone in reception... for you... send them through? Or are you coming out?"

"Who is it? Is it the Composer?"

"Don't know..."

"Well, is it a man or a woman?"

"A woman, with lots of containers of food, I think."

"Oh God! Is it lunchtime already?" Producer almost screamed.

"Quarter to twelve...."

"Please tell her to wait. Tell her... er... tell her we're right in the middle of a session... can't be interrupted yet...."

The studio youngster, his first day at work, ran briskly down the corridor to make sure the new arrival was duly intercepted.

The PA looked at her defiantly: "What are you up to now, darling? You're not sending her away are you? I'm quite hungry..." he pouted.

"Just shut up a minute will you Ronnie! I need to do some thinking. Need to gain time... oh shit! Listen, you haven't been here so you don't know. The Composer's been here since nine, and he just popped out to the bank because we couldn't do anything else with you guys not here. He'll be back any minute... oh no! She'll see him in reception. Quick! Run to reception and bring her in here. Then go back to reception and wait for the Composer. Tell him she's here... just alert him, and then let him decide what he wants to do... no, no forget it! He'll just shoot straight out again and that will be that! No recording. Ronnie, listen. Just take the food from her and tell her to leave. Tell her we won't be out for ages. Tell her anything. Just get rid of her somehow before he gets back. Oh, why does this always happen to me? Vital recording day and star Ustad two hours late and bloody Groupie lunch provider two hours early!"

The PA put an affectionate arm around her: "Darling, calm down. Why don't you go into the studio and be extra sweet to the Ustad, and just leave everything else to me?"

"Music! Pure Music to my ears, Bless you Darling Ronnie!"

54
RONNIE FIXES IT

"Ooh! Darling! So early... how nice! They're nowhere near ready for lunch yet. We started late you know..." the PA cooed on seeing the arrival of lunch.

The Groupie was very relieved to see PA. The Producer herself might have just snatched the food and said "Thank you, goodbye!" but with the PA one could always be sure of a decent chat, and who knows, even vital information about her beloved's whereabouts.

"Hello Ronnie," she cooed. "Hungry I hope? Come on, let's take all this in. It's time you guys had some lunch!"

"No, no darling, you see, we were all horribly late and the Producer is in a foul temper. She even yelled at the Ustad. Imagine! Yelling at such a great Ustad! I don't think she'll let anyone have lunch just yet. Why don't you leave the food here and we'll have it later? I'd love to ask you in, but it's like the Battle of Waterloo in there... not very social."

No doubt about it, Ronnie was doing his best to carry out his boss's orders, but the delicious smells wafting out of her metal containers were more than flesh and blood could bear....

"Come on, just a little taste. Right here... just for you. A sneak preview! Have some aloo-parattha. You must be starving!" coaxed the Groupie.

The PA was indeed starving and her offer of a torn-off piece of parattha was not unwelcome. He stood there munching and chattering about the difficulties of working alongside artistic temperaments: "If I wasn't an artist myself, I don't know how I'd cope," he boasted, delicately waving his ghee-covered fingers in the air.

"Here, try this chutney... and take a chicken leg from this one...."

She was hurriedly throwing open various containers, and the studio reception staff, who might otherwise have chosen to be tediously officious about having their work area turned into an Indian take-away, were tucking in just as eagerly as Ronnie.

With every new delicacy she offered, she asked a casual question – carefully avoiding any direct mention of her beloved Composer, the World's Number One:

"Have you done much this morning? Try this vegetable. How's it going, anyway? More chicken, come on! What raags did the Ustad play? Have some rice. Are you recording again tomorrow? Try some bhindi. Where are all the musicians staying? Do you like daal?"

Every so often she leaned over the studio visitors' signing-in book, lying upside down on the counter. She couldn't see his name, but then he was just as likely to sign himself in as "Mickey Mouse" or "Changez Khan."

"Hold on Ronnie – don't bother with that Coke, I've brought some ice-cold lassi – where's that thermos?"

The Groupie was now in full sway, presiding over her impromptu indoor picnic in the studio reception area with the magnanimous air of one who was fortunate enough to be feeding the only survivors of a nuclear holocaust. She smiled indulgently at every satisfied groan let out by the starving survivors. The long-nailed, bleached blonde sulky receptionist, the brand new studio junior who had already decided to stay in this job for life (the lunches were great!) and Ronnie the PA, who had been sent to shoo her away, but had instead fallen prey to the charms of her coconut chicken.

Just as the air was getting thicker with smells of freshly roasted whole wheat and ghee, the World's Number One Composer walked into the picnic through the front door, the Actress fast on his heels. At the same time the irate Producer tumbled into the area from a swing-door inside the building to see what the hell had become of Ronnie. The groaning, grunting, munching food orgy momentarily came to a halt.

"Hi!" chimed the Groupie, gazing adoringly at the Composer. Her face shone with a fresh radiance, belying the fact that she'd been up since dawn kneading parattha dough, and her hands trembled a bit as she held out a parattha towards him:

"Just in time for lunch ... or something...?" she asked as seductively as possible under the circumstances, with half the world looking on. Suddenly she became aware of the Actress, and disturbingly registered the fact that they'd arrived together.

The Actress linked her arm in his and spoke for him in possessive tones: "Oh no thank you! No lunch. We just had lunch...." She had recently started speaking in educated, upper class Urdu only.

The Composer broke free of the Actress and guiltily moved towards the Producer:

"We just ran into each other... I thought I should eat something... anyway, is everyone on base now? Can we start?"

"Yes," the Producer said icily. "Ustad-ji is quite ready. He has warmed up his fingers and the instrument has been tuned. Can you take charge of him now please? I need to be in the control room, and Ronnie, when you're quite finished, I need you in there. Things have to be labelled up properly."

She felt completely betrayed by the PA. How dare he stand here munching paratthas when she had explicitly asked him to get rid of the woman? Ignoring the Groupie completely, she turned to the Actress and deliberately spoke to her in English, "Shouldn't you be at your photo session?"

"I cancel – I want see recooording..." the Actress replied in her usual poor English.

"What's there to see? There's nothing to look at, you know. Music is for listening, not for looking," she concluded in patronising tones, hoping Groupie had also taken note of this vital fact.

Just as the Producer turned to go back in, the Groupie approached her with a plateful of food: "Please, have some. Try some. Where's the Ustad? Will you take some to him?"

The woman was bloody impossible, thought the Producer. If she had felt humiliated, she certainly showed no signs of it. If she had been enraged at the Composer for having lunch with the Actress she certainly didn't show it. And now, even though the Producer had clearly snubbed her, the Groupie's response was to kindly offer food in the softest of voices. It made the Producer feel like a nerd and she found herself getting really irritated for feeling it. But that wasn't all. Deep down she felt the stinging pain of little green monsters. How dare the Composer just "pop out to the bank" and then have the audacity to meet the Actress for lunch? And how dare her PA-Ronnie be seduced by the Groupie's food?

There was a sudden commotion at the swing-doors as the Ustad entered the reception area... "I say, where has everyone disappeared... I'm ready now, but where's the toilet in this place?" He stopped abruptly as he saw the full cast assembled around the low reception coffee-table, covered with scrumptious Indian-Sri Lankan cuisine....

"Oh great! Subhan-Allah! Wah! I think I'll eat first. And then I'll need a rest. Can we do the recording later? In the evening, I mean?" He was determined to be difficult. He had to punish the Producer just a little more for being so rude earlier.

"OK, that's it, it's a packer!" she was surprised to hear herself say it. It had sounded like someone else's voice. She decided there and then to reschedule the whole thing at some other studio and this time, she intended to keep the venue top secret. Things were going seriously wrong. Everything and everyone was getting out of control. The Actress had become so beautiful and sophisticated (in Urdu only) that the Composer appeared no longer able to resist her. The same woman he'd nicknamed "Chipkali", he was now happy to meet surreptitiously for lunch. And now, even her faithful PA-Ronnie was letting himself be seduced by the Groupie's food. It was all going horribly wrong.

55
THANK YOU... NO, THANK *YOU*

Sonia called up Ash late on Wednesday night: "Hi! Thanks a million for today. The dishwasher's working fine now."

"Yes, everything is working fine now, thanks to your dish washer..." he said cryptically.

"I hope you didn't have to hang around too long... he came on time yes? And you were able to do some work, yes?" Sonia was genuinely grateful to Ash for giving up a whole day to plumber-sit for her.

"Yes... fine," he sounded miles away – not his usual phone voice. "Everybody just uses her, they just use her and eat her food and...."

"Ash what on earth are you rambling on about? Who uses whom? Sorry, do you think I was using you just because I asked you to wait at my place for the plumber?"

"No, no, not you, them. The rest of them – they just use her..."

"Use whom for God's sake?" she was getting irritated with him for being so cryptic. When he was being like this it could only mean one thing:

"Ash, you aren't talking about one of your characters again are you? You're not trying to tell me that one of your imaginary women is being used by other imaginary people – Big Deal!"

"Thank you, thank you. It's you I need to thank. It's all beginning to take shape now. Zarine, your dream teacher is truly amazing. I mean, she doesn't directly teach or anything like that, but somehow, ever since I've been seeing her, everything is connecting up. It's just flowing... now, let me tell you about it...."

"No! Ash no! Don't talk about it – just write. If you want to talk, then let's talk about something completely different – help you relax. Take your mind off this imaginary woman. Now, for instance, tell me, did you know that women who wear skin-tone underwear are more given to elaborate sexual fantasies?"

"Skin-tone? But whose skin? A pinky-beige shade called skin-tone is hardly the job for a black woman."

"Don't split hairs Ash – why do you always have to make everything so difficult?"

"I'm just pointing out an accuracy problem – you can't call something skin-tone unless you qualify the colour of the skin first!"

"OK then, how about this one? Did you know that couples who make love on Saturday nights only are more likely to have green sofas then those who make love on weekday afternoons? Vegetarians are more likely to play scrabble? People who pick their nose incessantly are often immune to the flu virus, but much more inclined towards allergies?" Sonia was being deliberately silly and he sensed it.

"Oh stop it! I don't want to play this game – can't we talk about something else…?"

"OK then. Let's talk numbers. We all know about seven, but do you know about the number nine? You see nine crops up in the strangest of ways. Various cultures all through history have had nine. Don't you see?"

"See what? Of course they have nine. Everyone has nine. It's a number isn't it? It's bound to crop up now and then… so what?"

Even as he says it, Ash feels the inevitable discourse coming on: "That's it, that's just it Ash… you always fail to see the symbolism in things. You're hopeless at forming those larger links that make the basis of all knowledge. You'll never move on unless you learn to make connections between things. That's why you never finish your scripts. One must be prepared to see the significance of smaller things in order to relate them to larger ones. That's what art is all about!"

Is it Sonia? Really, Sonia? Ash is thoughtful. Thanks to you Sonia, I know about the number Nine. I know there have to be nine of them, and I know they have to be virgins – and they have to be fed. But you don't know what I know. Thanks to you, I actually know someone who has yet to fulfil her pact with God. She has yet to feed nine virgins… Sonia, wouldn't you just die if you knew who she was?

56
KLEENEX AND KALYUG

Maybe it was indeed Kalyug. The times were definitely a'changin'. The British had already quit, reasonably peacefully. Power was handed over to the ancient rulers of the Pearl of Africa's Crown. But British rule had, typically, left its mark. The descendants of the ancient rulers were in some ways more British than the British, and corrupt with it too. They didn't last long. They were driven away in a matter of months, a short-lived civil war resulting in a full-scale military take-over. This provided the British with the satisfaction of saying: "See? We leave them to it and what do they do? They just kill one another. And then, just to prove that they were still pretty decent sort of chaps – fairness and justice and all that – they offered political asylum to the deposed Oxbridge-educated African princes and their hangers-on. For the Mohanjis of this world, military rule was not at first seen as necessarily a bad thing. Military discipline fitted in quite well with the Mohanji red book of life's philosophy. In fact Mohanji himself was among the first to call on the new Dictator – so youthful and dignified in his uniform, yet he looked vaguely familiar...? Oh, but they all look the same!

As Head of the Morality Committee, Mohanji lost no time in offering the Dictator the support of his own community, and in a rare mood of generosity, he also hinted at special cut-price military uniforms for the newly expanded army. After the meeting, Mohanji had come away flushed with self-importance because the Dictator had told him that the country needed hard-working men, just like him.

A few weeks after that memorable visit, the Dictator decided to involve the new military government in the various private and personal issues of civilians. First, he decreed that red lipstick be outlawed. Anyone found to be sporting red lips would be considered a whore and jailed accordingly. If lipstick had to be worn, it could only be a light colour. Daily newspapers carried listings of those shades of lipstick sanctioned by the new military government which may be worn in moderate quantities – Shell pink, Bare Sands, Invisible Coral, Safari Brown, Khaki Dream. Those were all allowed. Max Factor, Yardley, Elizabeth Arden... are you listening?

After that it was announced that Black women who straightened their hair would be sent to prison without a trial, and possibly, at the discretion of the Commanding Officer for their area, be subjected to anal insertions of red-hot iron rods. The same hot irons that were used to straighten frizzy hair.

Fast on the heels of the iron-rods, skin-lightening creams were suddenly banned. At that point, Mohanji was slightly dismayed. Skin-bleaching cream was his largest earner on the cosmetics shelf of the Widow's shop. Still, never mind. What he'd lose in skin lightening cream, he would make-up by employing a cheap Afro-style hairdresser, to sit on the verandah and produce nice elaborate traditional African hair-styles – multi-coloured beads interwoven into plaited, frizzy hair. The Tribal Look. He would pay her two hundred shillings a month and she would do ten heads a day, six days a week, and the customers would pay him five shillings at a time. Not a bad profit margin, even by Mohanji's standards. Or better still, get one of his boys married to a nice Indian girl who knew how to do African hair.

Then the Dictator suddenly banned mini-skirts and Mohanji's joy knew no bounds! Ever since that wretched shameless fashion had taken off, people were buying less and less dress-fabric. Longer dresses would mean more fabric. He was truly thrilled, but officially, he maintained he was thrilled on modesty and morality grounds. It was immodest for young women to show their thighs. It was against Indian culture.

One of his black customers dared to argue: "But it's not against OUR culture. We're not Indian."

She was right. The Indians were hardly affected by the mini-skirt ban – their own girls usually preferred Indian clothes. It was mostly the poor Africans who could no longer wear what they wanted. And many wore minis for economy, not for fashion. It was easier to buy one yard of fabric for a small mini-skirt than the full nine yards required for a basuti.

But Mohanji's Black customer was quite right: "We're not Indian. We don't care about showing our thighs. We were ruled by the British, remember, and they gave us their dress?"

"Yes, but they've gone now. Why don't you go back to your beautiful national dress?" he suggested gleefully, not forgetting the required length of nine yards per basuti outfit… music to Mohanji's ears….

The Black African woman was not amused.

"Why does the Dictator worry about what we wear? Why doesn't he do anything about these Indian women who show so much belly – and sometimes even belly button – between sari and choli?"

"That's different. That is our ancient culture. There is no shame in that. We are proud of our dress," said Mohanji, and quickly went on to his favourite recent subject:

"I've met the man you know. He is great! He understands and appreciates our culture. Would never dream of interfering with Indian customs or traditions. Respects our hard work. Not like you people, just sitting around in the sun and eating bananas all day. That is why we had to come. My ancestors came to build your railway. You couldn't have done it. You people drink too much and sleep too much."

While Mohanji continued being a devotee of the Dictator, the new government went on passing various other sartorial decrees. At first, tight, drainpipe trousers were banned. Then, when the Paris catwalks showed flared, bell-bottomed trousers and they finally made their way to tropical Africa then, those too, were banned. Young men asked in dismay: So what sort of trousers CAN we wear? Normal. Just normal. Nothing too tight, and nothing that made a bell shape towards the ankle. Just straight, normal, loose trousers. Lots more work for the Widow. Various people brought in bell-bottoms for straightening out and the alterations trade was booming.

If Mohanji had done pretty well under the British and their stooges, then it could be said that under the new military regime his business was positively booming. The Widow's sewing machine on his shop verandah never stopped. Hemlines were constantly being lowered, necklines were being raised with the addition of frills, and sleeves were either being added to sleeveless dresses, or lengthened with tiers of fabric to reach the wrists.

But despite the euphoria of those early months of military rule, Mohanji felt a sense of unease – a kind of impending doom, made none the easier by the fact most of his sons were growing restless, and even a bit rebellious. They kept saying they had to leave the country. Things could only go from bad to worse. They argued there was nothing for them here. It would be a matter of time before some other new decree made it illegal for Indians to be shopkeepers. "Don't be ridiculous! Rogues! All of you! This is just another lame excuse to go to England to study and then mess around with shameless blonde-blonde white-white girls. I know you. I know all of you. Now that things are really taking off, you're not interested in carrying forward with the family tradition. Even rats only abandon sinking ships, not thriving ones. Shameless louts!"

All the boys had turned against their father – all except the green-eyed taxi driver. He was still very much in favour of staying put. The others spent more and more time studying, and less and less time in the shop. Mohanji began to panic. He decided to get the taxi driver married. That way, in time he would acquire a brand new set of grandsons to replace his own good-for-nothing sons.

The marriage was arranged hastily. So hastily that the taxi-driver and his prospective only met for five minutes, in her house, in the prosperous, big, neighbouring country. She agreed to the marriage at once. Mohanji was delighted. Her parents didn't even ask if they could visit their daughter's future home prior to the marriage, just to check out the living conditions. They seemed in a big hurry too.

The wedding ceremony was conducted that same evening, with only Mr Mohanji and of course his taxi driver son bridegroom present. They returned to the small town the next morning, complete with new bride daughter-in-law in tow.

Two more brothers were hastily moved into the Widow's room, already shared with three brothers, so that the newly-weds could have the small room at the end of the yard. Even though wives didn't officially sleep in the same room as their husbands but visited them quietly in the middle of the night, Mohanji decided to abandon this quaint tradition in the interests of fast conception of new grandsons. Privacy was essential for that sort of thing.

There was much excitement and consternation at the shotgun wedding, especially this surprising twist that the newly-weds had officially been given the same room. Such shame. Husband and wife openly sharing a room, and that too, with impressionable young boys in the house? What sort of example was that going to set to everyone? But apart from the question of shame, the main reason everyone felt put out was that they'd been done out of a wedding. No elaborate preparations, no henna, no open backyard cooking, no songs and no dancing. The deed had been done, swiftly and surreptitiously, and here they were. They had only gone to check out a prospective bride, and they'd ended up bringing her back with them. Very strange. Usually months would lapse between the first survey of a prospective daughter-in-law and her eventual approval for entry into a noble Dukavalla household.

Not strange at all, some people said. Just like Mohanji, to save the expense of a wedding. No, not fair, said others. He had spared no expense when the Widow had got married. He may be stingy in other ways, but he always spent money on important occasions, and everything was done properly, every single ritual was observed and explained for the benefit of the younger ones, so that they would understand and carry on the tradition into the next generation.

So what happened to the rituals this time, challenged the anti-Mohanji lobby? They only went yesterday, and today it's all done. How can that be? It takes at least four days to perform all the rituals properly.

The speculation gradually died down and gave way to other, more urgent gossip, notably the incredible wayward behaviour of the brand new daughter-in-law.

She had just turned eighteen. Fresh and youthful, with all the confidence that youth topped by beauty brings. Nobody could understand why she had agreed to marry a mere taxi-driver. Surely someone so beautiful could have had anyone she wanted? Why not a teacher or a doctor? From morning till night people came just to stare at her. As a new bride, she had no choice but to allow this traditional inspection, as the neighbourhood women looked her up and down and talked about her as though she weren't even there.

"I like the nose," said one. "Too long," said another. "But she's so fair. Is she half-European do you think?" said the third one. "Why didn't they even put any mehndi – no time I guess. Mehndi would like nice on her fair hands. Nice eyes. Very fragile face. Nice features – well chiselled. A little fat, maybe? No, not really, quite a small waist though. Babies will soon see to that!"

And so it went on. After three days of the non-stop inspection ceremony followed by fatuous comments, the daughter-in-law had had enough. She got up and announced she wasn't sitting around like a prize Turkey any more, and would someone please go and fetch her new husband from the taxi rank as she was in the mood to go out for a meal.

When Mohanji was told this staggering piece of news he decided to have a quiet word with her. New girl, you know. Doesn't know the ways of our household yet. How will she know unless we teach her?

"Look here dear daughter-in-law. Your husband can only return when he finishes work. And then we all eat together, here in the yard. It is important for a family to eat together. When family members start dining separately, that's the first sign of trouble. It spells the beginning of the end – Kalyug."

"But we've only been married three days, and we haven't been anywhere yet. We haven't been alone at all. These women just come and stare at me all day, and I'm sick and tired of sitting around," she pouted militantly.

"You can busy yourself with some light work, if you wish. I like people who get fed up with just sitting around. I can tell, you and I are going to get along just fine. There's a lot to do in my daughter's shop. Why don't you help her a bit? It will pass the time until my son gets home."

"What! I can't work in a shop! I'm asking you to give your son some time off so that we can go somewhere and have a proper honeymoon, and you are saying I should work in your daughter's shop, just three days after my wedding!"

Times had certainly changed. Mohanji could never have imagined that some mere chit of girl aged eighteen, his own daughter-in-law, would one day demand a honeymoon as an indisputable birthright. Didn't she even feel any shame in referring to her own honeymoon? And what's all this honeymoon-sannimoon nonsense? What a waste of money! Whatever they wanted to do on honeymoon could be done right here, in the privacy of that back room.

"Now look," he said soothingly, in his best kind-father voice. "We don't do this moon and honey ceremony. Anyway, I'm not saying you have to go and work in my daughter's shop. I just suggested it because you said you were bored."

"Yes, I'm bored. I need a car! I need a car of my own. You sold that one I got for my dowry. I need it right now! I need to get out and visit people and make friends. How can I do that unless I go to the big hotels and coffee shops? I need to go shopping. In the evenings I need to go out with my husband. To the cinema. And to eat. I need people to invite just me and my husband for dinner. Nobody's invited us. Don't you have any friends? Where are all your friends? Where's the European area? There must be some decent people living there. I like being with educated people who talk posh."

Mohanji couldn't believe what he was hearing. Just eighteen, and dropped out of school at fourteen, she considered herself good enough for educated people, and the European area.

"We don't go to dinner parties, and we don't invite people to dinner. If they drop in at food time, then they're welcome to join us. We only issue invitations for weddings and for virgins' feasts. We don't mix with the snooty Asians who live in the European area. We only do business with them. They come to the shop and buy their groceries. We ask after their health, they ask after ours, and that's it. We don't concern ourselves with their big talk of poetry and politics. We stick to our own kind. Like decent people, we eat dinner in our own house and then call on someone of our own community, just for a chat, and we never take more than a cup of tea in anybody else's house. Those are our rules. That is how we live. I explained all this to you in your own house when we came to see you. Weren't you listening?"

"No, maybe I wasn't listening. I fell in love at first sight with his green eyes. I heard nothing else," she said slowly.

Mohanji was shocked at her shamelessness. How could a young woman admit to having fallen in love in front of an elder like a father-in-law? Such frankness bred more shamelessness. And love? What was love? What sort of basis was that for a marriage? Silly girl! Instead of enthusing about the joys of being married into a noble family of well-to-do shopkeepers, she was claiming love as the reason for her marriage. What was the world coming to? Kalyug indeed!

She carried on, completely unaware of any disapproval: "You saw my parents' house. You saw how I lived. Surely you could see our style? How dare you think I could live in this hell-hole after living like that in my country? How dare you?" she burst into uncontrollable fits of sobbing. Mohanji awkwardly offered a handkerchief.

"What! What's this? A cloth hanky? Now you also want the delicate skin around my nose to peel off? You want to ruin my skin? Don't you know I have sensitive combination skin and this climate is making it worse? Don't you have any tissues? Bring me a box of tissues! Now!"

Mohanji walked out of the small room and crossing the backyard into the house, he walked through the door leading to the shop. He took a box of pink patterned tissues from the shelf and asked one of the sons to take it to the daughter-in-law.

So now it had come to his. Boxes of imported tissues that he stocked only for his customers, were now to be used and disposed of, in his own house. Kalyug had certainly arrived!

57
THINGS THAT CHEW IN THE NIGHT

The daughter-in-law's growing discontent soon became common knowledge – first within the claustrophobic small town community, then further afield. Her rich parents from the neighbouring country had visited her, and on seeing her living conditions had wanted to take her back there and then. But she insisted they take her husband too, because she loved his green eyes. Mohanji was outraged, to say the least. Yes, yes! Take her. Ruin your own daughter's marriage, but my son isn't going anywhere, isn't that right, my green-eyed one?

The son lowered his head with shame. Family crisis on a Sunday morning. No man should ever have to find himself caught between his own parents and his wife.

The daughter-in-law looked at him in tantalising fashion, trying to recreate the memories of the previous night.

"You'll come with us, won't you? You can run one of my father's businesses. You don't have to do this dangerous taxi driving all day. Come on, come with us."

"No, let's just stay here. Ask your parents to go away. They shouldn't interfere in our family affairs. THIS is your home now and you are part of my family. Let's just stay here together and work it out," said the green-eyed one.

Mohanji beamed with pride. The not-so-good-at school green-eyed one had always been his favourite – now he knew why. Shame on his other boys. Some of them had even had the audacity to be openly friendly with their thoroughly modern sister-in-law and to side with her in every argument. He had once even heard son number five saying to her:

"Yes, yes, you make a big fuss, then maybe we will all move into a real house. A bigger house. And you can have your own private apartment in the grounds of our big house. There are so many nice houses now the Europeans are going."

This was out and out rebellion. Defection! Desertion! Thank God he had at least one sensible son out of nine.

"Please stay," the green-eyed one pleaded, and the jade-olive-green-eyes weaved their magic spell all over again. She couldn't leave him. And she said as much.

Her parents disowned her on the spot, her mother wailing and screaming and wishing she had never given her birth in the first place. And her father just shaking his head from side to side and looking utterly stupefied at how his daughter could opt for this hovel instead of his own grand, self-designed mansion.

Both her parents were killed in a road crash on their way back to the neighbouring country. Mohanji was quietly philosophical: God's justice – retribution, for attempting to break up your own daughter's marriage.

When the tragic news reached her, she was anything but distressed. She was even glad she'd stuck up for her new family. But she was particularly that glad she'd chosen the scene of the big family argument to announce her pregnancy for the first time. It had worked like an Ace of Trumps. Not only because she was with child – a powerful position by any account – but Mohanji also felt he owed her some huge concession in return for defying her snobbish, now dead parents. In a complete break from the Mohanji family tradition, it was agreed that she should get a small car of her own, and her husband could take one evening off from his taxi-rounds so that they could go out together. But she also demanded that her husband give her half his takings for her own personal expenditure.

Mohanji knew when he was beaten. He agreed to all her conditions because, at least that way, the family would still be together, and family honour preserved. No price is too big a price to pay for the conservation of family Izzat.

Once the peace treaty had been enacted, things took a turn for the worse. She was never at home, thanks to her new car. She woke up at eleven, got herself done up, and left the house at one. She never took lunch at home. She usually drove off to some big hotel where she would meet new friends – idle women of the leisured classes, who sat around eating cream cakes and discussing slimming diets. Then she would go shopping for make-up, perfume, skin preparations – all expensive western stuff, big names and big price tags. And it was at one of those skin-care counters in the big chemist's shop that she first ran into Mrs Henara.

"Aren't you Mohanji's new daughter-in-law? I'm Mrs Henara. Your father-in-law is most kind. He allows my daughter to stay in the safety of your shop verandah while she waits for her school transport. He is a very kind man.

Nice to meet you," Mrs Henara had patronisingly turned on her north Indian Urdu charm to full volume hoping to probe into the family situation. She too had heard rumours of the famous Sunday morning family row, but she pretended to be above all that sort of thing. It would've tarnished her detached intellectual image if she admitted to being interested in the family affairs of Gujarati-speaking Marwari shopkeepers.

The daughter-in-law looked at her with unashamed awe: "Your daughter? My shop? Oh, shop! The shop's nothing to do with me. I don't work in any shop, huh! We just live there now. Soon we'll be moving out. As soon as my husband and I can find a decent house. Where do you live?"

Mrs Henara told her, and the daughter-in-law was sufficiently impressed to invite her for a cup of coffee there and then, at the Christian bakery across the road. But it wouldn't do to be seen in a public place with such a controversial daughter-in-law of such a lowly family.

"No, come over to my house, please. You're newly married. I should be the one inviting you to dinner, never mind coffee. Come on, let's go. Follow my car," Mrs Henara said imperiously.

Mrs Henara was everything the daughter-in-law had ever wanted to be. Well-spoken, educated, and such class! She didn't care about anything or anyone. She just did her own thing. Even smoked in public. Slim black cigarette holder and elegant chiffon saris. While everyone else wore multi-coloured large, busy, floral prints, Mrs Henara always appeared cool and composed in plain pink, or white, or sky-blue, or banana yellow. She even managed to make bright orange look like a pastel shade. And her sari blouses always fitted perfectly. Skin tight and showing lots of belly, but not a bulge or crease anywhere. Thirty-something with a perfect figure. The daughter-in-law felt privileged to be invited back to the house of such a graceful and elegant lady. She decided from now on, to try and model herself as much as possible, on Mrs Henara.

When they entered the long gravel drive leading to the house, the daughter-in-law felt this is where she truly belonged. This elegant lady, in just one casual meeting, had extended to her such a warm invitation in pure Urdu. Yes, this was definitely class.

When they arrived at the house, the Brat was playing in the garden. She was wide-eyed with curiosity and excitement. Why was her mother bringing a Mohanji home? Something was up! She'd better hang around just in case something important was going to happen. She ran into the house, ahead of the two women, and eagerly sat down in the drawing room, unashamedly showing an air of expectancy. What were they going to talk about?

"Hello Baby," cooed the daughter-in-law. "I've seen you playing on the shop verandah. What's your name?"

Before the Brat could answer, Mrs Henara had come down on her like a tropical thunderstorm, complete with hailstones:

"Hey, how many times have I told you to leave me alone when I have visitors? Go out and play."

"I've finished playing. I am bored. Can I stay and listen to you chatting?"

"No, you can't. Just go and tell cook we have a guest for tea. Ask her to make more sandwiches. And tell her we'll have that cake today. Go on, out with you! And stay out."

How could Mrs. Henara get on with her digging and probing if the Brat sat around listening to every word? However indirect the line of questioning only a daughter can know when a mother is being really and truly and unnecessarily nosey. That would never do. It would completely cramp her style. The Brat was a pest at the best of times, but if she actually got a chance to hear contentious family stuff, she was bound to go and repeat it all to her Mohanji boyfriends.

"So, tell me, how do you like our lovely little town?" Mrs Henara began in exploratory fashion.

"Oh it's nice, but I'm getting such dry skin. My complexion is my biggest asset you know. I don't want to ruin it. That's why I was at the chemist, buying all those creams."

"How are you finding living with the Mohanji family?"

What she really meant was how can you live in that dingy, crowded hovel behind the shop?

"Oh, they're OK, but they are not really my sort. As I said, we'll be moving out soon, as soon as we can find a place."

The daughter-in-law was struggling with her Gujarati-accented Urdu, which only served to make Mrs Henara even more consciously eloquent.

"I don't suppose you get to see too much of your husband. It's hard work driving taxis back and forth across those treacherous roads. Very dangerous too. He works all day, doesn't he?" Mrs Henara was truly an expert at probing.

"Yes, more or less."

She wasn't being very forthcoming. Mrs Henara decided to change tactics. Go back to before the marriage.

"Aren't you one of the Lalanis? I believe they're jewellers. Or is it furniture?"

"Both. We also have a record shop, and another shop that specialises in African crafts."

"Oh, I see!" She still couldn't see why this marriage had happened in the first place.

The daughter-in-law was dying to ask Mrs Henara various personal questions, but it wasn't done to question an older person, and especially a person of higher class.

"Your husband? Does he work late?" she asked finally, in a polite voice.

"Husband! What husband? Bastard! I threw him out. Enough is enough. I don't need a husband. Nobody needs a husband. They just mess you up and then they leave. And they're never happy with the one they leave you for. That's God's punishment."

She stopped suddenly realising she was talking to a newly married woman.

The daughter-in-law was monumentally impressed. An Indian woman, proudly declaring herself a divorcee. Such bravado! What style! Such class! This is how women should be. Financially independent. Self-assured. Loud-mouthed. Urdu-speaking.

Mrs Henara hastened to make amends: "Not that any Mohanji boy would ever do a thing like that. No, you people are very decent in that respect," she added hastily by way of redress. "I know them well. Such nice boys. The youngest one and my daughter are great friends you know. I'm sure one day he'll be a great man. So clever at school!"

"Yes, but I don't think my father-in-law will ever allow any of the boys to have their own life. He just wants them all to be shopkeepers of bigger shops. He's doesn't believe in too much education."

Now we're getting somewhere, thought Mrs Henara. Finally she's prepared to divulge household policies. But before Mrs Henara could pursue this opening, the Brat walked in, town-crier fashion announcing the earth-shattering news that the new cake had been partly chewed by some unknown creature, as yet unidentified by the investigating committee – cook, cleaner and herself.

"I think it was the cat, but the cleaning boy says it looks like it might have been a mouse…" she reported eagerly.

Mrs. Henara was furious at this interruption and more than a little irritated that the goings-on of various creatures in her larder should be discussed in the presence of an outsider – someone she was trying to impress.

"…but I think it has to be the cat. Mice don't like cake. They eat cheese don't they?" The Brat was unstoppable when she had a mystery to solve.

"And listen to this, you know what cook thinks? She thinks it was me! She is always accusing me, without any proof. If I was older I could take her to court for defi… dessi… dessication of my character, you know?"

Mrs Henara gave her daughter a stone-cold look. Mentally, both mother and daughter re-lived the dramatic scene that afternoon when she'd been caught yellow-and-red-handed, profusely breathing out garlic fumes. The Brat wilted somewhat at the memory of that spicy incident. The day of the tandoori chicken recipe revelation. Since then, the cook was convinced that every mishap in the kitchen was somehow linked to the Brat.

"Look, just stop going on about that wretched cake and ask that useless cook to bring whatever is whole and unchewed. I'm dying for my tea. Have yours in the dining room, and then get out and play in the garden. Don't come in here again." Mrs Henara was keen to go on hearing the modern daughter-in-law's objections to the traditional izzat-ridden Mohanji family.

"Do they make you work? I mean do you have to serve in the shop and all that?" she asked sympathetically in the manner of a social worker.

"No, no I can't. I'm no good at that sort of thing. And I can't sew, so I can't help my widow sister-in-law either. So I just go out all day. What else is there to do in this small town?" she replied listlessly.

"What about cooking? Don't they ask you to cook?"

"They do, but I can't. I mean I know how to cook, but I can only cook in a modern kitchen. You know, like where you can stand and cook. They don't have that. They squat to cook. I can't cook squatting. My knees get stiff."

"But then what about when you have to go to the toilet?" A small, curious voice had piped up. It was the voice of one who had spent many hours studying the logistics of the Mohanji toilet system. The Brat was still hovering near the door. Mrs Henara shot up and finally chased the girl out with threats of violence.

"No, as I was saying, " the daughter-in-law continued, "in my house we cook standing up. We have cooks but certain religious things we always do ourselves, you know. Like when we have special food on fasting days, it can't be prepared by Black hands. Special fasts you know. If you fast every Tuesday, then you can be sure of finding a good husband."

"Did it work for you?" Mrs Henara asked, rather unkindly.

"Of course. He is such a good boy. My parents came to take me away, but I said I would stay with him. I will never leave him."

The daughter-in-law realised, just a little too late, that she had just revealed a family secret. Nobody was supposed to officially know that her parents had come to take her away. She fell quiet as she sensed some guilt about admitting to a near-crisis in her still new marriage.

Mrs Henara, ever the well-spoken takaluff-trained diplomat, put her at ease.

"Oh well, these things happen. Every marriage has its ups and downs. So what, especially if you love him. How long have you been married now? A few weeks?"

"Two months."

The cook came in with the tea tray. Sandwiches and remains of the ill-fated cake.

"No, please," urged Mrs Henara, as the daughter-in-law reached towards the cake. "Please don't feel you have to eat that. That wretched woman should never have brought it in… honestly, I won't be offended if you refuse to touch it."

"No, no, really, it's OK. Yes, some weeks ago, I would have been sick on the spot, but now I'm in my fourth month, the sickness has stopped, thank God." She heaved a sigh of relief, patting her tummy with some satisfaction at the same time.

Mrs Henara, true to her tahzeeb and takaluff-bound upbringing, showed no reaction whatsoever to this startling revelation, pretending she hadn't noticed the inconsistency of a two-month old marriage with a four-month pregnancy. Instead, she changed the subject at once, and carried on talking about this and that:

"…anyway, since I kicked out my husband, my brother came from India to live with us. It's good to have a man around. He's my youngest brother. So clever. He teaches physics you know…" and she proceeded to detail her maths and intelligence theory.

But the distracted daughter-in-law was only half listening. Her mind was somewhere else. Something had gone wrong. What had she said? Something that shouldn't have been said was somehow said, oh yes! That's right! That's what it was. She had inadvertently mentioned about her parents coming to take her away. She should never have said that. Doesn't do for that sort of thing to get around!

58
FOR WHOM THE BELL TOLLS

Satwasa – or "goad-bharna" is literally to fill an expectant mother's lap. This special ceremony marks the seventh month of pregnancy, a lavish celebration in thankful acknowledgement that all is well. When seven months of gestation have passed, there's very little chance of anything going wrong.

But of course the Mohanji daughter-in-law is not in her seventh month of pregnancy, technically speaking. She is well into her ninth. Almost due, any day now. But nobody knows that – except, of course, nosey Mrs Henara, thanks to that half-chewed cake.

The Mohanjis, as always traditional and in complete observance of religious ritual, held a grand Satwasa in the backyard. A completely Green Occasion to bless their fertile daughter-in-law, and for others to come and congratulate her for holding on to her foetus up until now – right up to the safety mark of seven months.

"So big! Must be twins."

Other shopkeepers' wives have a field day at this special ceremony where it is actually not only polite to sit and stare at the mother-to-be, but to also freely comment on the bigness of her bump.

The ceremony entails the mother-to-be being dressed in a green sari with jewellery to match. Mohanji spared no expense. A special gold and emerald set had been ordered for the occasion. The most vital part of the ceremony involves having green bangles slipped on to her wrist by her mother-in-law. Only, Mrs Mohanji is dead, so the mother-in-law's duties are performed by a neighbouring Dukavalla wife. Strictly speaking, the next-in-line senior female in the Mohanji household should have been allowed this all-important role, but she's a Widow. And widows can never come too near the central figure in an auspicious celebration. So, an only-too-willing Dukavalla wife steps into the breach and performs the green-bangle task – a dozen on each wrist – with an air of solemnity coupled with a sense of pride.

The bangle-wearing is followed by the placing of various articles and holy substances in the pregnant woman's lap – to warm the lap, as it were, in advance of the baby arriving to take its rightful place there. A coconut, green scented herbs, rice, vermilion, perfume and a doll dressed in green, a crude representation of the baby. The women sing and dance. But the songs are all lullabies.

Grown-ups are really too stupid for words. The baby hasn't even arrived yet and they're already putting it to sleep! I can think of much nicer songs to sing on such a green day... if only they would let me. I could make up such beautiful songs about everything being green... I can hear special tunes in my head all the time these days....

But apart from the odd inconsistent grown-up stupidity, I'm really enjoying myself. It's my first Satwasa. Much to see, much to learn. Mohanji has been a bit mean on the food. I think that's because he spent too much on the jewellery.

"What we eat just goes through and comes out at the other end – emeralds are a good investment for the family," I have heard him say. He's right too – there weren't any shiny green emeralds lurking in the family shit when I purposefully went to the back to have a look. They've been really mean with the food. There should've been lots and lots of sweets because this is a happy occasion, but the main course is green-moong dal, boiled and crisp-fried. My least favourite. "Mug", they call it, and it's supposed to be aus... ausp... well, sounds like suspicious. I should have stayed on the shop verandah and played with my boys (no boys allowed at this ceremony), but I came along to this ladies-only do in the hope of lots of sweets. But the only thing even vaguely resembling a sweet is this one measly little green laddoo. Some woman is going round handing out one each, no seconds! Well, at least that's something. They're usually yellow or orange, so it's quite a novelty to have a special green one for this green occasion. I should eat mine slowly to make it last, but I've just scoffed it all in one go. It was so small, what could I do?

Once the ceremony and songs are finished, each woman goes up to the pregnant woman seated on a low wooden stool, takes out a ten shilling note, waves it around the pregnant one's head, and then places it in her lap as an offering for her unborn baby. And then they do a funny thing. They fold their knuckles over their temples to make a cracking sound. Apparently the knuckles have to crack audibly to draw away evil from the mother and her unborn baby. They're all doing this one by one. It's great fun to watch. Sometimes the knuckles refuse to crack and the errant woman presses them harder against her temples. Later she's heard complaining about a headache. Plain stupidity, I say.

And now it's my mother's turn. I know she never does what everybody else does. She always has to be different. I know she went out this morning and actually bought a present for the ceremony.

"Money? Money is so vulgar," she says. "I don't mind giving a gift if that's what's required at this meaningless doo-dah, but no way am I giving money!"

That's exactly what she said. And I know what present she's bought. She told me not to tell. It's a secret. I haven't told a soul, I promise!

She goes up to the pregnant star of the ceremony. She and Mohanji's daughter-in-law have become quite good friends. She's always patronising the girl. She loves championing causes, and an oppressed daughter-in-law is as good a cause as any. She bends down over the pregnant daughter-in-law with her special beaming smile – the kind of smile I often get when she reads my school report for English, but the kind that vanishes into thin air when her eyes reach the column that says "Maths."

My mother smiles radiantly and places the beautifully wrapped cubic package in the daughter-in-law's lap. The daughter-in-law is just about to raise her head and say thank-you when a really shrill-sounding alarm bell goes off inside the package, causing such shock and confusion that the daughter-in-law immediately goes into labour.

The backyard is hastily cleared of things. The mid-wife is called, as Mohanji never believed in hospitals and their eight-hundred-shilling charge for helping a woman to give birth. Birth! It's natural isn't it? Why should strangers make money out of something that is as natural as eating and shitting? Yes, shitting! Actually, it's exactly like going to the lavatory, so why lie down in some sanitised bed? Have you ever heard of anyone going to the lavatory lying down? What rubbish! So-called liberated western women are still fighting for the right to give birth at home, in a squatting position. As usual, Mr Mohanji was well ahead of his time. The special family birthing-chair is got out of one of the store cupboards. This is all so exciting! It's just like an ordinary chair but it has a cut out section in the centre-front, for the baby's head I guess. I wish they'd let me stay and watch the rest of the action.

The Satwasa guests are being asked to leave. Please, yes... yes of course we'll inform you as soon as there's some news... not now, please. Can we have some peace and quiet? Where the hell is that mid-wife Masi?

The crowd is reluctant to leave. They start dispersing slowly, obviously keen to re-assemble in some other backyard to carry on whispering: "But it's only seven months! Oh no! Hey Ram! Poor thing! God help them, please. Please let the baby be OK. Premature babies could be so weak and rat-like. Please let it live God. She's so young, poor girl."

They really mean well. They gossip like mad, but they mean well.

My mother has cornered Mohanji:

"But Mr Mohanji, this is dangerous! Anything could happen. I insist on driving her to hospital right now. Really, that's where she should be. Please, let me take charge...."

But Mr Mohanji refuses to be bullied by my mother. Good for him! I respect anyone who refuses to be bullied by my bossy mother.

"No, no thank you. Thank you for your concern, Mrs Henara, most kind, but it'll be fine. My poor wife had ten, I tell you, ten children in that chair and everything was fine. Don't worry... it's quite natural for us. Only educated people make a big deal out of childbirth. For us poor uneducated types, it's just another natural bodily function...."

My mother turns on her heel with a huff and swipes me away with her, just as I'm beginning to see my way clear to a second green laddoo. I know she's really miffed her special alarm clock gift had to go and announce itself in that vulgar fashion. She looks at me accusingly. I wonder if she knows I set the alarm for four-thirty pm sharp while she went off to get the special teddy-and-bunny wrapping paper? Well, she wanted to be different, didn't she?

59
BANANAS

"Hi, what's been going on? Haven't heard from you in over 18 hours... what's up?" Sonia sounded really concerned.

"I'm on to something," he said carefully. "Various snippets have combined together, and I think I've got a story... at last. You were right you know, about inspiration. Just a few hours at your place waiting for that wretched plumber, and my script started flowing...."

"Good! Now stop talking about it, and get on with writing it. I'll ring off now and let you get on with your work," Sonia used her best head-mistress tones.

"No... wait... I need to brain-dump...."

"NO! That's the last thing you need. What you need is a chat to rest your mind, now listen to this: what's the single largest selling product in super-markets? Come on, have a guess...."

"Oh, I don't know..." he sounded completely uninterested. She was obviously keen to dole out useless information again.

"No, seriously have a guess, please... I'd like to know what people think that product is... just for fun, come on Ashy...."

"Oh, I don't know, ...nappies, disposable nappies? Or... no, wait... washing powder? Bleach?"

"Wrong, completely wrong! Six leading supermarkets confirm that the largest selling item is... wait for it... Bananas! Yes, bananas. Because they're bloody good for you and because they come in their own biodegradable wrapping. Isn't that a nice thing to know? Aren't you glad I told you? What would you do without me Ash?"

"Yes, thank you. I'm thrilled. Now I'll be able to rest in peace... indebted to you... no, no, indebted to your dishwasher, actually. Wait a minute, I'll just go and get a banana. I feel like one right now...."

"ULG! You're such a ULG, and I love you for it!" she squealed, delighted to see one of her theories in action.

"ULG? I've forgotten that one... it's one of your special categories, isn't it? Let me see, is that the one about when a person sees someone on television drinking wine or eating a Chocolate Flake, then they want one immediately, there and then, to consume at the same time as the TV person?"

"Correct! Very ULG of you to want a banana straightaway, and I love you for it. Go and get one, I'll hold on."

"Actually I'm really glad you called Sonia, I need to sound you out... do you think... well do you suppose people can sometimes act completely out of character – can someone become the exact opposite of themselves – I mean the opposite of what they used to be?"

"I suppose we're talking about one of your characters again...?"

"Well, no, not exactly. It's someone real, but some years later, because of circumstances... take for instance a really miserly creature. If his stashed away millions did nothing for him, could he, maybe, then try to throw it all away...?"

"What, you mean like dump it in a river or something...?"

"Yes... except, could he perhaps do something more imaginative – same as throwing it away, but actually creating something in the process as well?"

"Yes, I suppose so... now, let me think. What's the easiest way to throw away large amounts of money? Charity!" she said triumphantly.

"No charity wouldn't classify as throwing away. Charity is putting money to good use. I said "dumping" it, but not exactly dumping it in a lake or whatever... using it, but not for oneself...."

"That's charity...."

"No, it's not charity. He is giving it all to someone else – a stranger...."

"That's called going bananas! Hey, bananas! ...Ash? Why so quiet Ashy-Pashy? Oh at least laugh with me. What's the matter with you these days?"

60
JEANS AND GENES

All the grown-ups are speaking in hushed tones. Every time a servant enters the room they switch into Urdu. Every time I ask a question, I get snapped at. The only thing I've been told is that we now have a military government. This military government is sometimes called a "coo" – I think that's a silly name for a government.

I'm not too sure what it means, but I suppose it could mean that soldiers are now in charge of everything. I don't see why that's such a bad thing. I think their uniforms are quite smart. Much smarter than the suits and ties of the old government. It's horrible wearing a tie in this hot climate. They make us wear them for school. Now, maybe, with a military government, I'll get a brand new military uniform for school. This cheers me up immediately. I float around the house imagining myself wearing a lot of shiny medals over crisp khaki. But why is everyone being so secretive? Something is definitely wrong.

My mother is lapping it all up. She loves a crisis. Sometimes I think she's really only happy when there's something horrible going on. She loves lamenting about the Middle-East and northern Ireland, but this time she's got something much closer to home to get her teeth into. Right here, in peaceful Pearl, where nothing ever used to go wrong, we now have a coo. She is glued to BBC World Service. She even records the news to hear it all over again. They say the same thing, again and again – and then she plays it back to hear it again – there's been a coo, they say, a military coo....

She is muttering something about having to send me away to boarding school in England, otherwise I might be forced to marry a Black man. But I'm only eight, I protest. How can anyone force me to marry? You never know with these savages, I'm told. They might do anything at any time.

But is it because they're Black, or is it because they're soldiers, I venture to ask. What makes them savages? They don't like us, I'm told for the umpteenth time. They hate Asians. But why should they hate us? Because we are successful and hard-working. "We made their country what it is," she says.

What? We did? You mean you and me? Yes, of course! Uncivilised brutes. "We educated them," she informs me in superior tones.

She goes on like this. If I ask too much, she yells at me. When she's not at her radio, she's solidly parked on her typewriter, noisily banging out letters to various schools in England. For the first time in my life, I reach out for the big heavy book. I can barely lift it. They call it an Atlas. I try to find England, but it doesn't show anything. No houses, or trees or cars or people. Just lots of blue with squiggly shapes in pink and yellow and red. Where is England? When I finally find it, it looks so small, how will I fit into it?

My aloof Uncle and my mother keep arguing. He wants me to be sent to India – boarding school in some place that sounds like Nannytail or Dare-a-doon. I like the sound of Dare-adoon. It's fun to say out loud. He thinks the discipline will do me good. My heart sinks. I don't want to go anywhere. I want to live right here. I want to be wherever my Mohanji friends are going to be. I haven't seen them for ages. I'm not allowed to go there now. The shop is too close to the market square, and the market square, according to my mother, is where all the Black trouble-makers hang out. She says it's not safe to go out at all. Sometimes we hear gun-fire. Everybody assumes it is from the market square.

I worry about my Mohanji boyfriends. I hope they're OK. Oh, and there's another thing. The Mohanji daughter-in-law has had her baby, but nobody is allowed to go and see it. I've recently started liking babies and I'm dying to see this one, but I'm not allowed. Every time I ask about it, everybody just looks the other way. Why? We have visited so many babies before. We always took them flowers, and special soft pink and blue blankets. I wish I had taken more interest then. Now I'm really into babies, I'm not allowed to go and peer at little fingers and little toes. It's not fair. Imagine! My Mohanji friends have become Uncles! It's an amazing thing for me that someone almost my age should already be an Uncle. How grown up that must feel!

No harm in trying again:

"Mummy, please can we go and see the baby?"

"No, I haven't got time. Very busy these days. So much to do. Have to sort out your future school."

"But please mummy, can't I just go and see the baby on my own?"

"No. You stay put! I don't want you stepping out of this house. These are bad times. They're kidnapping Asian girls."

"Why?"

"Because they just are."

"But I want to know why. Maybe if I got kidnapped then I could find out why.... Wouldn't that be good? Then we would know why they're doing it and we could solve the mystery and then it won't happen again...."

"Look, will you just shut up and let me get on with my letters? It's your future I'm sorting out here. If, God forbid, you were kidnapped, you wouldn't even live to tell the story...."

"No, but at least I'd know why...."

"Go out and play!"

"But you said not to go out."

"Don't twist everything I say. You can play in the garden. Just keep within sight of the house. And report back every half-hour so I know you're OK. Now get out!"

"Yes, OK mummy, but about the baby... you know I think babies are really sweet. When can we...."

"I said NO! Now do as I say!"

Shooed away, yet again. Brick wall, again. Try another avenue. I step out into the garden and walk round to the side of our big house. I make a point of lingering outside my Uncle's window. He's in there, doing his marking as usual. He notices my face pressed against the window and tries to shoo me away. I stand on my toes and stick my head inside the open window:

"Uncle, haven't you got any more physics lessons to send to the Widow?"

"No," he growls.

"But you haven't even replied to her last letter – I mean her physics homework."

"There's no need. Go away. I'm very busy."

"But Uncle you said her future depended on it. What will she do if she doesn't get to study science properly? She'll have to just be a slave in that shop. You said so yourself. Don't you think we should try and rescue her?"

"Just go away and mind your own business. Haven't you got anything to do?" My Uncle is most irritated by this line of questioning. He's obviously still very much in love with the Widow.

"But she wrote such a nice letter to you last time... I mean, I think it must've been nice because you smiled when you read it...." I know it's no use. I've been caught. He knows I know that he knows.

"Pest! Rascal! Do you think I don't know? Who else would write that sort of rubbish? Which woman would write, 'I love you more than all the sweets and toffees in the world – I'll give them all up for you. Will you be my lollipop?' Your only saving grace is that your spelling's pretty good. Your handwriting's not bad either...."

I hang my head with shame. So, he knew. And he'd given up on the Widow just because she hadn't bothered writing back to him. Men are such cowards. No staying power. Just because she doesn't play ball straightaway, he gives up!

Normally I would have been pretty shattered by his discovery that I'd been the real letter-writer. But I had more important things on my mind. I had a mystery to solve.

Why wasn't anyone allowed to see the new Mohanji grandchild? Was it possible it was a monster with three eyes or something? If that was the case then I most definitely wanted to see it. I had never ever seen a real monster. No, it can't be. If it really were a monster, Mohanji would set it up in the shop and make even more money by charging everyone who wanted to see it. No there had to be something else. Something big.

I walk round to the back of the house. I really don't want to play in the garden. I want to solve mysteries. When I grow up I want to be a detective and solve mysteries all the time. I invent a new game called Spying, which involves lingering outside the windows of every single room in the house, just to see if I can get any information about anything.

I overhear my mother and my uncle having a discussion about jeans. How can one talk about jeans in the middle of all this? My mother says the Black jean is always stronger. The darker jean predominay... predommy something. My Uncle says frizzy hair always pre-something over straight hair. And the nose. The nose is bound to look like it just came under a lorry. Whose nose? Which lorry? Has there just been an accident? No it can't be anything tragic like that or my mother would have her special worried for the whole world look.

Still, all this is most interesting. It is very rare for them to discuss jeans and hair. My mother is voicing her opinion very decidedly. She lords it over my uncle, because she's in biology. She says "I should know – it's MY subject."

So biology is to do with jeans? How interesting! I must ask for a new pair of jeans. That will please her. She'll think I am taking an interest in her subject at last. But when I decide to forget my undercover-agent spying game and poke my head through the window to ask if 1 can have a pair of jeans, she just snaps back at me:

"From where? All the shops are closing! The Indians are all going. Who's going to sell anything to us now?"

"But what about biology?" I ask innocently.

My mother's face grows radiant. She gives me a rare look of approval. She walks over to the window and leans out to talk to me properly.

"Oh baby, how clever of you! Yes, let me tell you about genes," and she launches into something called dee-en-ay and ex chrome-something's and why-something's.

A moment of truth. A turning point in my early educational development. There were genes and then there were jeans.

61
THE CHOCOLATE & CHILLIE BABY

I am that unfortunate woman who is not allowed to show off her baby. Wasn't it enough misfortune to be kanjoos-marwari Mohanji's daughter-in-law, without having to be ashamed of my baby as well? Reduced to living in this shack behind the shop. And to think I used to live in such a grand house, in the biggest town of the rich neighbouring country. I would never have believed that one day I would be married to someone who lived in a really small town. It's hard to live in a small town when you've got used to big towns. Back home it was so different. Bright lights, wide streets, lots of people. Not everyone knew everyone, like this wretched place where everyone knows exactly what's what. It's stifling. So many nosey people everywhere.

I have nothing to do. They want me to cook, and sew and clean the house. But I don't know how to do those things. I've never had to do them before. In my parents' home we had a lot of servants – all Black, of course. And here, in these two wretched rooms-behind-the-shop house, nothing. Even if I want a drink of water, I have to get it myself, from an earthenware water pot in the shaded part of the backyard. My mean father-in-law will not hear of a fridge. There's no electricity in the house anyway. Too expensive, he says.

My young brothers-in-law study by the light of kerosene lamps, and sometimes, when they want a brighter light, they go out into the blue neon of street lamps in the market square. That's where they have to sit and read their books – just like black Africans. It's not right. They're Indian, and they should have a proper reading light at home. I feel so sorry for them. They're all really nice boys. But just look at how they have to live – worse than animals in cages. I'll never get used to this. My parents' house was big and airy. In the evenings it was always brightly lit, not dingy and gloomy like here. Every time it was anyone's birthday or diwali or something, our wedding-cake shaped house would be outlined with hundreds of little multi-coloured lights twinkling late in the dark night. And little light bulbs on every branch of every tree. But my mean father-in-law Mohanji says that all that kind of thing is a dreadful waste of money and mother earth's energy. It's just for showing off wealth he says. He doesn't believe in showing off. Just the opposite. He believes is hiding it all away and living like a pauper.

I really miss my parents' house. We lived so well. But how could I go on living there? It would have brought a lot of shame on everyone. I had to get married, as soon as possible, and go away to another town, another country. What was I to do? It wasn't my fault. We girls are never taught anything. They never tell us the facts of life, and then when something happens, they say it's our fault.

I was told not to go out with boys. I was told never to be anywhere alone with a boy. To me that meant Asian boy. Nobody ever told me not to be alone with a Black house-boy. That was never mentioned. It was unthinkable that a good Asian girl like me should seek the company of a Black boy – and a house boy at that. But it happened. One day after my bath when I called out for a clean towel, it was the new house-boy, George, who brought it to me. He was always very friendly. He'd just finished primary school but couldn't afford to go to secondary school, so he had been forced into domestic service. Lucky for him, to find work so quickly with such a good Indian family. He was the junior servant, responsible for dusting and polishing. His duties also included cleaning all the family's shoes. So as he was coming out of my room having placed my carefully polished black shoes in their place, he heard me call out from the bathroom for a clean towel.

He brought one immediately, and stood with his back to the bathroom door to hand it to me. When I opened the door just a little, intending only to reach for the towel, the sight of his straight, strong back looked so nice I felt like talking to him. And anyway, being naked in the bathroom always made me feel a warm delicious feeling between me legs. I can't describe it, but it always made me feel sociable – in need of company, so I pulled George in, just to have a chat... really... only for a chat. He came in readily, saying he wanted to show me something. That was very forward behaviour for a mere servant, but I didn't mind. I liked him. He was friendly. What he showed me was quite nice too. It felt a bit strange at first, but soon I began looking forward to it, and we met regularly in the bathroom. How was I to know this had anything to do with babies? Nobody ever talked about that. When I had asked my mother how babies were born, she said I was completely shameless to ask such questions. When I persisted she said God just gave you babies automatically once you were married, and that too if he was pleased with you. And to please him you had to marry the right kind of person – the right person being one of your own creed, your own race, your own caste, your own religion – even your own language.

I just couldn't understand why God had decided to give me a baby when I wasn't even married. My parents never told me anything. They just said not to go out alone with boys or young men. I wasn't going out. I was in my own bathroom. And the servant George and I were just playing a friendly game. So how could it happen?

When I complained to my mother about my swelling belly, she said I should eat less. Then I remembered I had seen no blood for a while, so I came up with the bright idea that that was why my stomach was getting hard and swollen. I told her I thought all the blood was probably stuck inside me, so my stomach had become big and was making me vomit. On hearing this, she shrieked like a hyena and demanded to know which Asian boy among our family acquaintances had "spoilt" me.

I swore by every God I knew that I not been with any Asian boy, but they wouldn't believe me. And before I knew it, these people from the small town had arrived to look me over as a prospective bride for their son. I didn't like Mohanji at all, but the boy had a beautiful face – so kind, such soft green eyes. I decided there and then to marry him and escape from my mad mother who never told me the truth about anything, but just wailed and cried all day. Anything was better than this. But I'm regretting it now.

One day at the Mohanji's, they dressed me up in green – all green, green sari, green jewellery, green bangles. And the only woman I can relate to in this town placed a small parcel in my lap. A shrill alarm bell went off – my baby was announcing his arrival.

I was completely stunned when I saw him. How could God give an Indian woman a Black baby? Then I remembered George, and wondered if the two things were connected. But I had played the same sort of game with my husband, so why hadn't anything happened about that? Perhaps because you can only have them one at a time? So how do people have twins?

There was so much I wanted to know. But it was considered immoral for young women to want to know these things. I was already a married woman, and I still didn't know what made it happen. There was a new thing starting in schools now, but it hadn't been there in my time. It was called sex education. I thought it was a great idea, but people like my father-in-law and his Morality Committee were opposed to girls knowing about sex. If they knew about sex, they would go and do it. That was the thinking in all those respectable Indian homes. And if they didn't know anything about it, what then? What if they thought it was just another harmless game? What would happen to them then?

My baby is Black – well chocolate-coloured really. I never thought I could love someone with such a dark skin – but maybe because he's mine...? He's so sweet. Big brown eyes and such a funny nose! I know they won't let me keep him... what would people say? The Morality Committee will eat my father-in-law alive! Three of them came to the house the day after the birth and tried to coax me into giving him up to the Catholic orphanage. They said it was for the best.

"But he's not an orphan," I protested. "He has a mother and he has a father...."

"No, no, no father," they said. "A Black father isn't really a father... it doesn't count."

I clutched my baby tight, day and night, unable to sleep a wink in case they took him while I was asleep.

Four days after giving birth, there were incessant thumping noises cutting through my sleepless brain like shrapnel. Clouds of orange-pink dust stinging my sleep-deprived, wide-open eyes like fragments of shattered glass. Women chattering and gossiping and beating away at the chillies. While the neighbourhood women were savagely beating the chillies to powder, Mohanji and his friends were trying to beat me to death. They used the chilly-pounding noises to disguise the noise of their beatings, synchronising every merciless stroke in absolute unison.

But why should I worry? As long as my green-eyed husband is alive, I can come to no harm. He covered my body with his and they stopped beating me. Mohanji could never beat his favourite son. Soon after that, my husband and I moved into a rented flat.

62

A SONG FOR EVERY OCCASION

Pearl was an exceptionally musical place. And if music is about harmony then Pearl was also exceedingly harmonised between different races, tribes, religions and languages.

Everything and everyone made music. Every moment of time was filled with the magical sounds of being. Every living creature sang in unison, exalting the glory of creation. The crickets sang special songs to welcome the rainy season. The mosquitoes composed symphonies to celebrate the warm, clammy nights. The snakes rattled in syncopated glee, the geckos tapped their tongues in time to the buzzing, on-off dance of the fire-flies. And Nature's Light and Sound Show was aptly complemented by man-made sounds. The Hindu temple singers sang bhajjans, Muslim congregations pounded their breasts in rhythmically ritualised grief during the month of Moharram. Church choirs sang haunting melodies to the strains of majestic organs. And the Shabads of the Sikhs made hypnotic, mystical sounds in breezy Gurudwara courtyards.

And then those poor Blacks who hadn't been fortunate enough to have their souls saved by the kind White missionaries and add their voices to the majesty of Church organs, struck to their own pagan tunes. They had songs for every occasion – songs for every activity. There were songs for picking cotton, songs for the coffee plantations, for picking tea, for sugarcane – songs for planting and songs for harvesting. Songs for weaving, songs for grinding, songs for threshing, songs for churning. There were songs for work and songs for play. Songs to make light of heavy burdens – special songs for ant-like workers, a chorus of singers sweating in salty, smelly unison for their Asian and White masters. "Poley poley, Mzee, poley poley." And then there were songs for war – for marching – songs for going into battle. Not that there was any occasion for that... well, not usually.

It had been a most successful coup d'etat, and relatively bloodless as army coups go. Army divisions from Pearl's Northern Province and Southern Province had united to oust the anachronistic Black princes and their hangers on. Unity is strength. How else to get rid of these useless, corrupt chaps and their lavish lifestyles? All caught up in tribal loyalties and nepotism. This wasn't the age for princes – this was the modern age... and it needed a new state machinery – strict discipline. Stamp on corruption, wipe out bribery. Employ ruthless punitive measures, the kind that can only be enforced by a disciplined army.

The military take-over was complete in less than twenty-four hours. But there was just one small outstanding matter – and that was the appointment of the new Head of State. The head of the Northern Army had assumed he would be leader and his Southern counterpart would be Deputy Leader – a perfectly fair scheme, except for one small inescapable detail: the head of the Southern Army had assumed the exact opposite.

Given that the Northern Province was more populated and had a bigger army, Colonel North considered it his indisputable birthright to be appointed President of Pearl. But the Southerners, although fewer in number, had fought fiercely and were renowned for their bravery. And so Colonel South, much more charismatic and youthful than Colonel North, felt his appointment to this noble office ought to be a foregone conclusion. He even already felt and behaved like a President – the actual announcement of this fact on Radio Pearl would be a mere formality.

For a few tense hours it looked like all might be lost. Everything that had been gained in the last momentous twenty-four hours might just turn to blood and dust in a civil war of North and South. But common sense prevailed – most uncommonly for sub-Saharan Africa! But then, this was no ordinary African country – this was Pearl, and the Pearlites were essentially a musical, peace-loving people.

Pearl was indeed a very special place – anywhere else coup and subsequent counter-coups would've reduced the country to ashes, but not so in Pearl, thanks to its saviour who appeared in the form of a non-military, but better than average educated, good-looking young man. Both colonels North and South were satisfied with the compromise candidate from Pearl's rather insignificant Western Province, and both looked forward to pulling their puppet's strings. But he was no puppet, and luckily nobody needed to pull his strings. On all vital issues, without a single exception, he was in complete agreement with his new military employers:

EMERGENCY FIRST MEETING OF NEW MILITARY CABINET:
FIRST FIVE-YEAR PLAN: YEAR 1
AGENDA

1. Teach the bloody Asian Dukavallas a lesson.
2. Commission musician to compose special song for Asian send-off.

That's how this song had taken birth. The concept had first appeared as Item Two on the very first agenda of the very first military cabinet meeting, presided over by the quiet and unassuming young man, later, to become Dictator:

Farewell Muhindi's, farewell O Muhindi's
You've milked us dry
You've sabotaged our soil,
You've sold us our water,
Now go to England and try-ha-ha-yee...
ha ha ha, hee hee hee... ho ho ho ho
Just you try your tricks on the Whitiees
And then see what happens, what happens, what happens
We cleaned your shit, now you clean theirs
We'll love you always, but forget your airs
We love you so, but now you must go,
Farewell Muhindis, farewell Muhindis
Now go to England and tr..rr.rr..y
ha ha ha, hee hee hee, ho ho ho ho

There was no doubt about it. Pearl was truly exceptional. Even in hateful adversity, Pearl was a truly musical place....

63
CHOCOLATE COLOURED KALYUG

I don't know what crime I committed in my last life that God should have given me such a daughter-in-law. From the moment she stepped into this house, everything has gone wrong. She must have the most unholy feet. The Muslims would say "manhoos," we call it "ashub." Same thing, we're the same sort of people really – Hindu or Muslim, we're all Indians. I respect you in whichever form you appear, but God, why did you give me such a daughter-in-law? She stepped into this house and with her she brought nothing but disaster. I can only thank God my poor wife wasn't alive to see this shameful episode.

Why do decent Indian people bring up their daughters like this? Don't they know that their daughters have to one day go and join another respectable household? Why don't they bring them up to be reliable and trustworthy custodians of the honour of some other poor, hard-working man and his household? Is this the way to bring up daughters? She spelt trouble from the start. I should have known then.

First it was paper tissues. Yes, she had the audacity to demand disposable tissues when a good cloth hanky or the end of her sari would've done just as well. Then she wanted her husband's earnings to spend on her face creams. Then she wanted holidays with him. And one day, she finally took him away from us. To go and live in a flat. A flat! Is that the way for human beings to live? Layered on top of one another in soul-less blocks of grey concrete, with a metal coffin to carry you up and down those impossible heights? And I have to pay their rent. Out of my own son's hard-earned money, I have to fork out nine hundred shillings a month so that she can live separately from us.

Our house isn't grand enough for her. She says she's embarrassed to invite her friends here. What friends? Good for nothing, lazy, idle wives of rich men. Just for the privilege of giving them tea, she has to have her own flat. It's money down the drain. Where's the need to go and live like that when you already have a nice family house with a private room of your own? Still,

I managed to put up with all that. I suffered in silence. But now this? This is too much. Now she's given us a frizzy-haired, chocolate-colour-skin, grandson. I ask you, my son is fair, with green eyes. She herself is very fair-skinned – that's why I chose her for my son – and her hair is dead straight. Tell me, how on earth am I supposed to believe that this is my own son's offspring? My flesh and blood?

Be reasonable. How can it be my grandson? And it arrived so early. Premature they said. They think I'm stupid. How many premature babies weigh in at nine pounds and four ounces? I know, because I weighed him myself, on the shop scales. I may be just a shopkeeper, but even I know that premature babies are rat-like and thin, struggling for breath. Kept in small plastic containers with all kinds of tubes going in and out of their pathetic little bodies. Hey Ram!

But her baby, with a fat stomach and chubby legs, flat nose and big black eyes and clouds of frizzy hair, came out laughing. Yes, laughing. It was mocking us. I tell you it was taunting me. So you hate Blacks don't you? Well here I am, and I am half-Black, so what the hell are you going to do about it?

Even after all that, I didn't throw her out. My favourite green-eyed son would've been heart-broken. The Committee demanded I publicly expel her from my household. But I'm a reasonable man. I gave her the choice of giving up her baby to the local Catholic mission who have a special place for abandoned, illegitimate babies.

"It's not illegitimate! How dare you use that word? You are the one who is illegitimate! How can an innocent baby be anything? It's my baby and I'm keeping it. Go hang yourself!" she says. Such a vile tongue!

Only in this age of Kalyug and in this immoral country first ruled by shameless Whites and now immoral Blacks, can a wrongdoer behave with such effrontery. In India, back in our village, a woman as unfortunate as her would have just bowed her head with shame, and then jumped into the nearest water well, baby and all. That's the way to save the family honour. But she's completely shameless. Refuses to say sorry and insists on keeping her half-Black bastard. Then she goes and gets the government involved. She goes to some minister and complains about me. And this stupid army government cashes in on my shame and makes a huge example out of the baby. This baby symbolises their most cherished dream – more sexual intercourse between Asian girls and African men, and more bastard half-race babies. Damn her! I curse her!

Now I'm a marked man. They hold me personally responsible for prohibiting racial integration. I am told they're going to get me. They want revenge. It's all her doing. If she hadn't gone tittle-tattle, none of this would have happened. It was my own private family matter – my own shame, and now it's splashed all over the papers… Mohanji Rascist! Is this what integration is all about? Should our Indian girls become pregnant with Black babies and then be allowed to marry innocent, unsuspecting Asian boys like my green-eyed one?

I spit on this kind of integration. To me, integration means respecting each other's cultures and traditions. I have a lot of time for the real African culture, not this western rubbish they've all taken on. Real Africans respect their elders and the family unit is sacrosanct. The father is held in great reverence. Yes, these Blacks certainly had a lot of good sense, but those shameless Whites came and wiped out what little culture these people had. So what can they do? It's such a pity! Africans and Asians could live in such harmony if only all this inter-marriage nonsense goes away. We own the shops, we sell them stuff. They buy, we sell. They're happy, we're happy. So, where's the need for all this inter-marriage rubbish, bakwaas? How can one explain to them that our girls don't even marry outside their own caste? We don't even inter-marry within our own race. Hindus and Muslims are so united in this foreign land, yet we'd never dream of uniting our families by marriage. It would be quite out of the question. How can we even begin to contemplate marrying them to someone of a different colour and a different religion? It's unthinkable!

These Africans say Indian girls would naturally fall in love with Black men if given the freedom to do so. Ho! They aren't even allowed to fall in love with their own kind! Love is not the basis on which our marriages are made. How can one base such an important life decision as marriage on something so flimsy as love? What is love? What happens to marriage based on so-called love? One only has to look at western countries – just look at all those Hollywood people! Every one of those couples married for love, and where did it get them? What is this love thing? If it was real and everlasting then why would so many love marriages end?

And my poor green-eyed one. So noble, such forgiveness in his nature.

"So what if it's someone else's baby?" he says. "I like all babies. I want to be the father. The baby is blameless isn't he?"

That's what he says, my big-hearted, forgiving, angelic, green-eyed one. Such a God-like creature my son. He's not human he's an angel.

But she... she just walks out, baby and all, and shacks up with her new Black politician boyfriend. He already has three wives. Let her go. Let them be. Too bad she couldn't have gone quietly. Now the whole world knows about the baby.

And my dear son, my green-eyed one, I just watch him wilt. He used to be such a happy one. Now, he just works by day and then sits quietly through his evening meal. Then he goes to bed without so much as a word. What can I do? He loves her so much. He still wants her back. He says the politician will soon get fed up with her and she'll be back.

He's still waiting for her. He won't let me arrange another marriage for him. Lots of girls are still prepared to marry him. Hard working, good looking and young – who wouldn't want him? So what if his first wife turned out to be such a disgrace? Nobody's going to hold that against him. He's a man isn't he? Men can do no wrong – only women bring shame upon everyone by their wayward actions. God made woman to preserve man's shame. The minute a woman steps outside her four walls, it means trouble, take it from me.

Hey Bhagwan! Do you know what's happening in your world in the name of love? O you God of plastic, God of stone, you doll-like God, are you real? How can you smile like that in my poor dead wife's puja room, when all around you is being blown to ashes? Wake up God! It has happened. Kalyug, I tell you, Kalyug is here!

64
I HAVE A DREAM

The Dictator's dream was announced one morning in the main national newspaper. God had appeared in his dream and had ordered him to expel all the Dukavallas – Asian shopkeepers that is, and then, and only then would Pearl be truly liberated, and God's mercy would smile on the fields and flowers... and... er... the shops.

The announcement put Pearl's God-fearing Indian Dukavallas in a very difficult position. How to argue with God's dream? If that's what God wished, then it would have to be obeyed. Which person in his right mind could disobey God?

But was it indeed *God* who appeared in the Dictator's dream? Well, who was to say that it wasn't? That was the nature of revelations. If you claimed to have had something revealed to you from the Divine, then which God-fearing person would dare dispute that? That would be tantamount to disputing the existence of God himself, and declaring oneself an atheist. And in God-loving, God-fearing, ultra-musical Pearl atheism was second worst only to mixing up crockery between the races.

There were, nevertheless, those who timidly dared to suggest that the God who appeared in the Dictator's dream with this fearful message may have been some other god, not their God. But how could that be? God was only One! There was only one God, no matter how many dreams he showed up in. And the same God could go from dream to dream with the relative ease of one who was popping in and out of high street shops. So, there was no question of challenging the legality of this drastic order, leave alone crying for outside help, or appealing to rhyme and reason. It was no use.

"It's not my idea," said the Dictator, half-apologetically, in a resigned-to-fate sort of way.

"God says I must do it. Believe me. I don't want to... but God's wishes have to be obeyed. Sorry, folks."

God had become very important for the Dictator – more so since becoming the compromise leader of the coup. That spirit of compromise had also necessitated the Dictator's conversion to Islam as a gesture of neutrality and fairness.

Pearl's Northern Province was largely Protestant Christian, the southern Province predominantly Catholic, and coming form the rather small and insignificant Western Province himself, the Dictator decided that taking on a completely different religion would be the best course of action. Just in case the Northern and Southern colonels took their cue from Northern Ireland and found another reason to hate one another. No, don't take risks. Convert to a good, simple, straightforward, peace-loving religion. Safest thing, become a Muslim. That way, neither the Protestants nor the Catholics can get too big for their boots.

Both North and South were thrilled at the conversion. Good move. That way neither Christian sect would assume any unnecessary importance. Pearl was another word for compromise – in all matters, except where God himself intervened and ordained that things should be a particular way. Then there could no compromise. Orders were orders. The Dukavallas would have to go.

What about the others? Not all Muhindis were Dukavallas. The ones that occupied the biggest and best houses were teachers, and doctors and....

No, no, not them. They stay. Only Dukavallas go.

The non-shopkeeper-better-educated Urdu-and-Bengali-speaking Muhindis heaved a sigh of relief. They would get to keep their houses and their gardens and their mosquito-servants. They could hang on to this idyllic climate and their lavish life-styles. Their Brahmin kitchens. Separate crockery for the servants. Spacious servants' quarters rented out to poor Black families. Martini on the lawn. Pimms and Croquet. Chicken sandwiches at sun downers. Cricket. Bridge. Poetry.

The Martini and cricket set of Muhindis immediately threw their weight behind the Dictator and proclaimed his dream an authentic revelation from the one and only God. Yes, these bloody Dukavallas had exploited the poor Blacks long enough. Wretched Marwaris! Bloody kanjoos-makhichoos Banyas! Serves them right! Kick 'em out!

God was quite considerate, really. Or, he would have been, except that three days later, there was another dream. Again, it was the Dictator's dream, and once again it was on the front page of the morning paper. God had appeared again and added a footnote to the previous dream: The footnote read: "The word Dukavallas, used in this sense, is a synonym for ALL Asians."

Just as well our Dictator was rather well educated otherwise he wouldn't have known about reading footnotes, leave alone knowing what 'synonym' meant. Just as well our Dictator had had the discipline and the passion to pursue his studies by himself, quietly under the blue neon light of a street lamp, with books kindly donated by Mrs Henara. And just as well our Dictator had become a Muslim, because in Islam, there is no concept of the untouchable – even if you *do* do a job as filthy as sweeping up the Dukavallas' shit.

65
TONIGHT'S THE NIGHT

The Ustad knew all about grand entrances. He'd made enough of those on stage. The fact that the preceding entrance, that of his accompanists, the much-younger-and-nicer-looking percussionist and other supporting string players, caused more of an uproar than his own, never seemed to deter his majesty. He entered bowing and salaaming in all directions and remained doing so until the moderate applause petered away. Sometimes he carried on bowing even after the applause had died down. He refused to believe that people were no longer struck by his presence. That was his way at formal concerts, but at small, intimate, private recitals his assumptions of grandeur became even grander, particularly at informal gatherings where, officially, there was to be no playing or singing – just talk. But this kind of talk-only session often carried the promise that the Ustad, if inspired enough, would suddenly break into song, and some ever-willing hanger-on would disappear for a while and then reappear, complete with instrument, laying it in the Ustad's lap as graciously as possible. And as for the Ustad – oh well, what else could he do? Such an inspiring gathering. Such inspired people. When such lofty spirits gather together in a room then music was a natural and logical outcome.

The Ustad had played exquisitely that evening, and he had chosen a particularly beautiful raag – Bagesheri. A feminine raag, romantic, gentle, dreamy. It evoked visions of a beautiful woman clad in a diaphanous white sari, white flowers in her hair, fragrant, fragile. In her hands she carried a veena – an ancient instrument of some weight, which she held as though a feather. And she seemed to step out of the stars and descend down an imaginary staircase carved out of mist. At every note the Ustad struck expertly, she took another graceful step down the spiralling staircase of swirling, semi-transparent mist.

Musically, it had been a truly enchanting evening. The Ustad had perfected the technique of being conspicuously absent from his own performance. For the listener, this meant the added magic of receiving the music directly from the Divine. The Ustad seemed to have grasped that essential knack of not existing while making music. Too bad that wasn't the case in his non-music-making moments, when the fact of his existence and his grand stature was an inescapable fact.

He thrived on these gatherings at which some well-meaning hostess, usually a former groupie, would assemble a group of what she imagined were fans and devotees, and cook a superb meal at which she would have slaved all day. Only in this case, the Groupie had been bribed and bullied by the Producer into hosting the evening at her large house. The Producer badly needed an event at which the Ustad could feel important again. Their working relationship had been deteriorating and she had another vital recording coming up. She needed him in a good mood. In return for hosting the party, she had promised the Groupie that she would drag the World's Number One Composer to the event, somehow. The fact that the World's Number One spent most of the evening hiding in the garden while Groupie went from tree to tree and shrub to shrub armed with a plate of samosas was neither here nor there.

The evening music-party at Groupie's spacious mansion was exactly the sort of gathering over which the Ustad liked to preside. After the performance and the accolades that followed, he disappeared to freshen up and then re-entered the grand drawing room, heading straight for the seat of honour. He had a habit of just gravitating towards the most prominent, comfortable and centrally situated throne at which he didn't so much sit as sink, until he was quite indistinguishable from the piles of mirror-embroidered cushions. And then he waited expectantly to be asked probing questions on the mysteries of the origins of music.

Music was his favourite subject of discussion, not because he was eager to demystify its ancient anomalies, but because questions on this topic always provided the perfect cue for his favourite anecdotes and jokes. Of these he had dozens, and loved to tell them again and again. Those who had been at many such sittings with him already knew all the jokes, but when he delivered the punch-line, he would single out those regulars and fix them with a threatening gaze, intimidating them to laugh the loudest.

"So what if you've heard it before? I'm telling it again and you should consider yourself lucky to have the opportunity to hear it once more, from my own mouth!"

This particular gathering was exceptional in that the majority of assembled guests were non-Urdu speaking. This made him rely heavily on the Producer and the mostly absent Composer, for what he hoped were accurate translations of his own special brand of wit. He was, without a doubt, quite witty in the original, but most of his jokes lost something in translation. He often suspected that the translators were not doing a proper job, or were severely editing all his elaborate, build-up material to get to the punch line quickly. Hurry, hurry, always in a hurry these Westerners! In India too, people were becoming very hurried nowadays. And that was the cue to launch into his second favourite subject: the good old golden age when nobody ever hurried. He told of his grandfather playing alaaps of four hours. He spoke with pride of how royalty and nobility matched every single musical microtone with a gold coin. He boasted about how many elephants laden with silver urns of treasures appeared at their house as advance payment for his grandfather to play at the court of this or that nawab or maharajah.

And that would launch him straight into the story of how a one time top courtesan, a certain Tameezan Bai of Lucknow, had agreed to provide a mere "warm-up" session for his grandfather's recital of a special composition capturing the bitter-sweet essence of the nuptials of a long-separated couple. That composition was to have been the main highlight of that famous night. That was what people had come to hear. That is what they had been promised – a full all-night session with his distinguished ancestor. And what a session it would have been....

But there's such wickedness in this world. Evil eye. Ek nazar. Just one glance. Mountains can crumble. Rivers can turn to stone. Yes that night... that night....

66
THE BIG NIGHT

The courtesan's preparations had begun three days in advance. She was rubbed with turmeric, her body coated in sandalwood, then bathed and massaged with jasmine oil, her still-black tresses coated with coconut oil, re-bathed in goat's milk, scented with the fragrant smoke of udh-wood. Then combed and coiffured. Hands and feet decorated with henna. Last-minute fittings and adjustments to the very special outfit of gold-thread specially woven for the occasion. So what if she was only the warm-up act? She would be warming the stage for The Lighter Upper of the Universe himself. The torch that had carried her through many nights of despair – sixteen years of hoping and pining. Sometimes convinced it would happen, at other times despondent she would turn to ashes and dust before he even knew she was no longer in this world.

She was to entertain the assembled dignitaries with thumris and ghazals. She had composed a special ghazal just for this occasion. In fact, she had composed it years ago, thinking that the Ustad might send for her at any time and she wanted to be sure she had something especially stunning and original to sing for him. But all those years just passed, and it never happened. The Ustad had never ever expressed the slightest bit of interest in her songs or her body. Poor Tameezan – hoping he would just drop in, like any other client. Then, when she had been forced to accept that that was probably as unlikely as the sun rising at midnight, she had consoled herself with the thought that he would perhaps, some day, just send for her. And when that didn't happen either, she just spent long hours on the roof terrace of her kotha, singing as loudly as she could manage, in the hope that he would be passing in the street below and would catch a few strains of her undoubtedly melodious voice. This she did on many evenings. Vast crowds gathered in the street below for a free concert, but not a sign of the Universal Lighter-Upper Ustad.

And now, at last, by a wonderful twist of fate, they were both to perform in the same room. The room would be full of men. The women guests would sit at the back, concealed behind diaphanous curtains. And although she would be perfumed and oiled from head to toe, nobody would even get within a mile of her. This evening, she would be a bride, ritually dressed and adorned with finery befitting a bride for her wedding night. She had performed at every major court – pomp and grandeur and ceremony were nothing new for her, but tonight was a special night because she would be singing only for him. She was preceding him. She was preparing the ground for him. She would warm them up for him. And once her show was over, she would be seated alongside the men, in a prominent position to enjoy the rest of the night's entertainment.

He would have to look at her. He would surely hear the last few minutes of her singing, for she had been asked to sing until such time as the Grand Ustad was safely in place.

She had loved him ever since she had first heard about him. Everyone who knew the Great Ustad told impressive – often exaggerated – stories of his kindness, his wit, his humour, his good looks, his talent, his music, his wealth.

Once or twice she had managed to hear him play at formal occasions, but she had been confined to the women's enclosure, safely tucked away behind a lace curtain. How to attract his attention? And then there had been those many, many hopeful Thursday evenings: but how to make a man fall in love with you if you were only ever destined to catch a glimpse of his broad back?

She had sent him numerous messages and invitations to visit her and be entertained by her songs. She had even requested that he tutor her in music. As a last, desperate resort, she had even sought the spiritual intervention of a Holy Saint of Music.

She had tried every trick in the book, but there had never been a single word of encouragement from the Ustad. And towards the end of this message-sending phase, there hadn't even the normal courteous acknowledgement in flowery Urdu. At times she had felt immense anger. She, the number one courtesan of this grandest of states, for whom numerous men would've happily forsaken all their worldly goods, she who charged top rates and broke so many hearts – that she should have made such overtures to one mere Ustad, and he, heartless he… totally oblivious of her worth. Doesn't he know how lucky he is? Doesn't he know who I am? Hasn't anyone told him how beautiful I am? If I've heard so much about his music, why hasn't he heard anything about my beauty?

Sixteen years of waiting. Sixteen years of longing. A decade and more of wondering how their first meeting would actually feel… or indeed if it would ever happen. And then, out of the blue, this heaven-sent opportunity….

A not-yet bankrupt Nawab orders a gala evening to celebrate the birth of a son, three wives and eighteen daughters later. Every top musician had been invited to take part. At first she had asked the Nawab's messenger to go drown himself in a fistful of water. How dare the decrepit nobleman Nawab suppose that SHE could turn up to perform? She ought to be invited as a guest in her own right!

True, she was nearing forty at this time, but the Nawab, he of the newly acquired baby-son, being one of the old school and still captivated by the courtesan's old magic had sent for her because he wanted a star line-up for the evening's entertainment. The Grand Ustad Lighter Upper of the Universe had agreed to play on the condition that he would provide the grand finale and carry the proceedings well into the early hours. "Durbari you know – I have to play Raag Durbari for such an occasion...."

Once the Nawab's messenger sensed that the Courtesan was playing hard to get, he decided to bring the trump card into play and started chatting informally about the difficulty of filling four whole hours prior to the Grand Ustad's entrance – the Grand Lighter Upper, you know? It did the trick! Tameezan's ears actually cocked up visibly by at least a quarter of an inch. The Ustad himself? He Who Lights Up the Universe? You mean he's going to be playing at the Nawab's party? Oh well, I see, in that case....

But Tameezan was a hard-headed woman. A woman hopelessly and desperately in love she might have been, but she wasn't going to get carried away just because her most cherished dream at last looked like turning into reality. She agreed to turn up and sing, but only on the condition that she provided the penultimate item. She would come on just before the Grand Ustad, and then she would be allowed to stay put among the men to listen to the Ustad's exquisite music of which she had heard so much. This was readily agreed. The Nawab considered it a very small price to pay. Since she would sing before all the men anyway, what difference could it make if she carried on sitting amongst them for the Ustad's session? Anyway, she was a courtesan... it would be a treat. They could all go on gazing at her unashamedly if they got bored with the Ustad's music.

But nobody ever got bored with the Ustad's music. That would be unthinkable. His music had power over animals and humans alike. His music made snakes lose their venom, it brought wild animals wailing with submission out of their jungle abodes, and it brought half-dead people out of a coma. In fact, short of actually tilting the earth's axis by another so many degrees, his music was actually the First and Only Wonder of the Universe. So, what difference would it make if Tameezan was allowed to go on sitting among the men, in full view of the Ustad?

Big difference to her. This was her entire life's mission – to actually make eye contact with her beloved Ustad. To gaze at him, and to allow him to gaze at her. He would have to look at her – she being the only woman on view. And she would lose no time in making the appropriate gestures of appreciation. Soon he would be forced to notice that here at last was one woman who really understood music. She would stand out from the rest. He would realise how misguided he had been at spurning all her previous advances. He would see what he had missed. She would be there, before him, decked out in all her finery – dressed to kill – and he would be completely and utterly captivated by her charm and beauty. And then there was her sweet voice. That had never let her down. He would be sure to catch some of that when he arrived. She would have to time herself... measure her pace carefully, so that she launched into an appropriate verse of the ghazal, just as he entered the room. Yes, that bit of the ghazal would have to come at the precise moment when their eyes met for the first time. Yes! That's it! Practise! Work on it now!

67
THE GHAZAL

The Producer was pacing up and down in the tiny hotel room. Rooms should really be bigger. Pacing areas should be clearly marked. Furniture should be kept well away from the path of artistic motion. She was getting a bit dizzy at having to turn corners every so many steps:

"Look, this ghazal is really, really important. You'll just have to come up with something mind-blowing. It's got to be absolutely stunning. It's a very dramatic moment in the film. This is the first time the Courtesan is about to come face-to-face with this wretched man. She's been in love with him for years, and now's her big moment – it's got to be earth-shattering. What you just played me sounded like a down market film song from the seventies. If I'd wanted something on those lines I could have just gone to any number of fat, hairy pot-bellied film musicians. Why did I come to you? Am I mad? Why would I pay your exorbitant rates just for a film-song sound-alike? And where's that dramatic moment? You were supposed to build in the precise moment when they first look at one another. Now come on, this just won't do!"

The Producer was getting really agitated. The World's Number One Composer wore a calm resigned-to-fate look whenever she carried on like this. Totally unmusical herself, but convinced that she was the best judge of what sounded right.

He had prepared several stylised pieces – traditional and classical, beautiful sarangi interludes in between, haunting melodies and lyrics re-modelled and drawn from the greatest of Urdu poets. Lyrics that talked about eyes that have thirsted for years for one small glimpse of the beloved, how the wretched heart is about to stop beating now that the beloved has finally arrived into the eyes. And a desire to shut them tight to trap him therein. But if the eyes are shut, then how to look at him? And how to even remain alive long enough to catch that first glimpse? Oh foolish heart stop beating, just for one second stop beating so I can take a good look! First I'll look here, and then there – a hundred times I'll look here and there, and then, and only then, with some trepidation, I'll look at you. But how to look? How did Moses look up at God?

The Composer thought he'd done really well, and the Producer was being unnecessarily awkward and pig-headed. She was in her boss-mode as ever, and as usual, vague in the extreme about her exact requirements. But then, how does a musically illiterate non-musician communicate to a real musician what is actually wanted?

"Why don't you write the lyrics yourself?" he suggested with an air of exasperation, afraid of yet another row blowing up and she, as always, threatening to get herself another composer, while poor he, still very much in love with her.

"Honestly, if you like the melody, and if you think the general feel is right, why not just write the lyrics yourself? Or if you tell me what kind of idea you want to convey – maybe you don't like the thirsty eyes concept – let's find something else – I'll try to work it in...."

"That's just it. I can't decide what her mood should be. Sometimes I think I want her to sound defiant, sometimes bitter. I want her to sing about her own rarity and her uniqueness. Sometimes, I want her to melt utterly and completely. Like wax. Sometimes I want her to be the moth that throws itself whole-heartedly at the flame, certain of annihilation. But sometimes I want her to be the flame itself. Shama or Parwanah? Or both? Oh no! Too trite. Oh, I don't know... but one thing's for sure, what you just played me sounds plain corny. Whoever heard of thirsty eyes? Eyes don't thirst – quite the reverse. They shed water."

"That's the trouble with you foreigners who learn our languages. You may be an Urdu major, but you've never quite grasped the actual..." the composer should have known better than to have a go at her Urdu degree yet again, especially in her present mood.

"That's the trouble with you fucking Indians. Do you mean to tell me that every native speaker of Urdu or Hindi understands poetry, eh? Poetry has nothing to do with language. To understand poetry you need to understand the poet's heart. Humdilli, you know? First and foremost 'Hum-dil' and only then, 'Hum-zabaan', heart before tongue!" she was shrieking with exasperation and the Composer decided it was best to just agree with her. He offered a woolly compromise:

"OK, if you can't decide between the flame and the moth, why not combine the two attitudes? Let's have her being grateful at finally seeing him, yet aloof and detached over the way he's treated her in the past?"

"Easier said than done. You do it, or get one of your poet friends to help you, and call me when you're ready. It had better be good. I want this particular number to be a chart-buster. It's such a tense moment in the film – all eyes on her. And remember, we know what happens next. At the time that she's singing, she doesn't know that. Even in her wildest dreams, she could never have imagined that...."

"You're re-writing history...."

"No, not really, I think it's quite possible that... well, the Courtesan was most definitely, if unwittingly, responsible for it."

"That's just your theory. Why make out it's a fact? Aren't you the one who's always said that this is going to be the most definitive and complete true story of the Courtesan?"

The Producer always resented any direct challenge to her precious script: "Are you planning to be demoted from Composer to script-advisor?"

"Hey, I came up with the best script-advisor ever. You wouldn't have found him in a million years by yourself. The grandson of the original Universal Ronson Lighter. What a coup for you!"

"He's a crashing bore – thinks no end of himself!"

"But I did get him, and I engineered it so that he would play all the sitar solos for the film. He never ever plays for films. And he's taken such a shine to you. At least he's very willing to talk. And such anecdotes about the old days. I thought you'd be grateful."

"But he talks such rubbish. Everything he says, every story, every anecdote, every incident – every time he opens his mouth it's either to glorify his grandfather or some other withered old ancestor. He's incapable of playing anything without a long and boring speech about how his grandfather composed this bandish in the pouring rain, or how he thought of that composition after eating two dozen mangoes, or how the sounds from a nearby mosquito-net factory led to this particular raag...."

"Stop being bitchy. It's part of our Indian classical music tradition to give credit to our elders, to respect one's fore-fathers."

"I notice it's only limited to one's own fathers and one's own grandfathers. He's always bitching about other musicians' fathers and grandfathers. His family gets it right, everybody else's gets it wrong. Everybody else has diluted music to suit popular tastes. Everybody else is into fusion and "East-West".

Only he and his precious gharana still carry the torch. What rubbish! How can you swallow this bullshit when you're such a distinguished musician in your own right? You did OK, didn't you, without having to fall back on the family name? You never even mention your family – nobody knows you as anything but you. Isn't that how it should be? Where is your family, by the way...?"

"I've got to go. I'm performing in Rome this evening."

"What about my ghazal?"

"I'll think about it on the plane... if nothing comes, I'll think during the concert this evening – if not I'll try and think of something during tomorrow's performance in Frankfurt."

"Do you always do my work while performing at other people's concerts?"

"When else would I have the time?" he gave her a cheeky grin.

68
HE JUST FELL...

My father-in-law Mohanji refuses to go on paying the rent for my new flat unless I abandon my baby. I'm not allowed to see anyone. Nobody is allowed to visit me. Only Mrs Henara, brave, plucky woman! So classy! She broke all the rules and stormed her way in, walking straight past the Indian elders' morality committee mafia who were standing guard at my door.

You should have seen her – so regal, just like a real Queen. She walked right past them, waving her hands about and speaking in her beautiful Urdu. She ordered them to clear the way. They buckled down at once. Who could argue with that sort of woman? A woman who had kicked out her own husband, and only because he'd had a few mistresses! How many women could do that? What courage!

"You don't have to have to put up with this," she said to me. "They have committed crime after crime against you. First, you are not told the facts of life. Then you are deceptively married off. Now your in-laws want you to throw away your own baby – your own flesh-and-blood. It's not on! Ignorant bloody marwaris. I will write to the government for you. We'll get the best lawyers. You have a right to live as you want to live, right here, in this flat with your own husband and your child."

Mrs Henara always makes everything sound so easy. If she believes something, she just pretends it's the norm, and anyone who deviates from her idea of normality is just written off as completely mad or illiterate, or both.

She gave me so much strength. Soon after her visit, a government delegation came to see me. They asked me to go with them, to the neighbouring town where they have their new headquarters. There, they said, they could offer me full protection from the racist Indian Morality Committee. I went willingly, glad to be rescued at last. It was awful leaving my green-eyed husband behind, but I had to go, for the sake of my baby....

I was put in a luxurious guest house in the grounds of one of the government minister's big houses. He was an army man. All the government were army men, and before I knew it, there were dozens of photographers, journalists,

266

all the world's press, photographing me and my son and telling the world we had become outcasts thanks to the bigoted Asians and their blessed bloody culture and their stupid, out-dated religions.

The military authorities then produced another young man, who claimed to be the father of my child. I didn't understand. How could he be? But he said he was my lover. And all the journalists said this was a perfectly tragic love story about a young Indian woman and an upcoming African politician. Two people who loved each other and wanted to marry – and had already even had a child to prove their love for each other – but these bloody narrow-minded Asians would not allow it. And so, here was this poor young woman. She had run away from her in-laws' home and come to be with her real lover. She had been rescued from her monster in-laws, and from a short-lived forced arranged marriage to their taxi-driver son. That was their story. A perfect story.

But I knew it was only a story. Various English-language tabloids attempted to analyse the young woman's sin. What had she done wrong, exactly? The fact that she'd had pre-marital sex, or the fact that she'd had it with a Black man? Which was worse, from an Asian viewpoint? The young African journalists – most of them sons of government ministers and educated by Indian teachers from the British Raj – had a field day on the story.

I was so confused. This wasn't my story. I had never even seen this politician man before. He seemed nice enough, but why was he lying? Why was he claiming to be my lover? We had never even met before, how could he claim to love me? I didn't know what to do. Since nobody else wanted me I decided to play the game and live with him. At least my child would be taken care of otherwise my father-in-law might have tried to have my baby put to sleep in the night. At least here we would be under constant military protection. I felt safe.

But it didn't last. Once they'd made the point that Asians ought to loosen-up on mixed marriages, and the story had run almost everyday in the national and international press for two weeks, they quickly lost interest in my case and went on with their own internal power-battles. The man who had claimed to be my lover hardly ever looked at me now. He had a new woman. Then one day he disappeared, never to be seen again. He had apparently done something silly, like oppose the new military government on some small, petty matter. And he had, apparently, paid for it.

A few days after his disappearance, a group of men stormed their way into my guest house quarters and asked me to leave immediately. Before I could protest, I was thrown out onto the lawn. My baby was also thrown out at me.

I lifted my child and carrying him in my arms, I walked and walked and walked. Endlessly through the dark streets, fireflies lighting up the way, the song of the crickets piercing my ears. The world seems like a very strange place when you first walk all alone in the dark. I didn't know this Big town at all. I didn't know where I was going.

I must've walked for ages. The baby seemed to get heavier and heavier. Everything had gone wrong since this baby had arrived. Suddenly, I didn't want him any more. I just wanted one thing. I wanted my beloved green-eyed husband. I had to somehow get back to the small town. True, my father-in-law wouldn't want to know me, but my green-eyed one would be there. And if he rejected me because I'd lived with a Black politician for a while, then I could always go to Mrs Henara. She would surely help me.

Exhausted, I finally arrived at an Agip filling station, and an African taxi driver recognised me from the newspapers. I didn't have a single cent on me. The driver, who knew my husband from the small town taxi rank, offered to drive me home. He was really, really kind. All through the one-hour journey, he talked about my sad situation. He tried to persuade me that I'd be better off without the baby. The family would forgive me and take me back. Things were getting really bad in the country he said. Soon all the Indians would be kicked out. All family quarrels would be forgotten as every single Indian would, overnight, turn into a refugee. I believed him. He was a good man. My husband had always spoken highly of him. This man had friends in the army. He always had advance information on upcoming events. He said he would be happy to keep the baby and look after it himself. He and his wife needed a baby:

"Where is your baby?" he asked

"Er... I... er baby? I'm not sure. I think he just fell from my arms somewhere along that long road... you know, I walked for miles and miles.... I still haven't fully recovered from the birth.... I feel so confused sometimes."

Where was my baby? I looked down and my arms were still cradled – but no baby.

In a few minutes, I'd got out at the familiar small town market square taxi rank. At last... the last leg of my journey and it seems miles and miles away.

I can't wait to reach my destination and lay my head on the shoulders of my green-eyed one... quicker, quicker... my legs will just have to carry me... I'll collapse once I'm in his arms, but for now my legs will have to....

A strange sight in the early morning light. A man dressed in a suit and alongside him a woman in a red and gold sari – just like a bride... so much jewellery. Both carrying suitcases. They look vaguely familiar. Can't stop, must keep running to Mohanji & Sons General Stores... there's a funny smell, like guns have just been fired... in the distance I can hear gun-shots....

69

LOOKS LIKE FREEDOM – FEELS LIKE DEATH

It was all over in less than five minutes. All those years of hard work, and penny-pinching, and saving. Those dimly lit shops. Those sparkling copper coins. Those thriving little businesses. The shit piling up below the pedestals, awaiting the Bhangi. Morality committees, sex education films, Guru's, temples, mosques, gurudwara's… songs. The magical sounds of Singer sewing machines on the verandahs. It was all over in less than five minutes.

They smashed their way in just before midnight. They shot all the Mohanji sons. Corpses lay strewn everywhere – bloodied heads in sacks of flour, faces covered with red chilly powder and yellow turmeric. The boys whose destinies had dealt them the all important task of weighing out these colourful powders, lay lifeless in the midst of rainbow clouds of dust – faces and clothes splashed with colour as though it were Holi. Spicy aromas – haldi and dhaniya – mingling with the pungent, rotting cabbage smell of death. The Mohanji boys. Born in the shop, died in the shop. Aged from eighteen to eleven.

The gunmen spared the Widow, and they spared Mohanji himself. Their leader said he was under strict orders to spare Mohanji's life, for it was thought that the best punishment for Mohanji was to be dispossessed of his most cherished possession and find himself penniless and shopless in a cold, inhospitable country:

"So what man? Don't you know Napoleon said England is a nation of shopkeepers? So, now you can go and join your shopkeeper brothers. Only they are all White, and they think you are shit. Now go and exploit the White natives of England! Sell them their tap-water! Then see what happens, ha!"

Mohanji's life was spared so he would live to forever grieve the horrific murder of all his sons – his real wealth. Death would've been too good. Death would've meant a complete oblivion to suffering. No make him live. Let the bastard live, and let him suffer.

Mohanji was told he had to clear out in twenty-four hours. If he was seen in the country after that, he would be shot on the spot. No questions asked.

The Widow remained surprisingly calm. She had already packed, even before the shootings. Although stunned and in a state of shock, Mohanji felt a new-found respect for his Widow daughter. After such a horrendous ordeal, any other woman would've screamed and shrieked like a hyena. But not the Widow. She just stood there, calm as hell, a blank expression on her face, small suitcase in hand. And she hurriedly set about packing a few of his belongings. She'd taken out all her wedding jewellery from its special hiding place in the puja cupboard and now it adorned her, from head to foot. If you were only allowed to take what you could walk away with, then you wore all your jewellery. Nobody would dream of objecting to that. Black Africans were extremely reasonable about that sort of thing. They knew Indian men insisted on their women wearing a lot of jewellery. Jewellery was the women's way of saying "We're OK, our men care for us."

There was more than enough cash in the house for two airline tickets. Clever Mohanji! If he'd been stupid enough to bank it, then which bank opened at six in the morning? In any case banks had been ordered to freeze all Dukavalla accounts. If only everyone else had obeyed the rules of the Morality Committee and kept their money hidden at home, everything would've been fine. But no, some people believed in banks, especially the educated Muhindi's. They liked having cheque books and account numbers. It made them feel important.

There was no time to clear the debris. No time to arrange funerals for eight corpses. The Committee of the Wise and the Moral would have to see to all that. But that was just the beginning....

Afterwards there was massive confusion. Many more heaps of bodies were found behind other shops – many faces mutilated beyond recognition. The Maulana had panicked that the Committee of the Wise and Moral, all Hindus, would just cremate the bodies without first verifying the religious persuasion of the corpses. He didn't want anyone to be done out of a proper Muslim funeral. And the Temple Guru winced at the thought of one of his kind being buried by mistake. Things got even more tense between the representatives of the two religions. More than twenty-five years on, it was 1947 all over again.

And then when a solid mass of putrid, melting, oozing, spongy-squishy bodies, fluids flowing into one another was found in a nearby ditch, each Holy man, handkerchief tied on nose, invited the other in the most generous of terms, to do the honours. It was impossible to know which was which. Hindu blood, Muslim excrement. Or was it the other way round?

But Mohanji himself was spared all this insanity. Now that Kalyug had at last really and truly arrived, Mohanji himself, the most ardent disciple of the Dark Age of Immoral Senselessness and Shamelessness, was not destined to witness its machinations.

A few hours after the heartless shooting of the Mohanji Boys, Mohanji and his Widow daughter crossed the road to the bus station on the Market Square. The first light of dawn was only just struggling through the dark night and in it they saw a young woman sprinting past them towards the shop they'd just left. Neither Mohanji nor the Widow took the slightest bit of notice of this incongruous sight. Highly unusual it might have seemed – a young Asian woman in a ragged sari, hair flying in the early morning breeze, running towards the shop – but then nothing that had happened in the last few hours made any sense. Neither Mohanji nor his Widow daughter registered the frantic speed of the young woman. Neither did they stop to think that this was their very own daughter-in-law who had just passed them with the speed and determination of an Olympic runner.

The early bus was due in less than an hour. And it went all the way to the airport, on the other side of the big town, a whole hundred miles away. In Pearlite tradition, that was a major journey. That was the kind of trip for which one ought to have been packing for a month followed by a whole final week of lunch and dinner parties. That was the kind of short trip that called for elaborate farewell parties.

And yet, here they were, going away forever to an unknown future in an unknown country, but not a single dinner invitation to say good-bye. How could there be? Everyone else was going to England as well. England! If they had been coming back they would be known as England-returned. But how could you be England-returned if you weren't allowed to return? And who would be there to even see you return?

70
BABY TALK

She just dropped me – can you believe that? Just dropped me like one drops a handkerchief. It was the most frightening experience so far in my short life. Even more frightening than that afternoon when I was settling down to a cosy nap in my usual place and this deafening alarm bell rang out like it was the end of the world!

Well, it was the end of the world – the world as I knew it. That horrifying bell forced me to leave my comfortable home and arrive on this planet where nothing makes sense. Aliens! All of them!

Yes, she dropped me just like a handkerchief. At first I thought she was coming back… then as the minutes turned into hours, I knew I had been abandoned. I wanted to get up and run after her, but I can't even sit up yet, leave alone walk. Of all the species of mammals, God made the human infant the most helpless. I realise with some shame and a deepening sense of in-adequacy how, up until now, I've been utterly dependent on her. Well, nothing for it now. Just lie down and wait. Save the vocal chords. I love making a noise but it uses up too much energy. It brings on more hunger – raw, gnawing, nagging hunger. Wrong time and wrong place to get hungry.

A shuffle… grass crackling… footsteps? Goodie! I am to be rescued… oh no, please God no… it's a snake! Keep still. Keep very, very still. Snakes don't harm babies. They don't even harm adults. Not unless they feel under attack. Snakes want to survive, so do I. Survival.

That's what it's about, and I'm a survivor. Keep very, very calm. No kicking! Fists in mouth – keep quiet! Why do my stupid legs always want to kick in the air? Stop, stop!

The snake pauses a moment, looks at me pitifully, and then crawls on. I can sense it shake its head in a gesture of hopeless despair. I know what it's thinking. Even a snake wouldn't abandon its own baby in this heartless fashion. It would sooner swallow its own baby than chuck it away like a used tissue.

The snake's gone, but I can hear some movement… a car? Yes! Start screaming now!

Sure enough it works. But out of a group of six adult aliens, there is only one with any sense. He holds me close. He even mentions the magic word "milk."

The others are just plain stupid. Numb-skulls! They're only interested in my religion.

Dickheads! They stand around arguing amongst themselves. They're wondering whether I'm Hindu or Muslim – Black or Brown. Well, I ain't tellin'! Let 'em stew!

Don't they know babies have no religion? We don't need religion – there are more important things in life. Religion is not one of our top priorities. We need food and we need our bottoms dried – at frequent intervals. If you don't believe me, just go and ask any baby!

71
BUTCHER, BAKER, GURU & BABY

A motley crew of stranded travellers, late one night by the roadside. A truly terrifying experience, to be out and about at this hour on a dark and lonely road, and that too in this day and age, when Pearl was no longer the safe, cosy, predictable haven it had once been. Sheer lunacy!

Their car had had a puncture and the driver wanted everyone to get out while he worked on changing the wheel.

They stood around avoiding eye contact with each other. Not that there could have been much of that – it was almost pitch dark. Four men and a woman, sharing a taxi ride from the Big Town. In the good old days they would have travelled separately, each in their own latest swanky Japanese car. But now, this wretched petrol shortage coupled with rumours of stabbings and killings made it necessary to travel en-famille. All Asians together. We're all the same really. Stick together. That keeps the imagined enemy at bay. Unity is strength.

The Dukavallas were being kicked out of Pearl. Other Asian businessmen and women had been summoned to the Big Town in person, so that they could be given their own unique, individually tailored reasons for being thrown out of the country. The military government had introduced special licenses for all Asian businesses intending to operate in Pearl. The licence was to take the form of a special red black and yellow mark branded on the forehead of each kosher Asian so that the soldiers would know not to shoot at them. But in actual fact, the government had no intention of furnishing any Asian with such an honour. Quite the contrary. They took the utmost delight in making the applicants appear in person for an interview in the Big Town, for which they queued for fourteen hours only to be informed, with great glee, that they had to get the hell out of the country.

The humiliating indignity of this so-called "verification" process had left each aspirant grumpy and not just a little resentful: we have given this place our whole life. All our hard work, our sweat. What have we not done for Pearl? And now just look at them! Rounding us up like cattle and wanting to brand us with a special mark if they think we are good enough to carry on running our noble businesses in their blessed country. It's our country too! Well, it's not our real country – we're Indian and proud to be Indian. Our soul belongs in India, but we live here. Our livelihoods are here. We would starve in India.

India, in this sense, also meant Pakistan and Bangladesh. The Indian settlers of Pearl had not fully comprehended the Partition of 1947. India meant greater India – as it had been under the Raj. Within India there were several countries: the predominantly Hindu part was called Bharat, the Muslim part was called Pakistan, and the Muslim Bengali part was called Bangladesh. And then there was Kashmir – but nobody was sure about that, so they left that one alone. Kashmir was just a pretty place that provided great backdrops for Bombay film songs.

The grumbling travellers stood some distance from the diseased car, viewing the Black driver with increasing suspicion as he struggled with a torch in one hand and a jack in the other, while trying to balance a spare wheel between his legs. It didn't occur to anyone to offer him a hand – even if it was just to hold the torch. He was the driver, and it was his car, and it was his bloody job to sort it out. It was never too far from their paranoid minds that the driver might be part of some big evil conspiracy. Pretend the car breaks down. Have them all get out of the car – then, then who knows? Nothing quite like a perpetual persecution complex to conjure up a very real sense of danger.

The travellers were all owners of small Asian businesses and included three men and a young woman, and also a Hindu holy chap – chief resident at the Small Town Temple – who had appointed himself leader of the group.

The Guru had been particularly enraged at the summons to the Big Town to verify his business position. Verify? Verify? How can they verify God? I'm God's man and they want to verify me. Kalyug! I'm NOT a businessman he protested. I'm caretaker of the temple. It's not a business – it's God's House!

"But there's a treasury, and there are funds, and you run a school and a community centre, and you organise events... you sell prayers – yes, you charge people for praying for them... you charge people for delivering them from evil... no, it's definitely a business, like any other business. So get your ass over here and be assessed and verified," he'd been told.

"In that case," argued the Guru, "why hasn't the Maulana been summoned?"

Pointless question. Everybody knew that since the Dictator had converted to Islam, he had made many generous concessions to the Hill Top Maulana, just short of declaring Islam the official religion of the country.

The Guru had been seething with anger at what he viewed as a resurgence of militant Islam. Up until now, honestly, he had never ever felt an ounce of resentment or hostility against his Muslim brethren. But this kind of favouritism by the Dictator of one religion over all others, had caused in him feelings not unlike those in that land just across the Indian Ocean in 1947.

And then it happened. It happened as everybody stood around tired and grumpy. It happened at the precise moment when the Guru experienced a fresh surge of resentment against Islamic supremacy. A piercing wail of a sound. Like a baby crying… somewhere in the nearby bushes, just off the main road.

A trick! Beware! It's a trick to lure them into the bushes. With a fresh burst of suspicion, they glared at the driver again. They shrank back in terror as the driver threw his tools down and promptly went towards the bushes to investigate the noise. A tense wait followed.

Everybody looked at one of the men, a Muslim-Punjabi garage owner as if to say, "Well? What are you waiting for? Why don't you do something? You know about cars. Get that thing fixed quickly while he's gone and then let's all scram!"

But the Black driver emerged from the bushes just a few seconds later, carrying a bundle in his arms. That bundle, presumably the source of the wailing, was now silent, except for the odd gurgle – glad to have at last got some attention.

As the only woman present, there was an inevitable attempt at handing the bundle over to the young Muslim woman, owner of "Beauty Spot Salon." She had actually never held a small baby and stepped back with a shriek that sounded like she'd been asked to cuddle a cobra.

"No, no! Not me! How do I know whose it is? It might do something dirty!"

The Black driver shook his head ever so slightly. These Indians were impossible. What was she more worried about? The baby's ever-imminent excretions, or the fact that its racial and religious pedigree were something of a mystery? He stood there uncertainly holding the baby in his arms and looking to his well-to-do, worldly-wise, newly verified passengers for some guidance on the correct procedure.

The Guru asked for the torch and shone it straight into the baby's face. The tortured infant, who had already endured a mattress of thorns, blustery evening winds, painful hunger-pangs and the jeers of a big snake, to say nothing of a soggy, coarse towel nappy for over twenty-four hours, was not amused. It let out a shrill as fierce as the blinding light of the torch, almost like an air-raid siren or a trumpet heralding some vital announcement. Bang on cue, the Guru declared the infant a Chauthara – a disparaging Gujarati term for an Afro-Asian. Asian skin-colouring, but frizzy Negroid hair and a flattish nose.

"It's one of yours," he announced triumphantly to the Black driver. "Better take it somewhere where they look after them... you know, orphanage or something."

One of the travellers, owner of the Christian Bakery, stepped in: "How about dropping it off at the police station when we head back into town... they'll find the parents and the baby will be safely returned... that's the usual thing, isn't it?"

Another traveller threw his hands up in horror. "Such wickedness in this world... you dumb fellow, can't you see that it isn't wanted? It's been abandoned! If the parents wanted it, what's it doing in those thorny bushes at this hour?"

Another agreed and offered further clarification. "It must have been thrown away by its mother – probably unmarried. Threw it away in shame. No good taking it to the police. Better to take it to that Catholic Mission place. They look after orphans...."

"Why, why the Mission?" The Christian Baker had picked up some of the Guru's resentful tendencies against religions other than one's own:

"Why is it always the Christian mission that has to receive such unfortunates? If it was thrown away out of shame, then the mother must be Indian. Everybody knows only Indian Muslims and Hindus have shame. All the other races and religions are shameless, aren't they?" He looked directly at the Guru and added:

"What about your temples and your mosques? Why not take it there?"

The Guru had already anticipated just such an eventuality, and was more than ready to rise against this thinly disguised attack on Guruism.

"Well because we don't know if the baby is Hindu or Muslim. If it were Muslim and ended up being raised in a Temple, then Allah would never forgive the Gurus," he said with undisguised sarcasm, adding, "It should be taken to the Mosque and then the Maulana can decide what to do with it. The Maulana is a big man these days – does whatever he likes. He's the powerful one. Who am I? A mere Guru...."

"Wait, wait," chimed in one of the men, a Muslim. "We don't know that it's a Muslim, do we? In fact we don't even know if it's a boy or a girl...."

Here was a fresh idea. Up until now they'd just stood around arguing, but here was something concrete. At least this one mystery could be tackled with immediacy and relish. Everyone took a step forward in eager anticipation.

Once again the Guru assumed the role of Master of Ceremonies and aiming his torch between the tortured infant's damp legs proudly pronounced the bundle to be a boy. Everyone nodded to one another agreeably. It could have been a normal post-natal rejoicing session. It was almost like the wretched, hungry, soggy little bundle had only just arrived, this minute, into the universe. So, it was a boy! Wow! A boy. How nice!

The rejoicing came to an abrupt halt when they remembered he was still a little boy of ambiguous race and unknown religion.

The Black driver dared to speak. "First, let's get the car fixed. Then we should set out and look for some milk. I think the baby is very hungry."

All five of them fixed him with a hateful look. How dare he! A mere Black African driver! How dare he speak out of turn to them, his masters, in that morally superior way? To hell with milk! There were far more important things to be sorted out, like the baby's religion. Only Indians understood about that sort of thing. These Blacks! In a million years they would never understand the importance of family, religion, honour, shame, izzat.

But despite the high-flown ideas of shame and izzat, nobody had a better suggestion, and they couldn't go on standing there in the dark so the driver's suggestion – minus the milk-acquiring part – was grudgingly conceded.

The driver held out the baby. Nobody moved: "Well, please... I can't go on changing the wheel with a baby in my arms... can someone please just... take it...?"

They looked at one another. Then they looked at the baby. Then everybody took one step back – perfectly choreographed!

In the absence of volunteers, the driver laid the infant carefully and gently on the back seat. As soon as he did so, the baby immediately started screaming again – a scream of betrayal, a scream of despair, a scream of shattered hope. While he had been in human arms he had wrongly assumed that some sustenance was probably also on its way. The baby knew that whenever one felt the warmth of another body, then delicious food followed. But not so this time. He hadn't been in this world more than three months, and already, life was one big never-ending chain of surprises. God alone knows what awaited him in the prescribed threescore-and-ten!

72
EXODUS: BIDAAI

Nine days and nine nights of rituals, all kinds of rituals – some before the wedding, others after – but the high-point of every Indian wedding, Hindu, Muslim or Sikh, is the ritual departure of the bride: "Bidaai."

When all the ceremonies are complete and the bride and groom are man and wife, she goes away with him to live in his parents' house. If his parents are broad-minded then the newlyweds are given their own room. If not, tradition dictates that she learn to tip-toe to his room, anklets ringing, bangles jangling, in-laws waking, in the silent night.

The bride's departure from her parental home is a weepy ceremony – almost like a funeral, in sharp contrast to the usual beaming, champagne-drunk, happy, confetti showered bride of the western world, only too keen to hit the honeymoon suite. But for the traditional Indian bride, her final departure is indeed a sad occasion. From now on, she may not visit her parents without her in-laws' permission. Her parents are reminded by consoling relatives that their role as caretakers is at an end. Unlike sons, daughters are not personal property. You merely look after them temporarily, find them a husband and then bid them farewell. From then on, they're part of another family. This is what they've been reared for. And if they perform that role successfully then more glory for the parents. If they screw up, then, more often then not, they are returned to their parental home. A huge disgrace, and the biggest shame of all. God forbid that this should ever happen to any parent.

And so the bride departs, laden with jewellery, garlands of flowers and gold around her neck. Now she stops being a girl. She is about to become a woman, a big step forward. No need for sex education films. The knowledge comes of its own accord.

She steps over the threshold into her new home – her sasural – her in-laws' home. If they're Muslim, a Quran is held over her head. If Hindu, she stands before a senior female in-law waving an Aarti thali in front of her. Her final entry into this, her permanent home, is the culmination of her parents' life's work. Now they've done their duty, and she's here. She has to make a go of it. Once she has stepped over the threshold and entered this house, only her corpse may leave it.

And with that same sense of finality, one evening, at sunset, several thousand brides headed for their new homes. Anxious, apprehensive, a great step towards the unknown, and completely unsure whether they would be greeted at their final destination by a welcoming Quran or a thali of Aarti.

Mohanji's expulsion from Pearl had come at daybreak. By noon, the news had spread. Some people felt sorry for him, but others, mostly from his own community, said it served him right. But two days later it was announced that all the other Indian shopkeepers had to get out as well. They had been given two weeks to get themselves organised, but fearing that this was probably just another trap to get their daughters forcibly married off to Blacks, they started to leave that very minute, on the same day. And by sunset a few thousand families were already headed for the airport.

It was the same kind of sunset. This part of the world had looked like this at sunset for millions of years. Nothing new in that. A darkening sky pierced with arteries of red and gold, finally giving way to mauve and pink, and then suddenly, quite suddenly – no twilight – the pink capitulated before an opaque, inky darkness. Only this time, the red and gold matched the colours of the departing brides – brides being forcibly repatriated from the country that had become their home. They were only allowed to take what they could wear. So they wore their best clothes, usually their wedding outfits, along with all the jewellery they'd accumulated over the years. Jewellery bought by selling tap water to the natives. Although supposedly dispossessed, homeless and destitute, no other chapter in history had witnessed such heavily laden refugees – heavy with worry about an uncertain future, but even heavier with the weight of gold.

Two weeks to pack up an entire lifetime – a humanly impossible deadline – and then a massive, desperate, panic-ridden rush to the airport: a throng of brides all hurrying to get away, under a sentence of death.

They would have to move fast. But how does one move fast with forty gold bangles, twenty on each wrist, to say nothing of several gold chains and necklaces worn all at once, choking at their throats? Upper arms laden with solid gold bands. Hands weighed down by dozens of rings on each finger, and both thumbs. Faces pulled down by dangling nose-rings. Footsteps slowed down by heavy toe-rings and chiming anklets. Completely and utterly dispossessed but laden with gold. Oh, how they suffered!

The scene at the Market Square bus station resembled a typical Indian wedding. All the men in their best western suits, and all the women in shiny gold and red saris and heavy jewellery. While they waited for the airport bus, they stood around talking in small groups. Yes, it had to happen. They always knew this would happen. They had never trusted the Blacks and now they had been proved right. They had lost everything, but the two most important things – their women's jewellery and their daughters' virginity, the two most cherished possessions in the whole world – were still in place. So all wasn't lost yet. Their virgin daughters – all decked out in bridal finery, hymens intact – dressed to the nines, and no sasural to go to!

73
BEYOND MILKY WAY

Mrs Henara fought back the tears as she carried on packing the Brat's belongings. She was going to miss her only child. True, the Brat had only ever been a source of massive disappointment, but maybe that would have changed with time. Getting older always helped children. Some of them became quite sensible and considerate. Not that her child was inconsiderate, but just a bit too nosey. "Where does she get that from, I wonder?" puzzled Mrs Henara. But deep down, she knew she wouldn't have to look too far to trace the source of her child's over-curious nature.

She sat down on the bed, a brief respite from her packing giving in to some remorseful maternal reminiscing. She looked around the Brat's room with sadness remembering the many passions that had come and gone with alarming frequency. The collecting phase – shiny chocolate wrappers smoothed out and pressed flat, dried butterflies, old copper coins made to look brand new by polishing with guava leaves, soda bottle-tops.

And then this, her latest craze: cardboard cut outs depicting the solar system. The Brat had recently taken to gazing at the stars in the equatorial sky. A particularly cloudy cluster of stars, she had been told, was the tail end of the Milky Way galaxy. Milky Way. She had liked that name. It sounded just like a bar of chocolate. So, whether it was the result of that evocative chocolate name or that eerily pretty razzle-dazzle of zillions of twinkling stars, the Brat had recently spent masses of time with her head pointing upwards at the sky. A special woman had had to be called in to massage the Brat's neck so that she could hold her head straight again.

"Those who just gaze at stars end up stumbling on earth," Mrs Henara had sternly cautioned her, in typical bubble-bursting tones. "If you want to live in this world then you have to learn to look where you're going."

"But I don't want to live in the world. Everything has gone wrong since you told me we live in the world. I was much happier before. Oh why do we have to live in the world?" the Brat had, as usual, unwittingly posed a vital philosophical question.

Mrs Henara smiled at the memory of that question, and then looking at the Brat's half-packed open suitcase before her, was gripped by another surge of sadness. Yes, she would definitely miss her. She remembered the chubby-cheeked, round-faced gurgling baby, dribbling like mad, and everybody said it was because she was longing to talk. Then she became the hyperactive toddler who feasted on garden soil and ended up with a coiled caterpillar in her nappy contents. And then, the over-talkative young child who liked to use big words like "dessication of character" and Moses and his "Ten Condiments."

She remembered her in her frilly pink pyjamas. Cute as hell but already entertaining notions of being a sex object when she grew up. And she remembered her climbing eagerly into her mother's bed with alleged nightmares. She remembered the painful experience of having to lock her in her room so that she wouldn't squeal about the elopement plan. She remembered their walks in the garden and the feel of her small hand in hers.

Tears rolled down her face freely, stinging hot tears of guilt-ridden motherhood. Tears of remorse. Why couldn't she have been more understanding? Why couldn't she have shown more patience? Why did she find it so difficult to show affection? Why was she always telling the Brat to shut up? Yet she loved her child so much, it ached. Why had she never been able to put that love into words, or actions?

What had she not done to keep her baby? Otherwise that over-sexed surgeon ex-husband of hers would've claimed the child. If it had been a boy, then the father would definitely have claimed custody. And the Maulana, Temple Guru and Morality Committee would've sanctioned his claim. Sons were usually considered the property of their fathers. Girls stood a better chance of being reared by their mother, at least until they were fourteen or so. She was so glad she'd had a daughter... or was she?

Mrs Henara felt uneasy again. A familiar but vague sense of guilt descended on her yet again, like an ever-imminent black cloud gathering all around her and gradually fencing her in. She got up from the Brat's small bed. She made a resolution. The child would have to be told sooner or later, and since she was being sent away next week, she would have to be told the truth now, otherwise she would find herself in boarding school... and then, and then... no! She must be told now. Would she understand? Would she forgive her?

74
MY KIND OF GOD

Life is pretty pointless these days. No school, all the shops are shut, and everybody stays indoors all the time. Even that one mystery that made life worth living is at an end. It seems the Mohanji baby grandson is not pure Indian so nobody wants him. The daughter-in-law has been banished to the Big Town, because her baby is African. I asked my mother how God could give an Indian woman an African baby, and she says it's punishment for disobeying God's rules.

"What are God's rules?" I ask eagerly, keen to have a new subject of interest, a rule-making God.

"You know, I told you about the Ten Commandments. I even took you to see the film."

"But I know all the Ten condiments by heart. Which is the one about being given Black babies as a punishment?"

My mother doesn't answer. She hates it when I get too nosey. She's nosey as hell herself. She always finds out about everything, but then she keeps it all to herself.

Life is dull. The only silver lining on my ever-present cloud is an invite to this Sunday's Feast of the Nine Virgins. It's from the Widow. Maybe if I stare at her extra hard, I'll get some inkling of what her wish was all about. What on earth could she have wished for? And how could it have come true? I can't wait to find out.

I would like to change the rules of the Feast. I would like it so that the woman hosting the feast first reads out her wish and tells you how it has come true, and then and only then, serves the meal. That would be great fun. But my mother says wishes have to be secret, otherwise they don't come true. And after they've come true, they have to be even bigger secrets, otherwise the whole process reverses itself, somehow. Weird!

I wander around the garden aimlessly for a while, then go into the house out of sheer boredom. My mother is sorting through all my clothes. Oh good! Maybe she's picking out something for me to wear to this Sunday's lunch:

"No, not that one, please mummy! Can I wear the blue one again? That's my favourite... the bluebells...."

"What are you on about?" she asks, puzzled.

"This Sunday, lunch, you know. At the Mohanji's. Remember the Widow asked me to come? Can I wear the one with the bluebells because...."

"There is no lunch. It's all cancelled. Everything is over. There is no shop even."

"No shop? Where is everybody? What happened?"

"Nothing happened. They've all er... they've moved to England for good."

"But why didn't my friends say goodbye? Don't we have to have dinner parties for people going away? Why didn't we have them over?"

I'm inconsolable with shock and betrayal. All my friends, suddenly gone away... without so much as a goodbye?

"There was no time. They had to go suddenly... er... their British-entry visas just came up, so they had to go. There was no time to say goodbye. I'm sure your friends will write to you when they've settled down. I'll forward all your letters to you...."

"Forward? Where? What do you mean? Where am I going?"

"You are going to England. You're going to start boarding school there."

"England? You mean where the Mohanji boys have gone? Yippie!"

Then I remembered how England looked in that big Atlas, and immediately went off the idea again. I'll get out of it somehow... I'm sure she can't force me to go against my will. I'll think of some way out... right now, there were more important things to sort out....

"What about the Widow's Feast? If God made her wish come true and she hasn't fed nine little girls, doesn't that mean God will take away her wish and make it untrue again? Mummy, I really don't understand about your God. I can never figure out what he likes and what he doesn't like. Please... can you please explain it all to me again?"

"Not right now. I must get on with your packing. Just remember the Ten Commandments. Forget all this nonsense of lunches and wishes from God."

"But they're so much more fun than the boring Ten Comm... comm.ind... whatever. I like the sort of God who makes wishes come true. What use a God who just says do this and don't do that? Where's the fun in that? I used to love Mrs Mohanji and her new moon things. That's what God should be about. Do you remember Mrs Mohanji? She believed in God, but her God was special. He lived in the new moon. Every time she spotted Him she gave me sweets. I like that sort of God. There should be more gods like that."

"Yes, yes…" she says impatiently, "What you should remember is that people always invent the sort of God they'd like, and then they worship him. Men make all the rules and then they tell women God said this and God said that. I should know!"

"So is God a man or a woman?"

"In a man's world, he's always a man. He can't be anything else," she replies with conviction. "Didn't I just say people invent their own gods?"

"Invent? What do you mean invent? Do you mean he doesn't really exist?"

I'm shattered, yet again. My mother is so heartless in the way she kills off my most cherished beliefs. I want to believe in a God who lives on the moon and grants wishes, in return for which you feed nine little girls. It's neat. That way everybody's wishes come true, and little girls are always being invited out to lunch, with the added bonus of sitting on the ground and all eating from the same plate with their fingers. It beats knives and forks and having to mind one's p's and q's and my mother's obsession with fish knives and soupspoons.

So, no Moon God and no wish-granting God. Just some severe, stern, old chap who resides far away and just issues ten condiments – how boring!

And now, no luncheon party. And all my Mohanji boys gone.

Then I remember I'm also going to that same England. I cheer up immediately. Maybe they'll have a shop, the same as here, and maybe they'll live behind it in some English market square – do they have market squares? Well, anyway, maybe the Widow will have her luncheon party in England. I hope she remembers to invite me.

75
UNCONDITIONAL LOVE

Mohanji's green-eyed taxi-driver son returned home early that morning – the morning after the night of Holi – the night of a thousand colours, when unknown to him, his eight brothers lay covered in blood, spiced with the dust of home-pounded chillies. He is puzzled.

Why is the shop still closed? It's almost seven in the morning and my father hasn't opened up yet. That's strange. What are all those people doing outside the shop? Customers, no doubt, waiting for us to open up. I should go straight to the taxi rank – it's almost time for the morning's first round, but I should just look in and explain why I didn't come home last night.

Things have been pretty tense between us recently. I know I'm his favourite son, and I know he likes me the best. But these days we don't even talk. I don't know what to say to him. He has been so unreasonable about this baby business. That is why my poor, beautiful wife – delicate as a lily I tell you – had to go to the authorities. Not to spite him, but to save her baby. She was afraid the baby would be forcibly taken away from her and fed to the wild animals in the jungle. A mother has every right to protect her child.

I can't think why he minds so much. After all, I'm her husband, and if I don't mind that she was pregnant with someone else's child before we were married, why on earth should he care? Izzat, I suppose. I don't mind she was already pregnant. What's that got to do with me? That's her past. Everyone is entitled to a past, and every human being makes mistakes. How else would we ever learn? I never finished school, so I know better than anyone that the University of Life is the best place to learn.

My father blames everything on my wife. No one really understands her. Only I understand her. That's because I love her. Very few people really understand about love. They say I'll love you provided this, this and this... how can that be love? Love can only be unconditional. If it's anything else, it isn't love it's lust. They think they love someone else, but they really only love themselves. One day I'll show the world what I'm prepared to do for someone I love.

But where is everyone? Why does the shop look so gloomy?

The door falls open easily. I enter the shop. It smells strange. Lots of flies – more than usual. The lights are out. I tread on something. A fallen sack of flour or spice....? I reach for the light switch and turn it on. I look down. My foot rests on my younger brother's chest. What's he doing down there? Why is he asleep on the floor?

Hang on, they're all asleep on the floor sprawled in different poses – some bent over, some flat on their backs.

Where is my father? Where is my Widow sister? I hear a voice, one of the people hanging around outside. It's the sari shop man. He says they left early this morning. They were escorted to the airport. They have gone to England. They had to go. They were ordered out. Another voice says your sister looked very nice, all done up like a bride.

The voices are all strangely distant. I shut the door and ask them all to leave. I sit down and survey the scene of all my brothers' corpses. Suddenly I become aware of a persistent sobbing coming from somewhere behind the shop counter.

It's her! My beloved! She has returned to comfort me in my tragedy! I knew she would come. She is always there when I need her.

She gets up from behind the pile of fallen kerosene tins, her arms outstretched towards me:

"Come, come, let's get out of here. Let's go to England too. Let's start again," she says.

"What about the baby? Where's the baby? They didn't...?"

"No, I... I just lost him somewhere... he just fell...."

She tells me she's left her Black politician boyfriend. He's got a new mistress. She says she really only loves me. She says she could never love anyone else.

"Quick, let's leave. We'll drive away in your taxi, and then fly to England. Then we'll search for your father. He'll forgive me, and then we'll all be together again. We'll have a little shop in England. Let's hurry!"

I was so happy to see her. Even the fact that her Black soldier-turned-politician boy-friend had probably thrown her out didn't spoil my joy. Ordinarily, I would have been furious at any man daring to reject such a beautiful and innocent girl. But now she was back with me, and that's all that mattered.

We packed quickly and in a few hours we were speeding towards the airport. I didn't care about anything. I felt light as a bird. I was with the only woman I had ever loved, and she had come back to me. She wanted to be with me. What more can a man want?

76
FROM RICHES TO RAGS... TO RICHES!

All I ever wanted was for my sons to carry on our noble family tradition. A shopkeeper's son should also be a shopkeeper. In time, we could have owned the whole square. And Market Square would then be known as Mohanji Chowk. But it wasn't to be. Children, these days, when do they listen to their parents?

I failed completely. I failed to give my children my values. And then a single, most unfortunate outside influence – that cursed daughter-in-law of mine – just walked in and wrecked a whole thriving, happy, family. She went crawling to the military government. She made me their target. I personally became the object of their hatred. They expelled me, and they enjoyed it so much that they then decided to expel everybody else – just to watch the fun. Kick out the bastards, they said. Let's take over their shops and drink all the beer. Let's have a party.

I had so much money, but I never felt rich. I just felt poor all the time. I can't explain it, but somehow I always felt like my money wasn't really available to me. It had to be put away – just in case – rainy day....

And then that rainy day came. But all the money in the world couldn't bring back my eight sons – heartlessly slain in the middle of the night.

But God is kind. My favourite green-eyed one was saved, by a miracle. If his taxi had not broken down and he had not stayed the night in a nearby village, he too would've lain splattered by bullets, and coated liked tandoori chicken in our own home-pounded spices. Those savages... out and out savages, junglees, kaalias... leaving me alive to suffer. But at least my green-eyed one lives. I never saw him again... well, I did in a sense, and I do almost everyday, but he never sees me. He doesn't even recognise me.

After they shot my sons, they gave me twenty-four hours to get out of the country. What can you take when you are only allowed to take what you can carry in your hands? I was not allowed to take any cash. Even then, I managed to slip a few notes – pounds sterling – in my socks. And pretending to have backache, I used a special back-belt plaster, in which I concealed a few more notes. I wore my best suit, and my brave Widow daughter donned her wedding sari, and for the first time since her wedding day, she wore all her jewellery. And so we departed, like we were off to a wedding.

The refugee camp in London would have been the best-dressed refugee camp in history, only all our shiny clothes had to be covered with the second-hand charity overcoats they'd handed us at the airport. The English weather was indifferent to all our finery.

Then, on our second night there, we came face to face with my green-eyed son and his disgrace of a wife. So! She was back with him! Bloody snake! All else had failed and now she had latched onto my son once again and followed him all the way to England. When the camp authorities asked if we all wanted to be housed as a family, she screamed: "NO!"

My son just kept his eyes fixed to the ground, and she dragged him away, to set up home separately from us. Us? Who's us? It was just me now – my Widow daughter seems to have disappeared too – where could she have got to? I never saw her after that....

All alone in the world, what could I do? There was only thing I knew how to do – make money.

Now I have more money than I could ever have imagined possible. Much more than before! But I don't understand it. I don't even work that hard any more. It just keeps coming in. And because it comes so easily, I feel richer than I really am. It's as easy as that – if you feel rich, then you are rich!

77
DAGGERS DRAWN

The Producer was early for her meeting with the World's Number One Composer. He'd just flown in from Tokyo – Urgent stopover London six hours before flying to northern Sweden stop Special concert stop Ghazal ready stop. Even his conversation had been getting annoyingly telegraphic lately....

She decided to wait in the hotel lobby for a few minutes before announcing her arrival. Give him a few minutes to get settled. Hope he's managed to compose a decent ghazal this time. Bloody thirsty eyes stop pounding heart stop. Useless, pompous womaniser – stop. She halted her own telegraphic thought process with some irritation. She felt all alone in the world –nobody, not even her own especially commissioned Composer-lover seemed to understand. This vital ghazal had to be just right, otherwise forget it! The film would be remembered only if that one crucial ghazal was particularly apt, especially poignant, accurately timed and hauntingly memorable.

The Producer was full of misgivings towards her cheeky, baby-faced Composer. She was beginning to have serious reservations about the amount of time he was prepared to spend on her project. Tunes played down the phone by his secretary, DAT cassettes would arrive via courier from the unlikeliest of places like Mali, and Tunisia and Alaska. But even she had to admit that for the rest of the film, he hadn't done too badly on the music. His work was good, and he always delivered on time, somehow. There was just this small – but big – outstanding matter of the ghazal, THE ghazal.

The ghazal scene was the most crucial scene in the film, and it would have to be carried by a memorable, dramatic, soul-wrenching ghazal. Ideally, the ghazal should have been ready long before any of the shooting actually began. But because she hadn't been able to brief the composer properly on what it was she exactly wanted, they'd decided to put it on ice until such time as the project evolved and the story began to feel real. She was convinced she would have a flash of inspiration once things started taking shape. It was very difficult to think of these things on paper. You needed sets and rushes, and you needed to see the script played out for real.

The Producer sat smoking nervously in the hotel lobby. Suddenly, she became aware of the now familiar form of the Groupie slouching in a nearby armchair. For a brief moment both women looked at one another – a thousand thoughts racing through each mind. The Groupie showed undisguised delight, and losing no time she shot up from the chair all agog:

"Hi! How ARE you? What are you doing here?" she said in a forced, over-friendly manner.

"I have a meeting," the Producer said coldly in a guarded manner.

"With the Composer?" asked Groupie, her eyes suddenly lighting up and a hopeful pre-orgasmic smile breaking out uncontrollably on her neatly lip-lined mouth.

"Er... y..yes.," replied the Producer, feeling trapped.

"Oh, good! I've been here for hours, but I haven't seen him yet. This tedious receptionist won't give me his room number, and he's not taking any calls. I just found out he's staying here, so I thought I should come over and see if he needs anything. Maybe I'll come up with you and just say Hello...." She was already trying to lead the way to the main elevator.

The Producer was dumb-founded. Most unusual for her. How to get out of this one? She hesitated as if to say, no, not yet. I have some things to do first, I'm not going up yet, but thankfully, she didn't have to say anything. The Groupie joyously exuberant at her unexpected good fortune seemed quite oblivious to any obstacle as she gathered her dupatta about her and attempted to apply more lipstick while at the same time chattering away happily:

"I can always wait while you have your meeting. Then I want to take him back to my place for dinner. I've been cooking all morning – ever since I heard he's coming today. I've made aloo paratthas. He loves my food."

The Producer exercised the utmost restraint in not informing the Groupie that the Composer was probably dining somewhere in Sweden that evening. That bit of vital information would've sent Groupie, complete with aloo paratthas, whizzing to the appropriate terminal at Heathrow. Now the woman was attached to her like a Siamese twin, the Producer would have to do some fast footwork coupled with some quick thinking to prevent her tailing along to his room. Nothing could be revealed, no information, however non-specific, could be given out. The Producer was in possession of the valued room number. He had phoned her with it as soon as he'd arrived. He had also stressed that this information was confidential. He was giving her the number so that she could come straight up to the room. He was not receiving any other visitors. He wasn't taking any calls. Bloody poser!

But how to prevent Groupie tagging along? And how to let him know that she'd arrived for their meeting if he wasn't taking any calls? And how to go up to his room while Groupie was right behind her, watching her every move? Just as well she was half an hour early. At least there was time to think.

And then, as if life wasn't already complicated enough, a misty cloud of French perfume filled the lobby. The Actress wafted in, flicking back voluminous locks of hair, jhattka after jhattka, jangling bangles, anklets and shoulder-length earrings, turning every head as she marched up to the concierge and demanded a house phone to connect her to the room of the World's Number One Composer.

She looked stunning and moved with a new confidence, a completely new kind of graceful poise. Her voice was pitched lower than usual. Her tone had become refined, authoritative, her manner imperious, even haughty. Groupie and Producer both turned to watch and listen as a long argument ensued with the concierge:

"Don't you know me? I am fillum star! He may be Number Vun Composer, but I am Number Vun star in Bombay. Just tell him I'm here. That's all you have to do. Do it!"

The long-suffering receptionist stuck to her guns: she was not allowed to disturb him. He had most definitely said, "No Calls."

"I don't believe this. I am real star and HE is behawing like star. Look, he vill vont to see me if you tell him I'm here."

At that point, the Actress suddenly spotted Groupie. A thousand sharpened daggers were silently thrown backwards and forwards as they stood wide-eyed and open-mouthed glaring at one another in what could have been an almost perfect mirror image: two sets of dark eyeliner and two sets of dark lip-liner. American Georgio on the one hand and French Coco on the other, slowly mingling and causing a nauseatingly heady stench laced with the purest essence of mutual hatred.

The Producer cashed in on the diversion and slipped away towards a "Ladies" sign and then down a long, winding corridor. Finally it brought her to a wide, metal-grilled service lift full of baskets of white linen. She stepped in, tripped, and fell straight into a laundry bin while the lift doors closed automatically. Before she could press any buttons, she felt the lift move down. It kept going down for a long time. When the doors finally opened, she found herself in the hotel laundry room. Warm damp smells everywhere, with a soundtrack of whining, screeching, slushing washing machines.

A laundry assistant finally noticed her and showed her the way out. She came back into the hotel through a side door and managed to take another lift up to his floor, unobserved by the dagger-throwing women in the lobby. She knocked on his door, furtively looking right and left down the corridor. She was fifteen minutes early.

78
SAILING IN THE SAME BOAT

The Actress and the Groupie stood glued to the spot. If looks could kill then they should both have died several times, there and then.

The Groupie finally said: "Why do you throw yourself at men who don't want to know you? So de-meaning!"

"Huh! The deg-chi acting superior to the karahi! What about you? Do you think he wants you? Please, don't make me laugh...."

Bangles jangled as another aggressive jhattka was employed, sending more fumes of expensive French scent floating in the air.

"I'm his friend. We are very old friends. In fact in London I'm his best friend. I'm the only person he trusts," said the Groupie, determined to add an element of respectability to her persual of the slippery Composer.

"Friend huh? Then why you not already in room?" another French-scented jhattka.

"Because I have the common decency to not disturb a tired man. I never wake him up after a long flight. He's just flown in from Tokyo you know," the Groupie volunteered this information in the tone of one who is supremely privileged to know the elusive Composer's every move.

"Then vot you doing here? Why you here?" asked the enraged Actress, with an extra hard jhattka, sending long tresses of hair flying back over her head in the manner of a lifting black cloud.

"I came by to see if he wanted anything, but he's doing fine. Just resting. I brought him some paratthas. I was about to leave when you came in...."

The Actress fell silent while she considered this bit of shocking news. So, the Groupie has already seen him – she's already been up to his room. In that case she must know the room number. Time to sweeten her a bit... tone down the haughtiness and put on the helpless little girl number. Well she WAS an Actress, wasn't she?

"Oh, I see – oh that means you know room number – he told me but I'm forgetting, and now these stupid people won't give me... what's the number? Just remind me...."

"Of course I do. I've just been up there," the Groupie lied unashamedly and allowed more than a hint of triumph to creep into her voice as the full impact of this latest bombshell dropped on the Actress.

So, this bloody Groupie knew, but she wasn't telling. The Actress became agitated and now determined to humiliate this self-satisfied mother-figure of a groupie – the ultimate madonna. Everybody's mother and everybody's mistress-hopeful. Bloody parattha-maker earth-mother. The Actress abandoned her poor English and switched to her newly-elocutioned Urdu, in the interests of extra haughtiness and superiority.

"Oh, just look at you – you're pathetic. Just a Groupie calling herself best friend. What have you ever done with your life? All you do is follow famous musicians around, and how they talk about you – city to city, hotel to hotel, concert to concert, dressing room to dressing room. If only you could see how ridiculous and pitiful you look. I feel so sorry for you."

"How dare you! What have you done that's so great? Third-rate soft-porn cabaret scenes in exactly five films. And you think you've made it? I may have been from dressing room to dressing room, but at least I haven't been from casting couch to casting couch. Tameezan indeed!" The Groupie stuck to English.

"So, what's it to you? At least I have a career. At least I'm famous in my own right. I don't have to roll paratthas to win over friends and influence people. When Composer and I go out together, which we do all the time, I get approached for more autographs than he does. And he just loves tailing along to filmi parties and awards functions. He has made a lot of important contacts because of me. How do you think he got to do the music for the courtesan film?"

"So THAT'S it," cooed the Groupie, eager to twist this latest staggering revelation. "Oh, no wonder he has to be polite to you. I used to wonder why.... Well he's a nice guy. He hates saying "No" to people, especially those who pretend to care for his career. He's really too sweet. So childlike and innocent. Anyway, at least that explains why he has to be nice to you. I couldn't figure it out – it can't have been for any other reason. Now we know!"

The bilingual dialogue was getting louder and louder. At that point a member of the Hotel staff asked the ladies if they would prefer to carry on their conversation in the coffee lounge rather than disrupt fresh arrivals of suitcases in the lobby. There was a momentary lull. Now that they'd both got rid of those hateful feelings caused by being in a one-sided love affair with the same heartless man, there was no more joy of battle to be anticipated, only the melancholy business of counting the corpses.

The momentary lull in the slanging match drove home the point that the Producer had suddenly vanished – where? Had she left the hotel? No, no....

And in keeping with that famous cliché about feminine intuition, both women simultaneously turned their gaze towards the elevators. Where, but where? Eleven floors in this hotel. It could be any bloody room. Where to start?

Without a look at one another, and with perfect synchronicity as if moved by some unknown force, both women gravitated towards the coffee lounge, each struck by that same sense of feminine intuition that told her that she was somehow sailing in the same boat as her adversary. They were still enemies but there was now another, even more dangerous mutual enemy. Each woman felt intense and genuine sorrow for the other. They settled down to coffee. The Groupie lit up and began uneasily:

"I wonder where he's going next...?"

"Can I have a cigarette too, please? I'm supposed to have given up – that's why I don't carry any," the Actress interrupted chummily.

"Sure, it's always nice to meet another smoker," the Groupie leaned over with Dunhill.

"I'm not really a smoker. I can take it or leave it."

"I wish I could take it or leave it," said the Groupie wistfully. Musicians were even more addictive than nicotine.

The Actress picked up on the question of the Composer's ever-mysterious whereabouts:

"Yes, I wonder if he's staying the night. I wonder if he's free for dinner? I'd like to have dinner with him...."

"He can't go out with you tonight. I've cooked dinner for him...," she began belligerently then stopped, remembering their newly formed unspoken alliance against the Producer. She continued, as if suddenly overcome by fresh inspiration: "Actually, why don't you come and have dinner too? Then we can all go out to some club."

The Groupie was playing it safe. If putting up with this haughty Actress was the only way to see the Composer, then so be it.

"Oh, that would be lovely! I've heard so much about your food...", the Actress faltered uneasily as she remembered Composer's stories about how Groupie would cook the most elaborate dishes, feed and feed and feed him, and then expect sex in return, when all he wanted was to slink into a delicious sleep of the kind that can only happen after a rich, heavy meal swimming in ghee and coated with cream.

"How do you know about my food?" demanded Groupie uneasily, vaguely aware of a fresh complication.

"Oh, various people, you know. Good hostesses in London can never remain a secret – not even in Bombay. Anyway, a word of advise dear – woman to woman – you know," the Actress began, fingering the Groupie's dupatta critically to ensure it wasn't Polyester. Now that she had become even more beautiful, the Actress considered it her duty to dole out fashion and beauty advice to less fortunate, over-weight, older women.

"You know, you look best in saris – they hide all those bulges... er... I mean curves, you know, hips, very feminine and all that. But you must stop wearing those heavy Benarasi saris with twelve-inch gold borders. They make you look much older and so much heavier. There's nothing more ageing on a woman than a heavy silk sari with a wide border. Try plain chiffons, or soft pearl silks – much more slimming, more flattering. And wear your hair flatter, closer to the head. You would look much younger. You are really quite good-looking you know? When I first saw you with Composer, I was soooo envious. I know you must be nearly sixty, but you would pass for fifty, you know?"

The Groupie was still only forty-four, but she chose to ignore the cruel exaggeration about her supposed age. Instead, she said disarmingly, "Really? I look so young? How nice of you! Oh I don't believe it! You're just saying that. You know I really value your advice on clothes and make-up. You've become so elegant recently. You used to be so... well, so plain, quite fat actually. And you ate with your fingers. You didn't know how to use a knife and fork. Well that's what all the film magazines said. I never believed it of course, but since you've started the Courtesan film, you've become so poised and graceful... one can hardly recognise you now...."

The catty session disguised as a friendly coffee was now well and truly underway....

The mutual cattiness over, it was time to give a bit – to exchange confidences.

The Groupie volunteered the first snippet: "I wanted to be an actress once, you know...."

"Ooohh... why didn't you? You would've been so good in motherly roles!"

Again the Groupie chose to ignore the insult and launched straight into the subject that middle-aged women like best – their own life story:

"I fell in love with this wealthy computer person and married him. He was English you know," she said importantly, as if the acquisition of a White-skinned husband, albeit now an ex-husband, were some sort of trophy.

"How did you become so interested in music?"

"After my marriage broke up, I found peace of mind through music. I started going to concerts. Musicians are like doctors, you know? They just sit there and produce this soothing balm. Pure magic. But when the music stops, the magic continues – but only if I stay close to the magician. That is how I became friendly with musicians. It was never physical – just purely spiritual. Of course people said all sorts of things – everyone imagined I was sleeping with this Ustad or that Pandit – but in actual fact I can tell you, I only ever looked up to them as my healers – my fathers."

"And Composer, you know, the World's Number One, was he like a father-figure too?" the Actress felt a fresh surge of resentment for the Groupie's so-called friendships with supposed musician-healers.

The Groupie didn't like this deliberate reference to his nickname. It was well known in classical music circles that after her first night of a proper orgasm with him, she had, in a mood of joyful exuberance quite pompously and rather erroneously introduced him as The World's Number Composer at some glitterati event on the following day. The title had stuck, first being used rather disparagingly – almost tongue-in-cheek, but gradually, it had become his real signature. Still, how dare this once over-weight, finger-eating Actress bring it up in this direct, taunting fashion? But the Groupie decided to overlook the jibe and proceeded in a matter-of-fact way:

"No, he wasn't a father-figure. Far from it. He was very different. So young, so good-looking, so far away from home. Always so tired. Never ate properly. I felt he needed looking after. And I'm a very maternal type. He respects me for that you know? He confides in me about all those floozies who follow him around – specially the younger ones. He prefers mature women – even older women."

The Groupie felt delighted at being able to enlighten the Actress on the Composer's feminine ideal.

"What does he prefer them for?" The Actress was getting catty again.

"Oh, just friendship – company, you know. A man needs female company. Specially the caring sort of female."

"It can't be just for company. Come on, a man's a man after all. Didn't he ever try it on with you – I mean, try to get into your knickers?" The Actress just had to know one way or the other. She had always wondered....

Groupie let out a peal of deliberately hysterical laughter: "Oh he's been trying for over seven years – but I just treat him like a younger brother and laugh it off. I could never do anything like that."

The Actress frowned. Why was she lying? She was obviously trying to put herself in a special category. Not just another female fan following him around and offering her body again and again, not simply a whenever-he's-in-town-bed-mate, but a proper, caring companion. Putting herself in a separate league completely unperturbed by the floozies about whom he seemed to have confided in her. So could it be that he considered her a floozie too? The Actress had to know.

"Does he ever mention me?" she asked with some trepidation, dreading the worst....

"Yes, once or twice, not in any special context, just generally, you know...."

The Groupie cleverly managed to convey the impression that there was more, but she wasn't telling. She was enjoying herself now. She seemed to have won Round One.

"What did he say exactly?" asked the Actress, her lower lip quivering a bit.

"Oh nothing much – I can't really remember – nothing in particular."

Actress found this infuriating. Not only was Groupie deliberately holding something back, but she wanted her to know it, and she seemed just a little too pleased with herself. Maybe she was just bluffing? Try another tactic: when all else fails, attack!

"He told me about your coffee-tray incident," the Actress purred in her new, extra sultry, post-elocution tones.

"What coffee-tray incident?" Groupie's heart sank. Men were really not to be trusted!

"When you dragged him to your place after a concert, and then emerged stark naked from the kitchen, wearing only knee-high boots and carrying a tray of coffee."

There followed a one-minute silence – almost as a tribute to the abortive naked-with-coffee-tray manoeuvre.

Yes, that coffee-tray evening. The Groupie had been yearning for Composer's embrace and when it showed no sign of coming she had resorted to this desperate tactic. And on that occasion he had given in to her. What else could he do? He was a normal man. The fact that Actress knew all about it was really most annoying. How dare he reveal secrets like that? Should she attack back with a made-up story about the Actress? Better not, this woman was too sharp. Knew all the tricks. Safer to bring the Producer card into play – after all SHE was the reason why the two of them were even talking.

"Wonder what they're doing now? She's been gone a long time. Must keep an eye on the lifts. Let's see when she comes down. Should we wait until she comes down?"

"Oh, yes! Definitely! You know these arty-farty Producer-Director type of women. If they have two things to say to someone they call it a "business meeting" – things that could just as easily be said on the phone. But no, they have to have "meetings," – it makes them feel important."

Actress had temporarily forgotten her fight with Groupie and allowed her mind to renew her hatred for the Producer – arrogant bossy woman, always hurrying around with piles of paper in hand and dictating to her what she should wear and what her make-up should be. All for the sole aim of de-glamourising her. She decided to talk about the Producer, sensing that apart from the satisfaction that would come from voicing her venom, there might also be the added bonus of making Groupie feel even more insecure. A classic diversion tactic.

"He seems to spend a lot of time with her. If you ask me, he's quite taken with her. In fact, I think he's besotted. They must be having an affair. Why do men always like that sort of hard, bitchy masculine women? She's so ugly. Those jeans must be at least twelve years old. No make-up. Unwashed, greasy hair. And trainers! Did you see that? What sort of person wears trainers to a meeting in a five-star hotel?"

79
PERFECT RHYTHM

In Room 707, those same grubby trainers were being hurriedly unlaced by the Composer. He was always in a great hurry to get on with his lovemaking. Time was always limited. There was always a flight to catch. And he liked starting with her toes, so the trainers would have to come off first.

The Producer was most business-like about it. She had a lot to talk about and the sooner they could get the sex thing out of the way, the better. There was no point in trying to talk to him seriously while he had her body on his mind. Best to get that side of it over and done with and then sit up in bed, relax and talk.

She always got much more out of him this way. He was most receptive to her ideas in after-glow – this was the best time to persuade him to do things. Just before and just after were her two favourite times for getting the Composer to agree to almost anything. Only this time, she didn't seem to want to talk about work. When they'd completed a particularly riveting rhythm, congratulated each other for finishing at the same time, and christened the new rhythm "Jhaptal," she just wanted to gossip.

"There's quite a fan-club waiting for you in the lobby downstairs. Groupie's hoping to drag you away to her place for dinner, and the Actress is lecturing all and sundry on her popularity stakes in Bombay."

"What fun! Have they seen each other?" he asked, clearly chuffed.

"They'd just become aware of one another when I took my chance and escaped."

"Do you suppose somebody's called an ambulance by now?" he giggled with glee.

"You're really the pits – so heartless – so uncaring. Why do you treat them like this? Why not just come to the phone and say you don't want to see them?"

"Well I don't want to see either of them today – but who knows – I might need to see them another time. Might need them in some way. I might even fancy a parattha later on. Why burn any bridges? I believe in keeping every avenue open in life. You never know!"

"So, that's the secret of your heady fame and success, eh? Keeping doors open. Ladies in waiting. Film-stars and bored wives of rich men. Big deal! I think you're horribly selfish and completely self-centred. A gentleman doesn't lead ladies on. Shouldn't you have a frank talk with Groupie and tell her you no longer want to be followed around?"

"But I do want to be followed around. It makes me feel good. It's so exciting – so exciting to think there are two women in the lobby, both dying to make love to me. And here you are, in my arms, and you've just had it! We even finished together. Jhaptal! Don't you feel lucky?"

"Very lucky," she said sarcastically. "Now, about this ghazal...."

"It's not ready yet – but I'm working on it...."

"Then why did you say you wanted to play it to me this afternoon – what do you think I'm doing here?"

"You are here for my body."

"Oh, go to hell! I'm a really busy person you know. How dare you get me all the way up here under false pretences?"

"Didn't you enjoy it? The whole world raves about my rhythm!"

They both giggled and fell into each other's arms. She warmed a bit towards him.

"Yes, you do have tremendous rhythm. I can certainly vouch for that. But that's not the point. You explicitly said you had something for me. That's why I'm here. As for the other... well you know, I don't really mind if I have to read a good book instead. I'm not hung up on sex. I can take it or leave it... men just hate my independence."

"Oh, come on, you've seen for yourself – there's no shortage of women who want to sleep with me. And this is only London. You should see them in India! Even their fathers come to me and offer me their entire estates in return for marrying their daughters, or even for agreeing to have affairs with them. Can you beat that? An Indian father, bribing some man to sleep with his daughter because he can no longer bear her misery? A rich industrialist recently offered me both his daughters, at once!"

"Then why didn't you take him up on it? You'd get all his tedious hinge-making factories as dowry and then at least you can stop running around rat-assed doing thirty-seven projects at a time. You'd have it made! All the money in the world, and as much sex as you want from any number of fat, ugly, millionaires' daughters!"

"Chillies burning, chillies burning..." he sang the line in Urdu.

"Don't be ridiculous! If all those ghastly people have more money than sense, then why shouldn't some of it come your way? It would be easier than trying to earn your living through projects you can't even deliver on time."

"OK, where's your machine? I have a rough track for you...."

Her face lit up. He really was too much. Somehow, despite all the mayhem, he always managed to do his work. God knows when or where, but he had managed to put something together, somehow.

As soon as it began playing, she knew it in her bones.... THIS was it! This was absolutely the thing! It was precisely what she hadn't been able to articulate. It was almost exactly as it had sounded in her head. It captured that enigmatic mood perfectly. The lyrics were deep and crisp. The singing was exquisite – the music, pure ecstasy. She was momentarily transported to that world – hanging on every word of the ghazal. She was there, right there in the middle of the Nawab's party, and Tameezan was right before her eyes in a costume of shocking pink and gold, warbling the brand new ghazal, a rich pathos in her voice and her eyes hopeful with anticipation. Where... where would they make that moment – the moment when Tameezan first catches sight of her beloved Grand Ustad... where...?

And then it leapt out at her. Right here, there it was, that was it! It was so obvious and so perfect. The Composer had worked it in – he had carefully created that very precise moment within the ghazal – a pin-drop silence for a split second, three-quarters of the way in. Perfect timing! Just like his lovemaking. No wonder they said he was the World's Number One!

80
WHO IS ZARINE?

"Did I hear you right – 'nearly finished' – you said?"

"Yeah! That's right!" a triumphant Ash replied.

"What on earth is 'nearly finished'? No such thing! You're either finished or you're not finished. It's like saying a woman is 86 per cent pregnant."

Typical Sonia!

Ash was crest-fallen at the reprimand. Just before he'd rung her he was bloated with pride and self-importance. He'd finally worked it out – nearly all done. All that remained was to sit down and write. Feeling unfairly chastised he tried again:

"I mean I now know what I'm doing. The story is complete. All I have to do is write it. Nearly finished means I'm ready to write it – it all fits together now."

He could tell she'd already lost interest. He was right. Another plot. Another idea that was potentially a script. But it wasn't yet a real script.

"So why don't you just write?" she said in a disinterested voice.

"I can't write. I'm a film-maker. I went to film school. I didn't go to a writing school."

"OK, OK, so make a film – but how are you going to do it without a script?"

"Oh I'll have a script soon. I'll keep at it, don't worry."

"I'm not worried. Remember? I've heard it all before." Sonia sounded fed up.

"But this is different. I'm really on to something this time. Just wait till I tell you about it. You see it's about this...."

"No, no, don't tell me! Just do it! Write it! Submit it! Then tell me...."

"OK, if you don't want to hear about it I won't tell you. I thought you were interested in my work." Ash couldn't keep the hurt out of his voice.

"I will be – when it's done, but not before. So what else is going on?"

"Nothing else. I've just been working away. I wish you would let me discuss these things with you. After all, you talk for ages about this theory and that theory, but when I want to sound you out on one of my characters, you just don't want to know...."

"No, I don't want to know. I'm only interested in real people. I don't care for fictitious concoctions. Ash listen, real life is so much more exciting, who needs fiction?"

"But it's not all fiction. All my characters are real people, and they have real things happening to them. Oh, by the way, thanks for the Zarine contact. Really, quite a teacher! My plot has been flowing since I started the Zarine method...."

"Flowing, yes, but it's still not a script is it? It can't be a script until you sit down and write it, so what are you waiting for?" Sonia was being deliberately severe. It was only for his own good.

"Oh, I've still got to figure out an ending. Just a couple more sessions with your Zarine – the Dream Teacher, and then I'll have an ending. No problem, really. Do you still go to Zarine?"

"No, not as a client. I don't need to...."

"How much do you know about her really? I mean do you know who she really is...?"

"Who is ANYONE really? What does it matter? Her special technique works for you, doesn't it? So who cares?"

Oh Sonia, *you* care... you would care if only you knew....

81
BEWITCHED, BOTHERED & BEWILDERED

"Bismillah…" Tameezan muttered under her breath as she gathered up her voluminous skirts and stepped into the carriage sent by the Nawab. This was it. The night of a thousand nights was finally here. This night was Tameezan's biggest night – not because it was her first public performance in a very long time, nor because the Nawab had agreed to pay the largest sum of money ever paid to a courtesan for a mere ghazal recital. It was a big night because it was to be her first ever face-to-face, eye-to-eye contact with the man of her dreams – the Grand Ustad, the Lighter Upper of the Whole Universe. As the carriage jostled through the dark uneven alleys, she smiled to herself and starting humming her brand new ghazal softly, going over the vital moment of that first sighting again and again….

****

The Actress's make-up room was crammed with people – a terrific cacophony of sounds and smells and panic as she was being dressed for the first shot of the Nawab's grand party scene. The Producer managed to squeeze her way through the throngs to reach the army of hairdressers and make-up artistes for a final reassurance that nothing inauthentic would be used. No, no nail polish in late 19th century India, please. And lots of oil in her hair. It must glisten under the lights. Sharp middle parting and a tightly woven single long plait, hair extensions neatly added. Don't forget the oily shine on the face. Remember, it's hot at those Nawabi parties. And she's supposed to be nervous and excited, so a few beads of sweat carefully positioned on the brow please… let's make it look real.

For those poor long-suffering artisans of make-up and hair, there's nothing quite so tedious as a Producer-Director obsessed with historical authenticity.

The make-up artistes had hinted earlier that there might be some problems getting the Actress ready for this scene. They said she was bossy in the extreme in terms of what suited her and what didn't. So the Producer looked in to make doubly sure everything was in order. No felt-tip pens or red-paint. Real henna had been applied the night before, hands and feet, painstakingly decorated by henna-artistes brought in from Indian bridal beauty parlours in Wembley. The Actress had had to sleep with the henna on. It had been the most uncomfortable night of her life and she was getting fed up with the Producer's attention to detail. It meant she couldn't look glamorous. She wasn't allowed any skin-lightening cream. Her own medium skin-tone, she was told, was perfect because the Courtesan was not supposed to have been fair-skinned – just very, very striking. Yes, yes... you can look striking without being fair-skinned. There's such a thing as finely chiselled features... now come on! Stop being a baby! The foundation has to be two tones darker. No arguments!

And now as the Producer entered the cramped dressing room and stood whispering with the wardrobe assistant, the Actress's heart sank – whatever next? What does she want now? What is it that I'm not going to be allowed to wear in case I look too beautiful? Bitch! Can't stand me because I'm beautiful. I'm never going to work with a woman director again. Men are so much more obliging. In India they wouldn't care if I wanted a beehive and purple nail polish, as long as I looked nice.

The Producer marched up to the Actress aggressively: "Hi! The hair looks great! Well done all of you!" she announced in patronising tones.

"It's not finished yet," the Actress retorted icily.

"No, but it's just as I wanted. And you look so much like her I can hardly believe it!"

"Oh yes?" the Actress remarked unenthusiastically, thinking to herself, that means I look quite ugly, and she's pleased.

The PA was painstakingly threading expensive fresh white flowers to make a gajra – an intricate garland of petals – for the Courtesan's hair. The wardrobe people had supplied the same made out of paper flowers, but the Producer had almost had a heart attack: "OK, I know nobody can smell anything on film, but I want HER to be able to catch the scent of flowers in her hair. It's got to feel real to HER!"

"So?" the Head of Wardrobe was a defiant sort of lady. "So, just buy some jasmine scent and spray the sodding paper. What's your problem?"

"I don't need your advice on authenticity," she informed the wardrobe person coldly. "I went to SOAS, you know?"

And the long-suffering Ronnie-PA had had to shoot out to the nearest florist and purchase every stem of anything in white that even vaguely resembled the Arabian Jasminum sambac – the Producer's SOAS translation for the "Mogra" flower.

The Actress had now reached that enviable position that only few human beings are ever destined to savour: she was indispensable. She could do what she liked and for some mysterious reason, nobody ever threatened to fire her from the film. They'd spent all this money on training and grooming her. Why? It must be because she was a great actress – what else could it be?

She had recently taken to not showing up on time – often not showing up at all. She never missed an Urdu lesson or a dance class, but if a shoot had been booked and scheduled, she often excused herself at the eleventh hour, usually because she had to attend a concert in some other city. And since the World's Number One appeared in twenty different cities a month, that meant a lot of overseas trips and a lot of absences.

As her fame slowly grew and gathered momentum, concert organisers were only too thrilled to have her. She brought a sparkle to their events. She was famous for being famous, music or no music. It was soon an established fact that if the World's Number One Composer was performing or conducting, then the Actress was sure to be in the front row. Prices of front row seats doubled, trebled and then quadrupled on the black market.

Only three days before the ghazal shoot day, the Actress had gone missing, without a word to anyone. Even her best-friend PA-Ronnie had no idea of her whereabouts. The Producer refused to believe him. He was probably covering up for her. There was nothing quite so frustrating as having everything and everyone up and running while the main star goes missing:

"Look, does she want to be in this film or doesn't she? How can I use a substitute for her main singing shots? Be reasonable Ronnie, she'll be the first to whine if she thinks I haven't done enough close-ups of her new, ultra-sultry ultra-sexy look. Where the hell is she Ronnie?"

"Don't worry darling. The Composer has a concert in London the day before our shoot – she's bound to materialise then," soothed PA.

"God! It might almost be worth paying him a special fee to attend the shoot. That's about the only thing that would guarantee her presence on the set."

Even as she said it, the Producer felt an idea taking shape. Yes, why not? He should, strictly speaking, be here to supervise the actors playing musicians, just to make sure they were holding the instruments properly and their fingers were in the right place. She was going to do close-ups of hands with real musicians later on, but there were at least four shots in which the dummy-musicians were in frame with the Courtesan.

The Producer went on admiring the Actress's tightly woven plait and registered with some joy that the jhattka was no longer possible: "About today's scene. Can I just have a quick word?" The Producer had recently taken to speaking to the Actress in English only, because whenever she spoke in Urdu, the Actress with her special elocutioned voice and authentic Lucknow accent, always got the better of her. But in English, the Actress still had a long way to go and this made the Producer feel immensely superior:

"Look, I know we've been through this before but you haven't been around for awhile. It's absolutely vital to get this one just right. Remember, the rest of the film hangs on this one scene. The set has cost zillions of hundreds of thousands of pounds and we've only got this studio for a month before they start refurbishing for the other scenes, so we can't have too many re-takes. Now remember, every time you look up and look around, try to get that slightly anxious feeling... is he here yet? Could that be him? What was that noise...? And then alternate that with a couldn't-care-less feeling. So what if it's him? Who does he think he is? He's the one who's about to be struck by lightning! Just wait till he sees my beauty... that sort of thing, you know?"

"That makes no sense. Am I looking forward to seeing him, or not?"

"Yes and no. I mean, yes, you're dying to see him, you've been dying for sixteen years, remember? But no, you don't want him to know that, do you?"

"So what you want me to do?"

"I thought we'd been through all that," the Producer said impatiently.

"We had, but you just come in now and say something completely different. I'm totally confused," the Actress frowned. It was always like this. This was always a major drawback when the producer-director was also the writer. They would just go on making it up. They kept adding things to the story. They used film sets as inspiration, to fine-tune their wretched, improbable stories. And all this nit-picking while she was already sweating heavily under layers of silky fabric embroidered in gold, the metal of jewellery feeling hotter by the minute against her delicate skin – and she wasn't even under those merciless lights yet. She had been up since five in the morning. She had arrived at the studio on time, rearing to go. She had worked it all out in her mind. She knew exactly what expression to create, and now this bloody woman was rambling on and trying to confuse her.

"Really, you just confuse me completely," pouted the actress, with an imaginary jhattka – imaginary, because there was no cascade of hair to flick back from the left brow. Her wild, voluminous tresses had been safely immobilised with a thousand hairpins. On remembering this unfair imprisonment of her most important asset, the Actress quivered slightly about the mouth, causing fresh panic for make-up artistes whose worst nightmare was tears... oh no! We've taken hours, and now she's going to ruin it all! They arm themselves with tissues, waiting for the dreaded salty drops to arrive and erode away the expertly applied two-tones-darker foundation....

The Producer was in serious danger of fast losing that goodwill which she reserved for pre-shoot artistes.... "No, please, no, don't do this to me. Don't tell me now that you're confused. I don't need to hear this. Look, it's not at all complicated. You are there for him, right? You've only agreed to sing at this wretched party because he's going to be there, OK? You want to see him, and you want him to see you. But until such time as he actually arrives, you are slightly anxious, even nervous. But you act confident. You are supposed to sing beautifully – I hope you've memorised the words – and remember you have a captive audience of some of the wealthiest nobleman of Lucknow. And many of them haven't seen you perform for over ten years. You have their fullest attention, all eyes on you, so enjoy yourself. But remember that some vital part of the core of your being remains with your beloved Ustad, and your eyes search for him. Every time anyone enters the room, you look up to see if it's him. We'll take lots of close-ups of you later on, looking in different directions and they'll be cut into the ghazal in between the singing. There's some beautiful sarangi pieces to carry your glances through – sometimes anxious, sometimes hopeful, sometimes defiant... just emote the music... listen to the wail of that sarangi... we'll play you all the interlude music, of course...."

"Yes, OK.... I see...." she didn't sound too sure.

"Look, it's easy! Look happy and confident, but also, also..." and for lack of anything better to say in English, she added: "Look confident but also look bewitched, bothered and bewildered... you know?" She had always wanted to say that to some actor and having got it off her chest, the Producer decided to be charitable and take the heat off the Actress for a bit, so she changed the subject slightly: "By the way, did you like the ghazal?"

"Oh beautiful. I love it. But then it's always beautiful when he does it. He's the best musician in the world – Number One! I wonder where he is now? Maybe on a plane somewhere...?" she pined.

"No, he's in London and he might drop in later on – just to see how we're doing," Producer lied deliberately, just to test the impact.

"He's here? No! He's in London? He might look in? Really?" The Actress suddenly replicated that exact expression that the Producer had been trying to explain to her earlier.

"Yes, most professional you know. He wanted to see some of the ghazal being filmed. It's really his own you know? He pretends it's some poet friend of his, but I think he wrote it himself. Very talented man. Now, as I was saying… this ghazal scene…."

"He's here? Really? He might be coming to the shoot?" Her face had lit up, but with a definite degree of self-restraint. She couldn't hide her excitement, but she produced a facial expression of cool defiance mingled with nervous anticipation. And then, in an off-guard moment, she let out a gentle sigh and smiled to herself, completely unaware that the Producer was closely studying her face.

It was no secret that despite the Actress's endless concert attendances, the Composer usually managed to give her the slip. As she re-lived this bitter truth, her face became harder, yet more beautiful, and then it almost froze. Her resolve seemed to strengthen: Who the hell did he think he was? If he was the World's Number One Composer, then she was India's Number One Actress!

As she watched the Actress's face, now looking every bit as she had imagined Tameezan's might have looked on the big night, a sense of urgency gripped the Producer. Her little white lie about the Composer coming to the shoot would have to be made true somehow… it might just work….

She whizzed out of the make-up room to make what she called an "urgent telephone call". And for once in her life she was telling the truth.

82
TYPICAL BOLLYWOOD ENDING

The Producer-Director was getting impatient. Where the hell was that woman? They were already running late, and this was the most important scene in the whole film. Today's shots were the most important shots for that scene. She couldn't afford to be flustered for this one. Where was that wretched Actress? Hope and pray she wasn't getting someone to paint her nails purple or re-do her hair into a beehive....

The Producer firmly believed in shooting the most important scene first. That way you got the best of them. If you waited until later, everyone wisened up a bit and started to put forth the most ridiculous script adjustments. And they never respected you as much as they did in the beginning.

Ronnie-PA appeared on the set straight from the star's dressing room, looking suitably frazzled, sun-shades over his eyes, clipboard in one hand, stopwatch in the other, and a pen on a string round his neck:

"Not long now darling," he informed his Producer boss in the tones of one reporting progress on an important military campaign. "She's just had to pop into the loo. Too bad she couldn't go before. Now she's all decked out in her skirts and things, she's having a bit of problem gathering it all up just to have a pee. Two girls have gone in with her to hold up the skirt, don't worry."

"Oh, for God's sake, fuck the lot of you! Why do you treat her like she was made of glass? How the hell do you think they went to the loo when they had to wear those things for real?"

"Oh but be fair darling. She still has henna on her hands. How on earth is she supposed to lift up her costume? You're the one who insisted on the henna staying on as long as possible – you and your rich blackish-red colour – all very authentic darling."

"Stop being catty. I get enough of that from everybody else. Go and hurry her up again!" the Producer barked at the PA registering some irritation at his get-up. Why on earth did he have to wear those shades?

"The glare, darling, too much for my light-sensitive eyes...." he explained unnecessarily.

"That's right," she thought. "That's what happens to your eyes when you get your bum washed out too often in Harley Street!"

At long last the Actress arrived on the set and as if by a miracle, everything was suddenly transformed. If up until now it had all looked like a make-believe world surrounded by cables and light-stands and shabby jeans-clad workers, now it seemed as though they'd all taken a trip in a time-machine. The Actress's appearance had the uncanny effect of making everything real. And it wasn't just the result of costume and make-up. She seemed to work her whole being into another existence, evoking another historical period in a country that was thousands of miles away from this Home Counties film studio. She looked truly stunning, every bit the 19th century courtesan, and every bit like the one and only sepia photograph of Tameezan that had survived the ravages of time.

The Producer was thrilled to the core, but it wouldn't do to say as much now. She didn't want anyone suffering from over-confidence just before this most vital shoot. True they had been getting the Actress ready since five in the morning for an afternoon shoot, but it had been well worth it.

All the extras were already assembled, various minor characters in period costume, wandering around incongruously with mobile phones in one hand and cigarettes in the other. The Actress was put in to place for her main-shot: the traditional courtesan singing position, seated on a lavish rug with the skirts of her gharara and her voluminous dupatta spread out round her to show off the gold embroidery at its glittering best. Lights were switched on and off endlessly as the final adjustments began. Wide shots were taken to show various sets of extras in the back-drop while the Actress vaguely moved her lips to the same two lines of the ghazal again and again.

It had all progressed without a hitch. The extras were okayed and packed off while the crew repositioned themselves for the courtesan's close-up's. A whole verse of the ghazal had to be filmed in close-up, including the vital bit with that sharp intake of breath as the Grand Ustad, Lighter-Upper of the entire Universe, supposedly enters the room.

Shot after shot. Exactly as she wanted. The Producer found a new respect for the Actress. It was truly incredible: the woman was most certainly hugely talented. She had done all her homework. She looked magnificent. Beautiful, but slightly sulky. Cool, but also a little anxious. Apprehensive, but apparently relaxed. Yes, there was no doubt about it. She was truly gifted, and Bollywood had never known it! Never mind! Their loss was the Producer's gain. Now she wished she had been kinder to the Actress in their meetings. No drama school, no formal training, nothing. Just a born-actress, who knew how to enter a character body and soul. A true professional!

When the Actress was asked if she'd like a small break, she said she would prefer to carry on. She was enjoying herself. She liked being Tameezan. It was easier to keep going in that mood. A break would mean she would have to be herself again, and at the moment she just wanted to be Tameezan.

That remark was music to the Producer's ears. The Producer-Director who had only ever worked with enormous budgetary constraints was used to packing in a lot of work into the same day, and this way of working suited her just fine. She hated having to stretch things out just for the sake of it. She hated unnecessary breaks. It seemed to take hours to get everybody up and running again after their chattering and their coffees. It was too good to be true! Director and lead Actress were of the same mind. They had the same views on adrenaline. A perfect team.

"OK, now we'll go for the big one, where the Grand Ustad has just entered the room, and you are seeing him for the first time in your life. This is the man you have loved for years. Now he's finally here. Imagine how that must feel. But go on moving your lips to the song – that shouldn't stop. Just do it with your eyes. You're doing brilliantly so far. You're just wonderful! Absolutely priceless! You don't even need me to explain it. I'm just recapping for everybody else's benefit.... Make-Up! More sweat beads please, quickly! OK? You ready?"

She walked off the lighted area to check if the Composer had arrived as instructed, to wait in the darkness and then at the appropriate moment suddenly step forward and let himself be seen so that the Actress's surprise and delight would be as genuine as possible.

As usual, he was nowhere to be seen. Typical! Completely bloody unreliable! Oh, to hell with it! It was a nice idea, but surely an actress as talented as this could produce the perfect expression without any trickery?

The camera was rolling. Take after lake. All the takes were acceptable, but a certain something special was missing. And then it happened, without a warning. Just as they had started Take-Seventeen, a shadowy figure stepped out from the darkness, out of camera-shot, but in full view of the Actress.

And that's how they finally came face to face, for the first time in not sixteen, but twenty-one years....

Mohanji and his fashionable wayward daughter-in-law – finally face to face! He lurched forward, both arms outstretched – as though about to make an appeal – tripped on a cable and fell into a heap. As soon as their eyes met, he collapsed – exactly as the Lighter Up of the Universe had collapsed under the poisonous gaze of the Courtesan Tameezan's eyes, nearly a hundred years ago.

"Cut! That's the one! That's it! We'll print that!" squealed the Producer, from somewhere behind the camera-monitor, vaguely aware that some person had entered the studio and stepped out from behind the lights to face the Actress, head-on. In her euphoria at having got exactly the right kind of shot, she completely overlooked the matter of just who, or what had instigated that priceless expression on the Actress's face for the best close-up ever shot in the entire history of cinema!

But for some strange reason, as though frozen in a time warp, nobody moved. The ghazal track played on. Everybody stood as still and as silent as though the shot was still rolling. The camera was indeed still rolling, framed in close-up on the Actress, recording her every gesture, her every nuance, every twitch. Her big eyes were rounded with shock in a fixed gaze, while her mouth went on moving to the words of the ghazal.

And then another figure stepped out into the light. The Producer shook her head in a knowing sort of way... typical, bloody typical! As usual the Composer had turned up in the nick of time, as per her instructions, but just this once, they had managed without him. Her Actress had already produced a priceless expression without his help... but then, who was that other person who had just entered and so surprised the Actress, before collapsing in a heap?

Before she could say anything, she saw the Composer staring at that other person, now a lifeless heap on the floor, and with her stomach almost falling out on her well-worn trainers, she recognised the heap as Mr Moneybags himself.

The World's Number One Composer bent over the heap, full of wonderment, full of joy... he could've been a kid on his first trip to Disneyland. In fact he sounded just like a little girl... an eight-year old girl squealing with joy: "Oh Mr Mohanji..., Mr Mohanji... oh is it really you? You look exactly the same. You haven't changed at all... oh how I missed you Mr Mohanji. I thought of you all the time...."

The World's Number One Composer was now down on his knees, positively grovelling, crawling, tears running freely down his face, nose-dripping profusely and uncontrollably. Most uncharacteristic. Nobody had ever seen the Composer go down on his knees – well not in this context anyway....

"Mr Mohanji, Mr Mohanji... you don't know how I've missed your shop, your food, your shit... you made me everything I am today. You made me the world's number one. Oh thank you Mr Mohanji. Thank-you for the songs, thank-you for the rhythms... chilly-pounding, onion chopping, fly-swatting, sewing machine rhythms. Thank you for showing me the Moon God, a thousand thank-yous! If I were a woman I would feed nine virgins here and now.... Mr Mohanji... can you hear me, why don't you get up Mr Mohanji? It's me, remember me...?"

A strange paralysis gripped everybody on the set. The Composer kneeling down, and just behind him the Groupie who had followed him all the way to the studio carrying two cauliflower paratthas in a round tin. The Ustad who had invited himself to watch the ghazal shoot and then, catching a delicious aroma coming from the direction of the Groupie's tin, had decided to stay put; and Ronnie-the-PA who stood near his Producer Boss while she wore a horrified look of total puzzlement. The Actress, still sitting tight in her alluring singing position and still producing that priceless expression of stupefied surprise and the camera, still rolling... while Money Bags-Mohanji lay dead as a dodo.

"Mr Mohanji? Did I hear you say Mr Mohanji? Is that really THE Mr Mohanji?"

It was the voice of the PA. The Composer stopped sobbing. The Producer's expression now matched that of the Actress as everyone turned to look at the PA:

"He... he that bastard – he tore me away from my mother... the poor bechari Widow. He made my poor Widow mother give me away so she could work harder in his blessed shop... he was the one who made her do it...."

The PA's voice trembled as he shook with rage.

The Composer tore himself away from the heap that was Moneybags-Mohanji's body and walked over to the PA with a quizzical expression:

"Are you the same? You're the beautiful toddler that the Widow's in-laws came and took away? Where is she? Where is the Widow? Do you know? I must see her! She wanted me to come to a nine virgins' lunch, but it never happened...."

"Oooh, I don't knooowoo," wailed the PA with a high-pitched whine before throwing himself into the Composer's embrace and both men started wailing in chorus.

The Composer's wailing was frequently punctuated with sobbing speech:

"Where is she? Tell me, where? The woman of my melodies, the mistress of my rhythms... my muse of song... bluebells on black, green palm trees on white... where is she?"

The Producer stood fixed to the spot completely mystified and more than just a little annoyed at this turn of events. It was HER film, so why the hell was it turning into a tragicomic Bollywood farce? She was about to order all unnecessary bodies off the set when a uniformed nurse came in, wheeling forward an extremely good-looking, but completely zombified green-eyed man. On recognising her husband, Mohanji's Actress daughter-in-law suddenly shot up from her sitting position. Perhaps it was the heat of the lights... or the heaviness of her costume and jewellery – or then again, maybe it was just pure shock, but as soon as she stood up, she swooned and fell down again.

Mohanji's body lay where he had fallen and some distance from that, lay the richly-dressed and heavily made-up Actress who had just fainted. The PA, who would ordinarily have been fussing with wet flannels and ambulances, now lay sobbing on the Composer's shoulder. The Composer sat cross-legged crying like a baby near Mohanji's corpse.

The cameraman pulled back to widen the shot so that everyone was included. "Good, ain't it? Great stuff!" he winked at the Producer.

"Cut! I said CUT, you shit-bag!" the Producer shrieked, fully recovered from these bizarre happenings: "Enough! Bloody enough! Typical bloody last scene from a typical senseless Bollywood lost-and-found disaster. Great fucking family reunion. Final family group photograph!"

And to think that all her life she had gone out of her way to avoid any likelihood of comparison between Bollywood trash and her own high-brow ideals, and now here, right here, on her own expensive film-set, under her own direction, she had a real Bollywood ending. Life imitating art. It was more than art could bear. She stomped out. At last she was ready to just drop the whole thing and walk off in a huff.

83
TAMEEZAN'S GREAT GRANDSON

I have something to confess. I want to tell you the real truth about what happened on the big night – the night of the famous ghazal. The night that Tameezan the courtesan and the Grand Ustad Ronson Lighter, etc. etc. finally came face to face....

The Grand Ustad enters the room, followed by a retinue of attendants and hangers on. Various people start getting up as a mark of respect, paying no attention to Tameezan who is still mid-ghazal. The Ustad motions with his hands for them to keep still. Then he sits down to listen to the rest of her ghazal, but suddenly collapses in a heap. He dies on the spot, but his attendants deny it. They say he has fainted – the heat – the lights – perhaps a minor heart attack.

They carry him away. It wouldn't do for anyone to think that just one glance from Tameezan had finished him off. How would that look? How could they admit that he had died at the very first sighting of a woman he had refused to see for sixteen years?

Some weeks later his death is formally announced:

"The Universe is now in darkness. The one who lit the entire universe has now departed from this world. Long illness. He had been unwell for a while. Life and death are matters for Allah to decide. From him we come and to him we shall return...."

All that sort of thing.

But the actual cause of death? One glance. Ek Nazar. One poisonous look. Just one look from Tameezan had finished him off. Hers was a special brand of magic. Two eyes, deep, piercing, poised to kill. And one poisoned arrow set off from somewhere in between them. Two eyes that had shed oceans of tears. Tears into which she had dipped her quill to write the most beautiful Urdu ghazals of all time. Eyes that had thirsted for his shadow in the street below. Eyes that had remained behind a black veil every blessed Thursday night for two years. Eyes that served as windows of a soul that had writhed with pining and longing. As soon as those eyes fixed their gaze on him, he was consumed by their all-embracing fire. Fire of rage. Fire of love. Fire of betrayal. Fire of passion. Fire of revenge. Fire of death. There was no weapon like it in the whole world. It was true love. And true love never leaves a trace... no weapon, no visible wound, no blood.

Of course it could never be proved. It wouldn't have stood up in any court of law. Nobody dared say it, but it was generally suspected that the Courtesan had, somehow, killed the Ustad. Some assumed poison. Others imagined some special paste introduced into his paan, somehow. Yet others maintained a special herb sprayed into the seams of his clothes by a corrupt tailor, first rendering him paralysed, then dead as a dodo a few weeks later. But it wasn't a few weeks later. We know that. It was that very night. That very instant. It was at her sharp intake of breath, at that especially composed and built-in moment in the ghazal. Almost like she was drawing all of his breath away from him, and into herself.

I may be the World's Number One composer, but I'll be honest with you, I'm no poet. I didn't write or compose that ghazal. That WAS the original couplet, the one I found in my mother's locked chest – my treasure-hunt game that hot sultry afternoon when there was nothing else to do. The couplet that taught me to read a new language. That was the very couplet recited that fateful night by my own great-grandmother Tameezan, and it was revealed to me by the Grace of the Moon God. Otherwise I might never have known!

84
CHEATING GOD

"Hello. This may come as a shock to you – and I know it's six in the morning your time, but I have before me a script called "Tameezan." Written by you, you snake in the grass!"

Sonia sounded furious. It was almost a year since they'd last spoken.

There was a long silence. When Ash finally swallowed hard and opened his mouth to speak, his voice seemed to be coming from somewhere in the far distance. In fact it didn't sound like his own voice at all.

"OK, so you've read it," he gulped. "I'm sorry. But apart from upsetting you a bit, it's quite good isn't it? What do you think?"

"I think our friendship is at an end," she replied.

What Ash didn't even know was that while being his best friend and always being on the phone to him, she was also a professional script-reader and editor.

So *that's* what she does in between writing those crazy books about typewriters and staplers and saints and butterflies.

Nobody knew exactly what Sonia did for a living. And since her official stance was one of complete and haughty indifference to anything that might classify as visual art, how could Ash have guessed that his one and only completed script would end up with Sonia for critical assessment by a potential funding body? Not in a million years! She never even went to the cinema, so what would she be doing with a film script?

How could Ash have known that Sonia had a deliberate policy of never taking credit for anything? Yet he was uneasily aware of past references to this point, one of her many platitudinous orations: Complete confidentiality. You work best if you aren't connected with anything. People should never be allowed to perceive you as allied to this or that camp. Always undercover, always hidden. It was for your own protection. Sonia often said that the advantages of anonymity were so little appreciated that western journalists and feminists were stupid enough to assume that a veiled woman was, by definition, an oppressed woman. Can you think of anything more liberating than veiling yourself from head to toe in plain black and going place to place without anyone ever knowing you'd been there? The Black Burqa – the ultimate liberator!

Very few people understand the value of being incognito. Most people thrive on ego-feeding public approval. They want applause. They do one small thing and want to get interviewed about it for ten years!

But not Sonia. She wanted the opposite. Annihilate that greedy short sighted ego, and then see what happens. Who cares about the public? The public are just plebs. They'll consume whatever you feed them. They'll either rave about it, or they'll shoot it to pieces, but why should they know where it came from? Why is the identity of the artist important? Those who used her services – whether assessment reports on manuscripts or film scripts or political speeches – were more than happy to keep her name out of things. This brought in even more work, with the added advantage of not having to show up at tedious parties and meet boring people who gawked at small time celebrities. Once you were a celebrity, even of a lightweight quality, everyone wanted you to attend their septic little functions and tedious little talks, and even worse, their stale-samosa dinner parties so that they could field a guest-list of semi-famous names. Complete waste of time... time in which to be writing even more stuff... under yet another name.

Ash knew he had been caught out. He had nothing to lose. He still wanted to know whether she liked his script.

Sonia had never been a woman of few words, and in this case, he certainly wasn't getting off lightly.

"You creep! Constipated turd! You monumental, cataclysmic ass-hole! That's it! Our friendship has ended. The End! Fin. White lettering on black spacing. Fade down... bastard!"

"Sorry, it's just that I like you so much, well I had to put you in it somehow, so I made the neurotic Producer-Director a bit like you. You should take it as a compliment. And I made myself like the PA, Ronnie. Aren't you pleased I made you the Boss and made myself your chamcha? Ronnie is just like me except for the homosexuality bit...."

"Jerk! Go fuck a brillo-pad! Pilfering MY story! Nosing through my computer files. How dare you? You pretend you're performing the most supreme sacrifice in history by giving up a whole morning to wait in at my flat for the plumber, and then you spy on my private notes. How dare you?"

Her voice was cracking up. She was annoyed with herself for not sounding furious enough. Why was it so difficult to be angry with him?

"Look, please listen Sonia, I was bored. So I just trawled through your computer files. You had all these notes about Indian people in small town Africa. I found your people so inspiring. So I took my unfinished Courtesan story and added your people, and I think it hangs together very well. It will make a good film, no? I'll give you a special acknowledgement, all by yourself. In fact, I could start with the words '...a film inspired by Sonia's computer'...."

"I'm not like you, you know? I'm not hungry for credits. People should do what they want to do and just get on with it. Art is only art if it stands independently from its creators otherwise it's just a massive ego enhancing exercise. That's why I admire God. The cleverest trick God ever pulled was to convince a vast majority of the human race that He doesn't really exist. He is nothing. Yet He is everything! Because nothing, NO-thing, IS every-thing!"

"Oooh darling!" Ash deliberately let himself slip into Ronnie-PA mode. "It's so wonderful to hear you like this again. Are we still talking then? This is just like old times. You telling me about the mysteries of creation. I feel so much better already."

"No, we're not still talking! This is our final conversation. This is the last scene and then it's the end, you constipated caterpillar with an IQ of half a lentil. The End!"

"What, no epilogue? Oh, and, by the way, caterpillars sometimes turn into butterflies, and during your insect phase we discussed their excretions – how can they be constipa...."

"Belt up! I only called to let you know that I won't be recommending your script for funding or for anything else. I'm doing my report now and I'm advising my client to steer clear of it. Too contentious, and extremely insulting to Indian musicians and to SOAS graduates."

"It doesn't depend on your recommendation you know. I don't need any measly funding from any measly British source. I'm big time now."

"Big deal big time! I've never read such gibberish! Reeking of hatred and bitterness. You couldn't do anything else with Tameezan and her septic Ustad, so you took MY real story and gave all your lousy fictitious characters a past. You stole my real-life people to give your fictional two-dimensional, film-making prima donnas a context. You annexed my lovely, full-blooded people for your lusty ustads and your sulky starlets. That's the biggest crime you can commit against a human being. It's theft Ash, you stole someone's memories!"

"Hey, look, it fits beautifully. I loved your Mohanji. That sort of person always goes a bit mad and then acts completely out of character. So what if I made him Moneybags? It's clever isn't it?"

"Fuck off you-I'm-a-film-maker-shit-you. All you've ever done with your life is take clips from other people's films and package them into some sort of so-called presentation on TV with your name in five-inch high lettering. And now you steal other people's stories so you can make a film. How could you do this to me? I'm planning a serious book on the Indian shopkeepers of Africa. How dare you attempt to weave my reality into your no head-or-tail fantasy about courtesans and god's gift ustads? How dare you? Lousy creep... find your own bloody resolutions for your bloody pointless fantasies!"

"No, not fantasy, dream. Remember dreams? You were the one who was all for dreams, remember? I simply took your reality and sank it into a dream. Where's the harm in that?"

"It's supposed to be the other way round you shit bag! Dreams make reality! You can't take someone else's reality as a lazy substitute for your own, and then turn it into YOUR dream. I'll never forgive you. Why am I even having this conversation with you? My Mohanji story is someone's personal account of a tragic expulsion of thousands of people from the country of their birth – the Asian expulsion from The Pearl of Africa's Crown. How dare you just help yourself to it and make a hotchpotch with all your Lucknow and Ustad shit? And that's the other thing. Why are you making up Lucknavi courtesan stories when you know absolutely sod all about that part of the world? Why don't you stick to things you know about? What's this living by proxy? Other people's cultures, other people's stories... what happened to your own? Mohanji and the Widow are mine, and you can't have them!"

Ash loved this outburst. Now was his chance to strike....

"Yes, I see. I thought as much. I gathered you were the Brat. Were you really like that? Chillie powder on your dress... love letters to your uncle... Dolly Mixtures, Moon God... thee-hee-hee... and oh... garlic instead of cashews... thee hee hee hee hee!"

Sonia froze. In what could have been a Mrs Henara mode, she had to bubble-burst his gleeful mirth, somehow:

"Actually, if you must know, I've never even been to Africa. In fact, the Brat wasn't even a girl. That Brat grew up to be my husband. OK? Happy now? Go put that in your precious script!"

As soon as she'd said it, she felt a pang of regret. But what was she to do? She never could resist the temptation of shocking him with mind-blowing facts and figures. Besides, the desire to correct him always got the better of her – better than sulking and not bothering to put him right – and the shock and surprise in his reaction was certainly worth it:

"The Brat – Mrs Henara's precocious Brat-daughter – that was a boy? No! Really...?"

"Yes," said Sonia. "I should know. I was married to that Brat for three days. Three days only, but we've always been good friends. He was a little boy whose crazy mother dressed him up as a girl. Otherwise his father would've got custody. The Brat grew up and became the best musician in the whole world, the World's Number One Composer – thanks to the songs of the Widow's sewing machine. And thanks to the Moon God. Anyway, why am I telling you all this? We're through."

"No, wait! Don't hang up! The Brat was a boy? Mrs Henara's only child was a son? He was a boy and he turned up at all of those virgin-little-girl lunches? Oh no! That's disastrous! Cheating against God!"

"Cheating, eh? Look who's fucking well talking," and with that, Sonia slammed the phone down.

85
REVENGE OF THE HANDKERCHIEF

Ash could not remember his life without Sonia. He could not even begin to contemplate living in a world where Sonia was not available at the end of a phone line. Repeated attempts at ringing her had resulted in her answering machine being permanently turned on. There was only one thing for it – he would have to fly back from New York and just knock on her door....

She spoke through the gap in her chained door: "I refuse to discuss this any further. Get the hell out of my life! From now on, you're on my hit list. Just watch out! I know several contract killers personally. That's what happens when you steal other people's stories."

"Other people's? OTHER people's? You've stolen someone else's child-hood memories, and you accuse me of stealing? Just listen to you! And that's not all. Wait, don't shut the door! I haven't finished. Wait... what gives you the right to write about MY family in that candid fashion – describing their shit and everything? How Dare YOU! Your nosey Brat of a husband sniffed around MY family's shit and YOU'RE trying to get a Booker out of it?"

"Booker my foot! I would never... what do you mean YOUR family?"

Her flesh crept with goose pimples. What was this new twist? HIS family?

Ash leaned weakly on the wall outside her door: "Well, not really my family. How can they be my family? What am I saying? They rejected me... she dropped me... like a handkerchief... just left me to die..." suddenly he was sobbing violently, uncontrollably, and Sonia panicked he might choke.

"Ash? Ash, come on, come into the flat... please, calm down...."

There was a long pause while he downed several glasses of Evian water. He was dehydrated from the flight. He had been in New York to pick up a prestigious award for his new soft drink commercial – hazy images of winged half-human half-bird-like creatures flying across pink skies, over sumptuous landscapes and into setting suns, conveying an underlying message of global unity. While his masterpiece film script lay with Sonia for assessment, he had almost overnight turned into the most-wanted TV commercial writer-director. That's what the Zarine dream technique had done for him. It had shown him where his talents really lay.

Sonia couldn't find her voice. This must be a dream. It wasn't like her to be speechless. Ash had told her his mother was Indian. He had always been proud of his Afro-Indian background. That's what Sonia had always liked best about him – no chip on the shoulder about his mixed race origins. She also liked the fact that he'd grown up in the same country as her very own Brat, the Brat who had gone on to become the World's Number One Composer, thanks to the songs of the Widow's sewing machine. But how could Ash be...? Could he be? Yes that's right! He was just about eight years younger than the Composer.

"She dropped you, is that what you said... Surely not? You don't mean...? Not Mohanji's daughter-in-law? Ash, answer me or I'll die here and now!"

So that 's what Ash had done. He had woven an entire film script around his hatred of his mother – she who had literally just dropped him because he was the wrong colour. And then she had abandoned her devoted green-eyed husband and gone off to Bombay to become a film star. Ash had seen her, ever since his film school days, splashed across Indian film magazine covers wearing very little, showing off her beautiful body. Everybody's pin-up girl. Every man's wet dream, just like Tameezan the Courtesan.

Ash wanted revenge, but she was out of reach – how to get at her? And then one day, thanks to the kaput dishwasher, there she was, right there, inside Sonia's computer, making a confession. So that's how it had happened. It had happened because she didn't know where babies came from. And George the servant bringing her a towel in the bathroom had given her the knowledge – but only the knowledge of sex, not the fact that sex and babies were related. So what? Once there was a baby, wasn't it her duty to cherish and nurture the infant?

Death is too good for such sinners. Just as the Bhangi-Dictator Robert's troops had spared Mohanji's life, so his Actress mother also had to be spared. But she had to be slapped across her face first, somehow. And who better than Mohanji to do it? The same bigoted Indian grandfather who had rejected him, now came to his rescue in script form to help even out the score with his disgusting whore of a daughter-in-law. Sinners such as her have to live, and they have to suffer.

The only place to get even with her was in his imagination. Imagination would gradually transfer itself to celluloid. He lived in the hope that one day he would meet up with his Indian grandfather, now a famous and enormously wealthy man, and together they would cook up a scheme to teach her a lesson.

The scheme required a lot of money. If he dreamed it often enough, then one day it would come true. Someone would cast her in the role of a lifetime, and then leave her grossly overweight, high and dry – like an unfinished orgasm… shelved, postponed, permanently on the back-burner. Wasted. Just like him, wasting in that fearful jungle – under the bushes, surrounding by the rattling sounds of snakes.

She'd brought him into this world and then left him to die in the jungle. God alone knows what would have become of him if that African taxi driver had not had the presence of mind to hand him over to a childless English couple. They'd saved all the newspaper cuttings from the sensational Chocolate baby incident. That's how he had learnt he was the famous mixed-race baby that nobody had wanted. The Blacks said he was Indian, and his Indian Mohanji family, backed by the Indian Morality Committee said he was Black. But the White do-gooders had embraced him like he was their very own, because his predicament helped them to prove a long-cherished point: Brownies and Blackies can never live in harmony unless us Pinkies keep an eye on them. Quite right! They had created this mess in the first place, and it was their job to sort it out. And now their arty-farty institutions would host his most cherished dream. He couldn't get back at his mother in real life, so he would do it in a dream – and what else is a film, but somebody's dream? His mean Grandfather would cough up the money and the Whites would provide the outlets and the audiences to watch this dream unfold on celluloid.

The chicken had truly come home to roost….

Sonia switched on her computer "Come on Ash, no, really – I want you to read it" she coaxed him as one coaxes a child who's just been found with his fingers in the biscuit tin, only to be told, It's OK, go on, please have one.

"I want you to read the Brat's story," she said bossily. "I'm sure you want to know the rest. You and I are related in a funny sort of way you know? I just love that, don't you? Do you know it was MY ex-husband Brat who set the alarm that triggered off your birth? It was during your mother's Satwasa – do you know what a Satwasa is? Here, read it Ash… it's such a story! And to think I was writing your life story all the time, wow! Who needs fiction when facts can be so wonderfully weird?"

Ash revived a bit, partly due to the Evian water but mostly due to his best-friend behaving quite like her old self again.

86
MAKE MUSIC, MAKE LOVE

My mother's truths were always devastating. And they were always revealed at the wrong time. Like, we live in this place called the World. Or that there is no Moon God. Or that Charlton Heston isn't really Moses. But the one truth I desperately needed, she never provided. She lied to everyone, but most of all she lied to herself.

I don't know what would have become of me if I hadn't by the Grace of the Moon God, run into the kindly Temple Singer Kanhayya Lal once again. It seems he had always known. He had sensed my mother's madness. He knew she was Saloni's daughter. And he knew Saloni was Tameezan's daughter. Courtesans usually only had daughters. But that long line of daughters was interrupted when the family profession changed. Tameezan's grand daughter was a biology teacher in Pearl, and she gave birth to a son. It just goes to prove that parents cannot always hand down their own culture, lock stock and barrel. Mohanji could not persuade his sons to be shopkeepers any more than Tameezan could persuade succeeding female generations to embrace the powerful profession of courtesan.

Yes, Seema Henara was completely mad – first driven mad by her motherless childhood, then that same mother's tragic death – her body splattered all over the pavement, then finally driven mad forever by that beast they called her ex-husband.

I ran away from boarding school – how could I have stayed there, you tell me? I ran and ran and ran. I hung on to trains, I hid inside cars, and once I even hid inside a fridge on the back of a lorry. I polished shoes, I sold newspapers, I sold song-books outside cinemas. I even went with White tourist men for money… what was I to do? It was in my blood, wasn't it?

Just turned nine and completely alone in the world. Thrown mercilessly into the inhospitable heat and dust of Bombay. My mother tricked me. She said I was going to England. So I agreed to leave my beloved Pearl, only because I thought I would meet my Mohanji boy-friends the minute I landed in England. Let's face it, it looked such a teeny-weeny place in my atlas. But the plane landed in Delhi from where I was taken on a train to Dehra Dun. But I ran away to Bombay.

After my cool hilly gardens and my golden-red skies, my butterflies, my Milky Way, my Moon God, here I was in this stifling dump they call "The City of Dreams." How I longed for my Pearl. How I longed to be a little girl again... how I missed those lazy afternoons at the shop – the magical sounds of the Widow's sewing machine....

And then Kanhayya Lal found me – or I found him. Doesn't matter which. He placed his hand on my head and I knelt before him. Tears of bitter fury poured easily. He taught me the value of forgiveness. He dressed my wounds. He taught me to live with the scars. But best of all, he taught me music. Under his expert guidance I learnt everything about music... lots and lots of theory, and it was simply a matter of time before I was able to apply the theory to the sounds of my Pearl childhood.

And then the melodies came freely. They raced through my head day and night. They came faster than I could play them. I could play anything, anything at all. I could make tunes out of spoons, I could beat dustbin lids, and I could even make broomsticks sing. I could play a tune on any surface I touched. And before I was eighteen, they said I was an outstanding musician in my own right. Kanhayya Lal's Wonder Boy! That's what I became, just a few short steps away from being the World's Number One Composer. That's the sort of thing the Moon God can do. That's His department. All you need is faith!

I had come such a long way from that horrifying experience... a little girl in a Boys' boarding school. The teachers had been insistent: "No, you're really a boy... look, your mother has written to us, and see, see here in your pants, what's this? Idiot! Do you really think girls have this?

Idiot indeed! I had been naive enough to imagine that my mother, purely out of concern for my well being, had hoped that lots of new boyfriends at my new school would drive out the memory of my Mohanji boys. She knew I was always happier playing with boys, so, naturally, I was being sent to a Boys' school. Good old mummy! How was I to know that she HAD to send me to a Boys' school because I was actually, really, biologically a boy?

That should never happen to anyone. It can mess you up for life!

I don't care if they say I'm a boy. Fine, I'll be a boy on the outside if it pleases them, but inside I still feel like a little girl. I still love teen-age boys. I'm always attracted to anyone who reminds me of my Mohanji boys. Women throw themselves at the glamour surrounding the World's Number One Composer, but I still only like teen-age boys. And, I don't give a damn what anyone thinks! And Kanhayya Lal, the only person I really care about, says it's OK to love anyone and everyone.

Kanhayya Lal says love is all the same. He says it doesn't matter if you fall in love with a man, woman, or parrot – or all of them at once.

Love is love, he says, and it takes a thousand forms. Don't give it a name. As soon as you call it one thing, it defies you and becomes something else. Just feel it. Don't look for it he says, just let it find you. And when it does, take my advice, dear one, Love the One and Only.

And express your love by composing great music. Give – just give of your music, let the world hear it. Let your music wash over every living creature. Let your music make every branch swing with joy and every leaf flutter in ecstasy. Let it soothe aching hearts and let it bring peace to restless ones. That's the way to show gratitude my dear one... feeding nine virgins is neither here nor there!

87
BECHARI WIDOW

What you have to understand about the Feast of the Nine Virgins is that such a feast can only ever be hosted by a woman. It seems God is not interested in doing deals with men. A woman – and only a married woman at that – could have an understanding with God. He delivers whatever she wants, and then she has to feed nine virgins to keep her side of the bargain. Fair's fair. He delivers and she feeds nine little girls. And in my case he most certainly delivered, but I have yet to hold that feast....

I was only ever known as "The Widow." Sometimes I thought I was probably born a widow. I had become a widow at the age of twenty. "Bechari Widow" they called me. Young wives are supposed to try and reform their husbands. In that respect at least, I had completely and utterly failed. It was implied I hadn't tried hard enough.

I was the one who slaved day and night but my family behaved like they were all doing me a huge favour. I was returned to live with them when my alcoholic husband finally drank himself to death. My little son and I were just extra mouths to feed. And then my in-laws took him away from me because he was a boy, and my father was thrilled. Without a baby to look after, I would be able to work harder. That's when the dreaming began....

All the time I sewed and cooked I dreamed with my eyes wide open. Soon I could dream about whatever I wanted, awake or asleep. I had perfected the technique of willing my dreams.

I had always liked Robert. His father had, after all, died in our shop and as a result, Robert had had to leave school and sweep shit. He used to make his way quietly to the backyard, not even daring to look up at me while going past the shop verandah. For me he was special even then, and I tried on several occasions to talk to him when nobody was looking. But he only ever said one thing to me:

"Please madam, I don't want to cause you any problems... but some day, if I become something, I promise I'll set you free. Don't say anything, please... if anyone should see us talking...."

But who would look at me? I was just the sad, oppressed Widow, Bechari. Who would want anything to do with me? Except that precocious Henara Brat. She used to just sit on the steps of our shop verandah and stare at me. She seemed to be able to see inside my mind and catch my dreams. Why else would she have stared so hard? She always wanted me to sing... but she's such a stupid child... instead of naming the songs she would mumble: "Bluebells, sing the one about the bluebells...." Bluebells? Silly girl!

I knew my fashionable sister-in-law was planning to report my father to the military authorities for his racist attitude. I never said anything. Let her do what she is doing. Only good can come of it. I know she was behind the killings. But she hadn't realised they would kill all my brothers instead of killing my father. She had carefully arranged things so that her own husband, my green-eyed brother, would not be at home at the time of the massacre. She wanted to keep her options open. That sort of woman always needs a husband somewhere in the background.

I liked her in a strange sort of way. She had a dream. She was a dreamer too. She thought she had film-star looks. But she didn't have a special dream technique like I did – she merely day-dreamed about being rich and famous. But when I dreamed about something, it became real. Every reality is at first a dream and that poor unfortunate man who was reduced to sweeping up shit found himself in charge of destinies – hundreds of thousands of destinies, including my own. And he had scores to settle. My family was first on his list of things to sort out. But he promised there would be no violence – just liberation. He simply booted out the Dukavallas and set their daughters free.

Many of the killings were organised by opportunist Muhindis themselves. Keen to cash in on the chaos and keen to settle their own scores. And what of all those men who went missing, presumed dead somewhere in some ditch? Well, actually, many of them had used the chaos and confusion to abandon their wives and go off to greener pastures with other women.

And that self-righteous, pompous Maulana and that fearsome, bigoted Pandit Guru – all sweetness and charm – all pretended tolerance for one another, but seething with hatred underneath. And that brutal murder of Mrs Henara and her so-called brother, together, in bed? I'm convinced that was organised by the Haqs. Mrs Haq had never forgiven Mrs Henara for helping the Haq daughter to elope with her Hindu boyfriend.

What did my beloved Robert the Dictator do wrong? He just kicked out the Dukavallas. What's so awful about that? The Indians always said they dreamed of going back to India one day – well here was their chance! But it's a funny thing that not a single one of them actually returned to India – they ended up in all sorts of unlikely places, but not India. Instead, they made their Indias and Pakistans in Vancouver and in Bradford; from Chicago to Barcelona they live in a fictitious sub-continental haven of their own making. The Guru now has his temples in temperate zones. He wears an anorak over his dhoti as he clears away snow from the temple steps, while the Maulana now faces the reality of the 24-hour fast when Ramadan falls during summer in northern Norway. And their disciples go on dreaming about returning to "The Homeland" – this year, next year – in five years' time. When the children are settled. When we've saved more money. When... when... when....

That's why it is said everyone lives in a space inside their head. The live inside their heads now, and they lived inside their heads then, in Pearl....

But one day, quite suddenly, it was all over. Away from it all in a shot! It all happened so quickly, and I found myself in a cold, strange land. I took my chance and decided to "lose" my father. I lied to the authorities about my occupation. I said I was a student... and then, there was no looking back.

My psychology degree gave me the language with which to turn my inexplicable dream technique into a methodology. And with the right lettering before and after my name, exploiting the gullible natives of the western world was child's play compared to my father Mohanji exploiting the poor Black natives of Africa. These dissatisfied, greedy, self-seeking, wealth-seeking, fame-seeking, name-seeking materialist westerners. The more they have, the more they dream of having. I want I want I want.... I wish I wish I wish – all their sentences start like that.

And if I can help them to dream, then I can go on being of service. After all, that's what I've done all my life – been of service to others: first as Bechari-Widow Zarine, and now as Zarine, the Teacher of Dreams.

And I still owe God a Feast of the Nine Virgins. It's been more than twenty years since I promised Him such a feast in return for freedom. And now I am free. But where in Britain am I to find nine virgins? And how can I be sure they really ARE all girls?